The Grimm Files

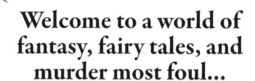

Welcome to a world of fantasy, fairy tales, and murder most foul...

Crow shifters. Bank heists. And lots and lots of stolen goodies. Just what I need to keep my mind off of the fact that Hook, my dead lover, might not be so dead after all.

But the crime syndication known as the Slasher Gang aren't just small-time crooks anymore, they're turning deadly. Everywhere they go now they leave a sea of blood in their wake. And nothing about what they're doing makes any sense.

A fae stronghold's been robbed. Dozens of the queen's royal guards have been killed. Whatever was taken, I knows it's bad. Like crazy, stupid bad. Like end of the world kind of bad. And I don't know how I know this, I just do. I can feel it, taste it in the wind, hear it in the changing tides. Something super evil, super deadly, and super scary this way comes. I only hope I can stop it, whatever it is, or Grimm as I know it might never be the same again...

The Long Goodnight: The Grimm Files

Copyright 2018 Selene Charles
Cover Art by Dan Dos Santos
Formatted by D2D
My super seekrit hangout![1]

---

1. https://www.facebook.com/groups/hattersharem/

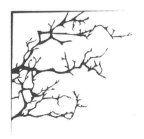

Prologue

GRIMM REPORTS
Cold Case File # 308: The Slasher Gang Heists
Detail of Events-

Seven robberies in a year, traversing realms and dimensions. Each time, the shifters get bolder. On the sixteenth of May, they held a group of fae nuns from the Holy Tree of Immaculate Conception at gunpoint, escaping the vanguard of uniformed dispatch waiting out front with ease. On the twenty-second of July, they took it one step further and held a high-ranking wizard's gnome hostage, forcing him to draw on dark magick to release locks dipped in dragon's blood, narrowly evading capture. Grains of dun-colored sand found at multiple scenes. Possible clue? On the twenty-seventh of August, committed worst act of terrorism yet. Holly Thorn, daughter of high fae Lord Banyon and Lady Seraphina caught in crosshairs of gunfight. M.I.C.E.—Mystically Issued Crime-Scene Examiners—on scene attempted to resuscitate, but she was later pronounced DOA at Winged Seraph's Infirmary.

Summary-

Task Force created. All active and retired investigators recalled.

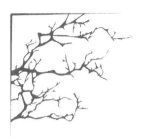

Prologue

Black Angus (leader of the Slasher Gang)

A YEAR IN A HALF EARLIER

I was on me knees. Me! And as if that were no bad enough I also had a bag over me head. I couldn't see a damned thing.

Me head were fuzzy too. I'd been asleep. It were the witching hour, no one sane was awake righ' now. Even the surliest of pirates were a'bed. But it weren't cuz we were good li'l bairns. Rather, because we'd been preparing for this day nigh unto a year now.

All the pieces was being set in motion. But to succeed with the riskiest of plans yet, the hermit golden king were needed to host a gala. No a problem, or so his lover assured us. If Lord Humpty lied we'd end him an' he knew it, so there was no incentive to deceiving us. So long as he told us truth and gave us the keys to the promised land, he'd be free to walk away once it were done. It'd been a sheer stoke of happenstance that'd landed that inflated bag of excrement onto our laps. Stealing from the King of all waters, Triton hisself.

Tsk. Tsk. Tsk. What a fool he'd been to think his deeds could ha' gone unnoticed, especially by us on our own waters. We'd forced him to our will, but better tha' than the fate that would ha' awaited him had the King of Fish e'er found out.

And once Humpty were done, he were done. I didn't keep wit slavery, I needed him for one task. Once we were done, we were through for good. To live his life as he saw fit. I didn't give a crow's arse what he did with his life, so long as he didn't try to feck with mine. And so far the thievin' bastard were keeping true to his word, it were all goin' according to plan.

There was time now to learn the schematics of the locale we'd chosen for the event. We would clean up and finally, finally see our syndicate become the most flushed families in all the hundred realms'. No more livin' hand to mouth, no more thievin', no more heists. We'd be set and we'd be done.

Me first mate kept pushing for us to do more, to up the stakes. The ante as it were. But she were young and excitable. She didn't understand that over-reaching had been the death knell of far too many crime families before us. Getting too big fer our britches were a good way to get all of Grimm down on our arses. An' that was a fight we'd no win. No matter how good we were.

Course, right now I were thinking Humpty were doing his damnedest to betray our gentleman's agreement. That double-crossing harpy, no doubt it were him responsible for my currently being trussed up like a Christmas turkey. I glowered beneath me hood.

One second I'd been asleep, and the next I was out here. Shivering, naked in the cold of night. Tossed unceremoniously down. I'd tried to get up, but I'd been cuffed in me left ear for the effort and I felt the warmth of blood still oozing out.

Me boat pitching up and down on the waters. Reason why Grimm PD or the Bureau of Special Investigations hadn't found us was because we were "grounded" birds. We lived not in the skies we ruled, but upon the waters themselves. Traversing the realms on the legendary Jolly Roger.

An old ship, but a well maintained one. The previous owner had met a grim end, but he'd been a lawman of sorts once and as such had been granted access between realms through the Jolly Roger.

I snarled as I heard the shuffling of boots come up and over the ladder of the ship, landing on the warped wooden planking, before turning and walking off in the opposite direction. The sounds of their steps fading into the distance. A foreboding shiver of black ice skated up me spine. I couldn't explain it, but I sensed deep down that this weren't simple mutiny I dealt with here.

Humpty hadn't just betrayed me, he'd done far worse. I just knew it.

A cold wind feathered along me naked body and I felt the squeeze of me feathers itch to burst through me pores so as I could fly far, far away. But whoever had grabbed me had placed a grounding cuff on me wrist. Nullifying me bodies natural ability to turn. Every time I tried I felt a sharp thrill of fire zap through me blood. I ground down on my back teeth so hard I were sure me teeth would turn to dust. I wiggled, fighting to work off the restraint and the rope so I could finally get up.

But whoever had bound me had done a helluva job. I couldn't even move the damned rope an inch, me skin felt raw at the wrists and wet. There was the stench of blood in the air. My blood.

Panting, breathing heavy from my efforts I tamped down on the panic that were trying its damnedest to take me under. I needed to remain calm, rationale. There were always a way out of any mess. Hells, I were the one and only Black Angus that done broke out of the maximum security prison of Grimm, warded by multiple level 10 witches. If I could do that, then I could surely do this.

I just had to think. I had to stop worrying and jus' think. I blew out a harsh breath, feeling meself getting slowly centered again.

I strained to listen, wondering what'd happened to me crew. There was too much silence. I had a gang of nearly a hundred. Surely, someone should have found me up here by now. Me men were loyal, always had been. And I'd no go squawking a'boot begging for help, if I did it that was the quickest way to be forced to walk the plank. No man respected a captain what couldn't hold his own.

But the mere fact that none of them had even crossed paths wit' me here were worrisome. Where the hells was I?

I smelled the brine of sea air. Felt the cool brush of the winds. And heard the rustling of the sails. I was most definitely out of doors, and on the deck. I weren't hidden below and out of sight. No, I was out where anyone and anything could see me if they'd had a mind to.

I wet my lips, tasting a hint of something metallic and irony. I'd split me lip somehow.

I glanced left and right, but saw nothing but darkness. Whatever they'd placed over me head didn't let in even a sliver of light.

What the hells was this? Again, I twisted me body, trying in vain to stretch apart the ropes they'd bound me with. But trying to undo those knots was like trying to tear through steel with me bare hands.

There was magick at work here. The very darkest kind. I felt it, like arsenic in me bones, crawling all over me. Holding me fast. Panic began to slowly bloom within me. Naught but a mere seedling of it and I kept telling meself I'd been in worse binds before... and yet.

I opened me mouth and tried once more to speak, but for some damned reason me tongue couldn't seem to form proper words. Nothing but grunts and groans spilled up me throat.

I shifted and felt the slide of a splinter slide up and through me kneecap. I winced and that flash of pain was enough to break something loose in me. I grunted, shifting and twitching almost violently. I'd tamped down me panic long enough, it was a ravenous beastie now and wanted out.

I screamed, but the sound were muffled, as though me face had been shoved into a mattress.

"Bluidy hells," a familiar voice snapped, "I thought you had more mettle than that, captain."

Gasping for breath, frozen all over, I blinked as my brain tried to desperately process what I'd just heard. It was no possible. This was no—

Suddenly the itchy bag were snatched off me head and though it were night, my eyes instantly teared from the gleam of too bright lights.

Once me eyes adjusted and I looked around, I noted that I was indeed still on me ship. And then I turned and all breath left me body.

The smiling face of my first mate gazed down on me. Lifting a hand, she traced my jaw. Fingers idly scratching at the scruff of me chin.

I shivered all over.

Her eyes were bright green. Sea green I'd always called them. Piercing. Haunting. And so much like her mother's—the evilest of witches herself, Baba Yaga. And even in the glooming of twilight, they practically seemed to burn like enchanted fire. She were sitting on the edge of a wooden crate, legs spread. Her trusted cutlass rested on her lap. With her unruly red curls she tamed with her black tricorn hat, and the billowing cream-colored blouse she wore, Anne were a pirate through and through. Me heart gave a pang to see it.

She grinned. "Hi daddy," she whispered and I trembled from head to toe. Desperately wishing and hoping that I'd hear a change, a difference in her tone, see her altered in her looks. But there were none. It was just Anne. Just me Anne. Me pride and joy. Me first mate. And me only child.

I shook me head.

She shrugged. "Oh, c'mon now. I'm only doing what any good pirate does, you should be proud. Really. Mama would have been."

Without thought, without reason I opened me mouth and spat. Cursing that vile woman. The only good thing that'd ever come of her treachery had been Anne. Me precious Anne.

I shook my head.

She sniffed and pointed over her shoulder. "Look, I don't have all night and well, neither do ye. The Jolly Roger is now under new management."

I muttered, tried desperately to speak but the geis holding me tongue mute was still firmly in place.

"Hm?" she leaned forward as she cupped her ear, green eyes glittering with what looked an awful lot like mirth, "What's that? Oh, right...you've been gagged, have ye no?" Her laughter, normally soothing to me soul, was a dark and twisted corruption of what I used to know.

She snapped her fingers and instantly the clamp on me tongue was lifted. I felt the sizzle of that dark magick get eaten away and for the first time I feared. I feared greatly. Me Anne didn't know spells. My heart hammered in me throat, my tongue were swollen, and me throat as parched as the dead seas.

"Oh, Anne. Oh, dear sweet, sweet Anne. What have ye done?" I murmured, heart galloping a mile a minute in me chest. Fear for me only child eating away at me soul like a cancer.

She shrugged. "I'm embracing the witch in me, daddy. That part of you, ye tried damned hard to stamp out. But I am part mama, and I'm learning awfully quick. Found me a new teacher."

I shuddered. Dear merciful heavens.

"Anne, if ye be telling me what I think ye are, then ye should ken that black magick always comes wit a price. One few ever—"

"Too late," she laughed, but the sound was hollow and full of something that I had no name for, but that I felt like the echo of frost in me soul. I shook me head.

"It's far too late," she whispered again, and this time I heard sumthin' that rattled me to me bones.

A thread of regret in me daughter's voice. But for me? Or for herself? I didn't ken.

"Anne. Annie. No," I murmured heatedly. "This be mutiny, Anne. I can no protect ye from this," I pleaded, trying desperately to reach through to whatever enchantment had gripped her black soul.

Her grin grew wider, but there were no light in her eyes. "I know it. But no to worry, Da, your loyal men'll be joining you in Davy Jones' Locker real soon."

I shook my head. "Ye don't be wanting to do this, daughter. Ye don't ken what the devil ye've made yer bed wi—"

"I ken well enough!" She spat, and stood instantly to her feet. Pacing in front of me like an enraged and restless tigress in a cage. "You tried to deny me my birthright, and I hate you fer it!"

I tried to stand, but the enchantment hadn't been lifted completely. I was held fast to the ground. I shook me head. "Daughter. Listen to me. Listen ta me, ye don't understand. I protected ye, lassie. Yer mother, she made a deal wit the devil and—"

"Oh, feck off!" She pointed a finger at me. "I'm so tired of yer damned excuses. We're masters of the skies. Kings of the seas. And all we do is steal things." She spat by my knee, that I now saw had gotten more than a mere splinter shoved through it. There was a piece of metal about the size of me pinky finger poking out of it and there were blood, everywhere.

I swallowed hard. She would no threw me into the ocean full of terrible beasties coated in me own scarlet, would she? It would be a foul and grue-some death, only reserved for the likes of traitors and pedos.

I glanced up at me daughter and she snorted, eyes trained on the blood with almost gleeful delight.

"I'm done merely stealing things. I wish to rule. As is my right. I will make all of them pay for daring to deny me. Starting with you! Get up!" She snapped her fingers and suddenly I was moving. Walking, but no because I willed it. Rather, because she had.

And that's when I knew. My daughter hadn't merely flirted with the darkness in her soul, she'd embraced it. Fully. An' she didn't ken what she'd done. She was naught but a babe. A child. Foolish and ignorant, unable to begin to grasp what she'd done.

"Anne, now listen ta me," I tried one last time as she walked behind me and took my wrist in her hands, yanking me forward with a sharp upward tug that made me rise high up on me toes and hiss. Me head grew dizzy with the sudden rush of blood and I had to shake it to clear the spiderwebs. Me lips felt numb and swollen. But I stuttered on anyway. "Ye... ye think ye ken the truth of it, Anne. But ye don't, lassie. Ye don't. Yer mother were a trickster. A bitch. She were a—"

A fist came crashing down on my temple and I saw stars. I staggered, nearly falling flat on me face as I struggled to remain upright. I shook me head, several times. Ears ringing and knowing I sounded drunk as I slurred, "It's no too late. Stop this, Annie. Stop."

She yanked me back, I slammed into her chest and her warm breath whispered into my ear. "You never knew me, Da. You never knew me at'all." Then she kissed me whiskered cheek and a terrible cry worked up me throat.

She shoved me forward. We were walking with some urgency toward the bow.

"Cap'n. Cap'n!" Those cries belonged to me men. Some I knew well, some I didn't.

I looked at them, ten in all. Loyal to the bitter end. They'd go down with me. I shook me head.

Pirates of the air or the seas weren't an overly loyal bunch, but that I had ten willing to lay down their life with mine spoke volumes. Though me heart broke to think of Anne's betrayal, me men and I would haunt the seas together. I would not be alone in the next life. And there was some comfort in that.

"What has been done here?" One, named Rufus—a swarthy skinned fellow with a jagged scar that ran clean from his temple down his right eye and toward the corner of his mouth stared at me with only the one eye. The left eye was gone. Snatched out of his head years ago by a hungry and bloodthirsty fae he'd lost a game of bones too.

I shook me head, silently telling me mate to keep strong. To hold hisself and his dignity together. His lower jaw trembled, but he dipped his head once and then notched his chin high. No one else spoke.

Me fate were already sealed and I knew'd it. But traitor or no, Anne were still me baby. And always would be.

"I dinna blame ye for this, my sweet girl. The bitch tainted yer blood. But ye are still half mine, and someday ye will ken it. Whatever ye do, sleep wit' one eye open. And dinna raise the dead, for if ye do, ye will be doomed to walk the lonely sands forever alone."

She laughed. "Fairy tales, bah!" And then she cried out. "Come, my boy!"

I turned, eyes going wide when I saw the shadow step away. And all breath left me body when moonlight struck the face of the one she'd spoken to.

He was tall. Handsome. And had a silver hook for a hand. But his eyes. His eyes were dead, just like him.

I cut my gaze away, stomach heaving within me. "Dear gods, what have ye done, Annie. What have ye done?"

She merely laughed. "Toss the rabble to the kraken."

The cries that went up from me men would haunt me forever, even in death. The sounds were terrible, unholy things to behold. The one who'd once been Hook walked over to me men. And now his face gleamed like the devil's unholy light. He stabbed me men through their hearts with his hook hand. Blood dripped like black tar to the deck.

Not a one made a peep. Only grunted as the light left them. Gathering like a blue haze in the sky before gradually fading back to the soul flame which ha' made it.

One after another I heard the splash of their bodies as they were flung overboard. And with each death me soul shriveled within me. No more fear in me. I was too old, too grizzled to fear Death's kiss, nay, me sadness were for another.

Annie turned. Blood red hair writhing in the wind like a nest of fanged serpents. She wore a broad smirk.

"Any last words, old man?"

I almost said nothing, but dark as her soul was, Annie were still part me. An' always would be. Wetting me lips I looked down at me feet. The sun were slowly starting to make its way up.

Soon the day would be ablaze with its fire. I'd always loved a good sunrise.

I looked at her. "Ye are young, I were young once too. An' sometimes that fire that makes us who we are, also kills us. Guard yer back, sweet girl, fer I fear ye dinna ken the devil ye've made yer bed wit."

For a minute she stood still and, for a quiet and brief but intense moment, I saw something in her eyes. Light. Truth. Fear. Me girl was scar'ret. She might not ken it fully yet, but she already knew all was not well.

"Kill him," she said without inflection.

I had no time to prepare for it, Hook's hand rammed through me gullet, tearing through me organs and shredding me up from the inside. I grunted, coughing as that hot stream of blood began to work its way up me throat.

He never said a word. Never batted his eyes. He stood there. Like a thing not wholly dead, nor wholly living neither.

I gasped, struggling to stand a'right. Anne's hands were suddenly on me shoulders. She would toss me o'erboard. But for just a moment, it were me girl looking down at me. Not the darkness. Not the blight that were her mama.

But then the light were gone and I were falling, falling, falling. When I hit the cold waters I instantly felt the brush and slide of a suction, the smoothness of muscle wrapped around me heel.

I looked up at the sky once more. Ablaze wit the colors of fire and in me heart, I forgave her.

Then I remembered nothing more save for the touch of the kraken's silky glide.

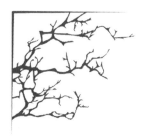

Chapter 1

Detective Elle

"WINGED-FAE BITCH!" I hissed, staring down at Caytla's mean, soulless eyes.

The fanged sprite only smirked back at me, looking like the cat that ate the canary. But the sprite wouldn't be smiling if she weren't currently hiding behind the might of the queen of the winged folk, Titiana.

Titiana's bloodred eyes narrowed into thin slits, and I shivered despite myself, clutching onto the golden pearls so hard I was seconds away from crushing them to dust in my hand.

The queen was dressed in full fae regalia. Her gown was a gossamer wave of morning dew that hid all the naughty parts, and her crown was made of spiders' silk. Her curly blond tresses tumbled down her back and were threaded through with miniature rosebuds and blooming sprigs of baby's breath.

Titiana sat within a golden acorn chariot that was harnessed to a platoon of buzzing, angry-looking bees. Beside her were her guards—all men, I thought. Hard to tell with how eternally youthful fae faces were. They were dressed in vines of ivy with breastplates fashioned from thorny oaks.

They might be small, but the fae had a taste for flesh of all sorts, and they were just as skilled at entrancing their victims with their particular brand of blood magick as I was with song.

Behind the ostentatious pomp hovered Caytla, my latest nemesis in a ridiculously long string of them. I just knew she was behind all of this some-how, the traitorous little cur—not that I could prove it. But I didn't have to. Her smug smile was proof enough so far as I was concerned.

I ground my front teeth together, fighting the anger raging through every square inch of me. I was going to be late for work, and that was not okay. None of this was okay.

I took a deep breath, telling myself not to give in to fits of temper since it would do no good and there wasn't a jury in the world that would come against the fae, not with the amount of magick and wealth the faery lands brought into all the realms.

By the hells, I wasn't one who cared for groveling, but I was stuck, and I knew it.

"The deal was..." I repeated for the third time, swallowing down the snappy retort I really wanted to give. "One golden pearl for two days' worth of water."

I'd never been accused of being a particularly patient sort of siren, but considering that I was dealing with one of the highest-ranking members in all of faery, even I knew when to shut up and dance.

"Aye." The queen smirked. "And so it was. But ye want a week's worth of water, for what... three pearls?" She held up three fingers and snorted. "Bah!"

"The price was never an issue before," I said slowly, my words nowhere near as tempered as I knew they should be. I was coming to the very end of my extremely fragile hold on what remained of my patience.

Tiny golden spiders crawled from out of the webbing of the queen's hair. I had to tamp down my revulsion at the sight.

"And what would King Triton do if he discovered we were continuing to aid the very daughter he struck from the history of her very own peoples?" Her words were a silky threat, and I couldn't help but grin, but there was nothing funny about any of this.

Titiana licked her tiny fangs, eyeing my body up and down, and I doubted very much she merely wished to play bed sports with me.

If I blew up, as I so desperately wanted to do, things would go south for me quickly. As much as I hated to admit it, the queen was right. The fae were my only work-around for my father's cruel banishment.

I inhaled deeply, biting down hard on the tip of my tongue. The hag was playing dirty pool, and she knew it, which let me know this had never been about the damn pearls at all. Titiana wanted something else, and I just had to try to be patient to figure out whatever the hells it was.

Screwing on a tight smile that I knew didn't reach my eyes, I dipped my head in acknowledgement of her words. "The queen is, as ever, most wise," I said silkily.

"Or, you know"—she shrugged delicately—"we could always just ask him." She tapped one long black-tipped nail against her chin, almost thoughtfully, as she stared unflinchingly at me. The stupid little bees buzzed their wings harder, the sound menacing and chilly.

I pinched the bridge of my nose and grunted. That would spell doom for me. I'd be an outcast in truth then, and that was a fate worse than death. That was more than enough incentive for me to strangle the ill will I felt toward her.

"If I might ask, Queen Titiana, what does my father suddenly have to do with any of this? You've always known who I was, not that I tried to hide it. You never cared before, so why now?"

"True." She dipped her head. "But King Triton has recently reached out to me, expressing concerns about his wayward progeny." She rolled her wrist as she mused aloud. "The king has discovered we've been aiding his pariah. And to say he's unhappy is, well, an understatement, to say the least. So tell me, Elle, why should we continue to render you aide?"

I bit my bottom lip so hard I tasted a well of blood. Heart hammering, because that was the last thing I needed in this situation, I licked it up and wouldn't open my mouth again until I was sure there was no blood left to scent.

Titiana's bloodred eyes glittered with avarice.

"We get so very little out of this arrangement, Elle, I'm thinking that perhaps we should just—"

"Bloody hells," I muttered and the queen's mouth pinched tight. "Not you, obviously." I flicked my fingers at her. "Tell me, Queen, what can be done to get what I need?"

Her grin was cruel and full of wickedly sharp-looking silver teeth. "Quid pro quo—isn't that what you detectives call it? Fish?" Her bloody eyes flashed with a flicker of fire at their center.

Gods above, I hated the fae.

Cheeky little bastards, they were.

I refrained from rolling my eyes but just barely. I was standing in the sand, feet tingling with pins and needles because unlike most of my kind, shifting was less than fun for me. In fact, most times, it was a bloody nuisance and hurt like the two hells. I was also naked. And though I might be a siren, and they fae, I had once been the princess of the deep. I knew my appeal and felt the raking, lecherous perusal of her guards like tiny little blades against my flesh. They wanted me. To screw or to eat, it was hard to say, but want me, they did.

Whenever one made a deal with the fae, one had to pay very particular attention to every unspoken nuance of what wasn't said. Dealing with the fae was tricky at best and lethal at worst. I had absolutely zero desire to enter into another arrangement with them, yet they knew as well as I did that I had very little position of power from which to haggle. I was almost entirely reliant upon their mercies, and they damned well knew it.

Losing what was left of my flagging patience, I planted a hand on my hip and glared at her. It wasn't necessarily a wise move, and I might have regretted it when the guardsmen lifted up their bramble pitchforks and aimed them directly at my heart. One word from their queen, and what was only the size of a walnut's shell could become as mammoth as a kraken's tentacle and as powerful too. More fools had died mocking the fae than one might expect, and since I was no fool, I held up my hands in a gesture of surrender.

"I am sorry, Queen Titiana. 'Tis only that I have urgent business to attend to," I said in the old speech, speaking to her not as a disgraced siren but as the royalty I'd once been.

Her wee nostrils flared, and her glare was as hot and raking as any sword could be. That damned Caytla—if I ever got my hands on that tiny winged fool, I'd wring her neck. I thanked the gods the fae couldn't read thoughts, or she'd know my apology had been less than sincere.

But finally, after what felt like an eternity, she dipped her head. "*Weel* then." She dusted off her dewdrop gown.

The pitchforks suddenly vanished, and the winged little men were once again eyeing me with lustful avarice in their beady black eyes.

I released a shaky breath.

She sniffed. "King Triton has vowed us free use of his eternal pools—"

I hissed. No way in the two hells could that be. I lived in one of the two eternal pools, and Nowhere—the second of the two—was forbidden to even me. This island was my home; it was the only place I could actually live. And the king—who I refused to think of as my father right now—had just decided that I should share my space with a bunch of perfidious, bloody faes! I clenched my hands so tight my nails dug painfully into my palms.

Not that I expected any less from my seed bearer. He was a rotten bastard, and I knew he must be taking great delight in my distress. He'd never liked me much. Always so much more attentive to my sisters than to me. I'd always been a thorn in his side. A nuisance. He'd been all too happy when I finally gave him the excuse he'd always wanted so that he could finally, finally be free of the curse that was me.

I bit down on my back teeth, clamping down on the hateful thoughts. This was not the bloody time to be thinking of that man. Not now. Not ever.

"But... I have a problem. One that none of my court..." She hissed, wrinkling her nose and fairly crackling with rage that lifted all the fine hairs on my forearms. "Can solve."

My eyebrows lifted—I sensed I might actually have a hand to play after all. "Are you asking me to come to faery lands?"

She lifted her chin—a proud, arrogant queen. But I saw the way her pupils slitted and the wrinkles lined her plump red lips. The queen was over a millennium old. She was vicious, cunning, and brutal when need be. But she'd not retained her reign so long by only being cruel. She was also fiercely intelligent, diplomatic, and practical.

"Faery? Nay," she hissed in her high-pitched singsong tone. "Nay. Never there." She shuddered. "But we have a small contingency in the Never Lands, and there's been an issue of late."

I didn't like the sound of that. Few creatures were stupid enough to mess with the fae. The fact that Titiana appeared legitimately concerned was more than just a little worrisome.

I cocked my head. "As in?"

She pursed her lips, looking as if she'd been sucking on a lemon. "There be a dragon skulking about."

I lifted my eyebrows, flooded with relief. Dragons were dangerous, yes, but that was nowhere near my jurisdiction. And considering there was only one dragon that I knew of patrolling the Neverlandian skies, I didn't think they were in any true danger. "Likely Whiskers—he's harmless. Plays with the Lost Boys, lives in one of the fanged-tooth mountain ranges. I'm sure if you just spoke with him, he'd be more than happy to relocate."

"We don't mind the dragon, fish eater. He's merely a nuisance. Usually. But my guards have noted his behavior growing erratic as of late—patrolling the skies at odd hours, blasting out jets of flame as though he does battle. But never is there anything around."

I lifted my eyebrows, waiting for more. Realizing rather quickly there wouldn't be more, I couldn't help but wonder why she was making such a big deal of this. "Look, I actually know Whiskers. Not well, but he's never been anything to worry about. As far as neighbors go, you could have done worse. And if he's blasting fire, he might be killing insects. I don't know. Or more likely, he's eating. You do know that many of Never's creatures go invisible at night."

"That's not the answer I want to hear," the queen said silkily and practically vibrated on her seat.

I knew what she wanted, for me to agree to go and check things out—waste my time and hers, because there was no way in the twins hells that Whiskers was a threat of any sort. I wanted to snap that I didn't have time for this bullshite, that I and everyone else in Grimm were far too busy to take time out from our stupidly hectic schedules just because a few suddenly decided that a lone pacifist dragon was an issue where he'd never been before. But her wee little guards had lifted their damned bloody pitchforks again, and gods tooth, I hated the fae.

And why did she even require that of me? Was she setting me up for something? She had her guards, faes far more capable of handling a dragon than I could. Fae were treacherous beasts and I wouldn't put it past the queen of the winged folk to have an ulterior motive.

I thinned my lips.

"I ken your previous relationship with the dragon," she said, as though answering the very question I was thinking. "It is why I ask that you and not one of my guardsmen handle this."

I squinted at her. "How did you know what I was thinking?" There were times I wasn't sure that fae couldn't actually read minds.

"You're naught but a baby. Reading your expressions is disgustingly easy. What is your answer?"

"*Hm,*" I muttered, thinking that there were a lot of things I didn't know as well as I sometimes thought I did. It wouldn't surprise me if the fae could lie—about everything. And their supposed inability to lie was just another lie they told.

I swallowed my instant retort and instead practiced the kind of patience I saw Maddox use day in and day out. The fact was, I didn't have much choice, and she and I both knew it. Not if I had any hope of actually leaving my prison. Plastering on a tight smile that I hoped looked less false than it actually was, I said, "Will it get me my shirt?"

She did some sort of weird nod and rolling of her eyes gesture, which I hoped was a yes.

"Fine," I huffed. "I'll check into the mountain, when I can find a spare minute, and not a minute before. But I want two weeks of air now, not one."

She knew I was good for it. Only a fool would dare try to pull one over on the queen of the sprites.

She thinned her lips, and the little pitchforks were now looking not quite so miniature anymore.

Scoffing with obvious disgust, she flicked her wrist. "So mote it be, you bloody fish. I hope you rot in the two hells—*after* you solve my problem, of course."

"Don't really see how Whiskers is much of a problem. You sure you wouldn't rather reconsider? I can promise you that this is going to be a complete waste of my time and yours."

"Then that is my problem, is it not?" She snorted with mirth. "Caytla, craft her the gown and take the pearls too."

"Gown?" I shook my head. "I do not wear gowns, and like twin hells I'm giving you the pearls too."

"Oh, ye'll do it, Detective. Ye'll do it." Then she turned around in her buzzy little chariot and flew into the heavens, leaving a glittering trail of golden fae light in her wake.

And just as I was about to snatch up Caytla and wring her scrawny little neck, the fae had already fled in a violent buzz of wings. The pearls had been snatched from out of my hand without my even knowing it too. Fecking annoying the bug might be, but she was fast, blazing fast.

Lying in the sand at my feet was a gown, a cocktail gown the shade of a smoky-black pearl with a cinched heart-shaped bodice and a skirt that would barely cover the goods. How the hells was I supposed to work in this shite?

"Damn you to the two hells, Caytla!" I growled into the dead silence of the night, but if she heard me, I never knew.

Bloody hells, a dress. I never wore dresses anymore. Not ever. The boys at work were sure to tease me about this one.

With a growl of disgust, I picked up the revolting thing and grimaced as I slipped it on.

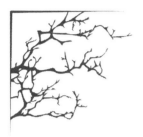

Chapter 2

Detective Elle

YES, I MIGHT BE WEARING a dress, but I also had on combat boots laced up to my knees and a black leather jacket with metal studs on the collar and wrists. Since I was wearing all black, my electric-blue hair looked even more unnatural and exotic than normal. For once, it actually didn't look like a frizzy mess but was soft and fell in silky waves down my back.

Hatter, who'd figured out fairly quickly my morning routine, was waiting for me as usual by Georgie's coffee cart, legs crossed at the ankles, leaning casually against the silver frame as he and Georgie chatted about nothing in particular.

His clothing was immaculately pressed. He always wore trousers, jackets, a white button-up shirt, and a scarlet satin cravat tied around his strong neck. My heart gave a flickering bump of approval. There was no denying my partner was gorgeous, with his five-o'clock shadow, the strong, masculine planes of his face, and those unusual blue and green eyes. I'd be a liar if I said I didn't enjoy looking at him—because I did.

But we were partners, and fraternization was a no go, especially after what Tanner and his wife had done. The office of internal affairs had been up our asses for the past two months. Any infractions, even something as insignificant as "borrowing" office supplies, had caused many good people with badges to be sacked.

Whatever Hatter and I might or might not have had was tabled for the foreseeable future. Ichabod and I had had a couple of flings, but because we'd never been open about our trysts, we'd flown under the radar. But the amount of digging IA had done had been more than enough to scare us straight.

For now, Grimm PD was a well-oiled and strictly by-the-books kind of an operation. At least until Delilah Longbottom, IA watchdog and level-10 black witch, got reassigned, which at that rate was looking like exactly never.

I grunted.

One foam cup of coffee sat untouched on the counter beside Maddox. I wasn't sure how the man had done it, but he'd figured me out pretty quickly. I knew without even needing to ask that it would have a double shot of squid ink and would be topped with a creamy layer of sea foam. My mouth was already watering thinking about it. My morning had been shite, and I knew my day wouldn't see much of an improvement.

Georgie was the first to spot me. His bushy orange eyebrows practically lifted into his hairline, a look of dumbfounded shock on his craggy face.

I glowered at him, daring him to say anything. Let him try—he'd be missing a tongue if he did.

Maddox, aware that something had caught the cave dwarf's attention, turned to glance at whatever had distracted Georgie. He did a double take, first turning aside quickly then instantly turning again as a slow, curling grin crawled over his handsome features.

"Fecking hells," I snipped and held up my finger at him. "Not one word, Detective Smart-Arse."

He mimed zipping up his mouth, but his dark eyes glittered with barely disguised humor. I rolled my eyes, fighting my own grin in response to his. Hatter had a way of making me less cranky than I was normally inclined to be. I didn't know whether that was a good or bad thing, but it was definitely a thing.

"Wha' crab pinched ye on the arse this mornin'?" Georgie asked in the familiar grit-inflected voice of his.

With a curl of my nose, I jerked my chin in thanks toward Maddox and snatched up my cup then took a large swig of it, practically chugging the now-tepid ambrosia.

"Think she'll pass out from not breathing?" Georgie asked Maddox with a note of incredulity as I continued to mainline the inky manna from heaven. If I could just shove an IV of the stuff straight into my veins, I probably would.

"Heard sirens don't need to breathe much, anyway," Maddox said, his tone full of good humor.

I didn't think I'd ever seen Maddox come to work once without wearing a smile on his freaking handsome face all the time. It was as if nothing was capable of bringing the man down. He'd at least been somewhat normally depressive when he and I had first met in Wonderland. But ever since he'd come to Grimm, he was different—not in any way I could really put my finger on and say this or that was the reason for the change, but he just didn't seem to carry the weight of the world on his shoulders anymore.

Everyone at the precinct loved him, even Ich, which, yeah, made me a little jealous if I was being honest. Me, they called the she-hag. Apparently, I had anger issues.

Pft.

Only after I'd inhaled the very last drop of the good stuff did I finally take a deep reflexive breath, then I sighed deeply.

Maddox shot me a questioning look. Some days, I'd order a second, but not today. I shook my head and tossed the cup in the garbage bin.

"Java was strong today—new vendor?" I asked the dwarf.

He grinned, revealing his strong, blunt teeth—teeth fully capable of ripping into a fish's tail with ridiculous ease. Once upon a time, dwarves and sirens were bitter enemies. Resentment ran deep between our species and even still amongst some, like my father, who'd likely choose to stab Georgie rather than smile at him.

Triton would be so disappointed in me, but then again, when was that new?

"Yah, not sure about it. Did you no—"

"I liked it," I said, slipping my hand into my jacket pocket. I pulled out the first gem my fingers encountered—I always kept a handful on me at any given time—and slid over what actually happened to be a diamond. Usually, our going rate was blue sapphires, but for diamonds, I expected a little more information, and well he knew it.

Georgie's eyes lit up with avarice as he quickly snatched it away then pocketed it so fast his hand was little more than a blur.

I snorted. "Any news today, dwarf?"

Georgie had one other skill set that made him invaluable to me, and that was his ability to hear the rumors that ran rampant through the underbelly of Grimm, even quicker than most detectives could. Many times, his clues had been the breadcrumb I'd needed to point me in the right direction to help me solve a case then or even one in the future. Dwarves were short, squat, and to most people so unintelligent that they rarely bit their tongues around them. It didn't matter that it was absolutely untrue—prejudice ran deep in Grimm. But I knew better.

If you could get a dwarf in your hip pocket, you were usually one step ahead of the rest of the pack. I couldn't do half of what I did without him, and the dwarf knew it too.

"Ye be meaning the Slasher Gang, eh?"

I shrugged. It was no secret Grimm PD was focused nearly exclusively on bringing down the now-labeled terrorist group. I wasn't sure when it had happened, but what had once been a small-bit bank robbing enterprise had suddenly turned coordinated, highly skilled, and extremely dangerous, probably within the last half year or so.

All I knew was they were a priority-one catch. Several task forces throughout most of the realms of Grimm as well as the Bureau of Special Investigations, or BS for short, were focused on their capture.

"No much," he groused, scratching at his ginger-bearded cheek with one thick finger. "Savin' for one bit that may or may not mean nuthin' to ye, but I heard tell at the Rusted Sarcophagus las' nigh that sumthin real big was fittin' to go down. Smoke an' mirrors was the proper term of it. Mean anythin' to ye?"

As far as tips went, that wasn't one of his best. It could mean something or nothing at all. "Too vague to say, Georgie, but should you hear anything else, you know where to find me."

"Aye, that, I do, Detective. That, I do."

I tipped my chin and glanced behind us. Up till now, we'd been the only ones at the cart, but I could see a small crowd headed unerringly in our direction. The salmon stream of early-morning commuters had finally arrived.

I shoved my fists into my pockets, walking slowly toward central station. Maddox matched my steps. I blinked, licking my front teeth, ignoring his obvious looks.

He sighed, and I shook my head.

"Not right now, Maddox."

He took off his perpetual black-silk top hat and brushed his fingers through his slightly long dark-brown hair, causing the ends to poke up in all different directions.

I didn't want to snap at him. I really didn't. But I was sick to damned death of talking about Hook already. One day, he was going to push too far, and I was going to explode, and I really didn't want to do that, not with him, because after the initial shock of hearing Maddox's proclamation that Hook was still alive had worn off, I knew two things: one, he was wrong, dead wrong, and two... I couldn't. I just couldn't.

"You know, at some point, we're going to have to talk about this," he said slowly.

I stepped onto the sidewalk, avoiding a large, brackish puddle of water. There must have been a downpour last night. The world actually smelled clean, like salt and petrichor, two of my favorite scents in all the hundred realms.

"Yeah, well, that day's not gonna be today." I gave him a look, the kind of look that clearly told him to back off about that subject.

He held up his hands, but a look of frustration had pinched itself between his thick black eyebrows. "Whatever you say, Detective."

Damn it all, he'd called me Detective. Not Elle. He was pissed—at me. And yeah, I knew I was acting like a heinous bitch this morning. Dealing with the fae hadn't helped, but I'd had a rough night regardless—none of which was his fault.

I thinned my lips. Things had cooled off between Maddox and me recently, probably beginning right around the time he'd told me of my dead lover's return.

My stomach quivered, and I bit the inside of my cheek. The last thing I wanted was this tension between us. If I was being honest, for a woman who'd never fancied herself being the type who needed or even wanted a partner, I kicked arse with Maddox.

Our methodology was sometimes messy, and while we didn't always agree on things, no one could deny we got things done. If I had to be saddled with a partner, even I could admit I couldn't have gotten a better one.

I sighed and held up my hands. "Look, my night was shite, and this morning wasn't much better. Georgie had the right of it. I got up on the wrong side of the bed this morning. Can I get a mulligan?"

I grabbed his forearm as he went to take his next step, clamping down hard on his elbow, my eyes imploring. I wasn't used to playing nice with others—everyone knew that about me—yet for some strange reason I found myself trying harder with Maddox than I had with just about anyone ever.

He stopped walking, not looking at me as he ground his molars. The shadow of his trimmed beard caused his strong jaw to look even more razor-sharp than usual.

And just as I was sure he'd brush me off and walk away, Maddox sighed, glancing side eye down at me, lips still set in a thin, tight line of displeasure. But his shoulders were no longer stiff and erect, and at least he was looking at me. That was progress, so far as I was concerned.

"I know you think," he said in that deeply cultured Landian voice of his, "that I harp on you. I vow, Elle that I am not. But I am daily haunted by visions of this male, and I don't think it's wise for you to continue pretending that—"

I glanced up and down the busy, smog-choked streets before sighing deeply. I'd vowed when Maddox and I had become partners that I would try. So I tried.

Pinching the bridge of my nose, I held up my hand, cutting him off, and shook my head. "Maddox, I respect you. You're my partner, but more than that, you're a damn fine detective, and I trust your gut—implicitly."

"I sense a *but*," he grunted, and I shrugged.

"But..." I clamped down on my tongue. Talking about this always churned up all the bad memories—that sense of quiet desperation that I'd felt when I'd watched Hook breathe his last in my arms. I squeezed my eyes shut, shaking just a little. "But," I repeated firmly before looking back at him, "I... I cannot believe that this is real. Because if I believe this is real, I'm not sure I could be okay. Ever again."

He inhaled deeply, glancing over toward his left, looking beyond frustrated with my constant denial of his vision.

Leaning up on tiptoe, feeling desperate he hear me out for once, I grabbed his face in my hands, forced him to look down at me, and opened up to him completely.

"You and I, we understand what it is to lose, right?"

His nostrils flared, and a smile that was less a smile and more a snarl flitted across his full lips. Maddox rarely spoke of Mariposa—the daughter he'd lost to still-mysterious-to-me circumstances. It was a sore subject for him, and I never used his daughter to dig at him, but I had to make him understand where I was coming from.

"I held him as he breathed his last, when he stopped breathing completely. And I held him when he turned to sea foam in my arms. A tender mercy, I'd granted him, returning him to the world he loved most. Then, Maddox, I swam away. I swam away from him. I left him scattered to the tides. Do you get that? Do you understand what I'm saying? I left him." My breath hitched, and I shuddered, clutching my arms to my chest as I thought about that terrible day. "I. Left. Him."

Maddox's lashes fluttered, and the stern displeasure shifted into empathy. "Gods," he rumbled, and I swallowed hard.

Not even Ichabod had known that part. I'd never shared Hook's death with another.

"So please, I beg you, if... if you ever cared for me at all, please leave this be."

He closed his eyes and nodded once. "As you wish, Detective Elle."

Not just Detective, not quite Elle, but it was good enough. I gave a hard nod.

He looked at me for several seconds then slowly lifted his hand and brushed his knuckles down my cheek, just barely grazing me, not lingering long. But I felt the heat of his touch move all the way through me and knew that my siren's mark upon my forehead was starting to glow.

"I hear you," he said, and I gave him a wimpy smile of thanks.

After that, we turned and headed as one toward the precinct and walked up the steps at the same time. Maddox opened the door for me, and immediately when I entered, I heard catcalls and chuckles, and even a few of the more daring cops wolf-whistled.

"Damn, Elle, never knew that's what you were hiding beneath those arse-ugly trousers you always wore," someone rumbled to the right of me. It sounded like a troll's voice. Trolls all spoke with the same inflection, as though they'd swallowed a bag of rocks for breakfast.

I frowned, confused for half a second until I remembered what I was wearing. Glancing down at myself, I growled, then with a tight smirk, I gave them all a one-fingered salute.

Maddox snickered beside me.

"You gonna let her do us that way, Hatter?" someone else guffawed. The tone was soft, delicate. Faery blood. Recently, we'd gotten a rash of new cadets, and it was hard for me to place who was who anymore.

Maddox shrugged and grinned affably. "If there's one thing I've learned in my life, rookie, it's that you never place a leash on a female—especially not a siren."

"Hey, Maddox..." This time, it was a female beat cop—Jane, Janey, something. I was shite with names. All I knew was she was a Valkyrie with clear-glass eyes and she was one badass bitch. "You should check Elle's purse. Heard she's got your balls in there."

"Touché, Róta," he said with a smirk.

There was ribald laughter, and even I grinned at that.

Róta though? I frowned and leaned in toward Maddox. "That's her name? Róta?"

He snorted and said beneath his breath, "You've been here years... me, two months... and still you don't know Róta. She's only been working at this precinct for seven years. Let me guess. You thought her Emily or some such?"

"Jane, actually. Janey." I shrugged. "You know I'm shite with names."

He smirked. "That, I do, Detective."

He still wouldn't say my name, but I didn't sense anything other than easy banter when he'd said it. I rolled my eyes, but I grinned.

Bo suddenly popped her head out of her office. It was as if she had a sixth sense the instant that Maddox and I showed up. Her finger was crooked, and she urged us to her silently while holding a phone on her shoulder as she spoke into the receiving end in short, angry bursts. Then she promptly disappeared.

I turned to glance up at Maddox with my eyebrow raised. "What did you do now?"

He snorted but said nothing more.

We got to her door, and I tapped on the frosted glass panel. Bo, who was dressed in a white pantsuit, glanced up and ushered us in.

She'd dyed her hair recently and had instantly looked at least a decade younger for it. It was no longer graying blond but now a striking shade of raven's-wing black that shimmered in the sun with hints of dark green and indigo. She'd lopped most of it off, and it was an elfin length that framed her square features, giving her an androgynous look that worked for her. Her eyes were large and warm brown and bloodshot, attesting to the weeks we'd all been working like dogs to bring down the shifter syndicate.

"Yes. I hear you. Yup. They're going. That's what I said, Draven." She all but growled the last word before tersely snapping, "Later." Then she hung up the phone with a resounding finality that made me want to clap.

Draven, also known as Commissioner Marcel, was a hard-assed vampire who'd once upon a time been a warlord of some not so insignificant standing and still thought he could lord it over us peons.

"I take it Commissioner Hard-Arse is giving you guff again?"

Bo, who had her forehead in her hands and was rubbing the bridge of her nose with her pinky fingers glanced up, one eyebrow lifted as she clearly debated whether to chew my arse out for my lack of respect or just let it slide.

She rolled her eyes, and I elbowed Maddox in the side, feeling as though I'd just won a minor victory.

"You could say that again. He's lobbying for the royal-advisor position and is on my ass to bring down the Slasher Gang sooner rather than later. You know how political power grabs go." She sighed and shook her head. "Anyway, we're not here to talk about the commissioner." She flicked her wrist then paused, eyeing me with a calculating gleam. "Like the dress, Detective."

Now it was Maddox's turn to elbow me with a cocky smirk.

I wrinkled my nose. "Don't remind me. Damn faeries made me wear it."

"Well, ironically enough, the dress has come in handy today." She leaned back in her seat, arms laid over her stomach as she tapped her thumbs together. The shepherd-staff pendant resting between the *V* of her breasts gleamed a dim blue. "What were you and Maddox working on again?"

Scratching the back of my neck, I got a bad feeling. I glanced sideways at Hatter. "Oh, um—"

Maddox cleared his throat, stepping forward, total professionalism. "New lead on the bank of Grimm rob—"

"Right." She dipped her head. "Right. Change of plans."

I inhaled, pretty sure I wasn't going to like where this was going. "You do realize it took me weeks to get my CI to come out of hiding long enough to even talk with me?" I tapped my chest. "This lead is solid. I feel it in my bones. He mentioned something about sands I'd want to see."

"I get that, Elle. I do," she said, mouth stern and face serious. "That's why Crane'll take point on it now. Good work, both of you. But there is a more pressing matter at the moment."

She opened a drawer in her desk and pulled out a calendar then jotted something down quickly.

She was trying to throw me a bone, but I wasn't happy. Yes, if there was anyone I could trust to take my Intel, it was Crane, but I'd been working five weeks on that lead, and losing out was like a kick in the nuts.

Rumor had it there'd recently been a major shift in power players and that the syndicate wasn't as unified as they'd once been. Lately, there'd been witnesses talking about magick, some high-level super-bad-juju kind of stuff, as in possibly the work of a dark mage, which, if true, could mean things were about to get so much worse than any of us could even imagine.

And this was bad because dark mages weren't technically supposed to exist anymore. There'd been a purge in the last century, and let's just say things got really heated, as in burning-at-the-stake kind of heated. It had taken the might of many different species working together to bring them down. Grimm had suffered nearly catastrophic and irreparable damage thanks to the bloodlust of the dark ones. No one really believed what we were dealing with now could in any way be linked to a dark practitioner because they hadn't simply been burned—all their arcane knowledge had been as well to prevent another uprising.

But Maddox had been getting flashes lately, images of pending doom that made me feel breathless when I thought about it for too long.

Rage stirred through my bones, my blood. This was *my* case, dammit, not Crane's. Though I liked him, that wasn't the point. I shook my head, biting down on the inside of my cheek.

Bo lifted a dark eyebrow, staring unflinchingly at me. "You have something to say, Detective?"

Maddox shifted on his heels, his hip just barely grazing my own, which for him was as good as yelling at me to "shut my damn mouth and dance."

He had such a hard-on for Bo. He was always talking about how intelligent, how fashionable she was, just like the Landians—which, technically, she was—and how wise she was. It would almost make a girl believe her partner and her boss had a secret bumping-fuzzies kind of thing going on, except for the fact that Bo didn't swing that way and didn't seem to notice Maddox much at all other than as one of the best minds in the precinct.

I smiled, showing nothing but teeth, fingers flexing tight by my side. "Nope, course not, boss."

She didn't look the slightest bit convinced by my half-hearted attempt at docility.

"What do you need from us, Captain?" my freaking perky partner chimed in. I swallowed a growl.

"Tonight, King Midas is hosting a gala."

"Oh, for fecks sake," I groaned and she shot me a dirty look, but I shook my head. "Please, don't tell me we've just been yanked off our lead for some babysitting bullshite."

Her nostrils flared. "I don't think I need to remind you, *Detective*," she said crisply, quickly putting me in my place, "that so long as I wear this badge"—she tapped the captain emblem pinned to her lapel—"you do what I say. The days of you running off and doing whatever the hells you please are long gone."

"The hells?" I growled. "I've never done that."

She lifted her chin. "I had a very enlightening chat with the bureau yesterday. You're skating a very fine line here, Elle."

She didn't say she was only trying to help me, but I heard the words loud and clear.

I shouldn't say anything, but that was bullshite, and she knew it. "Oh yeah. Let me guess—Crowley, right?"

Maddox glared down at me, but I refused to look up at him. I knew what he was thinking. So yeah, maybe I shouldn't have let the street rat Aladdin go when I'd clearly been told by the department that BS was on their way to interrogate him, but he'd only been a boy. A homeless, dirty child desperate to get food to his family, and in no way was he connected to the Slashers. It was just unfortunate that he'd decided to wear a vest threaded through with their black feathers. Everyone was so jumpy about the Slashers that even a child came under extreme scrutiny for having a momentary lapse in judgment. So yeah, I'd released him, and I still wasn't sorry about it.

Crowley, of course, had blustered and raged at me for it, but I'd just feigned ignorance that he'd wanted the kid thrown in solitary. No way in the twin hells was I going to let that arsehole detain a child, and he might have been pissed about it and even known I was lying, but that in and of itself wasn't a crime. I'd broken no laws, and that was the part that, no doubt, chaffed Crowley's hide. The arrogant prick. He *would* tattle on me like a little bitch.

"You know I can't tell you that, Elle. You're a damn fine detective. You and your partner."

I opened my mouth, but suddenly, Maddox's foot was on mine, and he was pressing down just shy of bruising my toes. Whipping my head around, I glowered at him and yanked my foot back. He looked less than impressed by my show of temper.

"I daresay one of the best we've ever seen."

"You mean the best," I muttered, and Maddox lifted his foot to try again. I whipped my finger up and tensed, letting him know in no uncertain terms that things would end badly if he stomped on me again.

Smart man that he was, he didn't make another attempt at it.

"Look, here is the truth, if you want it. Yeah, this is babysitting bullshit, but no, it can't be helped. We know the Slasher Gang is targeting high-profile locales—banks, high-end exhibits, galas such as the one King Midas is hosting this evening. It only makes sense that we will need eyes and ears that I can trust on scene. Rumors are floating on the streets about some big heist getting ready to go down. Our analysts are sure this is where it'll happen."

Some of the fire went out of me. It did make a certain kind of sense. The type of event where jewels, gold, and unimaginable wealth were out on full display would be like ringing the dinner bell to hellhounds. Yet... I glanced over at Maddox. He was looking straight ahead at the wall over Bo's shoulder, his one hunter-green eye blazing like sun-stroked emeralds.

He was witnessing something yet to come. I frowned, questioning how much I could really afford to believe his premonitions. Hook was impossible, and if even one of Maddox's premonitions was false, it brought into question all his other ones. Just how much of what he thought was right actually was? What if he'd just been extraordinarily lucky?

Yet the odds of having that kind of luck were next to impossible, which put me right back to square one. Just what was going on with Hatter's ability?

It only just dawned on me that the captain had stopped speaking. I glanced down at her, but she was looking at Hatter, consternation pinching her eyebrows.

Maddox had already outed his strange abilities long ago around here, almost from the very first day. So everyone in the precinct was well aware of his proclivity toward "spacing out," but I knew it made most of them uncomfortable.

"He'll be done soon. I'm sure of it," I said in a low voice, then without skipping a beat, I placed my hand upon the uncovered sliver of his wrist, as though I were trying to gently pull him out of the visions, when in truth, I was doing anything but.

Maddox had tattoos on his body, one on each arm, and a few others in certain other lovely parts, none of which were pertinent at the moment.

But the arms in particular were also "special." They were images of a female devil on one and an angelic being on the other, both of them wearing the face of his one-time partner Alice.

He'd never explained the reason for the tattoos or why both figures wore her face. All I knew was those tattoos were just as magical as his eyes. No one in the precinct knew about that little secret. Hatter hadn't shared it, and I wouldn't betray his confidence in that way. It was because of the markings—which could literally glow at the drop of a dime—that Hatter always wore his long jacket at work.

But when I moved my thumb, I scraped against the heated image upon his flesh, and I saw what he saw. There was darkness, the howling of winds, and fear—fear so thick, so cloying that it felt like being coated in heated tar.

My heart rate kicked up, my pulse sped so hard I grew dizzy, and I felt myself sinking into the darkness of waves that were not actually waves. They were other, but I didn't know what.

Suddenly, the vision blanked out, and I felt my partner give himself a slight shake, the same as he always did when he'd been freed of the vision. I surreptitiously released his arm, but he knew I'd peeked. Hatter had told me once it was like stripping his flesh off his body and laying his soul bare when he shared a vision.

Which was probably why he loathed doing it and had refused to tell anyone that he could. But he'd never minded sharing with me, said if we were partners we shouldn't have secrets when it came to our cases.

The thing of it was, that hadn't felt like anything at all related to our case. I shoved my hands into my pockets, knowing I couldn't ask him about it until we were alone.

Bo looked between us two before asking, "You good now?"

Maddox grunted.

"All right, well," she said slowly, as though regathering the lost threads of thought. "Anyway, masquerade ball. All the details to the event can be found inside..." She reached back into the drawer of her desk that I was sure had been spelled to be bottomless—I could have sworn I'd heard a wolf's howl once when she opened it—and pulled out a pure gold envelope that gleamed like molten metal in the light. "The invitation with coordinates as well. I don't think I need to tell you guys to remain undercover. If there is a theme, keep in character. If the Slashers are there when you arrive, you mustn't do anything to stand out. Keep the king safe at all costs, and for the gods' sake, don't let any of his jewels go missing, or Draven will have us all for lunch."

She handed Maddox the invite. He took it and slid it into his black dinner jacket. Then she nodded toward the door. "You may leave, Maddox."

I turned to follow my partner out the door, but Bo cleared her throat. "Elle, a minute, please."

I blew out a hard raspberry. Maddox glanced back at us worriedly, but like the good little soldier he was, he left without another word, silently shutting the door behind him.

Turning, I shrugged. "You wanted me?"

Bo stood, leaning forward on the surface of the desk with her fingers spread. "It's been two months, Detective. How are you holding up?"

I knew what she was and wasn't asking. She wasn't asking whether Hatter and I got on, because that was obvious to anyone who bothered to look. She was asking, however, about the other thing, the very thing Hatter had tried to talk to me about this morning. And I would think a conspiracy was afoot between the two of them except for the small matter of us having literally just arrived.

I wrapped my arms around my chest, wishing like the twin hells that Maddox hadn't reported his vision to Bo. By the books, he had to. But as a friend, I wished he'd kept that little tidbit between us, mainly because I didn't want to revisit it, ever again.

I'd done my mandated counseling, I'd been given the green light to return to work, and that had been that. Instead, I had to deal with a boss who was really, really good at coaxing details out of me that I wouldn't have even given my own mother—if I'd ever actually had one, that was. It was part of Bo's shepherdess training, no doubt, but bloody hells, it was annoying.

I shrugged, not even sure what to say.

"If you need to speak with—"

I held up my hand. "Let me just stop you right there, Captain. I appreciate the concern, but *he* is a nonissue. *He* is also very much dead. So please, if we could just—"

"Detective Maddox Hatter's visions have a one hundred percent success rate. I understand that this is hard—"

I snort laughed, but heat burned the backs of my eyes. "Oh, do you? Do you really? Are you seriously going to stand here and tell me that you understand what I'm going through? Please don't patronize me, Captain. You've had your partner how long now? Thirty? Thirty-five years? You have no idea what this feels like." I chewed the words out, feeling as if I were ripping at a scab that had just barely begun to heal over. I had to make them stop, all of them. I knew they were just trying to be there for me, but giving me false hope wasn't helping. In fact, it was only hurting me.

Sirens weren't supposed to be capable of falling in love. We were creatures of the flesh, of the lusts, almost solely. So the fact that I'd done just that had left me vulnerable in a way few of my kind, or any other, could ever fully appreciate.

I'd committed the one act any good siren knew to never, ever do. I'd fallen in love, and I'd paid the ultimate price for betraying what and who I was.

"Thirty-one," she corrected softly before lowering her eyes and staring at a lamb-shaped paperweight on her desk. She was still for a few seconds, then I saw her fingers clench before she finally turned to look back up at me. She blew out a heavy breath. "You're right, Elle. I don't know. What I do know is this. I can't lose you. You are vital not just to Grimm PD but also to me personally. You're smart. You're crazy intuitive, and Melanie and I have been discussing my retirement for some time now, and there are only a few names that come to mind when I make my suggestion to the commander for my replacement."

I blinked. That wasn't at all been what I'd been expecting to hear. I wrapped my arms even tighter around myself, feeling oddly vulnerable. "You? You really think I could be captain someday?"

All my life, I'd been a screwup, to royal protocol, to what was expected of me, but mostly to my own father, who'd felt he had no choice but to curse me for bringing such dishonor to our family name. The list of people who hadn't looked at me like a major screwup was piteously low. It probably didn't help matters that I was as prickly as a barracuda with a toothache most days.

I swallowed hard.

She thinned her lips. "Well, that time isn't for a while yet. But yes, Elle, you definitely make the short list. So whatever the hells it is that's got your head out of the game, fix it. If it's Hook, fix it. If it's Maddox—"

I snorted, quickly shaking my head.

She just gave me a look that I in no way wanted to decipher. "If it's Maddox," she said again, "fix it. If it's something else, then godsdamnit it, fix it. But just fix it, Elle. You hear me? Don't give Crowley any more reason to hang around. You got that? I don't know why, but that man has a serious hard-on for you."

I clenched my molars. She was right. As grumpy as that thought made me, she was absolutely right. I'd been getting into bad habits again. Maddox's vision had thrown me for a loop. I knew that, and I was obviously doing a piss-poor job of hiding it. All I had left was my work, and I took pride in that. I blew out long breath through my nose before giving Bo a hard nod.

"Pretty sure the masquerade tonight is a high-class S&M theme. Black and white and gold only. FYI," Bo said, raising her chin at the door. "You and Maddox are free to go and find what you need for tonight if you don't have anything appropriate. Looking forward to reading your report in the morning. And I don't think I need to tell you this, but don't let him die, Detective. A royal death on our watch is the last thing this department needs to deal with."

After snapping a sharp salute, I turned and made for the door.

When I stepped out, I gently eased the door shut behind me. The precinct was a buzz of activity. Hatter, just as I'd expected him to be, was leaning against the wall, clearly waiting on me, reading the invitation in his hand.

"S&M and gold, black, and white," he murmured, lifting a sharp-peaked eyebrow and looking at me.

"So I heard. Bo gave us permission to go and shop on company funds for tonight. I have nothing."

He tucked the envelope into the pocket of his jacket then tapped his chest with two fingers and said in his whiskey-smooth Landian drawl, "I might have something. Care to visit Wonderland?"

I used to hate Wonderland. Now, I didn't hate it so much. I smiled softly, almost looking forward to visiting the quirky realm.

Lifting up on my toes, I nodded but pointed down the hall. "We'll need to get an all-access key card from Thantor, then yeah, I'd like to see Alice again."

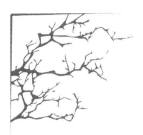

Chapter 3

Detective Maddox

WE WERE TRAVELLING through an intra-dimensional portal, making our way toward Wonderland at the speed of light.

Elle was looking down at her crossed feet, a tight pinch to her eyebrows and around her tense mouth. She wasn't happy, hadn't been since my return, and I'd worry that it was me, but I knew the truth.

Maybe I shouldn't have told her what I'd seen, but I abhorred lies, especially lies between partners. That wasn't the way I wanted to start things off with us. Now, though I wasn't sure if I'd made the right choice. Things between us had hit a stalemate and were pretty much at their frostiest.

Interoffice romances were verboten, and I understood why. Relationships were a complication that didn't need to become an added burden between work partners. Alice and I had been such a disaster that I was in no hurry to jump into any new romantic entanglements, yet Elle had made me feel alive again. Even now, when things weren't at their best between us, she made me burn with verve. I felt centered around her, more capable, better able to work through complex puzzles, to not get so pulled into the chaotic visions in my head, always lost to the world because I was too full of prophetic images scrolling through my head. Elle quieted all of that, and I knew it was because she was my intellectual equal. I didn't need to work through the puzzles alone because I had her.

It wasn't just lust that drew me to Elle, though there was that. Sirens exuded pheromones that made them catnip to everyone, but Alice was a sex therapist. Flesh and the carnal weren't anything new or even all that arousing to me anymore.

What turned me on more than anything was a meeting of the minds, someone with whom I shared interests, hobbies, someone who understood that a thinking being was a far more complex organism than just what gender or sex dictated one should be.

I opened my mouth, but nothing came out. It was hells not knowing what I should and shouldn't do where she was concerned. One thing I did know—Hook was off limits. I clamped my lips shut. Maybe I had been wrong. After all, it was two months since I'd told her and six months since I'd begun to have images of his return, and my visions had yet to manifest. I'd never been wrong before, but there was always a first time for everything.

The thought made me sick to my stomach because I realized now just how much I'd always depended on my visions, always believed them infallible. But what if they weren't? What if I was no longer the same? Maybe it had been Wonderland's soil that had fed my magick, and after being gone for so long without the twisted madness of Wonderland sinking its feelers into me, I was losing that part of me that I'd taken for granted would simply always be there.

The tension between Elle and me was so thick I could cut it with a knife. I'd love to know what in the hells Bo had told her, but if Elle wanted me to know, she'd tell me—eventually. I was sure of it.

To the rest of the world, Elle might appear prickly and distant, only ever giving others a superficial impression of herself or what she thought, at best. But she wasn't that. If anything, Elle had trust issues, and unless she fully trusted you, she'd never give you more than a cursory idea of what and who she really was. In that, however, she and I were the exact same.

The starlit doorway opened. Immediately, I was blasted with the familiar scents of home: the smog of heavy machinery belching their black fumes into the perpetually overcast and gray skies of the city square; the street vendors selling their greasy wares; the petrichor of fresh rains; and all of it mixed in with the stench that all big cities boosted, no matter how clean they tried to be.

The buildings were all crawling toward the heavens like long, gnarled, and twisted fingers. Several dirigibles steamed and puttered gracefully through the skies, modes of transportation reserved only for the wealthiest of Landians.

For a second, I suffered a small pang of homesickness when I stepped out. This had once been home, and it had also once been the epicenter of my cntire world, but with the loss of my daughter, Wonderland had lost all its appeal for me. I would always love it because of the memories of her forever tied to it, but I was happy to be freed of the shackles that had burdened me for so long.

Grimm was my home now. It was where I felt free and alive, for the first time in a long time. But I still had connections to Wonderland, one of which would come in handy tonight.

"Come," I grunted and quickly crossed the street to avoid oncoming golden carriages wheeling the obnoxiously wealthy a few meters here and there, their legs all but useless after so many years of disuse.

It was always easy to spot the truly filthy rich. They were generally dressed in the most ridiculous fashions that they believed made them the epitome of desirable, and they never looked anyone in the eyes because they were far too good for the common rabble.

Elle was hard on my heels. In seconds, I spied the wooden placard of the Crypt swaying in the gentle breeze above Alice's nondescript sex shop.

I opened the door and stood aside, allowing Elle to enter first. She breezed right through, and I smirked. There'd once been a time when she would have hissed at me for daring to open doors for her. I'd call this progress, meager though it was.

I'd rung up Alice before coming, so this time when we entered there was no scent of labulum coral and black anemone being pumped through the vents. That combination turned my partner into the darker, madder version of her—a version that could kill, that *had* killed.

The shop was buzzing with patrons, more than was normal for this time of day. I glanced around at the scantily dressed men and women of all species. The low sounds of sex were a constant refrain in the background. But after years of hearing sex, I was no longer affected by it.

"Busier than usual," Elle remarked in a low voice, as though she said it more for her benefit than mine. I nodded anyway. Elle looked as similarly disaffected as I was. Considering she was a siren with a siren's appetites, I was not at all surprised.

Alice popped out from behind a shelf. A black wardrobe bag was draped over her forearm, and she wore a dress fashioned entirely from a silver netting of nothing but sewn-together diamond chips.

Dusky of skin with striking ice-blond hair that fell in luscious thick waves down her back, she was as beautiful as always. Her eyes were dark blue and shaded with a thick layer of smoky black eye shadow. Her lips were as red as blood.

"Oh, there you are," she said, eyes widening, and she patted her hair back in place, as though she'd been startled by our sudden arrival. Alice no longer wore her blue ribbons she'd been known far and wide for, because it had been those very ribbons that had nearly been her undoing.

"Maddox." She smiled softly and leaned in to kiss my whiskered cheek, laying her palm on my shoulder to pull me down to her, calm and poised once more.

It had been many months since Elle and I had saved Alice from swinging on the hangman's noose for a series of murders she'd been framed for by a dirty beat cop in Grimm.

"Alice," I said deeply, sometimes still surprised by the silent truce we'd seemingly entered into, and gave her a quick hug of greeting.

If anyone had asked me whether it would be possible for Alice and me to find a peaceful coexistence again, I'd have declared it to be an impossibility. We had so much bad history between us. Yet here we were, never the same but no longer so far apart, either.

"Elle," Alice said in her cultured voice and dipped her head toward my partner, who snorted and pulled her in for a quick hug.

I thinned my lips in shock. Elle wasn't the demonstrative sort. A ghost of a grin touched Alice's composed mask. Blue eyes full of pleasant surprise stared up at me, and I shrugged. Elle often surprised me. Alice patted Elle's back awkwardly, but I knew her well enough to know she hadn't minded the touch.

They broke away just seconds later.

"It's good to see you again," Elle said and sounded as though she really meant it. "How are things?"

Alice shrugged a slim shoulder, sighing deeply but still wearing the ghost of a grin. "The same—yet different too. Seems murder really helps drum up business. Who knew."

Elle snorted. "You'd be surprised what a hot commodity a sexy possible murderess suddenly becomes with a business like yours."

Alice laughed, the sound artlessly sultry. Alice didn't try to exude sex. It simply came naturally to her. "I'm figuring that out." Then she glanced at me and dipped the wardrobe bag toward me. "I had to call in a favor with a client of mine, but I'm sure this will be a perfect fit. And for you, Elle, I have one of my own costumes, if you're daring."

Dark-blue eyes glittered with challenge. "I'm fairly certain you couldn't possibly have anything for me I haven't seen or tried at least once before."

"I'm counting on it. I doubt many would be willing to try, yet I'm certain you are one of the few who could wear this and not have it wear you. Besides," she said with a shrug and a full-lipped smirk, "Midas is rather a bit of a snob when it comes to his infamous soirees. You want in close with the king, then trust me on this."

Elle chuckled darkly. "I'm well aware of the king's dark proclivities. But we go on business and not pleasure. He will invite us in whether we're gauche or not. He'll have no choice on the matter."

"I rather thought you might be. And true enough, but you'll get a much more cooperative king this way." Alice grinned then dipped her head at us both. "Come, follow me to the dressing room."

Her round bottom flexed with her steps, causing the diamonds to wink and glimmer in the haunting lime-green lighting. Rolls of fog swirled around our ankles. Everything about the Crypt was designed to appeal to the baser side of our sexual natures.

Alice would often switch up the décor on the inside. Sometimes there'd be a Roman orgy theme, other times a dark, dank dungeon, and so on. Today it looked like a haunted forest with creeping willow vines shuddering from beams above us, and the creaking, rustling sounds of wind through trees ringing all around. Come to think of it, most of the beings I'd seen when we'd entered had been of the woodland variety.

Clasping my hands behind my back, I followed the ladies at a sedate pace, studying them both. Elle was pale and exotically beautiful: long dark-blue hair, eyes so electric blue they seemed to create their own light, and skin that glimmered with mother-of-pearl undertones. Even dressed in the ridiculous combat boots, leather jacket, and cocktail dress as she was, she commanded attention from all.

But Alice was no shrinking violet. Where Elle was light, she was dark and just as exotic. Alice wasn't originally from Wonderland. She'd come from another realm entirely, smuggled in for her unearthly beauty and sold to the highest bidder by a marauding band of pirates who'd profited most generously for it. She'd been trained in the arts of seduction, and the student had eventually exceeded the master.

Alice didn't remember her other life, and my research into her true origins hadn't dug up much. Who she'd been born to, and what she might have been groomed to have one day become had been lost to time immemorial. But Alice was content with her lot. She was a freed woman who did as she pleased, "And that," as she'd said, "is worth more than all the gold and jewels in the all the worlds."

Her steps closely matched Elle's, and every so often she'd intentionally brush up against Elle, her breast casually grazing Elle's forearm. I knew Alice well enough to know she was putting out subtle cues that she was willing to enter into a liaison if the siren was also willing.

I clenched my jaw and swallowed hard. They would make a lovely pair—none could deny it.

Stopping at the end of a long hall, Alice pointed to a closed door. "Through there. You'll find all you'll need."

Elle dipped her chin and opened the door, and immediately, the scent of roses punched me square in the nose as she walked inside. This was Alice's personal changing room.

I made to follow and glanced at Alice, who was still standing there, a faraway look in her eyes.

I frowned. "Aren't you joining us?"

Blue eyes cut to mine. "What? To watch you both change? I've better things to do with my time. Besides, she does not wish for me to be there. And I do not go where I am not wanted."

Glancing into the verdant garden thick with freshly imported long-stemmed white roses and many other floral varieties, I searched for Elle's familiar blue hair, but she was lost in the thick maze. "You don't know that."

Alice was the epitome of culture and refinement, so when she gave a snorting type of scoff, I noticed. Her hand was on her hip. "I do know that, and the fact that you can't see what's so clearly obvious to me in just a matter of minutes worries me exceedingly."

"See what?"

She smiled gently and patted my cheek. "My dear one, you were never knowingly blind with me."

I frowned, brows gathering into a tight *V*. "If you are perhaps alluding to there being something between my partner and me, you are sorely mistaken. We work together. Who Elle chooses to sleep with is none of my concern." My words were steady, confident, but my hands clenched into tight fists by my sides.

She inhaled deeply and glanced down at my now relaxed hands. Her full lips thinned. "As you say, Hatter." She looked as though she meant to leave but gave her head a slight shake and grimaced before saying, "Does she know? Who you really are? *What* you are?"

A slight tick in my cheek muscle betrayed my inner turmoil as I glanced left and right to make certain we were truly alone. "She knows about Mariposa, if that's what you're implying."

She shrugged. "I figured she would. She's a smart one, that siren. But you know that's not what I meant."

I could play dumb, but she and I both knew it would be disingenuous. I knew what she was asking. Elle had seen a few aspects of my otherworldly nature, the darker part of me I worked like the twin hells to keep hidden.

Licking my front teeth, I adjusted my cravat with fingers that suddenly felt numb and cold. "I don't see any reason why that needs to come up. As I said, we only have a working relationship. I was thoroughly vetted before becoming a Grimm detective. I've been as honest as could be, but who I really am is no one's concern, least of all my partner's."

"You keep telling yourself that if it helps, Maddox. But if you should decide for more with her, be honest. It helps. Not just anyone could accept what you really are."

I heard what she wasn't saying. It wasn't just Mariposa's end that had spelled doom for our relationship. Most days, I kept a tight leash on my emotions. But when my only child had died, a part of me had died with her, and that part, for a time, had been control of the darkness. Alice had seen the very worst of me. I did not blame her for walking away then, and I did not blame her now.

I chuckled darkly. "Alice, while I appreciate your kindness with me, I must assure you that in this you are wrong. Elle and I do not work as a pair outside of Grimm duties. I may have briefly entertained the idea of there being more. Once. And I vow to you that had there been, I would have told her all first. But there is not, and I do my partner a service by my silence. You know that I do." I thinned my lips and nodded hard once, the subject closed so far as I was concerned.

She shrugged, dropped her hand, and took a small step back. "Then I guess there's no more to say." Her eyes suddenly sparkled as she shoved the wardrobe bag into my chest. "Hope you like what I've chosen. Though knowing you as I once did, I figured you'd be game for a little role play."

Narrowing my eyes, I stared down at the bag in my hands. "What did you pick out for me?"

She laughed airily. "You'll see soon enough, my darling." Then she kissed the tips of her fingers and brushed past me, gliding as though she walked on air back into the den of sexual delights that awaited her.

With a coughing grunt and a curious heart, I slipped through the open door. It slid gently shut behind me. The world was a living garden that burst with neon-blue butterflies gliding lazily through the twilit skies. Everything smelled of the finest imported flowers from all corners of the hundred realms: the lush scent of jasmine, the heady fragrance of roses, the gentle lushness of honeysuckle, and so many others.

But beneath it all, I smelled Elle—water and darkness. I'd learned her scent long ago. It was in me now, and I knew that no matter what, I would always find her.

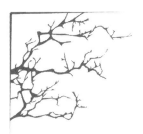

Chapter 4

Detective Elle

I HEARD THE SNAPPING of a twig before I felt the presence of another person.

Turning on my six-inch black-leather thigh-high heels, I saw Hatter walk toward me like a feral, loping predator.

My heart rate quickened. I would say it was the flowers. Everyone knew the flowers of Wonderland drove everyone mad. But though the garden dripped with their rich verdant scents, those were not native Landian blooms.

He watched me unflinchingly as he drew nearer to me, his dark eyes looking almost black in the moon's heavy glow.

"I love the strange madness of this land," I admitted, as though in a trance.

He stopped walking at the sound of my unwitting confession. I hadn't meant to say that, but my pulse had been beating so fast in my throat as he'd drawn closer to me.

I never had to tell Maddox where I was or where I was going. Yet somehow, he always found me.

He grinned, and the play of shadow and moonlight along the sharp lines of his face made him appear devilish. I pressed a hand to my stomach.

It was rare that Maddox and I ever found time to be truly alone together. We were always busy, rushing from one scene to another, or if we were at our office, there was a constant stream of chaos just outside our open door. Maddox had never come to my eternal waters again, and I never went to his apartment.

I thought the madness of him, the way his nearness had infected me like venom during our very first case together, had waned in me. But I saw now that it wasn't true at all.

If anything, I was more aware of him.

"You didn't always," he said in that thick drawl that had me feeling suddenly weak in the knees.

I'd been aware of Alice's cues earlier as we walked toward the dressing room but hadn't felt much. But all Maddox had to do was look at me with dark secrets shading his eyes, and I felt wildness stir through my blood. That ancient siren's magick had only ever gripped me once before—with Hook.

I shuddered as I thought about my dead lover, and that finally gave me impetus enough to break away from Maddox's hypnotic lure. I turned my back to him and stared into the vanity that sat in the middle of the expansive gardens. Bulbs glowed a soft golden hue on the mirrored frame.

There was nothing sitting upon the desk save for a velvet-lined black mask with threads of swirling gold upon it, an opened can of glittering golden paint, and a small, dainty black riding crop.

There'd also been a pair of ridiculously high heels that I now wore. I'd had to buckle the damned things—they were leather and lace and buckles and stupid. How would I be expected to fight—if it came to that—in something like this?

Still, I had to stick to the theme, and the outfit certainly did that.

I touched the tip of the paint jar. "I suppose I am meant to paint myself?"

Suddenly, I felt the overwhelming wave of his presence cover me, and when I glanced up, Maddox stood right behind me, so close I felt the brush of his heat pressing against my own.

His multihued eyes burned with a lick of orange flame right at their center. Only once had I seen Maddox burn with fire that he'd created. My pulse kicked into overdrive as I recalled just how primal, how... animalistic he'd been then.

Rather than putting me off, it had called to me, enticed me, hypnotized me. Sometimes I thought that maybe I'd dreamt it, but then I saw him like this, shaded by madness and moonlight, looking like some demon that had crawled straight out of the twin hells, and I thought that maybe my partner was so much more than what I could ever imagine.

He reached around me, took the jar of paint into his large hand, and said in that deep, whiskey-drawl of his, "This is not for you."

I frowned and turned, almost immediately regretting my decision to do so, because he was so big and overwhelming, and... and... my fingers twitched as I felt the first stirrings of my dark hunger slink and slither through my veins like an unfurling snake.

As if sensing my turmoil, Maddox took three giant steps back, still holding tight to the pot of gold paint. "I know what Alice has planned for me. She always teased that one day she'd get me to play dress-up with her. She's now gotten her way."

I quivered and clutched at my stomach, feeling like an untried virgin. I didn't know what in the hells my partner did to me whenever we came to Wonderland, but somehow I always felt like a wreck around him when we were here.

"Hatter," I breathed, not pausing to think through my words, "your magick is strongest in Wonderland, isn't it?"

"I'm not sure, Elle," he whispered darkly then tipped his chin toward the mask. "But you should get dressed. We still have to try to find this bloody place."

He faded into the bushes, leaving me alone. I turned and stared at my face in the mirror. I looked pale, my skin too purple beneath my eyes, my lips a dull red. My hair looked fine, though—maybe just needed a little smoothing out to tame the cowlicks.

Alice was right. Midas was a vain man and didn't want to just be beautiful—he wanted to be surrounded by nothing but beauty.

For all his vanity, though, I actually had a soft spot for the golden king. He was fiercely intelligent and had a ribald sense of humor that appealed to me greatly.

My hands shook a little as I shrugged off my leather jacket. Though I preferred my combat boots and black leather, Midas would not.

Unfortunately, I couldn't wear the garment Alice had laid out for me, either. The dress the faeries had made me was nonnegotiable—that was, if I actually wanted to breathe. And though I appreciated the gesture of wearing nothing but glittering rope between my arse cheeks, I simply couldn't. The outfit certainly would have made Midas notice me, though. She'd been right about that. Breasts out and arse covered with nothing but floss.

I remembered Midas from my years at my father's court. An old man even then, he should have long since given up the ghost, yet rumor had it that Midas's heart was unlike any other. His heart, it was said, was as immortal as the gold he loved so well, keeping him locked in an age that was neither too young nor too old.

Midas had always liked my looks, but then I was a siren and appealed to pretty much anything that had a pulse. But that didn't mean I couldn't make myself look even better than I naturally did.

It had been a long time since I'd bothered to try, but tonight, I would try, because I was going to be the brightest pearl at that gala. I was going to make Midas want me close.

I opened a drawer and rummaged around for makeup, knowing Alice had to have some around. Sure enough, I struck gold. She had several cases' worth of quality rouges, color pots, lip dyes, and so on.

I'd never been much for the styles of my court, which had been decidedly elaborate and ostentatious, but any female of marrying age was required to know at least the basics of beautification.

My eldest sister, Andrina, had been the best of the seven of us at applying hers and had taught me several of her tricks, one of which was that I didn't need to have a steady hand when applying eye paint. I could just smudge the edges to give myself a smoky-eye quality. If I was going to wear a mask, there was no sense in getting more elaborate than that. Most of it would be covered, anyway.

I grabbed the silk mask and held it up to my face, checking to see how much of my eyes would show, then made sure to apply the richest application of deep-hued indigo powder to those sections. I also added silver glitter at the edges. With my naturally blue eyes, the color combination gave me an otherworldly quality.

Once I was satisfied with the edges, I quickly tied on the mask. Once it was in place, I applied long false eyelashes that had golden phoenix feathers laced throughout.

I blinked and wiggled my eyes. The falsies held fine. I looked like an electric peacock, which was just what I'd been going for.

I took a pot of pale-pink rouge and gently applied a little. I didn't want to look like a hooker. I *did* want to look like a high-class harlot, though. Midas definitely had a type.

The pale-opal quality of my skin played nicely with my color palette. All that was left was the lip stain. I found one called Sugared Berries, not quite pink or purple but somewhere in between the two.

I quickly applied it and held my mouth open until it dried. The stain smelled of the berries it was named after. Cocking my head, I glanced at myself in the mirror and was startled to see a woman I'd not seen in ages. The last time I'd bothered to paint myself had been when I was still the apple of my court. Father had hated me, but everyone else had loved me—or at the very least, fawned at my feet.

Snarling, I wanted to wipe the damned paint off and just go as I was.

"You ready?" Maddox's deep voice rolled through my body like a heated wave, caressing my insides, drawing me in.

My breath scissored out of me as I opened my eyes and stared at him, rendered speechless by his transformation.

Hatter's style was always impeccable, but I'd never seen him like this before. He had on trousers that molded so perfectly to him they almost seemed like a second skin. His chest, arms, and face were coated in gold paint so thick you could not make out any of the tattoos on him. It gave him an alien, otherworldly beauty. Whenever he breathed, he shone like fire. But that wasn't how he'd looked when he'd burned like an inferno months earlier. This fire was molten gold, and my pulse skittered loudly in my ears.

His dark hair was slicked back, and he wore a black crown that wasn't dull but gleamed like a polished onyx stone.

He watched me watch him, and I could have sworn that his pupils were large black pools threatening to drown me in them. I clenched my jaw.

"You look—"

"Ridiculous," he said with a roll of his eyes, and I snapped my mouth shut, because that hadn't been the word that had come to my mind.

"Did you get your back?" I asked him.

"I'm fine," he said with a nod, "but I could use help with this." He turned his palm over, and in his hand was a men's black silk collared tie with a large

Victorian broach on it. Chipped diamonds framed the black gem at its center.

I blinked, feeling unsettled. My stomach was squeezing in on itself. He smirked at me. His look said he knew I wouldn't do it. I narrowed my eyes, and steeling my nerve, I snatched the damned tie off his palm.

Devilish brows lifted, but a cocky grin stole across his handsome golden face. I looked him up and down. Even with my newfound six inches, Maddox was still taller than me.

"Kneel," I commanded, voice ringing out with just a hint of the siren's command in it.

I wasn't hypnotizing him to obey, but I was challenging him right back.

"As my partner commands," he drawled as he smoothly knelt beside me.

He made a very pretty sight on his knees. Big and strong male that he was, submitting to me, it was empowering in its own right. I'd never failed to appreciate the S&M subculture, but I had to say, I liked it even more right now.

I took one step to the side so that I stood right behind him and spread my thighs. That way, I framed his body within the *V* of my legs. He rested his muscular back against me. His flesh was hot and silky to the touch.

I glanced at my thighs, noting that the paint hadn't transferred from him to me. Of course Alice would only have the best on hand. I wet my lips, lowered the collar, and wrapped it around his strong, corded neck. I felt his warm inhalation wash across my wrist, and I couldn't help but shiver.

"Is this too tight?" I asked, voice huskier than I'd planned on it being.

His warm fingers grazed mine, and it was as if a jolt of lightning had suddenly run through me. I tried not to, but my thighs twitched at his touch.

How long had it been since I'd had sex? With anyone?

I frowned, realizing it had been too long, too damned long. I was a siren, for the gods' sake. I needed to feed the bottomless hunger every now and then just to keep my bestial side in check. But I'd been so busy, so focused on work, that somehow it had completely slipped my mind. I knew if I'd fed my beast, these innocent touches wouldn't be affecting me so much.

"Tighter," he said, and I grunted, more to relieve some of the sexual tension flexing like a hot flame between us.

"You make that sound so dirty." I smirked and squeezed the tie tighter, banding my fingers around the front of his neck so that his windpipe bulged against my palm.

He sucked in a sharp breath and shook his head, and I could have sworn he rumbled a sound of appreciation so low that it vibrated straight through my thighs. My knees felt as though they were in very real danger of giving out on me. I needed to end this situation quickly.

I'd never seen a collar quite like this one. It didn't buckle. It laced together and was done in such a way that, done right, the laces would form an intricate knot at the back.

I frowned, wondering what the knot was for—until Hatter reached down and picked up something and handed me a black leather leash just a second later.

"You want me to walk you?" I asked in disbelief.

"I believe," he said in his whiskey-drawl, "that is exactly what this costume was designed for. But if you'd rather not, I'm sure I could find someone else to parade me about."

I snorted, shaking my head softly. "Alice has a cruel sense of humor, I think."

"Well," he said as he adjusted his collar, "if there is one thing I can trust Alice to handle, it's how to dress me for a costume ball, especially one like this. Besides, our outfits will be tame compared to what I've seen at most S&M balls I've been to before."

I slipped the leash out of his grasp, quickly looped it through the knot, gave it a good tug to make sure it was secure, and nodded. "Do this often then, do you? You can get up now, by the way. I'm done."

As he glanced at me over his shoulder, with his hands on his slightly spread knees and no shoes on his feet, it was so easy to imagine that he wasn't my partner but my lover. I swallowed hard. Hatter and I hadn't gotten to finish what we'd started ages ago, but it was impossible to now, even if I'd had a mind to. Which I didn't. I absolutely didn't.

"I've done a great many things, Elle, and if you ever truly want to know them, all you have to do is ask."

My skin prickled at the thought. Just what kinds of things had my very straight-laced partner done before? At least, he appeared straight-laced on the surface, but I'd suspected for some time that Hatter was far from a vanilla kind of man. Considering he'd made a life with one of the hundred realms' most infamous madams, I was almost certain that his sexual conquests were as experimental and numerous as mine.

"After all, you are my partner," he said softly.

I thinned my lips. Partner. The reminder was like getting ice water dumped on my head. "Yes, we are that, aren't we?" I took two small steps back and smoothed down the bottom of my dress, feeling fidgety and strange. "I guess its time we should go."

He stood in one lithe motion, his movements darkly seductive. It had to be Wonderland that did that to him, turned him into sexual napalm, because the alternative wasn't one I was sure I comfortable with.

"You've got the key," he reminded me, and I reached into my bodice, where I'd tucked it beneath my breast.

I flashed the gold card at him. I loved Thantor sometimes. Travelling through way stations would have been a giant pain in our arses. At least this way we could arrive at Midas's gala exactly on time.

"Got it," I said then glanced at his trousers and failed to see any pockets. "Where did you hide the coordinates?"

"Latitude forty degrees, one minute, sixty seconds north. Longitude seventy-six degrees, thirty-seven minutes, thirty-five point thirty-nine seconds west."

I frowned. "And you're sure of this?"

He tapped his forehead. "I've got a brain for these sorts of things, Detective. Trust me."

"I do."

I swiped the key card through the air. The key had been created by the familiar of a high-ranking wizard. They couldn't in and of themselves create magick, not like their masters, but they could harness small amounts of their masters' magick, enough to create a special key that would help us access parts of the hundred realms shut off to almost everyone else. Being part of Grimm PD didn't often come with perks, but this was definitely one of the rare few.

A tunnel of swirling starlight opened before us, beckoning us to enter. Hatter went to take a step, but I grabbed his elbow and gently turned him toward me. I'd been thinking on the ride into Wonderland that I owed him more than I'd given him this morning.

In his own way, he was showing me he cared. I wasn't used to accepting kindness from anyone. But he was trying, and so would I.

"Before we go," I said softly, looking down at the carpet of jewel-green grass at our feet, "I just wanted to say—"

"You don't have to, Elle. I understand," he said gently.

Pursing my lips, I looked up at him with determination. "No, but I do. For so long, all I've had to rely on was me. That was it. I was betrayed by the one man I thought loved me more than anyone else in all the realms. And I lost the one man I'd ever really loved." I shook my head, reliving the memories all over again. "It made me cold. Bitter. Callous. I know that." I frowned, finding it so difficult to say the words, even though I knew I should.

He grabbed my hand and closed his bigger one around mine then covered both of ours with his other one as well. I swallowed hard, drowning in the jeweled depths of his eyes.

"Great loss affects us all in different ways, Elle. I get that. Maybe more than anybody. You never have to apologize for surviving the best way you knew how."

I nodded slowly, my tongue swollen with so many unspoken words.

Looking at the entrance to the starlit tunnel, I knew one thing. There was no way I was going to work through all of this right now.

"If we don't leave soon, we'll be late," I said.

Nodding, he reached behind himself and grabbed hold of the black leather rope tied to his collar. "Agreed. But in case I forget to tell you later, you look very handsome tonight."

I felt my lips twitch, stupidly pleased by his words. I'd been called many things in my life—beautiful, otherworldly, sexy. But never handsome. I pressed a fist against my midsection. There was something endearingly old-world about Maddox that I never would have thought I'd find attractive, yet here I was, contemplating doing something so beyond foolish again. I knew where this led for me—the same place it always did. I knew better than this.

If I had any shred of decency left to me, I'd walk away, put up my shields, and push him away. It was for the best, for the both of us.

"Let's go, Elle," he said, handing me the tip of the rope, and for some damn reason, it felt like more than just a rope when I took his offering, as if it was a metaphor for something more. I shivered.

"Yes, Hatter, let's go," I whispered back.

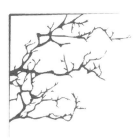

Chapter 5

Detective Elle

WE STEPPED OUT OF THE tunnel. I clung tightly to Hatter's rope, knuckles white from my tight grip.

The first thing I noticed was the spicy, fiery scent of brimstone. The next was the wafting heat that seemed to permeate the room and come from the very ground itself. There was a dull red glow and the sound of thickly burbling water. I frowned. Not water exactly, because I didn't feel even a drop of it in the air.

My skin felt hot, itchy. I swallowed hard and automatically rubbed a hand against my skirt, reveling in the silky smoothness of my enchanted waters threaded through the fae fabric, calming myself with each steady stroke. I would be fine, though I definitely didn't want to be here long. I felt Maddox draw closer to my back, his warmth pressing against me, but unlike the dehydrating heat of this strange world, his was welcomed.

I glanced around, studying the area, wondering if perhaps we'd been given the wrong coordinates. I heard no music, saw no other guests. I knew Midas well enough to know that this couldn't possibly be all, though the exotic locale would certainly be something I'd expect of the eccentric king.

I had an inkling of where we might be, though I'd never had occasion to come before.

The sky was a ghostly shade of navy blue with large skeletal beasts flapping massive bat-like wings as they gracefully glided by so quietly that unless I'd been looking at them, I would never have known they were there at all. Their eyes glowed like pinpricks of dancing flame.

What trees there were had been completely stripped of their leaves. They were black and twisted gnarled things with enormous roots that tore free of the blackened soil.

"Where are we?" I whispered, "Is—"

"This is Hel," Hatter said deeply, voice a velvety dark burr.

I glanced at him from over my shoulder. He had his eyes closed, and there was a pained look on his face. His jaw muscles were clenched tight, and now that I'd noticed that, the rest of him looked tense too.

"Are you having a vision?" I asked, hand lingering close to his forearm, ready to share in it with him.

He gave the merest shake of his head and opened his eyes. They blazed like jewels, and there were pinpricks of fire at his pupils, the same as there'd been in the beasts that had wheeled overhead. But they didn't glow the way they did when he was having a vision. This was his internal fire, and it looked to be going haywire.

"Just a little unwell of a sudden."

I gently frowned. "Do you need to go back to Grimm?"

He shook his head. "I'm sure this will pass soon. I'm fine."

He did sound stronger. But it was clear that whatever was going on with him, he didn't want to make a big deal of it, and as long as he could do his job, I wasn't going to make a big deal of it, either.

Nodding, I inhaled and turned to look back at the expansive dead zone. It was one of the two hells of Grimm, somewhat more habitable than its sister realm, Hell. Hel was said to be inhabited by creatures of air, land, and water. Whatever those bat-winged beasts had been in the air, it did look as though there was some form of life here.

"Okay, so why are we in Hel? Are you sure you didn't get a coordinate wrong?"

"I didn't get it wrong."

I shrugged and tossed my arms up. "Where now? What else did the invitation say?"

"That there'd be an escort for us. We just needed to answer a riddle."

I rolled my eyes, remembering Cheshire's constant riddles whenever I wanted to ask him anything. "Great. And why the hells is there a riddle when we were given an invitation? Doesn't that negate the whole 'invited' thing?" I asked grumpily.

He shrugged and said, "He's rich."

And I didn't even need to ask him what he meant, because he was absolutely right. The filthy rich did whatever the hells they wanted for the simple pleasure that they could, and for some bloody reason, it amused them to watch the peons sweat. And I should know, considering I'd once been heir apparent to the mightiest water realm in all of Grimm.

Pursing my lips, I looked to the left and right, sweating my arse off and getting more uncomfortable with each second that passed. Maddox's gold paint had to be sweating off too. If someone didn't pick us up soon, there was no way in the twin hells that Midas would invite us into his inner circle, not looking like drowned rats by the time we actually got there.

I tapped my toe, growing more and more fidgety with each second that ticked by. Where was this bloody escort, anyway?

A small mewling growl of displeasure tore up my throat. It was never wise to go traipsing through a realm one was unfamiliar with. Each realm was full of traps, and this being Hel, I doubted they'd be much fun.

"Be patient, Elle," Hatter said behind me. "The escort will be here."

"I'm just oozing patience," I snapped and wiggled my fingers. "Can't you tell? And how would you know, anyway? This is Hel. Just what kind of bloody escort should we expect, anyway?"

I glared at him, and he only smirked. "Oh yes, you overflow with it. And I know."

He said those last three words with complete authority, as if he really did know. And that was impossible, because until he'd landed a job at Grimm PD, Maddox had been realm bound, as most Grimmers were, which meant he was blowing smoke up my arse to try to get me to calm down.

I opened my mouth, not sure what else I meant to say, when I suddenly smelled the thick stench of thousand-year-old eggs—a delicacy in certain parts of Grimm. They were black on the outside and putrid green on the inside. Ichabod had a taste for them and would often use them like a weapon against me on the days he felt petty, masticating on them like a feeding cow, stinking up the entire precinct, and getting more than just my wrath for it.

Central station now had a strict no-putrid-eggs-for-lunch policy.

To me, those little bastards smelled like the wind passed by an ogre after a particularly malodorous meal of rancid meat and fatty bone marrow. I grimaced, placing my knuckles against my nostrils and breathing shallowly.

Maddox's pupils were glowing with fire again. What was wrong with him? He always had tight control of his flame, but today, I'd seen him flicker with it twice, and I knew that whoever we'd been waiting for must have finally shown up.

Frowning, I turned back, expecting to encounter a nightmare crawled straight out of the bowels of Hel, not a beautiful male, skin as dark as night, each muscle clearly delineated and brushed with a light dusting of gold-flecked powder. He was nude, save for a codpiece he wore tied around his waist, with the most absurdly huge erection that was impossible to ignore even if I'd tried, which I wasn't. I marveled at its thick realistic looking veins and the way it bobbed as a real cock would as he did a quick bow of greeting.

Good grief, he could impale someone with that thing. Who'd want to try that? But then I felt my body tingling at the thought, and I smirked. Apparently, I'd gone far too long without sex if even that thing could rev me up.

On his face was a black-and-white mask of a lion's face mid-roar. Eyes glowing the red of hell flame stared through the eyeholes. He was a demon, or some form of demon hybrid. Of that, I had absolutely no doubt, and he was staring unflinchingly at Maddox.

I couldn't read his face behind the mask, but his body was tense, tight, and I wasn't sure, but it seemed to me that he was definitely twitchy all of a sudden. I frowned, glancing back at Maddox. What the feck was this? Did they know each other?

"My name is Rasputen," he said, drawing me back to him and shutting down my curiosity for the time being. His voice was thick and gravelly, purring and exotic. My nipples turned into tiny little beads of instant wanting. I inhaled deeply, and this time when I did, I didn't scent putrid egg but dark fields of rich clover. My heart started to race, and my thighs began to quiver. My channel flooded instantly, and it was hard not to pant like a bitch in heat.

I gripped tight to Hatter's rein, wondering briefly how he was handling it.

Everything about this escort was meant to entice, to make you want, need, to the point that you'd go mad for a taste of the dark promise he had to offer. But the promise of heaven was actually more like hell when it came down to it, because that beautiful creature was a thing that had crawled straight out of the fiery pits, just as I'd expected something that came from Hel would.

"Incubus," I gritted out, fighting his inherently decadent nature with some of my own, allowing just a drop of my siren's will to spread through me, clearing out the haze of lust that had tried to infect my blood and bones. I shook my head free of the cobwebs and glared haughtily at him.

How embarrassing if I'd dropped my panties right here and right now for it.

Sex with a demon like that was a big fat nope in my book. Demon blood was infectious and addictive, and considering demons weren't capable of love, if they dragged you under their dark pull, it could quite literally spell your doom.

Rasputen dipped his head. "Siren," he said, and I could hear the smile on his lips. "A riddle I have for thee. In hell I hide. In heaven I am. But I am not in box. What am I?"

I frowned and turned to glance at Hatter, an unasked question in my eyes. *What the fecking bloody hells?*

He licked his front teeth, his golden face deep in thought, his eyes faraway. I could see him working through the riddle in his head.

Riddles were tricky beasts. Get them wrong, and there were no second chances. With Cheshire, if I said anything other than the answer, he'd consider I'd lost. Some riddlers would accept questions, and some would even give hints when asked. So which type of riddler was Rasputen? I looked back at the incubus.

He was still, flaming eyes on me alone. "Speak if you must, siren," he intoned in the voice of a male who sounded as though he'd just eaten a bowl of gravel.

"May we have a hint?"

"No. And you have only seconds left."

I blew out a harsh breath. Damn Midas to the twin hells. If I got sent back to Grimm Central empty-handed, Bo was going to have my proverbial nuts in a vise. Normally, I was good with riddles, but I wasn't good with them while under pressure. I could swear I felt the seconds ticking past, each one a loud boom in my ears.

Boom.

Boom.

Boom!

"Heaven. Hell. Not in box," I mumbled, trying to see the correlation between the three. The first two were obvious enough, but box was throwing me. Why had he worded it that way specifically, *not in box*, instead of the grammatically appropriate *not in a box*? Was that a clue? "Bloody hells. Hatter?"

I glanced over at him, hoping like hells my brilliant partner was closer than I was.

"Ten seconds," the incubus intoned, and when I glanced back at him, he held a timepiece in his hand, the golden sands spinning through the narrow opening at an alarmingly fast rate.

Heaven and hell, possible wings? Demonic and angelic? But box, what the hells did box have to do with anything? A halo? A broken halo? Box, though. Box was killing me.

"Dammit," I snapped. "Um, uh. It's..." I shook my head. "I don't know. It's—"

"The letter H," Maddox suddenly said, and the timepiece vanished from Rasputen's hand. He rolled his hands together, creating a whirling vortex between his palms that glowed like the red fire in his eyes.

"You may pass," he said, and the vortex spread from his palms, growing bigger and wider, creating an arched wooden doorway with a dark eye at its center that stared down on us. The eye was rimmed in a thick band of kohl with sweeping bands of turquoise and gold as well.

The creepy eye blinked, looking eerily at us. Its pupil was jet black, but its iris glowed golden.

"The eye of Horus," Maddox mumbled. "Midas is truly showing off his wealth tonight."

Rasputen stepped aside and spread his arm, silently telling us to enter.

Through the doorway, I could see the lights of the party, hear the low chatter of the revelers, and smell the rich decadence of the food.

"Lead the way, my goddess," Hatter said to me, his voice a silky command, and I twitched at the velvet purr behind his words. Then I realized he was playing his role, and now it was my turn to play mine.

"Let us away, pet," I purred, remembering the one and only time I'd played dom to a sub and hoped I was doing it right. I wasn't exactly vanilla, but in this strange world, I was pretty sure Hatter had far more experience than I. He gave a low growl of approval, and I smirked. It might be more fun than I'd imagined.

Tugging on his rope, I guided us into Midas's ostentatious gala of strange and exotic wonders.

Detective Maddox

THE MUSIC WAS LOW, sultry, velvety, and it blended seamlessly into the background. The foods were all aphrodisiacs: raw oysters chilled on the half shell; golden champagne with floating pomegranate pearls; cucumber slices with cheese swirls and a slice of smoked ruby red salmon; strawberries dipped in chocolate so dark it was nearly black. There were bacon-wrapped roasted asparagus tips with a chili demi-glaze glistening over the top and some sort of miniature pie that smelled of succulent meats and exotic spices. And the tables weren't made of wood or metal, but bodies, beautiful human and humanoid bodies. If you wanted to eat, you'd have to pick your hors d'oeuvres from off their breasts, thighs, and flat painted stomachs. It was excessive, indulgent, and completely over the top.

But that was just the food. There were court jesters dressed in black, white, and gold paint walking on fifty-foot stilts and acrobats swinging from above on swings made of roped pearls.

We were still in Hel, but it was a refined and elegant depiction of fire and brimstone. There were theater troupes dressed as glorious angels doing battle with equally beautiful demons, their black and white wings spread out as though ready to take flight behind them. They held swords in their grip, high and gleaming in the hazy red lighting.

There were hundreds of couples socializing in groups or smaller bands, all of them dressed in their erotic finest. Most of the women were in leather, some dressed from head to toe in it with only a zipper at their noses and mouths to breathe. Others were dressed only in transparent silks that did nothing to hide the curves of their bodies. Then there were a few like Elle who were clearly the dominant, dressed in suits with ties or leading their subs around by a length of golden chain. I was more dressed than most of the men, many of whom were as nude as Rasputen had been, wearing the absurd-ly large codpieces and animal masks painted in gold and mother of pearl.

It wasn't as warm in this place, which made me wonder what kind of air filter the king had used. Hel was never this pleasant. But endless coffers meant nothing was impossible.

I scanned the room, looking for Midas, knowing a retinue of guards would surround him and his entourage. It should be easy enough to get in close once we found him.

Though Elle was far more dressed than most of her gender, she burned brighter than all the rest. She was a phoenix risen from the burning eternal flame, mesmerizing and impossible to ignore or even forget. She'd released a small amount of her siren's charm, causing her skin to gleam like an abalone's inner shell. Everywhere she led us, she drew stares. We meandered lazily through the crowds, looking to be in no rush, as though we were truly noth-ing more than revelers trying to gain our bearings, overwhelmed by the scope of the gala, which appeared to be endless.

Though I'd yet to spot the king, I wasn't only looking for him. I was look-ing for potential Slashers hidden in plain sight. But it was difficult to know if they were truly there or not because everyone was in costume, and I doubt-ed any of them would be foolish enough to come wearing plumes of feathers, considering all of Grimm was now wary of anything that even remotely re-sembled bird shifters.

As far as wealth being on display, it was more than even I could have fath-omed.

There were fountains that rained not water but streams of liquid gold, and statues so lifelike that I wouldn't be surprised if Midas had frozen betray-ers forever in gold.

There were looks of anguish and agony twisting their forever-silent faces. Faceted diamonds winked in the red glow of Hel's perpetual flame from every conceivable nook and cranny, on the floors, embedded within marble white pillars. Even the flowers that had been brought here were not actually flowers but gems so delicately shaped that they dipped and swayed as real blooms would in the lush jasmine-scented breeze that had also somehow managed to be pumped in.

The king had spared no expense. Captain Bo had been right—this place was ripe for the picking. So though I couldn't see, smell, or sense them, I knew the Slashers would not be foolish enough to pass up a once-in-a-lifetime opportunity for untold wealth such as this.

After ten or so minutes, Elle headed toward a stone statue of an angel wearing a demon's face that sat beside the human table filled with finger foods.

"Pet," she whispered huskily, stopping her meandering trail and glancing back at me over her shoulder, "I tire."

The siren's mark upon her forehead, which was usually hidden, burned as brightly as a lightning strike. Her hair glowed deepest blue like the scales of an electric eel. She was absolutely mesmerizing, and it was difficult for me to remember my role for a moment.

Heat rolled through my body. Though I wasn't often affected by sexual charms, I felt the prickles of hers pressing against me. Elle was a powerful siren, one of the strongest in history. Just one look from her, and I felt the drawing of blood between my thighs, making me hard and excited. Not that anyone in here would care if I walked around with a cock stand—I wouldn't be the only one.

"Does my goddess wish to sit?"

Normally, Elle's face was expressive and easily readable. But she was different in here, imperious, aloof. She looked like the princess she truly was as she thinned her lips and dipped her long, elaborate eyelashes behind her black silk mask.

She placed a hand on my shoulder and squeezed just slightly.

Understanding what she wished, I dropped gracefully to my elbows and knees, and moments later, she sat upon my back. Her weight was slight, and I purred my approval as any good sub would.

I'd never played submissive for Alice because I'd never believed myself to be one. I still wasn't, but maybe I was more of a switch than I'd thought.

Ahead of us, a top and bottom were acting out their sexual fantasies in front of a small but gathering crowd. He was paddling her backside with a dainty leather paddle, her skirts were above her head, and she was making no noise. But every time the leather struck her backside, she'd lift up on her silk-clad toes. Her skin was as pale as moonlight, her naked arse a pretty bright red. She was draped over the edge of an elegant white couch large enough to host a small orgy of writhing bodies on it.

The spectacle had helped draw most of the eyes away from Elle.

She stroked my back with her fingers, her movements rhythmic and calming. She was acting her part. To anyone not in the know, she'd appear no more than a top caring for her bottom. Her long legs were crossed, and I knew the sight we must make together.

"We mustn't look desperate. Midas abhors desperation, but he esteems confidence," she said softly, her voice so low that I had to strain to hear her, letting me know she wasn't speaking to me as the dominant but as Elle, my partner. "The king is slowly making his way through the crowd, headed in this direction. He should arrive within ten minutes or so. Can you hold me for that long?"

I grunted. "Your weight is nothing."

She laughed lightly. "If the boys back at the precinct ever heard about this, I'm pretty sure that your reputation for being a ladies man would be well and truly tarnished. How in the twin hells do we always seem to find ourselves in these unusual situations?"

Grinning, I nodded, though I knew she could not see me. "I'm sure I could survive it. And Bo clearly thinks we do weird well."

"I think you could survive a great many things, Maddox," she agreed softly, then I felt her shift. "And yes, rumor has it that you and I have been dubbed."

I lifted an eyebrow. "Do I want to know?"

"The twisted duo."

"Fitting," I said drolly.

"I thought so." I could almost hear her smirk. "Seems incredible that we've only been partners for two months."

"Feels like forever sometimes."

"*Hm.*" She sounded contemplative.

When Elle was in Grimm, she was spun up, like a taut string ready to snap. But when she and I went out on missions, she completely transformed. She smiled more, laughed more. She was easy to be with. In fact, she was fun. Several of the cops teased me mercilessly about getting saddled with the ice queen. It used to piss me off until I realized they just didn't get it—get her.

Elle didn't just give herself to others. They had to earn it. And few of them in there had. Ichabod mainly. Bo too. And now me.

I didn't have to look at her to know she was still alert and scanning the room, but Elle had the capacity to look relaxed even in the most taxing of situations. No doubt her royal upbringing played a role in that talent of hers.

"How did you spot the king? I looked for his entourage but could not find one large enough."

Her laughter was charming and electrifying. The fine hairs on the back of my neck and on my arms stood on edge.

"Midas is not your typical royalty. He's... eccentric," she said, sounding fond.

My brows gathered. "How so?"

"Well, for one, he won't be surrounded by an entourage. At least not yet. He likes to mingle first, play his little games, pretend to be one of the plebs. Then when it amuses him to reveal himself, he will. He did it all the time at Father's court, sometimes appearing as a court jester, other times as a commoner. Today, he is in drag. I pegged him almost from the moment we got here."

"You don't say. How very clever. I'll admit I was not looking for a female. Why does he do this?"

She laughed. "So that he can laugh at our expense when the jig, as they say, is up. People talk far more freely about the king when they do not imagine that they are speaking to said king. I've seen him turn people to gold for daring to say the wrong thing. He truly is a devious sort of male."

I snorted. "Then I am lucky I have such a brilliant partner. Otherwise, I might have told him that I found this party clichéd, the food ridiculous, and the entertainment hackneyed."

She wiggled on her bottom and gently swung her now-uncrossed legs back and forth. There were none as well versed in artless seduction as a siren. She radiated innocent ingénue.

The crowds were growing larger in front of us, and there were a few titters from those with virgin eyes and cries of "Well done, mate" from the more well versed among them.

Elle continued to brush my back with her fingers, and I scanned the faces of those drawing nearer, looking for the disguised king among them. But Elle was still too loose. She wasn't "on" right now.

"I saw your vision in Bo's office earlier."

"I did not try to hide it," I said, wishing I could actually look her in the face and not down at the marble floor full of strange golden flecks of sand.

"Third one this week—same thing, though, right?" she said. "Any idea yet what it could be?"

Feeling a twinge in my left knee, I desperately wanted to shift but knew I couldn't, not until Elle gave me the command, and therein lay my reason for why I didn't make a good submissive—I did not like to wait.

I grunted. "None."

She sighed loudly. "It's very annoying, isn't it? Seeing these visions that clearly mean something but not having the key to deciphering them?"

"It *can* be. Though the key eventually turns up."

She was very quiet after that, and I knew she was deep in thought. She'd even stopped gliding her fingers over my shoulder. But I was curious about something and had been all morning.

"Why a dress? Today of all days? Did you know we'd be sent here?"

I felt her twitch, and then she sighed, her magical fingers picking the rhythm back up again. "Ah yes," she said, and I could hear her grin. "I wondered when your inquisitive mind would get around to asking me about that. It was the faeries' doing—well, Queen Titiana's, actually."

"She speaks with queens. Why am I not surprised," I said with amusement.

She blew out a heavy breath, and her fingers were suddenly replaced by the leather glide of her paddle down the small of my back. My skin broke out in a wash of goose flesh. I swallowed hard. It was merely an act between us, yet somehow it didn't feel that way.

She was twirling the tip of her crop in silken, slow motions down my sides, letting the small length of rope trail along the backs of my thighs. I shivered.

"I have to wear this wretched dress for two weeks because it holds my waters, you see."

"Why two weeks?" I asked, somehow able to focus on what she was saying even though I felt wrecked and alive with dark sensations she'd pulled from deep within me.

"Because," she said, drawing me out of my dark thoughts, "I've been thinking a lot about what you said to me."

I thinned my lips, not sure what I should say here, so I went for neutral. "Oh?"

"I know you know what I'm talking about. It's okay, Hatter. I know what I said this morning, and I meant all that."

"But?" I prompted.

"But." She sighed, replacing the tip of the crop with her palm, moving her fingers down my spine, massaging small circles on me. I couldn't help it. I moaned.

She shifted on her seat, pausing in her circles, and I bit down on my tongue. But then she resumed again, and I nearly sighed with relief. I should probably have pretended not to like it quite as much as I did.

"But," she whispered, "I can't stop thinking about it, either. And sometimes I swear I hate you for it."

I squeezed my eyes shut, feeling torn apart and eviscerated by her gentle touch and her impassioned words of odium.

"Why? Why would you tell me such a thing? Knowing what we had or hadn't had yet? You've torn me open, Maddox, and it was cruel." The tassel of her small crop was suddenly drawing up the backs of my thighs, a threat, a promise. I shivered.

Then she stopped. Stopped touching me. Stopped moving. Just stopped.

In a low voice, barely above a whisper, I heard her say, "I had briefly considered beginning a search for him at the end of our shift. That's why I needed this fecking garment. So I could have weeks and not days if need be."

She growled, and I felt her body grow tense, rigid. She was angry—angry with me or her situation, I wasn't sure. But Elle was pissed, and I felt guilty for it, though rationally, I understood I'd done nothing wrong, either.

But then, neither had she. I'd known what my words would do to her, what revealing that vision might cause to happen between us, and as much as I loathed the place we were in, I also knew I'd do it again, in a heartbeat, because partners were honest with each other.

"And now..." she said loudly. "Now I owe the queen a favor. I get a free ticket to Neverland to see what the hells a dragon is doing at a stronghold. Which is so much fun for me." She laughed bitterly, but it wasn't the dragon that made her this way.

I narrowed my eyes. "Do you wish company?"

The thought of Elle investigating a possible dragon sighting without any backup made me sick to my stomach. Dragons were dangerous, cruel, and cunning.

"You would do that?" She sounded shocked.

I nodded, trying to glance at her over my shoulder at her but unable to. I scowled. "Yes, Elle, I would do that."

She laughed again. This time, it sounded more angry than anything else. "I tell you that I'm going to investigate your claims, to resurrect my dead lover or whatever the hells I might find, and you say, 'Can I come?' What the hells is wrong with you, Maddox? How do you do this? How can you tell me in one breath that you want me and in another be so damned willing to help me find a male you know cannot share me? How?"

I wet my lips. So that was what all of this was about then. Elle was angry, not just with me but also with Hook and herself. Because she was torn, and it made her feel guilty.

I closed my eyes. She was wrong if she thought I did not care. But I was not the type who could ever, ever give in to the depths of my emotions. If I did, it would become a consuming fire.

"You could always whip me." I said it softly, but my voice was steady. It wasn't a command—I'd actually meant for it to be more a joke, a way to break the tension, but the second I'd said it, I'd had a flash of her doing just that, and I was more than a little curious.

"What?" she snapped, sitting up straight. But I saw her glow radiate and knew that her siren's charms had suddenly grown stronger. Was she curious too?

I bit down on my back teeth, ready to confess it had simply been a badly worded icebreaker, but then I felt the smack of metal-spiked leather tassels across the backs of my thighs.

The pain of fire soon gave way to waves of indescribable pleasure. Hissing, I arched my back, rising up on my knees, confounded by the emotions coursing through me—shock and... bloody hells, arousal? I shivered.

"I did not tell you you could move, my pet," she hissed, the words trembling with emotions that were very, very real.

"Yes, my goddess," I panted, straightening out as best I could. My body still tingled, and I was amazed by the new and strange sensory emotions ranging through me.

She did not speak, and I did not move, half afraid she'd whip me again, half afraid she wouldn't. My pulse raced like a rocket in my ears.

"Will you behave, or should I punish you again?" She said it softly, voice a silken caress that I felt move across my nude back, pulsing against me like a demanding wave.

I swallowed hard.

"I vote for punish—he makes quite the pretty sight when you do." Another voice, as cultured as mine, broke through our stolen moment.

I frowned. Glancing up from my position wasn't easy, but I made out the exquisite fabric of a gold-brocaded silk skirt and knew that if the person wasn't royalty, they were at least someone very high up on the food chain.

Elle whipped around, the tassels now gone, and I felt strangely empty. Exceedingly curious, that.

"King Midas," she whispered with a light, tremulous laugh, and then she was up. "You may now stand, my pet," she said with all the concern of an evil stepmother toward her adopted Cinderella.

I was slow to rise to my feet, head dizzy and swimming with the sudden rush of blood, legs tingling and arse still prickling with heat. A cock stand I'd not expected to have refused to go down even an inch. I doubted very much that it was quite what Bo meant when she'd told us to blend in. Then again, no one looking at us who did not already know us would ever mistake us for the law. There was that, at least.

True to Elle's word, the king looked like a very handsome she. Midas, as I'd only ever seen in papers, was an androgynous sort, able to seamlessly become whatever gender he desired.

He was dressed like a buxom blond, but the affectation wasn't grotesque or absurd. His painted face was flawlessly and skillfully done. He wore a gown of brilliant red that faded into gold toward the hemline. The gown it-self was a thing of artistic genius, scandalously indecent in the back yet de-mure in the front. The whole of his back was on display, down to the very tip where arse met spine, giving a peekaboo glimpse but only a glimpse. The front of the gown slid all the way up to his neck but curved around a pair of breasts that could rival any female's. It had to be an enchantment since I'd seen pictures of the king and he was tall, lanky, and normally flat of chest. The effect made him look like a succubus come straight from the mouth of Hel itself to tempt us all.

Thick ropes of golden-blond hair were gathered up in an intricate crown of braids that was threaded through with priceless gems and pearls. He also wore gold satin evening gloves that slid up to his elbows, no doubt to keep anyone safe from accidentally grazing his lethal hands, which were gripping tight to an elaborate fan tipped in gold lace.

Elle leaned in to hug the king warmly, and he returned the gesture in kind. There was an old friendship between the two—it was obvious.

"La, my darling, it has been far too long. You know, I have never forgiven Triton for the shame he brought upon you. And to now be forced to mingle with the rabble—how do you bear it?" He sounded truly distressed. I might have laughed at his obvious theatrics except that he gazed at her with kind-ness in his golden eyes. He was genuinely worried for her.

Elle dipped her lashes and smiled ever so slightly, her courtly training once again on full display. Midas, being king, outranked her. Elle did not hold with courtly manners much. In fact, she had a serious hatred for the Charmings', but she liked Midas, and I had to wonder why. What did she know about him that I didn't?

"Well, you more than most understand the why. I did wrong. He pun-ished me for it. End of story." Her spine was rigid, and only I could see it because of my vantage point. But Midas's eyes glittered with something that looked a lot like empathy, forcing me to reevaluate what I thought I knew versus what I'd actually only heard of in rumor.

The king was not at all the overbearing and pompous arsehole everyone claimed him to be—or at least not with her.

Midas tapped Elle's breast with his closed fan. "No, my dear, there is wrong, and there is right. Rules be damned. You were the brightest pearl amongst them, and if they couldn't see that, then they be damned. I will no longer run trade with your father. I abhor the very sight of him."

"Midas, why... why do you tell me this?" she asked with a small shake.

He smirked, glancing up beneath his long lashes at me, and there was a glimmer of approval on his face as he scanned me up and down. The king clearly enjoyed what he saw. But I kept my face composed, because I was naught but a "submissive" at the gala and unless "my goddess" willed me to speak, I could not break character.

"Do you think, my dear Detective," he said softly, leaning in conspiratorially, "that you and your partner could grace me with your presences later in the evening? A dance? The four of us?"

"Four?" she asked.

He grinned, the look shy. "I plan to introduce my new beau later. But I thought perhaps you'd like a private meeting first. See if I get your approval."

"Do you need my approval?" she asked with a hint of laughter.

He rolled his eyes. "Don't be ridiculous, darling. Still, I'd like to know I had it all the same."

She nodded slowly and reached up, took his elbow in her hand, and gave it a gentle squeeze. "Then I accept your invitation, my old friend."

Midas dipped his head to Elle's forehead, the two of them breathing in one another's air. I did not think it was an accident. It looked more ritualistic, like a deed they'd performed many times in another life, one she'd long since left behind. I wasn't sure. But they stayed united for several seconds, enough to get noticed by passersby. Two beautiful women seemingly locked in a lovers' embrace.

Elle had a past, an entire life I'd only ever been peripherally aware of, but I could see a glimpse of it here, and I couldn't help but wonder who she might have become had Triton not done to her as he'd done.

Midas pressed his gloved finger against her lips once before quickly stepping back and spreading his arm. "So tell me, how does my little soiree stack up against your father's? Be kind now—I might behead you if you don't tell me mine is best."

Tilting her head back, she laughed with an open gaiety that was quite frankly mesmerizing to behold.

"Well, how could you ever know if I were being honest now? Yours is the best, of course." Her eyes glittered, and her lips turned up just slightly at the corner.

Midas softly snorted. "No cannibalism masquerading as entertainment—at least there's that," he said with a wrinkle of his pert nose, and at first I thought he was surely exaggerating until Elle sighed.

"Yes, there is that."

Just what kind of court had Elle been brought up in?

"All you have to deal with here are demons who want to suck out your soul. How very thrilling, *non*?"

She chuckled. "So you're telling me there is more than Rasputen here? Why Hel?"

He shrugged. "Because the Slashers would be fools to attack me in Hel, that's why. I was well aware of the risk tonight. That doesn't mean I came unprepared to handle it. There are currently no fewer than ten high demon lords and at least fifty half-breeds meandering in and around. More than that, a high-level sorcerer cast a spell on this venue." He rolled the wrist holding the fan with an elegant twirl. "Let's just say that if you've come here tonight to pilfer anything, you'll very much live to regret it. So I'd say that between the demons and the sorcerer's spell, we're all absolutely safe."

"Famous last words, my friend. You and I both know that there are those out there stronger than a handful of demons and a sorcerer's parlor trick."

He snorted indelicately. "The list of which is piteously low, and well you know it." He slapped the fan upon his palm. "I think you're merely determined to see the glass as half-empty, my dear, and that will simply never do."

Midas was right. He had nearly gone above and beyond what was required to ensure the safety and comfort of his guests, and I could tell by the tugging at the ends of Elle's rosebud lips that she knew it too. I could feel the tension emanating in waves off of her, but outwardly, she kept herself composed.

"So in other words," she said slowly, "you didn't need us at all."

His laugh was light and feminine. "Obviously, my dear. But I missed your pretty face, so here we are." He shrugged unrepentantly.

"Oh, Midas, I should write your gorgeous arse up for abusing our very valuable time and resources in this way." She shook her head, allowing just a little of her annoyance to spill through her words, before she took a deep breath and said in a low voice, "Though for reasons quite beyond me, I can never seem to get angry with you even when you desperately deserve my wrath, you awful, odious male."

Midas laughed lightly and tapped Elle's nose with his fan. "Enjoy yourselves, and mind that you do not let your slave wander..." he said with a sideways look at me. "Far."

I lifted my brows, sensing the king would not mind if I happened to wander into his bed.

Elle, as if sensing the undertone, sidled in closer to my side and planted a very firm and obvious gesture of claiming upon my nude chest and rubbed her palm over it. "My pet will cause you no trouble. You have my word."

My brow lifted. Was she... jealous? *Hm.*

"Ah." Midas grinned and nodded at us both as his hawklike gaze studied the two of us. "So it is like that then. My apologies. I figured it wouldn't hurt to try. Enjoy yourselves. This is my gift to you, Elle, for years of cherished friendship."

Then taking her hand in his, he lifted her knuckles to his mouth and pressed a dainty kiss there. She nodded her thanks.

Only once he'd moved off did I dare to look at her in the face.

"How long do we stay?" I asked, wondering whether we should just call Bo and end it now. "We might still have time to make the assignation with your—"

"No." She looked up at me, her jeweled eyes gleaming, but exhaustion was clearly stamped on her face. "We stay. High demon lords or no, there is no way in Hel that we can leave the king. Because if anything does happen and there was no Grimm PD on sight, Bo's right—Draven would roast our balls over a spit and feast on our bones. Midas is a clever bastard. But he's a bastard."

She sounded tired. I sniffed and looked around, wondering who in the twin hells the demons were. Demons weren't always the stereotypical red-skinned human-monster amalgamations straight from your worst nightmares with cloven hooves and tails and smelling of brimstone. Though some did, most didn't. Most could very easily pass for human. There were telltale signs, though most of them had learned to control their baser natures by adapting a more refined air. Why? Simple—money.

Money talked.

Very few things mattered to a demon so much as the gain of money, and demons could rarely afford to be trusted, but they would dance a jig for the highest bidder. They had zero shame when it came to selling out their "loyalty," but Midas didn't strike me as the type who wasn't also keenly aware of their flaws. Still, Midas, unlike most kings, had an endless coffer at his disposal. I'd imagine that kept the demons on his payroll very contented indeed.

"Let's dance, my pet." Elle held her hand out to me, and I dipped my head, then I took her in my arms and twirled us gracefully around the dance floor.

But we were not simply here to enjoy ourselves. We were scanning the room, looking for anything unusual or out of place.

After half an hour of people-watching, Elle tapped my shoulder. I turned to look down at her, but she was looking off to her left.

"At my eight," she whispered then pulled my head down toward her. My lips grazed her long, slender neck, and fire crawled through my bones at the touch of her sweet and briny-scented flesh. My skin prickled with heat as I pretended to be nothing more than her amorous submissive.

I ran my hands around her trim waist and slid them slowly up her spine, making her hiss and lean into my touch. She twirled us so that I could see what she had, and when she did, I saw a lone inky-black feather curved delicately upon the marble ground and, in a small neat pile beside it, more golden grains of sand.

"They're here," I growled.

Chapter 6

Detective Elle

THE MOMENT WE SPIED the feather and the sand, we both went on high alert. We couldn't afford to stop dancing or in any way stand out from the rest of the revelers. But my skin crawled with goose bumps as I scanned the cold porcelain masks of those surrounding us.

Everyone danced as we did. Laughed, talked, ate, and had sex as they pleased, with no shame or ulterior motives other than to satisfy all lusts of the flesh.

We could be surrounded, for all I knew, but I knew in my gut the Slashers were there, and judging by the way Maddox had suddenly tensed up beneath my palm, I knew he knew it too.

His breath was a hot caress on the shell of my ear as he whispered, "Do we tell Midas that his wards have failed?"

I turned my hip into his so that he would know to twirl me, and Maddox did just as I'd hoped he would. I took the turn slowly, studying the crush of humanity, looking for a sign, a hint, anything.

How in the hells, with all the safety precautions in place, had the Slashers gotten through? If a sorcerer had indeed spelled the venue—and if Midas said it, I did not doubt it—it should have been impossible for a Slasher to get in here. My skin prickled and my scalp burned as I felt my magick begin a slow churning glide and crawl through me.

Impossible though it was and as unlikely as it seemed, I knew they were here. I scanned the masked and unmasked faces, pulse thundering in my ears as I looked for more than mere specks of sand and a single black feather.

Rarely did my gut lead me astray, but as I watched dancers twirl and glide gracefully across the marble dance floor, a niggle of doubt began to chew away at my insides. Maybe it had been a prank? Some fool who thought it would be funny to try to spook the others?

But I couldn't believe that. The Slasher Gang was becoming as notorious as the bogeyman killer of days past. They'd become a nervous buzzword. People all over the hundred realms were justifiably worried about the gangs growing a thirst for violence and bloodshed. And the crowd didn't strike me as the type to make light of the recent uptick in homicides.

"Anything?" I murmured to Maddox, twirling my finger up and down the column of his strong neck.

"No," he rumbled. "You?"

I swallowed, shaking my head as I momentarily glanced at an elegant-looking couple dressed from head to toe in white and gold. They didn't even have an inch of skin on display. Not odd in and of itself, but their movements were... strange. I couldn't really describe it, but they looked as though they weren't dancing so much as gliding—on air.

"Maddox," I murmured. I felt his stare like a brand upon my face. I shook my head, wondering why it was that the couple should stand out so to me. Not until the third pass of their forms did it click.

Their costume was decidedly avian in nature. I frowned.

Birds.

My stomach was gripped by painful nerves.

Maddox squeezed my fingers, silently telling me that he was seeing it too.

Men and women in yards of exquisite Arabian silks with golden-dipped plumes of feathers resting like crowns upon their heads glided past. On their faces, they wore golden masks with eerie facial expressions upon them—surprise, laughter, annoyance, jeering.

I wrapped my arm around Hatter's waist and snapped him back to my side, careful to keep my face composed, to not let on that I was aware, that I was anything more than a mere spectator in the crowd.

The tune of the music changed, becoming sultrier, with beautifully erotic undertones. It was a tango of strings and wind instrumentals.

Maddox, who I was learning was an exquisite dancer, took lead, gliding us seamlessly through the steps, covering up my lack of skill or finesse with his so that it actually looked as if I knew what in the hells I was doing.

Brushing my fingers over his gold-painted hair, I pressed my cheek to his.

My heart raced frantically as now there weren't just one or two bird-clad dancers with us but six, then ten, then twenty, then I stopped counting.

They were marching like ants out of a disturbed mound, and I didn't have a damned clue how they'd shown up or how we'd even missed them in the first place.

I frowned. "Maddox," I murmured, grazing my lips along the very edge of his.

He growled, acting as though he were lost in my touch, but I felt my partner's tension and knew he was just as aware of our current predicament as I was.

His fingers grazed the curve of my ass, making me feel electrified, making my throat ache with the burgeoning desire of my siren's charms. I could feel the song resting upon my tongue. It would be nothing to open my mouth and fell them all, drop the birds to the ground, stone dead.

But I wouldn't simply kill them. I'd hurt them all, the innocents along with the guilty, and I couldn't do that. Hatter twirled me, and I felt the cold, comforting glide of my firearm that I'd tucked into its holster on my inner thigh. That was only a very desperate plan B, if push came to shove. There were still far too many civilians in here. The odds of me hurting one of them were far too high. But the feel of steel was comforting to my strained nerves.

I'd half expected the night to be a bust, but it was looking as if Bo's Intel might have been good after all.

Maddox snapped our arms out as he moved us seamlessly through the steps, then his fingers were brushing through my hair, and his nose was nuzzling the side of my cheek. "Do you have your eye on Midas?"

My stomach feathered with curls of wicked heat and desire. I swallowed hard, scanning the thousands of porcelain-masked and unmasked but highly painted faces in front of me.

And finally, I spotted him—he was dressed as his true self, getting ready to make his way toward the elaborate golden throne of his to welcome us all to his ball and say whatever the hells kings often said. If the gang was going to strike, they were going to strike soon—very, very soon.

"The adder is making its way to the den now," I hissed, being cryptic in case there were any unwanted ears listening in, as all around us more and more masked birds swirled and danced. "Where are the damned demons?" I hissed so softly it was barely a breath of sound.

I wasn't sure what I was looking for as far as the demons went. High Lord demons weren't your typical red-skinned freaks. Rumor had it they could be as beautiful as the very angels themselves, though I had no personal experience with actual demons myself. Few of the hundred realms did. Not many could afford to keep even a low-grade demon on payroll, let alone a few dozen.

Maddox brushed my hair aside, his calloused fingertips wreaking havoc upon my sensitized flesh as his lips brushed like flame along the curve of my neck. I felt the scraping of sharp teeth and hissed, digging my fingers into his spine, not sure whether I meant to push him back or draw him forward.

My brain and body were completely at odds with one another, but I knew it was nothing more than him keeping us in character. So I told myself to breathe and to let him set us up as he felt he should. I trusted Maddox, knew that whatever he was doing, he was doing it for the good.

Then something that felt an awful lot like the glide of a fang pressed against my carotid, and my pulse jumped hard. I groaned, rubbing my head against the curve of his shoulder and purring, all while wondering how in the hells Maddox had fangs.

"I count no fewer than fifteen moving in. Look for the ivory-fanged masks," he whispered heatedly.

I purred when his large palm slid down my left arse cheek before cupping and holding a good portion of it, forcing my thighs to part so that his knee could take up residence between them. I shuddered, fighting my body's natural inclination to grind down on him so that I could alleviate the mounting pressure building.

But I forced myself to keep focused, and sure enough, I saw the fangs moving slowly in toward Midas, drawing a tight circle around him.

The tension in the room was electric, and all around us, I could feel the energy of the dancers responding to the subtle sensual cues of the music.

There were hands brushing against us, bodies moving in closer, some birds, most not. My mouth tingled, the need to sing growing more and more desperate within me.

Maddox pressed me tight to his body and whispered, "You're starting to leak, Elle, and that has given me an idea—if you're game, that is."

I growled, biting down on my front teeth. Knowing exactly what he was referring to, I could feel my magick gathering, coalescing into a tight sphere within me. My siren's charm wanted to explode from within me. It was building momentum. I hadn't felt this wound up in I didn't even know how long. But it was his touch, fake or not, that was doing it to me. And that damned sexual feast for the senses all around us. I was feeling overwhelmed and was losing my very tenuous grasp on my desires.

He wanted to use my powers, and I was all but willing. Only once, when Cat Pillar had siphoned some of my siren powers, had I ever flipped around him. Pillar had taken too much, stolen more than I'd offered. As a result, I'd become darker, the more murderous version of me. It had taken a trip to Alice's shop and placing me into the arms of the enigma Celestria before I'd reclaimed my sanity. But we'd learned since then that if he gave me warning and didn't startle me with the amount of power he pulled from me, I could actually handle the shift enough to be somewhat cognizant of who I was and what I was doing.

It was a revelation in terms of helping me to gain a foothold on my abilities, a feat I'd never before believed possible.

There was still one problem, though. There were too many civilians, too many innocents that could get hurt. And a lawsuit wasn't something Bo would take kindly to.

"People," I whispered.

He nodded. "I can clear them out."

As long as we could get the dancers and musicians clear of the worst of my song, it might work.

"Do it."

He grinned and very loudly said, "Is that the king?" Then he gasped. "Are... are those bags of gold?"

Everyone who was likely not a Slasher turned, and the tide began a slow rolling exodus toward where the unwitting king would soon hear demands for gold.

I chuckled and murmured beneath my breath, "Clever boy," then louder and in a husky drawl, "I care not for gold, my pet. Only that you dance with me."

Then I couldn't wait any longer. Leaning up on tiptoe, I grabbed hold of the shell of Maddox's earlobe with my teeth and bit, hard enough that he hissed and rose up on the tips of his toes.

"Elle," he hissed a warning but didn't sound all that displeased with my aggression, either.

His fingers dug into my waist, making me jerk against him, both from pain and the pleasure of feeling myself so manhandled. It had been so damned long since I'd felt this level of passion.

So bloody long.

I smirked, choosing to ignore his chastisement. He was making me spark like a firecracker. It was the least he deserved, the fecking bastard.

Nuzzling the tip of my nose against his chest, I murmured, "We need to call this in, get backup here stat."

His hot hand was moving, gliding around my waist, sliding up toward the edge of my breast. We were moving in unison, he and I, in and out, swaying and grinding, neither of us mindful of what we were doing. We'd been tap dancing around our feelings for weeks, and it had only been a matter of time before all the tension had finally come to a head.

The party was the absolute worst place to have this happen. We needed to keep our heads in the game, remember why we were here. But I was a siren who'd been pushed very nearly to the edge, and he was... well, I wasn't entirely certain what Maddox was, only that he was my catnip and apparently, I was his.

"No time," he said as he leaned his face so close to mine that I felt the mint of his breath wash over me. "We need to get to Midas now. You're sure you're okay with what I'm about to do?" He gripped me tight.

I nodded and purred my approval of his off-the-cuff plan. So long as it got me what I craved, too, I'd have agreed to sell what was left of my soul right about then—that was how turned on I was. Careful not to rip out the false eyelashes, I gently pulled my mask off and dropped it to the floor. I would need to see from all angles, plus I couldn't touch him as I really wanted to. With a purr, I began to rub my cheek against his like a cat in heat. I pressed my hands to his chest. *Yes,* I was silently saying. And he knew it. He saw it. His pupils flared.

The birds were closing in on us. We were nearly surrounded. It would be obvious if we suddenly started plowing a trail through them toward the king, waving our badges about. We couldn't afford to let them know just yet that we knew who they were. But if we moved toward the king as two lusty siren-sparking lovers, well... none would be the wiser for it.

"Do it, Maddox," I whispered. "Do it now."

He slid his strong, powerful arm around my waist and pulled me in so tight against him that not even an inch of space existed between us. I felt the ropey strength of his muscles vibrating against me. He was like a snake ready to snap, and it thrilled me endlessly.

"As my goddess wishes," he rumbled in his darkly cultured voice, which made me shiver and my flesh skate with heat.

With a hungry moan, his mouth found mine. It was a mere peck, a ghost of a kiss, really. Barely a graze, yet I felt my skin start humming, felt my legs grow soft and pliant, the transformation very nearly upon me. I might have worried about his sanity, getting me to this type of frenzied peak, but Maddox could handle me as long as he didn't push me to the point of no return. I wasn't sure how, but I didn't give two damns how it was possible right now, either.

My siren charms were at their peak. One more touch of him to me, and I would become a nova of lusty flame and wild desire.

"Is that it?" I teased, digging my fingers into his back and daring him to give me more. "I know you've got better. I've tasted of you before, or have you lost your—"

I didn't get to finish my thought, because he was suddenly kissing me, eating at my mouth like a ravenous beast. And I sang beneath his touch. I couldn't help myself. He'd unleashed my tempest with a simple touch.

I hummed, the sound low and sonorous and hypnotic.

Around me, I sensed the humans dropping one by one to their knees as they were gripped by the siren's song, by my song. But they were outside the range of true danger. Now it was merely an annoyance.

I had them all so easily at my mercy, and with a mere snap of my fingers, I could make them mine to command, mine to control. I was desire, beauty, sex, and death. I laughed even as I sank deeper into the darkness that was a siren's true and sometimes cruel nature.

I knew the magick I was channeling was strong, because Maddox hadn't simply revved me up. He'd made me burn, and my waters were curling around me, and everyone who heard my song moaned, moving farther and farther away from us. But Maddox didn't seem bothered. If anything, he clung harder, kissed deeper, swiped his tongue against the seam of my lips, then he was dueling with mine.

I felt us moving, but I was lost to the madness. I hadn't given in to my charms in months, and it was like a pressure valve that had just been released. From the corner of my eye, I saw a few unwitting humans who'd gotten too close drop like stones. But it was too late for me to stop.

Maddox's hands were in my hair, and he was growling angrily, destroying me with his touch, and I sensed that we were walking up some steps. Somehow, he was still moving, still cognizant, still thinking as a detective should.

But all I could think of was him—him in my arms, him beneath me as I feasted on his body, licked at his flesh, and sucked on his blood. My fangs slid out, and I sliced through his bottom lip and tasted the tang of his salt and iron upon my tongue.

He growled but didn't push me away. Instead, he drew me closer, deeper, as if he enjoyed my violence, my aggression. And I felt him against my thigh, long and strong and thick. He liked it. And I smirked because I liked it too. A lot.

A part of my brain understood that I was losing my grip, but he wasn't fighting it, and a more primal part of me was glad, thrilled even.

I curved my clawed hand around the back of his head, wanting to be as physically close to him as I possibly could be. It was dangerous to tango with an excited siren and never to be done by the faint of heart.

But Maddox held his own, using my powers as his weapon as he continued to clear a direct path toward the king.

"*Stop them!*" I heard someone snap, then all hells broke loose.

Detective Maddox

I DIDN'T KNOW HOW THE Slashers hadn't fallen prey to Elle's siren charms, but suddenly, we were surrounded, and Midas was barking out orders. "*Demons! Attack!*"

Elle and I broke apart. I saw her blinking, confused, no doubt taking a second to assess our surroundings, brain still banked in the fog of lust. Her eyes were glowing a brilliant blue. Her marking was lit up like a flash of lightning, and even her hair crackled around her head. She'd barely begun to unleash her magick and was still a force to be reckoned with. Her nostrils were wide while she scented the air as she turned, keeping her sights peeled for the king.

But he'd hidden behind the rush of bodies still swarming at us. There was madness as all around us, the revelers screamed. Those who'd been gripped by her song were free of the enchantment and were up and running and turning an already chaotic scene even more frenzied in their desperation to get to safety. I had no idea how many Slashers there were because a horde of them had suddenly appeared as though from thin air.

The demons turned into streaks of black smoke, swirling around figures who fought with nothing but killing air, their dying screams echoing macabrely through the dark-red night. Midas had a golden sword in his hand as he hacked and slashed at his attackers, holding his own. Mere yards separated us from him, but it felt more like miles with the wave of humanity that constantly pushed us back.

We would see the crown upon his head bobbing up and down, and then he would disappear into yet another wave of fleeing revelers and bloodthirsty Slashers. I rose up on my tiptoes, scanning for any sign or glimpse of him. All around, I could hear the grisly echoing clang of steel meeting flesh with a sickening, bone-jarring thud.

"Do you see him?" she asked, her voice hard and sultry, a blend of detective and siren.

I shook my head. Someone fell shoulder-first into my middle, pushing me back on my heels and making me grunt. It was a woman with tears running down her face, the whites of her eyes large and nearly swallowing up the iris. Her skin was so pale it looked as though she had no blood in her at all. Her bicep was bleeding profusely, but she didn't even seem to be aware of it as she scrambled back to her feet and continued to slip and slide her way toward safety.

"Godsdammit," Elle snapped, and when I looked at her, it was to see her wrestling with her own mad stream of partygoers. She shoved the males back hard. "Out of my way." There was no madness of the siren left in her eyes anymore.

We slowly made our way ever closer toward the king.

The demons weren't slowing their attacks even an iota. If anything, the closer we got to Midas, the more chaos ensued. It was as though he were the eye of the storm.

I went to reach for Elle's elbow, seeing a massive group of at least eight get ready to cut between the two of us, possibly separating us. But she must have seen it, too, because she did an elegant sweep and roll with her arms and somehow cleared a path right through them.

We were probably within fifty feet, if not less, of the king when I felt the fine hairs on the back of my neck lift up. Growling, I glanced behind me, and that was when I spotted two attackers coming at Elle and me from behind simultaneously, their wickedly curved claws extended. They were dressed all in robes of black silk and fur, with elegant golden masks on and hoods pulled over their heads. There wasn't an inch of them I could see to use as a character description. But I knew these were our Slashers.

"Elle, at our six, we've got company," I barked as yet another naked female cut between the two of us.

Elle's face was a stony mask of irritation. She took one look at me and nodded. "Well then, as they say, the jig is most definitely up." She reached into her bodice and pulled out her badge, holding it high, and glared unerringly at the Slashers who were now mere yards from us. "Hands up!" she cried. "Grimm PD. You're under arrest."

At the sight of her badge, those who'd still been fleeing around us suddenly stopped and dropped to their knees, tossing their hands over their heads and screaming out that they were innocent.

The black-robed Slashers didn't even slow down a little. If anything, it seemed as though they'd picked up speed.

And from one second to the next, they were upon us. Two came at me, and five went for Elle.

After shoving her badge back down her bodice, she became a whirling dervish of death as she danced between arms and legs, punching and kicking out. It would have been so much faster if she could use her firearm, but she was wise not to. There was too much potential that a bystander and not the Slashers would be hurt or possibly even killed.

I wanted to aid her, but I had my own worries. Lethal steel claws tipped in something viscous and clear made a grab for me. I turned but not quickly enough. One of the claws found me and dragged a long vertical tear down the center of my chest.

With a grunt of shock but also of rage, I rolled out of reach of their hands and moved my hips into the hips of another, executing a perfect over-the-shoulder throw. But when the black robe fell to the marble floor, there was no grunt or cries of alarm or even of rage. Because the robe that had covered a human form just seconds earlier was now nothing but a small pile of discarded fabric, and a large black bird was winging rapidly away.

I needed to take down the bird, capture it, and question it, but it was already out of range, and the next set of hands was on me, and this one was far more deadly.

The robed attacker moved like my shadow, anticipating my each and every move. I would move left, and so would it, back and forth. I'd punch it, and it was like a mirror that could hit back. And each time it did, its blows grew in strength and ferocity.

At one point, it landed a perfect blow to my lower ribs. I grunted as I felt the bend in my bones and had to bite down on my back teeth to keep upright and not lose my lunch.

My ribs ached, my head was pounding, and my breathing was deep and gasping. My head was screaming out in agony, swimming with stars as the mirror image followed my every lead. But it wasn't only following my lead—it was actively doing something to me. Every second in its company, I felt myself growing weaker, as though it were siphoning my essence, drawing my energy away from me.

I frowned, recognizing the stamp of very dark and potent magick emanating in waves from it. What the devil was this thing?

If I didn't attack, neither did it, yet I felt that like a coiled spring, should I even make a move, it would come at me with ferocity that would leave me breathless.

I tried to find Elle from my periphery, but we'd been separated, and I could no longer even hear the king's clanging steel—only the screams and the cries of the wounded.

"Who are you?" I asked, changing tactics. I wasn't going to be able to beat the thing this way, because the more I gave of myself, the more it stole, and I could not afford to give it any more of me. If I did, the results could be catastrophic.

But it didn't answer. So I tried again, eyeing the tall, straight figure. The robes clung to its clearly muscular frame. I was surprised it merely stood there. It was obvious to me that it had the upper hand, but it wasn't even attempting to fly away as its compatriot had. It just stood there, staring at me through dark eyeholes that made it appear sinister and wicked.

I looked at its boots made of black leather with silver rings and studs on it. It stood in the fighting stance before me, but it didn't make a move. So long as I remained calm, so did it.

It, too, wore an elaborate golden mask, but there was something different about this Slasher, something I couldn't quite put my finger on. The way it moved, it was more elegant, more... defined?

"What do you want? The gold?" I tried again. "Why are you here, really? And more importantly, how did you get through the king's security?"

This time, the Slasher didn't mimic my movement, because I cocked my head to the left, and it cocked its to the right. Then it took a slow and measured stepping sort of glide forward, and in my heart, I understood that whatever temporary stalemate we'd shared was coming to an end.

Most of the civilians were cleared out. There were many fallen bodies around me, but I didn't smell a lot of blood or the offending sweet decay of the newly deceased, which meant either they were playing possum, or they'd fainted. Some were dead but not as many as there could have been.

I tamped down the burn of my powers, which ached for release. But I felt the heat sliding up behind my eyes and knew that soon my pupils would glow with its flame.

My nostrils flared.

The Slasher was so close to me that I could smell it—sweet, sickly sweet. I curled my lip, grimacing at the scent of almonds.

I knew that smell, recognized it instantly as the musk of death. I narrowed my eyes. "What are you?" I whispered, and it raised its gauntleted fist. The fire in my eyes burned. My fingertips began to burn. My insides swirled, my blood rolling through my veins like a serpent's venom. Little licks of fire began to glow within me. All I would need to do was let it go, and I could drown the world in it.

My lips pulled back, exposing my teeth. "I do not wish to end you, Slasher, but I will," I warned. "I will."

There was no laughter, no quiver whatsoever. If the masked creature heard me, it didn't seem to care. It all happened so fast. The robed figure reached for me, long claws extended, viscous fluid leaking. *Drip. Drop. Drip.* Each drop hitting the marble floor hissed and burbled as the acid ate right through it like a hot knife cutting through butter. I could only wonder what that substance was doing to me. Was I growing weaker not because of the creature but because of that initial strike of its claws to my chest?

That made more sense. And if that was the case, then what in the hells was that stuff?

I lifted my hand, palm aching with the fire that I would not release until I'd placed my hand upon the creature's chest, then I would propel a jet of flame through its body, its bloodstream, its bones, killing it from the inside out, leaving nothing behind but a still-intact outer shell, its innards completely burned to a cinder.

And just as I was about to finally release that torrent of fire, as my hand began to glow bright, fiery red, Elle was suddenly there behind the black robed figure, her face a mask of deadly beauty as she mimed for me to clamp my hands over my ears. I had less than a second to do as she bade before she opened her mouth and the full fury of her deadly song dropped the robe to its knees.

Her song was so shrill that all around us, goblets of crystal exploded into a million tiny projectiles. There were cries, and then there was silence.

I stayed where I was for a moment, blinking in a daze, realizing I was still me somehow, and Elle was glowing like a goddess of burning blue.

"You okay?" she asked, voice still trapped somewhere between the sultry rasp of the siren and the elegant refinement of the detective.

I frowned, sliding my hand over my paint-slicked hair and nodding. "The king?"

"Safe." She shook her head, toeing the robe, who now lay prostate at our feet. The only sign of life was the gentle, rhythmic glide of breath expanding its chest in intermittent bursts.

"Casualties?"

She shook her head again. "I don't fecking know how its possible, but very, very few. Lots of flesh wounds but nothing that won't heal." Elle swallowed hard, her blue eyes glowing like activated phosphorescence, attesting to her heightened emotions. I knew we were both wondering how the Slashers had infiltrated the event, but neither of us was asking it yet, because my brain was having a hard time accepting what had just happened.

Few, if any casualties. Slashers inside of an event more tightly controlled and warded than a dragon's lair. And apart from the one lying at my feet, no actual Slashers to speak of. Nothing but discarded robes lay scattered about with piles of sand at their center.

The wealth out on full display had been left unmolested. What was this? What had just happened?

"None of this makes sense," she muttered, staring around with a hard frown stamped on her forehead and pinching the corners of her eyes.

Around us, there were dozens of discarded black robes.

"Agreed," I grunted, beginning to feel the pain of my injuries as a low but building throb literally radiated off every inch of me. I applied pressure to my side, hissing and trembling as the pain of my injuries were starting to make itself manifest. My head, my chest... hells, even the balls of my feet ached.

Her eyes hooked to mine, and she gazed at me holding onto my side. "You hurt?"

"I'll live," I muttered.

She shrugged and shook her head. "We need to go debrief the king, see if he saw anything leading up to this. Then we have to call this in. Damn it all," she growled, glancing down at the robed figure at our feet. "None of this makes any fecking sense whatsoever."

"Every other black robe is a pile on the ground," I said slowly, thoughtfully, "so why is this one not as well? Why didn't it shift and fly away?"

Her lips twisted, then she knelt. "I don't know. But at least we've got one of the bastards, and this ought to make Bo shite her pants. It's a helluva lot more than we've had in a year." She laid a hand upon the chin portion of the golden mask.

I shook my head. "Elle, maybe we should cage it, ship it over to the witches first. Because you're right, this was too easy. Too different. I'm not sure we should trust—"

She slipped the mask off, then all the blood drained from her heart-shaped face, and she said one word that sounded like a gun blast in my ears.

"Hook?"

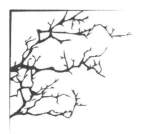

Chapter 7

Detective Elle

I BLINKED. THEN I BLINKED again because I was sure that it was some type of dark-magick mirage.

But the softly parted mouth, the elegantly handsome face in repose—I'd seen it so many times in reality and in dreams that haunted me still every single night.

He had a shadow of dark scruff on his square jaw. His nose was long, slightly crooked along the bridge, his mouth full and looking softly pliant.

I swallowed hard, brain reeling, lost for words as I drank in the sight of the only male I'd ever truly loved. I shook my head, hearing sounds echoing around me, but it was like listening to leggers—full time land walkers—talking on land while I swam beneath the waves. Tinny and distorted.

I frowned, hungrily sweeping my gaze over his prone form. It wasn't possible.

My hands were somehow on his chest, and I grabbed his right arm and shoved the end of his sleeve back, then there was a flash of silver from a long s-curved hook, and I heard another sound, like that of a choking, dying beast.

Hands were on my shoulders, shaking me roughly. "Snap out of this, Elle. Snap out of this!"

It was Maddox. I could recognize the whiskey-like grit of his voice. But there was something else in there other than mere worry, an undertone of emotion. I shook my head, latching onto his wrist.

How was I on my arse? When had I fallen? I couldn't even remember, but he was kneeling in front of me, holding my face in his hands, his multicolored eyes gleaming with licks of fire at their center.

"It's not possible," I croaked. "No. Not. Possible."

His nostrils flared, and he glanced over his shoulder at the still prostrate form of something that was not my Hook but wore his face.

"He... he died. He died, Maddox. He died." It was as if I was pleading, begging with him. I didn't know what I was saying or even doing, but his face was a blur as my waters filled my eyes and I shook my head.

I was losing my grip, my skin was crawling, and this time, the powers of my siren felt darker, tighter, far more dangerous, as it had the time Maddox had been forced to take me to Alice's to help fix me. I could feel the rising thrum of its madness leaking through my pores.

Maddox's hands began to burn with heat. My skin sizzled, ached, but the pain brought focus, clarity.

"Listen to me, Elle," he whispered heatedly. "Listen. Do you hear me? Are you with me?"

Every time he asked me that, I felt myself being pulled back, away from that abyss that would swallow me whole, obliterate my ability to think rationally.

His green eye was blazing like a jewel. He was seeing another vision of the future, but I didn't want to share with him this time. Around us, I felt the pounding of heels, the rushing movement of heavy bodies coming at us, coming for Hook.

I shuddered.

Hatter shook his head. "Only worry about me right now. Look at my face. I'm here. Are you're okay?"

I swallowed and nodded once, still jittery but hearing him.

"Good. Just breathe, Detective." His thumb kept softly brushing at my clavicle. The glide of his hot skin against mine was like an anchor drawing me back.

I took one last shuddering breath then angrily swiped at my cheeks with the backs of my wrists.

"We don't know what this is, only that it is the darkest magick. That might not even be Hook, Elle. I sense great magick, foul and tainted, emanating off that form. Whatever did this, whoever did this, its just trying to get at you."

What he said actually made sense. Why anything would want to get at me specifically was beyond me, but he was right. There was no way that was my Hook. None. He'd faded in my arms. That strange man, then, was Maddox's vision of Hook finally realized. It had to be.

I felt myself better able to think rationally once again. It was impossible. He'd faded to sea foam. In fact, if I went back to my eternal pools, I knew I'd feel the essence of him still move upon the waves.

I dug my fingers into Maddox's wrist, holding him fast to me, needing his strength as I'd rarely needed another's before.

The mania of just seconds earlier was fading. I was getting stronger again. Hatter's hands slid up the curve of my neck. The touch of his skin on mine was warm and comforting. I gripped him tight and nodded silently again.

"I'm okay, Maddox," I whispered. "I'm okay."

"Elle, are you all right?" It was Midas's voice over my shoulder, a note of anxiety in it that finally made me recall where we were and why. Hatter and I broke apart slowly. He lifted me gently to my feet, keeping one arm around my waist to help steady me. I didn't need his arm to keep me upright. I was okay. But it was oddly comforting, so I said nothing.

"I..." I took a deep, shuddering breath. That wasn't my Hook. That was an imposter, nothing more. And with that thought, I felt the full returning of my thoughts and senses. The temporary scrambling of my wires was no more.

"She is well. She took a heavy blow from that... thing," Hatter growled softly, gesturing toward the prone body of the thing that was not my Hook with his thumb.

"I will fetch my doctor and—" Midas sucked in a sharp breath. His entire body went rigid and tense. "What? What is this dark magick?" he hissed, backing up quickly on his heels as he made a sign of the cross upon himself.

I shook my head. Midas had known my Hook. In fact, Midas had been the one who'd first made introductions.

His eyes cut to mine, shock clearly stamped in them. His face bore tiny scratches on his cheeks and one nasty gash on his forehead that would definitely require stitches—adding more of a rugged appeal to his pretty looks than he normally had. "Elle, is that—"

"No," I cut him off sharply, curling my fingers tightly around Maddox's elbow, drawing my strength from him. "No. That isn't him. I don't know who or what that is, but it isn't him."

Midas frowned, looking deeply disturbed, before giving a slow nod. "As you say."

With one last silent squeeze, I finally and very reluctantly pulled away from the strength of Maddox's arm. He'd been injured in the fight too. I could see the pinched look around his eyes and mouth, the slight graying of his flesh even beneath the tint of gold paint that had begun to flake off in spots. In all the drama, I'd failed to note how gingerly Hatter was treating his left side. "What has happened here, Midas? How did they get through?"

Looking every inch the regal king, he turned his full lips up just at the edges in a slight snarl. "When I find out, there will be hells to pay. I can assure you heads will roll for this."

It wasn't an idle threat. Midas might be a good-time king, but he took his reputation very seriously, and right now, he was no doubt feeling as though he bore a scarlet letter.

Biting my lower lip, I glanced at Hatter from the corner of my eye. His face was blanched, and he was gripping his ribs still. I could have lost him, too, tonight. And the very thought of that made me ache, made me furious, but not a heated anger. It was a cold, icy fury that ate away at my mind. As a woman of the law, I couldn't encourage Midas in his pursuit of blood, but I felt that same need for vengeance.

"Are you missing anything?" Maddox asked, voice steady, though now that I'd noticed he wasn't doing well, he actually seemed to be looking worse by the second.

I sidled in closer to him, wanting to wrap an arm around his waist. But we were no longer pet and goddess. We were on the clock again, and we were just partners.

Not lovers. Not anything.

I bit down on my molars, curling my hands into fists.

Midas tossed one arm out to encompass the chaos of what was left. The people that had been huddled on the ground earlier were slowly making their way to their feet, running away and not looking back.

"Too soon to tell," he said, deep in thought, before glancing back down at the still form of the thing that was not my Hook. A worried frown twisted his handsome features.

I looked not at the thing that wasn't Hook but at my old friend. As if sensing my study of him, he looked back up at me.

"How was this possible? And furthermore, why here? All my most prized possessions are on full display for all the realms to see, yet they appear to remain as they were. Nothing but piles of robes and sand are all that's left, and then there's him." He jerked his chin toward the thing that wasn't my Hook.

I shook my head, not having a clue, either. "I have to call this in. I will be contacting you in a few days once you've had more time to go over everything and make sure nothing was stolen. But if you learn anything, if you find anything—"

Stepping forward, Midas made to reach out for me. But he wasn't wearing gloves or even gauntlets, and I quickly stepped back, placing my palm upon my throat. The pulse point beat like a hummingbird's wing as I stared back at him.

Midas gripped the air, curling his fingers so tightly back into his palms that his knuckled whitened. He bit down on his molars so hard that the muscles in his cheeks twitched. He gave me a short bow. I'd hurt him, but it couldn't have been helped. One touch of his flesh to mine, and I would be no more.

"Of course. I will tell you anything you wish to know." His tone was brusque.

I closed my eyes for half a second longer than was normal and nodded. "Thank you, my old friend. Maddox, please prepare the prisoner for transport."

I looked at him, and he nodded. His movements were slow, and because I'd worked with him so long, I could tell that he was in pain, but unless one really knew him, they would never know he was only moving at fifty percent. He didn't want to draw attention to himself right now, and I would honor his wishes. It was business as usual between us.

"Goodbye, old friend." I turned one last time toward Midas, who nodded back at me.

"If your father could see you now," he said.

I snorted. "He'd curse me all over again."

He frowned, shaking his head just slightly. "No, my dear. I'm not sure he would."

Then turning on his heel, he called out to his demons, "Clean this mess!" Then he marched off, head held high, and just like that, the golden king was gone.

Maddox had covered the thing that wasn't my Hook in a shimmering net of gold, a transporting spell. The false Hook still slept, looking so still that I suffered a pang, a memory of him closing his eyes for the last time, relaxed forever in my arms as I'd whispered the spell over him to turn him from flesh and blood and bone into sea foam.

With a growl, I swiped the key card through the air and stepped through, Maddox and false Hook close on my heels.

But once we were in the travel tunnel and safely ensconced away from the outside world, Maddox's wounds finally made themselves fully manifest to me.

He stumbled against the tunnel, his knees giving out on him, and he would have fallen on his arse had I not been there to grab him.

I frowned, planting my hands on his chest. "Maddox," I hissed, "what's the matter? What are you hiding?"

Gasping, breathing so heavily and quickly that I was afraid he'd make himself faint, he began chipping away at the peeling paint upon his chest.

"What are you—"

My words died as I saw, even in the dim lighting of the starry transdimensional tunnel, that Maddox had been wounded more than I'd known. The gold paint had created an illusion of wholeness, but without it on him, I could see the angry, red, and swollen tissue around a small but clearly inflamed vertical tear.

"What is this?" I hissed, locking eyes with him.

He snarled, but his face was twisted up into a mask of barely checked pain. "As I fought with Hook, he reached out and nicked me. I thought nothing of it at first. But damn," he seethed, dropping his head back against the tunnel and breathing heavily, palm covering his wound as he squeezed tight, as though applying pressure to try to alleviate the pain.

I swallowed hard, and my stomach twisted and dove in on myself. I'd fought four of those abominations, and I'd seen a viscous fluid leaking off the clawed tips of one of them. Most would claim that the thick clear fluid had no scent or odor, but I was a creature of the deep and had instantly scented the oh so slight as to be nearly undetectable tang of a stonefish's venom.

"Hatter," I whispered, "may I?" I tapped his palm. I needed to look at the wound, because if it was stonefish venom, I had to get it out, and I had to do it right now. There was no time to waste. The longer it stayed traveling through his veins, the worse off he'd be, until eventually, the venom would move straight to his heart and he'd be completely transformed from man to stone—forever.

Snarling, he dropped his hand, and any hopes I'd had that I was wrong fled at the sight of his skin now turning a chalky gray right around the edges of the wound. He'd been stabbed in the chest, meaning the venom would reach his heart far more quickly than usual.

We had medical witches back at Grimm who were fully capable of reversing the poisoning. This kind of venom took seconds, at most minutes, before the damage was so great that it was irreversible. But those precious moments had been wasted with me sitting on my arse, having the mother of all freakouts. And I was furious with myself for losing my head as I had. Because I was shite at composing my fear, I lashed out.

"Godsdammit, Hatter," I snarled, my panic turning to rage, as it so often did with me. "You could have told me this happened. Godsdammit!"

He was breathing heavily, his lungs rattling with each inhalation. "I... I can fix this. I just need to burn..." His words hitched. "Burn it out of me."

My nostrils flared as I smelled the internal ossification process already starting. The chalky scent of calcium punched me in the nose. I covered his wound with my hand, adding some pressure.

He rose up on his toes, his face blanching, then he slunk down the tunnel, landing flat on his arse, his strength leaving him instantly. "Elle," he croaked. His skin was tacky with sweat, and the paint was rolling off him, making him look as though he bled gold. "I need to—"

I heard it. The goodbye. I'd suffered it once before, and like hells would I live through another one. I shook my head. "No. You hear me, you stupid bastard. Don't you dare say anything else."

"Elle," he murmured, eyelids slipping shut, "I'm not... not who you think—"

His neck was dark gray, and bulging bruised veins stood out in stark relief upon it. The venom was moving so bloody fast. I sank to my knees in front of him, yanked his chin into my hands, and physically opened his eyelids. The whites were pricked through with busted capillaries. Panic was a ravenous consuming beast in my head.

"I don't give a rat's arse if you're the bloody queen's consort. You're my partner," I hissed. Why did the dying always feel the need to confess their sins? "You have to tell me yes, Maddox, you hear me. Tell me yes. Tell me to heal you. Because this is going to hurt like a son of a bitch and make you wish you'd never been born. So say yes. Tell me to make this better. Tell me I can. Tell me!"

What I was about to do was highly illegal. I was essentially going to commit a crime, using the force of my siren's powers against him. And considering that BS had forbidden me from ever tapping into a soul again with penalty of death if I should be found out, well... it could get me into a helluva pickle. But if I didn't do it, he would die before we ever even set foot upon Grimm soil again.

His body was a weight, his head heavy, as though the ghost had already left him. I shook my head. "Wake up! Say it, Maddox. Bloody say it! Say yes!"

His lips were blue, and beneath my palm, I could feel his heart slowing. His skin was no longer supple and warm but stony and cold.

I shook him violently. "Please don't be dead too. Don't be dead too," I whimpered. "Oh please, Maddox, please."

Then there was a flicker, a slight flutter of his lashes, and I screamed, lifting up on my knees. "I'll take it," I hissed. "I'll take it. This is going to hurt, but it's the only way, you hear me. So don't fight me. Whatever you do, don't fight this."

There was no more time. I called the siren, called her in all her deadly glory to me. I burned with her darkness, her powers. My marking burned like flame upon my forehead, and I opened my mouth, singing a song, a deadly beautiful song, calling him back from the dead, stealing his soul right back from the Pied Piper himself.

He began to twitch at first, then he began to scream. Then... he didn't stop screaming, even as blood ran like a river from his ears, his nose, and his eyes. I was unraveling him, tearing him apart from the inside.

And I gloried in the feel of that dark craving, the violence of severing soul from body. I drew on the string of his light, wrapping it tighter and tighter around itself, forming a ball of brilliant gold.

I was aware that it wasn't normal, the gold. Souls were blue. Human souls weren't the color of the gods. But I didn't stop to ponder or to wonder. Because there was no time.

And as I drew on the ball, I felt the hunger rising. Sirens consumed not only the bodies of their victims but their souls too. I'd once been brimming over with hundreds of them, maybe even thousands.

Our souls were so small, so pitiful as to be nearly nonexistent. We ate souls because that was how we felt most. That was how we learned, how we knew what joy, desire, and want were. We consumed souls because when we did, we learned how to live.

My mouth watered even as Hatter roared and his body began to smoke, to churn with his powers. But he wasn't fighting me. I knew what he could do, the nova of raging fire he could become. Which meant he was still aware, still in there.

I swallowed and closed my eyes, shuddering and trembling as I fought a need I'd not felt in ages. I was so empty inside, almost always.

Just a taste, a tiny brush of his soul against my dried lips would be enough to set me to rights, would take off the edge that I fought on a nearly daily basis. The hum of exquisite and great power in my hands was so damned tempting.

I continued to sing until the last bit of his light slid into my palm, and it was as if I held the sun in my hands, the fiery heat so intense, so mesmerizing. Like liquid gold, it swirled and danced.

Hatter was silent, panting, and I could feel the burn of his eyes upon me as he studied me, wondering.

I knew what I looked like, kneeling over him, his powerful soul trapped in my palm, my marking and eyes aglow with my power, my hair swirling like electrified and charmed snakes. I looked like death, like beautiful death.

I had his soul, and he couldn't stop me if I wished to consume it. I'd never tasted of soul so powerful as his. Even without touching my tongue to it, I felt the immense pressure of it like a ten-ton weight in my hand. I wet my lips, throat dry and aching for that first sinfully velvet drop of ambrosia.

I drew a clawed finger down its brilliant warmth, hissing at the enormous strength of its power flexing against me. I looked down at Hatter's face. His eyes were open, shining with question and pain. So damned trusting. I growled, trying to fight instinct and desire that demanded I give in, that I stop denying myself the pleasure I was born to consume.

My fangs had slid down. All I would need to do was lean over and prick his neck with them. I could end his suffering, his misery. It would be a mercy. Then with no form to hold him, I could eat his soul. He wouldn't need it anymore.

I blinked, and he nodded and closed his eyes, exhaustion clearly stamped on every line of his forehead. I could feel the transdimensional tunnel shuddering. We were close to Grimm.

I was better than the monster inside of me. I had fought her for so long, denied myself for so long, that if I gave in now, if I even took a drop of his soul upon my tongue, I would unleash from its cage a beast I could never again push back in.

With a heavy breath, I hissed, then forming my left hand into a fist, I punched into his chest, tearing through flesh, muscle, bone. He screamed in agony, nearly flying off the ground as he shoved up on his shoulders and the balls of his feet.

His fires began to sputter, began to flame on. Soon, he would be a nova I could no longer touch. Guarding his precious soul against the cage of my body, I grasped hold of his hearts and pulled.

Hatter went slack beneath me, his screams no more.

When I yanked his hearts out, I saw the stone of them. Three-quarters of one and the entirety of the other had already been turned. Another few seconds would have ended him.

The tunnel quivered, the lights of the stars exploded around us, and we were dumped right onto the steps of Grimm PD—Hatter with a large gaping hole in his chest and me covered in his gore and blood and kneeling over him, with his soul orb hidden in one hand and his hearts in the other. And beside the both of us was the prostrate and still-silent body of the imposter Hook.

Then someone screamed.

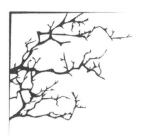

Chapter 8

Detective Elle

IT HAD BEEN TWO DAYS since our return to Grimm.

The rumors of what I'd done hadn't been pretty. They ranged from me snapping and reverting to my deadly siren side—which was ironically true, in part, anyway—to my being a double mole for the Slasher Gang. There had been an office vote as to whether I'd snapped and needed to be put down. Apparently, I only still drew breath thanks to one vote. If I knew who it was, I'd be tempted to bring them cookies.

Bo had debriefed me extensively. I'd been forced to go through a rigorous series of exercises and tests to ascertain whether I'd really done all of that to save Detective Maddox or whether I'd snapped.

Even the bastard Crowley had made a brief appearance, glowering and growling at me, recommending that I be handed over to him to be "put down as feral." But I'd cleared my tests. The witches had determined—and rightly so—that I'd not snapped and I was one hundred percent in my right frame of mind when I'd done it. In fact, the doctors of the Hawthorn Hills Hospital had said it was only my fast thinking that had saved Maddox's life at all. Another minute with those hearts in his chest, and he'd have died. My only true joy in the last two days had been in watching Crowley being forced to return to BS empty handed.

I'd hidden Hatter's soul, though it hadn't been easy. The temptation of shoving his soul inside of me had been great, but I knew I couldn't push my luck. So I'd rummaged in one of Ich's drawers for something suitable to contain it, and just as I knew I would, I had found just that something. A golden, and rather insignificant looking, locket. I'd given Ichabod detailed instructions on where to take it and where to place it. He'd never even asked me what was inside. He simply nodded and did as I'd asked of him.

Hatter could live without a soul long enough to heal, and none would be the wiser that it had been taken from him. At all costs, I would protect my partner, and now that I'd had more days to think things through, I knew that he had a secret, a secret I wondered if even Bo knew about.

But with the amount of poking and prodding he was getting, his golden soul would have been sussed out quickly, and if he wasn't ready to share the truth of it with them, well then, by damn, I'd make sure no one ever learned of its existence. They would simply think him soulless, which was better than the alternative.

I wasn't certain what Maddox truly was, but I had a few ideas, all of which, if true, would be more than just shocking. They could even be extremely dangerous.

"Next!" a chirpy voice cried out, yanking me out of my thoughts. I stepped to the front of the line. I didn't want to leave Hatter's side, so I was downstairs at the Witches' Beans instead of getting my double squid-ink latte at Georgie's.

I looked at the bubblegum-pink-haired witch as she looked at me. She was short, just barely coming to my chin. Her eyes were bright green and her lips full and a strange shade of bluish purple. I thought that maybe she had some fae in her blood, but I wasn't entirely certain, either.

"What can I do you for?" she asked with a large and overly friendly grin that made me want to punch her in her pretty face.

I always hated the really happy people. More often than not, it was little more than a façade meant to hide the darkest parts of them. Or maybe I was just a jaded cop who desperately needed caffeine. Probably the latter.

I frowned, glancing over at the menu for the hundredth time. "Do you have any sea blends? At all? I'd even take pond scum if you had it," I said with an edge of desperation.

"Sea blends? Um, no," she said with a nervous laugh then pointed at the strange menu full of weird symbols and characters. "We've just got the regular roasted beans, with some extra juice if you want it."

The café was crowded, and I could feel the tension of the couple in line behind me. Clearly, I was taking too long. If I didn't need the caffeine, I would leave. I'd never had regular coffee before and doubted I'd enjoy it. And what in the hells was juice?

I sighed, shoulders slumping. I hadn't slept in two days. Well, technically three. Time was ticking with my case. I'd still heard nothing about imposter Hook, and Maddox was sleeping and hadn't stirred even an inch, and I was basically at the end of my rope. I was hanging on by a thin thread of hope. Add to that that Bo wanted me to head over to Midas's castle in about an hour's time to see if maybe he'd learned anything in the days since the attack, and I was going fecking insane.

"I've never been to a mundane café before," I said slowly. "How does this work exactly? All I see on your sign is coffee, and"—I pointed to the sign, which was nothing more than emoting faces, some mad, sad, happy, etcetera—"what the hells is this? What juice are you talking about?"

"What the hells, man," the woman behind me hissed loud enough for me to hear. "Comes to a witches' bar and doesn't know what in the hells she's doing. Hurry up!"

I narrowed my eyes, tapping my fingers on the countertop, telling myself not to turn around and snap her head off her neck for being so bloody annoying.

The petite cashier smirked. "The faces are just asking you what kind of mood you'd like."

"So what, it's like a shot of emotion or something? You can do that?"

"Goddammit, is she slow or something? How stupid do you have to be, like seriously?" that same bitch behind me hissed, then I heard the man beside her whisper, "Glenda, stop it. We only learned about this last week ourselves."

The cashier grinned with a twinkling gleam in her bright-green eyes. "Something like that. You seem a little stressed. Perhaps I can help."

I ground my front teeth together. I could hear the foot-tapping behind me growing louder.

If I weren't wearing my badge, I'd probably lose my head, but I was wearing a badge, and I was so damned tired. "Yeah, whatever. Just give me whatever."

"Coming right up." Then she turned and in a loud voice that cut as clear as bells through the cacophony of noises, called out, "One large dark with a shot each of forbearance and *qui vive*!"

My eyebrows rose on my forehead. What was that, and did I even want to know? It was a witch hospital, so it stood to reason there might be witches working in the café. Had they spiked the flavorings with their spells? I was starting to rethink my drink order. But I was also thinking I might kill something before the day was through if I didn't get my drug.

So I said nothing as I watched a skinny and pale-skinned brunette with long pigtails that fell past her breasts whip up my drink in what seemed like no time at all. Then she grabbed two clear bottles full of glittering colored liquid that made me think of dyed unicorn tears. One was golden. The other was a deep aquamarine blue. The pale barista squirted a drop of each into my cup, gave it a quick stir, added a lid, then tossed it over her shoulder to my cashier, who grabbed it without even turning around.

I blinked. "What was..." I shook my head. "How?"

She didn't answer my question, but her eyes sparkled as she looked at me and said, "Here you go."

A little stunned by how odd that had been, I reached into my pocket, pulled out a wad of cash and tipped them both well. That had been the most entertainment I'd had in days, sadly.

I grabbed hold of the cup and sniffed it tentatively. All I smelled was the bitter, slightly burnt scent of black gold.

Needing the jolt of caffeine more than I mourned the loss of my delicious squid ink, I took a large swig. The texture was velvety and rich as it slid down the back of my throat, like warmed caramel with hints of bitter dark chocolate. I sighed as that wondrous elixir worked its magick on me.

The shots of whatever had clearly been a gimmick. I couldn't even taste them—though to be honest, I had no idea what forbearance or qui vive was supposed to taste like—but I could grudgingly admit that the coffee wasn't as noxious as I'd expected it would be. I took another, bigger sip, loving the feel of it warming my belly, then I started to move.

"Finally! Rude much?" the female behind me asked with a snort.

I turned, holding the cup in my hand. She was a redhead, broad in the hips and ample in the chest, with the kind of body even a siren could appreciate. Her eyes were so blue as to be nearly violet, and she had a smattering of freckles along the bridge of her very straight nose. She gasped, her pretty eyes widening as she finally caught sight of the mark on my forehead.

"I... I... I thought you a nymph," she mumbled as she licked at her pearl-pink lips.

The man beside her, large and roguishly handsome in a nerdy, boyish kind of way, grabbed her elbow. "Bloody hell, Glenda," he mumbled, "you would pick on a siren."

There was a vein throbbing in the side of his neck, and he was slightly shoving her behind his back, the stance protective. I almost laughed. Did they think I would eat her?

Just a second earlier, I really wanted to punch her in her pretty face. But now, all I could think was how flattering her flowery blouse looked on her.

"Well, have a nice day then." I tipped my cup toward them and scooted off. "Nice shirt, by the way."

She patted her top. "Thank—thanks, I think." Her red eyebrows gathered into a *V*.

"It was the forbearance," my cashier said with a breathy little laugh. "Gets 'em every time. Now, what'll you have?"

I shrugged, having no damned idea what she was talking about but suddenly feeling as light as air and weirdly happy, all things considered. Standing up on my tiptoes, I hummed under my breath—making sure to keep my tone to safe human decibels—as I meandered my way back toward Hatter's private room.

When I got in, I was pleasantly surprised to see him sitting up as two nurses flitted over him, one monitoring his vitals as the other wrote something down on a clipboard.

The nurses were dressed in long gowns of black velvet. Their corsets were colorful, though. One was a beautiful indigo and the other a rich hunter green. They had the witches' hat perched jauntily on their heads, and I couldn't help but smile when I saw it. They were pretty witches.

"Maddox!" I said with a happy chirp and raced over to him. He looked at me with something akin to horror on his face as I leaned in and gave him a quick peek on his cheek. "You're awake. You look well."

When I pulled back, he still looked confused and rubbed at his cheek with his fingertips. "Elle, are you—"

I grinned, sipping more of my delicious brew.

"Are you his mate then?" The nurse in the indigo gown glanced at me.

I chuckled. "Sure, if that means you'll tell me that my partner is fine."

Hatter snorted. "She is not my—"

"He'll be just fine. Are you the siren? The one who saved him then? What you did to save him is practically legend now." Her dark-purple eyes sparkled.

I humbly shrugged, but my grin was practically taking up my whole face. "Well, I don't wish to brag, but yes, that was me." I laughed heartily, feeling weirdly positive and happy.

"Most astonishing, stealing his heart from his chest as you did. My goodness, I'm not even sure I could have managed such a feat. And to not even bruise an artery in the process." She placed her hands on her cheeks and shook her head, awe shining in her eyes. "Well, it was nothing short of a miracle. Might I... might I shake your hand?"

Giggling, I turned and winked at a still far too silent Hatter, then I held my hand out regally toward her, knuckles pointed downward. "You may."

"Ah. Yes, well," she said and clasped my hand, turning it sideways and giving me a hearty shake. "An honor."

"Adira..." The green corseted witch sighed. "Leave them to it then, shall we? Her man needs his rest. He's only just woken up. Nice to meet you both."

"Zephinira, but—" Adira squawked as the other nurse pulled her out by the collar, and the door slid shut with a loud boom behind them.

I was eyeing the interior of the recovery room, which looked just like Maddox's bedroom garden in Wonderland. There was a large full moon hanging above us, and well-groomed hedgerows. Massive butterflies with electric wings zipped by, and the air smelled of earthy flowers.

"And just what in the devil has gotten into you?" he asked.

"*Hm?*" I blinked and took a longer pull of my drink. Gods above, but this thing was addictive. Never thought I'd like anything but the sea blends. I'd most certainly be grabbing another before I left.

"You, what has gotten into you, woman? Who are you, and where is my partner?"

"Oh, you silly boy." I laughed effervescently and slapped lightly at his chest. "It's me, obviously. And I love your choice of décor, very Wonderland. Very you. Does anyone in here know yet that you descend from the gods?" I took another swig of my coffee. "*Mm*, this is lovely. Would you like some?"

Tipping my cup toward him, I waited expectantly.

"No," he said slowly, "I think I'll pass."

His eyebrows were pinched tight, and he looked a little pale all of a sudden. His entire body had gone tense too.

Pouting, I shook my head. "Why so glum, chum?"

Not bothering to ask permission first, I sat down beside him, wiggling my body in close to his and then sighing once my thigh was flush with his.

He looked taken aback and hardly even breathed as he watched me.

"Elle, I don't think you know what you're talking—"

I shook my head and placed a finger against his mouth, leaning in until our mouths hovered close to one another. "I thought you would die. I thought..." I swallowed hard and shuddered. "I thought I'd lost you, Maddox."

I brushed my fingertips against his very bristled cheek. He needed a bit of a shave—not much, as he preferred to wear his goatee, but he was looking a little rough around the edges.

His shoulders, which had been tense just seconds earlier, slumped, and he seemed to literally wilt before me. "I thought I was dying. I'm... I'm sorry I didn't tell you what had been done to me sooner, but I didn't think it was anything to worry about."

I nodded. "Because you're a god and you can't die, right?"

"What? No, Elle. Bloody hells, what is in that coffee you're drinking?"

I looked at the cup, smiling happily. "It's just mundane coffee, which I was never particularly keen on trying, but I swear to the gods, or you, I suppose, that it's the best damned thing I've ever had in all my life." I laughed lightly, realizing in a corner of my mind that I was definitely not acting like myself.

"Elle," he grumped, "for the gods' sake, please stop saying that."

Grimacing, I nodded. "Right. You're right, of course. Can you imagine the chaos that would ensue if the world learned of a god walking amongst us? Oh, how they'd panic so. So how exactly did you get banished, Maddox. That's all I really want to know."

He pinched the bridge of his nose and closed his eyes, his face looking deeply troubled. I took another long slug of the bean brew then sighed as I rested my head against his shoulder for the briefest of moments.

"I won't tell. I vow it," I said to put him at ease. "But I do know. You lied to me. You're not human at all."

I was looking directly at him, so I saw when he finally opened his eyes. They sparkled, but he looked tense and miserable.

"Elle, you have to stop saying such nonsensical things. It's not true."

His eyes shot around the room, and that was when it dawned on me that we were being monitored, and though I couldn't work up the energy to really worry about anything at that moment, deep down, I suspected that if my hunch was right, we absolutely should keep his secret a... well, secret.

I cleared my throat and lifted my head. "Dear gods, I do think you're right. I have been drugged." I said it rather loudly then laughed, as though to mock myself. "Of course I am wrong. You are a man. Just a man. Just a wonderfully beautiful man who I still wish to have relations with. But a man when it's all said and done. And I really like this coffee. My gods." I moaned with desire so fierce one might think I was about to orgasm right on the spot from it.

I made to take another sip but Maddox grabbed it from my hand, brought the lid to his nose, sniffed, then with a shrug, whispered, "Bottoms up."

I gasped as he downed the rest.

When he finally came up for air, my eyes were narrowed, and I was wagging a finger in his face. "You're evil. I hate you." But the threat lost its effectiveness because I couldn't stop giggling as I said it.

Then he was the one smirking, taking my finger in his hand and placing a tender kiss upon its tip.

I shuddered but not with revulsion. Biting my lower lip, I stared at his full, lovely mouth, then I muttered in a hoarse voice, "I am glad you are well, my friend."

"Thank you for making the hard choice, Elle. I've said it before, and I'm fairly certain I'm going to keep saying it with you, but I'm so glad you're my partner."

He framed my cheek in his large palm, and I sighed as I snuggled into his hand.

"And Elle," he whispered softly.

"*Hm?*" I blinked, staring at his handsome face and thinking that I was sure I'd never seen anyone nearly as beautiful as him before—save for Hook, of course, and now that I was thinking of Hook, I was also thinking of false Hook.

I waited for the rage to suffuse my body, but it never came. Instead, all I could think was that I needed to speak with Bo and figure out why they'd clearly enchanted a man to look like my dead lover.

Glancing both ways, Hatter moved in closer to my side, and I could smell his sandalwood cologne. It was rich and earthy and sexy, just like him. I had to tamp down on a sigh.

His warm breath caressed the shell of my ear as he said, "You're not entirely wrong, either."

I blinked, and he pulled back, staring at me with worry glittering in his two-toned eyes. Still, very aware of the watchers, I swallowed down the hundreds of questions his statement had elicited in me and instead nodded.

"Okay," I said. "Okay."

"By the way, you have been spelled. I tasted patience and alertness and possibly a few other emotions in there, and all things considered, that's not a terrible thing to be influenced by right now." He brushed his knuckles down my cheek, his touch feather light and barely more than a graze, before he pulled his hand back to his lap.

I placed my fingers upon my cheek, still feeling the tingles of where he'd touched me. "How long will it last?" I asked him.

He shrugged. "A few hours at most. It wasn't much, just enough to take the edge off. Which I imagine you must have needed in a bad way. I'm sorry. How many days was I asleep?"

"Two. And I have to go soon. Bo's sent me to speak with Midas—"

As if on cue, the door opened with a loud wooden groaning. When we looked up, I wasn't sure who to expect to find, but it wasn't Bo. That was for sure.

"Captain." I shook my head and quickly scooted back to the edge of the bed, dangling my legs over the side. "I was just saying my goodbyes to Hatter. I'm headed to King Midas's no—"

She looked hard between the two of us for a few seconds before she held up her hand and shook her head. "Hold off on that trip, Detective. We have far more pressing matters."

I cocked my head then glanced behind me at Maddox, who looked as lost as I felt.

When I turned back around, Bo was striding elegantly toward us. She was dressed in a steel-gray jumpsuit with a smartly knotted tie. Her shepherd's-hook pendant gleamed quicksilver in the *V* of her breasts in the dim lighting.

"There was an incident. At Neverland. Three Lost Boys." She thinned her lips. Her gently lined face grew stoic, but I'd heard the barely there hitch in her voice and shook my head.

"Oh no. Are they—"

"Dead?" she finished my thought without preamble and cleared her throat before shoving her fists into her pockets. Her voice was steady and controlled, but I saw the pain glittering in the depths of her warm brown eyes. "Yes, Detectives, they are. A realm is in mourning, and I would not ask you to go, all things considered, but our department is stretched thin as it is, and there's a... well, a matter."

I frowned, saddened by the loss of the boys. Though they weren't technically boys—they were eternally youthful men, really. Still, I'd always had a soft spot for the Lost Boys crew. I'd once known their leader, the Pan, quite well, and him—there'd been multiple pans, actually—I did not like. No matter the incarnation, the boy had always been a devil. But thankfully, the Lost Boys hadn't taken completely after their leaders.

"What's the matter?" Hatter asked.

She looked at us both as she said, "We have probable cause to believe the dragon caused it."

I blinked and leaned back a little. "The dragon? As in *the* dragon, Whiskers? That beast might as well be a teddy bear, that's how frightening he is. Whiskers would never hurt a soul."

Bo shook her head, her gaze glassy and faraway as she whispered, "Whiskers was captured late last night. There is video of him. Incontrovertible proof of his crimes. He will be put down, Elle. I am sorry."

I gasped and shook my head. Titiana had told me to go to Neverland, to see to Whiskers. Guilt that I'd waited too long scratched at the back of my mind. But with everything that had happened recently, seeing to a pacifist dragon had been at the very bottom of my ridiculously long list of things to do.

"Dragons are rare and ancient creatures, Bo. The realms will riot if the courts do this terrible thing. You know they will. I just can't believe he's done this. Not him. Not Whiskers."

She thrust out her jaw. "I've come because he's specifically requested your presence, Elle. He wants to speak with you. And what I believe, or even you believe, is completely immaterial to this case, and well you know it. Facts—that is all we deal in, Detectives."

She thrust out her jaw again, and my stomach ached. It wasn't possible. I mourned the loss of the boys. Of course I did. But Whiskers was my friend, and he was still among the living, and I had to get to the bottom of something that made absolutely zero sense to me.

"What was his motivation for this crime?" I asked. "Has he confessed? Video aside, what might his motive be? And also, I hate to ask this, but I'm on Slasher detail. Is this connected in some way that you'd suddenly pull me from my meeting with Midas to see to Whiskers?"

It wouldn't be the first time I got pulled off my case. Not that I was annoyed, but I was annoyed.

Hatter cleared his throat. "I wondered the same thing. Are we looking at two separate incidents, or do you believe, Captain, that our cases are somehow linked?"

She glanced at him and nodded. "There are signs that perhaps not everything is as cut-and-dried as the prosecution would try to make it be. They're fast-tracking this case, as you knew they would. High-profile murder victims and a dragon responsible for the crime—it's juicy tabloid fodder, and you know how the commissioner and BS get in times like these. They want to fix the problem, and they want to fix it now and to hells with right or wrong. So long as someone swings soon and they can assuage public fears, that's really all they're after."

She wasn't saying anything that wasn't true. We all knew it.

"What is to become of Whiskers?"

I knew one thing about my old dragon friend. He was a pacifist, a true one. He'd cut ties with the marauding and blood shedding of his brethren ages ago. It was why he'd left the fire realm hundreds of years earlier. He'd been in search of a simpler life, a more peaceful one.

What he'd done and who he was—the two simply weren't computing in my head.

"He will be tried for his crimes, and if found guilty, he will be dealt with."

Code for he would swing. I sighed, conflicted and confused by the horrible turn of events.

Bo cleared her throat and looked down at Hatter. "The doctor tells me you're recovering well. Should be cleared by tomorrow night at the latest."

"I am well, thank you," he said, voice slightly dull and scratchy sounding.

"Good." She shrugged and nodded. "Good. Elle, say your farewells. I'll see you to the door. I have one last matter to discuss privately with you."

Nodding, I looked over my shoulder at Hatter. His color was finally returning. I was grateful that he appeared to be on the mend. "I'll come back for you tomorrow."

Looking between the two of us, he nodded solemnly. "Stay safe, partner."

I wanted to take his hand and give it a squeeze or even lean in and kiss his whiskered cheek. But Bo's eyes were far too intelligent and piercing, so I simply nodded at him, brushed off the wrinkles of my dress, and followed Bo out the door.

It would be the first time in months that I'd be doing a mission without Maddox by my side, and I didn't like it. I didn't like it at all. I paused at the threshold of the door, spine tense and knees locked, words on my tongue.

Bearing down on my molars, I nodded without turning around, then I pushed out the door, exiting a garden and entering a cold, sterile hospital wing once more.

A rush of busy bodies moved to and fro. Owls carrying large trays of food in front of them winged by. It was clearly the lunch hour. One flew past me in a blur, entering Maddox's room.

Shoving my hands into the pockets of my leather jacket, I stared at Bo's lined and worried face.

"Elle, I wanted to ask you a question before you left."

"Shoot," I said with a nod.

"The... uh, doppelgänger I suppose is a polite a way of calling the male you brought back with you from Midas's ball... did he speak with you? Say anything at all?"

I frowned, wondering why she should be asking me such a question. "Surely Matilda has extracted those memories from it. And no, I don't recall anything."

Cocking my head curiously, I studied her as she studied me.

Her eyes were thinned. "You don't seem as upset by this as I'd expected you would be."

I shrugged. "Should I be? I don't believe it is him. You know as well as I that I witnessed his death with my own eyes. I was there. There can be no mistaking that he died. And a human cannot come back from that kind of wound. You know it. I know it. Therefore, the only logical conclusion is that it is a doppelgänger, the magick will wear off soon enough, then we'll see what we're really dealing with here."

Bo wet her lips before saying, "Right. Of course." Her smile was quick and didn't quite reach her eyes. "As you say."

She sounded strange, and I couldn't put my finger on why that was. Had she learned more than what she was telling me?

"Has the magick worn off then? Did the witch crack the riddle? Who is it?"

"Oh, what? No." She pursed her lips tight. "No, of course not. Matilda is still drafting up incantations. Whatever spell is on the male, it is quite strong."

"She's a level ten. She should have cracked the spell or gotten damned close to it by now," I said with some incredulity. Matilda was just about as powerful a witch as they came. There weren't many stronger.

Bo rolled her wrist, as though batting my words away. "I'm sure she'll work through it soon enough. We both know how capable she is. It's just a little stronger magick than she's used to is all."

What in the blazes could craft magick stronger than hers? The list, if such a thing were possible, would be piteously short, I was sure.

I nodded, noting the tightness of her forehead.

"Anything else, boss?" I asked, rising up on my toes. "Because I should probably get going otherwise." I pointed a thumb over my shoulder.

Her eyebrows gathered, then without warning, she leaned in close to my mouth and sniffed. Suddenly, the question mark on her face cleared, and she snorted. "I should have realized the siren would consume the loco beans downstairs. Now I get why you're acting so strange. What did they give you?"

"Maddox says it was alertness and patience, though I'm not spell—"

"Oh, but you are, Elle." She patted me on the shoulder. "Welcome to the obsession that is the Witches Beans. Now, go." She stepped back. "You will debrief me of your findings upon your return. And be quick about things. No chasing after thin leads as you are often wont to do. I do wish Hatter could have gone with you. He does a far better job than I do at keeping you on task."

I snorted. "That, he does. But this should be a cut-and-dried interrogation."

"I've learned through the years that matters are rarely so simple. Especially when they come to your investigative style. Not that I mind how very thorough you are, but I do have to kiss a lot of IA ass when it comes to you, siren." Her light laughter let me know she was mostly teasing, but she was right. I did often rub internal affairs raw. My money was on it being more my father's doing than my own shenanigans that caused me to be a bug under their microscope, but I could be wrong—doubted it, but I could be.

"See you in five hours then, Elle," Bo said.

I shook my head. "Two tops."

"Yeah, that'll be the day." She guffawed, and after pulling out a golden key card from her inside vest, she swiped the air, opening up a travel tunnel. She didn't look back as she stepped in and the swirling starlight swallowed her up whole. Her laughter echoed around me long after she'd gone.

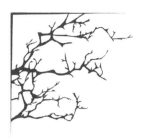

Chapter 9

Detective Elle

I LOOKED AT WHISKERS. He was a Chinese dragon with scales of gold and jade, and long, beautiful golden whiskers projected from his snout, glittering like molten metal in the dim lighting of the jail cell.

Covered in spelled witches' chains, he was pinned fast to the cold concrete floor. I'd only ever seen him flying the winds, proud and majestic, a regal warrior who'd protected Neverlandian skies from threats above.

Now, my old friend looked miserable and dejected. I shook my head. I'd managed to secure ten private minutes with him in a detainee cell. Outside, two rock orcs stood guard, massive arms crossed over their massive chests. The sands of an hourglass slid steadily through the narrow opening—my time with him was quickly running out.

"What is this, Whiskers? What has been done to you?" I rolled my wrists, helplessness consuming me at the sight of him.

He turned his beautiful lion-colored eyes upon me. I could see each fleck of gold glittering in their depths.

Iron scraped loudly against the cold concrete as he shrugged.

"Do not move, prisoner," the left orc growled. His pig's face was twisted into a tight snarl, and his tusks clacked together menacingly as he spoke. "Eight minutes, Detective," he snapped, and I nodded.

I looked back at my friend. Dragons aged but very slowly. I knew that Whiskers was one of the oldest, but I'd never known a true date. Dragons took years to reach full maturity, and only then were they truly considered a danger to others. But Whiskers had never been.

I'd seen him fly Lost Boy after Lost Boy through the skies, patiently putting up with their silly games of kill the dragon. It wasn't an uncommon sight to see him on the ground, surrounded by a bevy of Lost Boys poking and prodding at him with their wooden swords as they'd loudly declare the beast quite dead.

Lost Boys were eternally youthful, so long as they remained upon Neverlandian soil. A few did, but most didn't. Eventually, many of them would return home, usually once they'd begun to lose their memories of their past lives and their families. There was something unusual in Neverland soil. The dirt was often used by witches for their forgetting spells, and only dragons appeared to be immune to its terrible powers.

Dragons were not native to Neverland, but they were mystics and could glide between realms by travelling the ley lines. Since they were creatures and not humans, there was no law prohibiting them from doing so. Though they were fearsome in looks, dragons were generally well-behaved members of Grimm society. That was what made the case so baffling.

I'd seen pictures of the crime scene. The photos would haunt me for the rest of my life. They'd been some of the most gruesome I'd ever had the misfortune of looking at. The violence of the boys' deaths... I clamped my front teeth together and forced myself to take three quick and shallow breaths, pushing the bile back down.

"It is good to see you again, Princess Arielle," he said in the deeply accented voice of his kind. "I thought you'd forgotten about us all."

It was a rolling thunderous type of speech pattern that was both aggressive and eloquent to the ear at the same time.

I smiled sadly. "It has been some time since anyone has called me such. I'm just Detective Elle now, my old friend."

"As you wish," he said steadily. "How are you?"

I shook my head, realizing I truly must have been spelled if I wasn't having a meltdown at finding myself back in the one realm I'd promised myself I would never again return to after Hook's death.

"I am confused." I pointed at him with a small shake. "Finding you here and hearing the rumors of what you've done."

His massive jaw clenched tight, causing the jade and golden scales to glimmer almost prettily. Curls of steam emanated from inside of his large nostrils.

I blew out a harsh breath. "Tell me," I leaned in to whisper quickly, "that none of this is true, Whiskers. Tell me you did not do as they are all saying you've done."

His regal face was stoic, his eyes full of glittering pain as he grunted, "I do not remember doing any of what they say I've done."

A knot that had been forming in my stomach began to unkink until he shuddered and said, "But I was captured on video. The proof is, as they say, in the pudding. It is me. It is very much me. I did this. I killed my friends. And for that, I should pay."

I shook my head. None of it was possible. I knew Whiskers. Dragon or no, he couldn't have hurt a fly. I needed to look at the video. I refused to believe this could be. There had to be a reason for all of it, like he'd been spelled, or... I thought of the not Hook and frowned hard. But no sooner than I halfway started to entertain the idea that maybe not Hook wasn't not Hook and maybe, just maybe, Whiskers hadn't been spelled, did I absolutely dismiss the notion out of hand. There was no damned way. None. He could not have done it, not Whiskers. Any other dragon, possibly, I'd believe it, but not Whiskers. I steeled my resolve and loudly cleared my throat.

"Don't be ridiculous," I said. "It's not possible that—"

"But I did!" His voice was a terrible rumble that caused the ground to quake and the thick walls to tremble. There were cries from the prisoners outside, and the orc guards twirled, batons held at the ready.

"Damn ye, beast!" The right one snarled and slapped his baton against the metal cage with a loud and heavy *clang*. "Try that once more, and see if ye don't like a taste of yer own medicine. Ye'll find I'm much hardier than a mere whelp of a boy." He spat.

I shot to my feet. "Threaten him once more, and I'll book your arse for harassment. See that I don't, you sniveling bastard."

I must have been spelled, because my words definitely lacked the heat of my usual threats. Yet my words seemed to have hit the mark anyway, because the orc's nostrils flared as his eyes turned the color of heated tar. With a last snarl, he banged his baton against the cage once more but didn't utter another sound as he turned.

I glanced at the hourglass. I had five minutes left.

I slumped into my seat with exhaustion. "You won't hang for this. I vow it, old friend. I know you—"

He snorted, causing plumes of smoke from his nostrils to encircle my ankles.

"You knew me, years ago. You've not returned since, and you do not know me now." His words, though true, felt like a spear had just been driven through my heart.

I swallowed hard and shook my head. "You... you know why." I said it so softly, I wasn't even sure he'd heard me, but his earflaps twitched. "Even so, I am sorry."

He blinked his large golden eyes back at me. It was horrible to see such a magnificent creature like Whiskers bound in chains. It was unnatural, and I hated it. I took a deep breath, reminding myself that I could do nothing other than question him at the moment. I couldn't release him. If there indeed was video—which only a fool would lie about—the evidence was damning and solid enough that no judge would issue bail. Not for something like this, something this high profile and that would touch on the hearts of all the hundred realms. Cases that involved children were often the hardest and worst to solve because biases and deeply held beliefs usually got in the way of conducting an impartial investigation. If there was even a whiff that someone had done something heinous to a child, even the most sane witnesses tended to become unreliable.

"Don't be. I never asked for your apology," he rumbled and moved his massive chin to lie atop his front right paw.

I took in a shuddering breath. "I know you are hurting, Whiskers, but if you could just tell me something, anything that could help with this case..."

Jets of white smoke issued from his thick nostrils, causing the scales to glint like gems in the dim lighting.

"There is nothing, other than I slept, and when I awoke I had blood on my claws, Detective. Flesh between my teeth. And the taste of marrow upon my tongue." His words were a terrible rumble of self-loathing and self-hate. "For days, I scented wrong in the air. For days, I felt—"

His words brought to mind Titiana's words of him acting unusual.

"The queen of sprites told me that you'd been patrolling the skies more frequently lately, blasting jets of fire all the time. Why?"

He looked at me as though he didn't understand what I was asking. "I don't recall ever having done that, Detective."

I frowned. "What? But why would she lie about that?"

A hard rolling growl trembled from out of his chest. "Sadly, she might not have. The truth is, I have gaping holes in my recent memories. The past two weeks are mostly a blur to me."

My stomach bottomed out, and I clenched my eyes shut. That was not good and would definitely not help his case.

I reached over, clapped my hand on his massive shoulder, and gently scratched the smooth jade-green scale. Whiskers had his eyes shut, but he took in a trembling breath.

"You say you recall nothing other than waking up and finding blood in your claws. Is this so?" I asked him soothingly, needing him to remain focused but not wanting to upset him any further than he clearly already was.

"It is so," he rumbled, and I nodded.

"I'm going to ask you one last question, Whiskers, then I will leave you to your desired solitude."

His massive golden eyes gazed back at me, making me feel as though I were sinking in some way. Whiskers had to be thousands of years old. If he'd wanted out of this place, a couple of spelled chains were hardly enough to hold him back. He might not get out, but he'd bring down the entire house of cards and everyone in it before he was through.

Anyone with any sense could see how much what had been done panged him, and surely that should count for something. I rubbed his shoulder soothingly, over and over, conveying without words that not everyone thought him a monster.

"Just..." I shifted on my seat, not wanting to ask him but knowing his answer could be crucial to my investigation. I cleared my throat and pressed on. "Just before the attack, did anything strange or odd happen to you? Anything that, looking back, feels out of order or just plain wrong? Anything at all, no matter how insignificant," I rushed on when he opened his mouth and began to shake his head as though he meant to deny it.

But then he paused, eyes taking on a faraway look, and he spoke without looking at me, as though he was reliving a moment.

"Strange that you should ask. No one else did, and I would tell you it was nothing, but it was odd enough that even now when I think of it, I feel baffled by what it was that I saw."

My pulse jumped, and I curled my fingers into my palms. "What did you see, Whiskers?"

He blinked, and this time, it was as if he'd come back to himself, severing the memory, and was fully back in the present. Golden eyes glimmered intelligently back at me. "Just before this particular day began, I walked from my nest, stretching my wings, and I saw blood upon the cliff. It was everywhere, like a slaughter had taken place just outside my door. But I'd heard no battle in the night, and apart from my recent memory lapse, I forget nothing. It could be that as the queen says, I'd roasted something, that I'm responsible for this slaughter. But then how could I forget this?"

It was true—a dragon's memories were said to be eternal. And when I'd spoken to Whiskers before, it had been a legend I believed to actually be true. He'd seen the rise and fall of countless civilizations and its peoples and could describe them all to me in exacting detail. But more than that, if I came back for more of his tales, no matter how long between the telling of them, his stories had never changed.

But finding a slaughter outside his cave would mean nothing in a court of law. It was proof of nothing. I shook my head. "What are you saying?"

He ground his jaw so loudly that I could hear the creaking and groaning, and I grimaced. He was agitated, looking from left to right, aware, no doubt, of the surveillance we were under. Anything he said could be overheard by the guards watching us on the monitors in the other room.

Wiggling on my seat, I slid forward just a little and affected a nonchalant attitude as I crossed my legs and planted my chin onto my palm, looking calm and collected, bored even. But I'd shielded his facial expressions from the view of the cameras, then I allowed my marking to glow. Only softly, though—I didn't want to alert any guards to what I was actually doing.

Whiskers, fully aware of my abilities, gave an imperceptible nod, a silent communication between the two of us. I arched my eyebrow. He was a Chinese water dragon. I, too, was a creature of the deep, which meant we could communicate in a completely different way than landers did.

"Again I ask, Whiskers, what are you saying?" I kept my voice steady, speaking through my lips so that the monitors would think nothing amiss.

But my trident's mark burned, and I spoke not only with my mouth but also with my mind, able to mentally project to him as well because of our joint affinity to water.

Speak quickly, Whiskers, or we shall be caught. What aren't you telling me?

His golden whiskers twitched. *It wasn't merely blood I found outside my door, Detective. But feathers. I've heard of the Slasher activity, and though I cannot fathom what could have possibly brought them to a land not known to host much in the way of coin, I highly suspect it was them. In fact, I'd been finding feathers for many weeks now. But this last time, there seemed to be a great deal of them, enough to make me edgy and curious. And more than that, I found sand. In my nest. Hundreds of feet above sea level. It's not possible. Not unless I trucked it in, which I would swear I did not.*

My heart jerked so hard I twitched in my seat, but his face remained impassive. I should not be seen reacting. I was vaguely aware that I was vocally chastising him for wasting my time. Splitting my consciousness this way wasn't easy. I had to work incredibly hard to remain focused so that I could concentrate less on the talking and more on the mental. Whiskers was also speaking to me in tongue, not just mentally. Hopefully, anyone who saw us would be none the wiser to the truth.

Go on, I thought to him.

Rumor has it the Slasher Gang has grown more active, flying between realms, even, so I was curious, and I followed the trail of blood and feathers. It led me to the fairy stronghold. Detective I... He swallowed hard. *I believe I was spelled to create some type of diversion. It is the only thing that makes sense. The last thing I remember seeing was a massive pile of golden sand, and then I remember no more, until I was charged with murder.*

He shuddered and stopped speaking.

I frowned, clamping my lips shut. I had a thousand more questions to ask but knew I had no time left to utter any of them. Before Midas's gala, I'd only ever seen dun-colored sands at the scenes, but Maddox and I had seen gold at the ball, and now the dragon spoke of gold too.

What did this mean?

"It is time." The left orc interrupted us as though on cue, and the heavy grinding of metal on metal rang discordantly through my ears, making me bite down on my front teeth with a grimace. "Have you got what you came for, Detective Elle?" he rumbled in the deeply sonorous tones of a mountain orc.

Standing slowly, I looked down at Whiskers's bowed head. He had his eyes closed and appeared to have fallen asleep. He was clearly done speaking, and so was I.

Sighing, I shoved my fists into my jacket pockets and nodded. "Aye."

The orc pointed to the door. Chewing on my bottom lip, I wanted to say goodbye to Whiskers, but I couldn't bring myself to do it, because it could quite possibly be the last time I ever said it to him. And I didn't want that.

I wouldn't lie—it did not look good for him. Very few attorneys had ever successfully gotten their clients off with the "magick made me do it" defense because it was terribly hard to prove an enchantment after the fact. Unless Whiskers had been captured actively under the spell, witches with that level of magick could quite easily erase any marks of such a curse once the task was completed.

With a heavy heart, I nodded toward the orc and turned to go. Only once I was outside the maximum-security stronghold did I reach out to the PD.

I would have loved to speak with Maddox and figure things out together, as we so often did. He could usually see things that I couldn't, bringing in a different perspective and helping me to look at a case outside the box.

I needed to speak with someone, though, and I didn't have enough to badger Bo about any of it just yet.

Swiping my key card through air, I thought not of Grimm PD or even Maddox's room but Ich's home. He had the day off, and right now, he was the only one I could think of.

When I stepped out of the travel tunnel, I stood in front of a nondescript brownstone building with a staircase that consisted of seven steps—a lucky number, he'd said, something about integers and sieving process and prime numbers and I didn't know what. Mathematics was quite beyond me.

The entire block looked the same, rows of brownstones with few, if any, distinctive features to them, with small black wrought iron-fences and uniformly planted maple trees in the sidewalk in front of them.

Ich's was easy enough to distinguish because of the way the address of his home tilted crookedly down the front of his wall like a metal slide. He wasn't much for home repair.

I jogged up the steps and knocked once. Ichabod, who'd clearly seen my arrival, opened the door immediately. He was shirtless and wearing a pair of loose dark trousers. His feet were bare, and he had a towel wrapped around his neck as he gently rubbed at his head. His dark hair was still damp from a recent shower, and he smelled of brandy and good, clean soap.

I glanced around his flat looking for any signs of visitors. "Bad timing?"

"Not at all. Come in. I saw you arrive not a second ago. Tea?"

I shook my head. "No, I'm fine. Just a quick question, then I'm back to Neverland."

He nodded as he walked us back toward his kitchen area. Or at least, it was what I called his kitchen because of the stove. But honestly, Ich lived in a library. He had books everywhere, popping out of every conceivable nook and cranny. He had books on the shelf, in the cabinets, on the floors, all of them bound in leather and looking older than even my father, who was well into his three-hundredth year.

"So is that where you are today?" His intelligent blue eyes roved over my face. "Never thought I'd see the day you willingly went back there."

I sighed and pinched the bridge of my nose. "Long story. But I have a friend in trouble. Big trouble, actually, and I'm following a hunch is all."

He pursed his lips as he neared his counter and pointed to an opened newspaper. On it, the headline read in big, bold black letters: **Dragon Rains Death!**

I wrinkled my nose and shoved it away. "Rubbish headline. Nothing more than shock value, that."

"Whiskers, is it? You knew him?" he asked, reaching for a teacup and pouring out a cupful of steaming water from his still-whistling kettle before dropping a silver ball packed with loose green tea into it.

I nodded. "Once. A long time ago." Leaning against whatever bit of available open counter space there was, I crossed my legs at the ankles and stared ahead of me without really seeing much.

"Friends with a dragon—you never cease to amaze me. You do know that's quite rare, no?" He gave me a rakish grin. With his long hair hanging down and the shadow of a beard on his face, he made me think more of a pirate than my usual nerdy companion.

I shrugged and gave him a small ghost of a grin. "So I've heard."

"But..." He stirred his tea before taking a small sip. "I get the impression we are not here to exchange pleasantries, so tell me, Detective, what it is that has actually brought you here."

Astute observer as always, he was right, of course, so I agreed with a nod.

"You've been the one collecting the samples of grains from the crime scenes, no." It wasn't a question because I already knew he was.

"Indeed, I have. Why do you ask?" He took a large swig of tea before giving a deep sigh. I smelled hints of lemon rind waft up from the steam. He reached behind a stack of books and pulled out an amber-colored bottle, uncorked it with his teeth, and poured a generous serving of brandy into his mug. This time when he took a sip, he grinned.

I shook my head. "I was just interrogating Whiskers, and he mentioned seeing them. And the other night when Maddox and I were on mission at Midas's gala, I saw some then too. In fact, in reviewing many of the case reports, the grains seem to be the one constant tying what on the surface look like completely unrelated scenes together. I was hoping that maybe you could elucidate on the matter and, further, tell me what you learned from my contact the other night,"

He snorted and chuckled. "I have rubbed off on you, siren. Haven't I? You, looking at the small, almost insignificant parts of the scene rather than just tearing off after the obvious clues."

"Well, I did have a very good teacher for many years who taught me to look beyond the discernable."

He tipped his head before setting his mug down. "To answer your question, yes, I think the grains of sands are significant. And your contact was absolutely useless. He never showed."

I thinned my lips. The next time I saw Hector, the one legged ghoul, I'd be giving him a piece of my mind. That bastard had played me for a fool. I shook my head and sighed. "I am sorry about that. Trusting a ghoul to actually show up might have been a bit naïve on my part, but I hoped after what I'd done for him, he'd do the right thing at least once in his long, undead life. Anyway..." I flicked my wrist. "So we are definitely certain now that the grains are indeed sand?"

"*Mm.*"

I didn't fail to note the noncommittal answer.

Then he was rushing off, marching with a briskness that told me the nerd in him had grown excited with discovery. I grinned as I followed his mad dash toward his bedroom.

And I knew this because this wasn't my first time at Ich's place. But just as with the kitchen and living quarters, his bedroom, too, was a floor-to-ceiling maze of leather-bound books and journals. He had a desk with a few vials full of powders and other odd bits, an ancient microscope, and a Bunsen burner on it, no doubt to perform his experiments on. It was the only area of his room that was somewhat neat and tidy. His bed was covered in books, and there was a ratty couch sitting catty-cornered with a blanket tossed haphazardly over its back—clearly where he really slept. Even so, I counted no fewer than ten books scattered across its cushions.

He walked toward a shelf that a mound of books had hidden from my sight and ushered me toward him. I moved to stand beside him, then my forehead wrinkled when I studied ten clear bottles full of tan sugary sand.

"Are those—"

"The sands from the crime scenes?" he finished. "Yes. Yes, they are." He clasped his hands behind his back and lifted high up on his toes. I knew Ich well enough to know that for reasons quite beyond me, he was excited about something. And it all had to do with the sand.

"And have you tested their properties? Anything unusual about it? Spelled? Anything?" I asked, running my fingers along the cool glass.

"*Mm.* All the same. Just sand. Nothing but sand. It's all it is."

I frowned, thinning my eyes, because he sounded far too excited for it to just be sand. Planting my hands on my hips, I shook my head and glanced at him. "Then why do you sound so happy about that?"

He lifted a finger and practically skipped back toward his desk. I followed, wearing a confused grin. It was always a pleasure to watch his eccentric mind at work, even if more often than not I was completely lost.

"Yes, you're right, of course. Why am I happy about that? Well, until today, I wasn't at all. I couldn't understand why in the devil we kept finding piles of sand at each crime scene. Was it simply debris left behind by the Slashers? But really, that made no sense, either, because they're far too intelligent to be so damned clumsy. It's why they continue to evade capture as they do. But the sand is significant. It has to be, right? It's a"—he rolled his wrist—"calling card, if you will. A way to let us know that not only are they aware we're watching, they don't give a rats arse about it, either. Because no matter what we do, we can't stop them. Hubris, of course, but hubris can be defeated."

Then he reached toward his desk and pulled out the drawer, and a tiny vial of yet more sand rolled with a *plink* against the wood. But this sand was obviously different. This sand glimmered like freshly minted gold by candlelight—the exact same shade as the stuff Maddox and I had seen scattered around the gala.

He picked it up with obvious reverence and tilted his hand toward me. "Now, guess what this is, Elle."

"Sand?" I shrugged. "Golden sand," I said to be more specific.

His eyes sparkled. "By all appearances, you'd think so. Now, this sand was found at the last crime scene. The gala, in fact. And just like all the rest, it was found in neat and tidy piles. But it's not beige. Why is that?"

I could feel his excited tension, and I knew that he suspected he might be on to something significant. But I still hadn't a clue what that could be. It wasn't uncommon for both Ich and Maddox to be ten, sometimes even twelve, paces ahead of me. I was by no means stupid, but they solved crimes as they played chess—it was a fascinating process to behold.

"Because Midas accidentally touched some?"

He moved briskly over to his desk and yanked open yet another drawer and pulled out a small glass slide, which he set inside his microscope and powered it on then stepped back.

"*Mm.* Maybe. But that's not what's got me so excited. Because, you see, this sand is very, very different. And it has nothing at all to do with Midas touching it or not touching it."

He waggled his eyebrows, and I harrumphed. "Ich, get to the point already, please."

Taking a step back, he pointed toward the microscope. "Look for yourself then. Maybe you'll see what I did."

Frowning and even a little excited by the mystery, I leaned over and stared into the eyepiece.

Being a siren, I was very attuned to the terrain of the underwater worlds. Some sands were red because they were so rich in iron. Others were green, connoting a rich deposit of olivine close by. And based on the colors, I could generally approximate within a few meters where the sand had been picked up.

There was only one problem. Nowhere in Grimm—that I was aware of—were there golden beaches. And as I stared at the slide, I grew more and more confused. Because this was most definitely not sand.

Sand had an unpolished and gemlike quality to it beneath a microscope. That should have looked more like yellow-tinted glass beads. Instead, it was deeply metallic and shaped quite like actual gold. Leaning back, I looked at him with an obvious question mark on my face.

He nodded.

"That's not sand."

He snapped his fingers. "No, it is not. Yet it is."

"No, Ich, I know sand. That is not sand. That is gold dust."

Shrugging, he said with a grin, "Or is it, Elle?"

I was about to school him on the facts, when he unstoppered the vial of gold he still gripped in his hand. He turned it over in his palm and slid out just a few grains, leaving most of it still in the vial. Carefully, he replaced the stopper and set it down on his desk. Then turning to me, he held up his hand and with a mile-long grin, whispered, "Elle, bring me my tea."

I snorted. *You can get your own damned tea.* I thought the words. I did not say them. They rested heavily on the tip of my tongue. Yet I felt confused of a sudden, my brain in a fog. And when I looked down, in my hand, I held the mug of tea he'd made for himself back in the kitchen.

I blinked then blinked again, hand shaking a little and causing the tepid contents to slosh over onto it.

"What? When... did you place this mug in my hand?"

I was standing right beside him. I'd not walked away. In fact, I hadn't moved an inch, but he was smiling like a cocky peacock back at me.

"I didn't put that in your hand. You walked into the kitchen and grabbed it for me."

"Like hells I did. I never moved."

"Oh, I assure you, Elle, that you did." Then he twisted on his heel and quickly jogged toward a surveillance monitor sitting on a thick stack of old newspapers. His fingers ran like a blur over a keyboard, then he stepped back and pointed.

I saw myself walking away and heading into the kitchen. I returned not a second later, holding his mug in my hand. I saw myself on the screen and knew it was true, but I had no memories of it. It was as if that period was completely erased from my mind.

"Bloody hells!" I snapped. "This is the proof then. This is what was done to Whiskers, isn't it?"

Ichabod nodded and ran his fingers through the grains, which were golden no more but beige, as the other vials had been. "I believe so. The only problem is, this sand was found not in Neverland, as I said, but in Hel. Unfortunately, M.I.C.E. hasn't been able to find any sands at Whiskers's nest or even in Neverland at all. But if we can find some and I can tie it to this same type of sand, then we could potentially get Whiskers off. But only Bo knows of this right now. Please tell no one of my findings. If the press catches wind of this, we could lose the only element of surprise we've got left. This could very well be the first misstep the gang has made and the very key to cracking this most perplexing of riddles."

I shook my head. "Of course, though I must tell Maddox."

"Understandable. But speak in whispers. There is something about this case, Elle, that makes me very, very uneasy."

"On that, we agree." I gazed at the beige particles in his hand. Setting the mug down on the desk, I pointed with my chin toward the grains. "Put those on a slide, Ichabod, if you'd be so kind."

"You wish to see it for yourself. That is fine. I, too, didn't quite believe it the first time it happened to me. I did not have the benefit of another soul around when I inadvertently activated the grains the first time. It took several hours before I lost the tail. It's always why I've set up cameras in my home."

"Do I want to know what you're talking about?"

He shuddered. "Probably not, no. It was truly the stuff of nightmares. But as they say, seeing is believing." Quickly, he set up a new slide for me then replaced the previous one with the new one and stepped back.

A quick glance told me all I needed to know. What I was looking at wasn't gold at all but unpolished gems. I licked my front teeth and turned slowly to look back at him. "The gold is the spell. And once used up, it returns to its true form. Sand."

"Indeed, it is sand. But from where and why? I still don't know."

Chicken skin pebbled my body, and a sense of slinking unease began to wind its way through my gut. Now that the excitement of discovery was wearing off, I was coming to a very uncomfortable realization.

"Ichabod..." I said his name slowly, but as he'd done to me so many other times before, he nodded, already anticipating my words.

"Yes. This would have been cast by a very high-level witch indeed. The enchantment is quite sophisticated and nearly untraceable. The perfect crime. Except that someone serendipitously dropped unused sand, and now we can hopefully start to unravel this very peculiar mystery."

"*Hm*," I mumbled, staring back at the slide with a heavy frown. "Peculiar, indeed. All righty then. Keep me apprised, if you could. I'll go now."

He gave me a curious look. "To where? I heard Maddox is still laid up. Would you care for company?"

"It's your day off."

He shrugged. "I'd rather be working. You know that. Besides..." He reached over and trailed a hot finger down the back of my hand and stepped in closer toward me.

He didn't finish the thought, but I could feel the rising thrum of awareness prickle through me at the unspoken invitation. I shivered, reaching out and placing my open palm on his naked chest, savoring the warmth of his body heat.

It would be all too easy to give in. With Ichabod, sex was never a complicated matter. I closed my eyes, voice scratchy as I whispered, "You have no idea how much I'm tempted. But…"

I stepped back and dropped my hand. My life was far too complicated for any of what was happening. Even no-strings-attached sex. Especially that.

There was a hint of disappointment in his intelligent eyes, but he smirked and dipped his head. "Of course, Detective. And you know, on second thought, I still have much work to do here. Let me know if you should find anything at all pertinent to the sands."

Blowing out a heavy, frustrated breath, I nodded. "Of course." Gods, why did relationships have to be such stupidly complicated matters?

I turned on my heel, swiped my key card, and returned to Neverland. I had one last stop to make before I could return to Grimm.

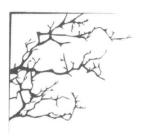

Chapter 10

Detective Elle

I STARED AT THE MOUNTAINOUS stronghold in the distance. It was nothing but jagged shelves of loose gray shale with thickly striated rust-colored bands punching through the sky like serrated and broken teeth. Large canyons wound around it like a serpent's tail. There were massive bat-winged creatures the darkest shade of ebony flying in formation around the mountain's highest peak. The sun was setting, and the sky was a blaze of deep orange, rich indigo, and pale blue. Sniffing the air, I scented the iron-rich tang of blood and the rotten sweetness of viscera. There had been death there, but being that it was faery land, Grimm PD wouldn't have been notified. The fae had their own brand of justice, and it was a sight bloodier than ours. That was certain.

Where most of Neverland was little more than forested jungle with canopies and ropey drawbridges that formed massive citadels in the skies, this section was an emerald-green sea of rolling grass and flowers in every shade and bloom imaginable, with massive trees as ancient as Neverland itself standing sentinel. Insects with their chitinous armor gleaming like polished rubies flew by in a blurred rush, all of them unerringly heading in the direction of the massive fae stronghold.

I shivered and gently grazed my palm against the comforting hilt of my weapon strapped to my outer thigh. No matter how big, strong, or terrifying, all fae had one rather significant weakness.

I'd already loaded my Glock with iron bullets. Clenching down on my back teeth, I studied the landscape, looking for any signs of intelligent life, guards or even a regular passerby. Anyone would do at that point, so long as they were of fae heritage and could grant me temporary asylum to pass through.

Coming unescorted into fae lands during the day was less than fun, but at night, it could potentially be a lethal endeavor. Faeries, no matter how cute and innocent they looked, were predators first and foremost.

It might be Neverland, but make no mistake that this section, at least, was ruled by Titiana, and she'd done me no favors by asking me to drop by without offer of a guard.

I felt the strength of fae magick in every breath I took. The saturation of potent earth energy seeped up like a wet blanket from the ground itself, making me feel as though I were breathing through a thick fog bank.

My skin tingled as I continued to gaze at the endless expanse of land and sky. The night was far too quiet, too still. Something was wrong. I could taste it on my tongue, feel the urgency of it ride through my bones.

Again, I sniffed the air, and this time, I caught wind of another scent—moss and dank, rich earth and even more subtly, petrichor and iron, a smell that only resulted from a mixture of water and earth and blood.

Kneeling, I reached out to caress the blades of grass beside me—as dry as a bone. I tapped my finger upon the soil, which was as dry as the sands Ichabod had stored at his home. There'd been no rain here for days, maybe even weeks. The grass was a fae hybrid, making it hardier than normal fescue should be. By rights, I should be looking at brown and withered fields. But even so, fae lawns could die. They weren't indestructible. I kept running my hands across the blades until I paused, feeling something slightly damp brush against my palm. I wasn't sure what it was, so I very lightly ran my hand back the opposite way, and this time, I definitely felt something warm and tacky.

The sun was barely lighting up the night, but even so, when I turned my palm over, I saw the distinctive rusted hue of blood, just a tiny smear of it but indisputable. It was thick and viscous, clinging to my flesh like freshly tapped syrup.

I brought my hand to my nose. It was sweet and extremely iron rich. I was pretty certain I knew what it was, but as Maddox had once taught me, apart from M.I.C.E. with their fancy tests and equipment, there was only one other surefire way to know for certain. I stuck out the tip of my tongue and took a quick lick.

The effect of it was immediate on me. My marking flared like a flame, burning as bright as a fiery torch. The winds began to rustle, and my hair undulated around my face like the sensuous curling of a Medusa's hair. The faery gown I wore turned smoky, fitting me more like dense shadow that glittered with pinpricks of great fae magick.

I looked as surreal as the creature I was hunting.

It had been blood I'd tasted, but it had also been more. Standing slowly, I once more looked at the tree line but with different eyes, scanning for that telltale sign of alienness.

What I was looking for had once been nearly hunted to extinction by fae hunters, hunters who'd sell the blood of that creature on the black market for a very pricy sum. Those hunters had eventually been terminated by Queen Morgana the Olde, Titiana's predecessor. She had her reasons, I was sure, though I rather thought they had less to do with altruism and far more to do with the fact that they'd infringed on her own stock too.

Then I saw it. It was so easily overlooked, if one didn't know what one was looking at.

It was a tree, just like all the others, but its branches were unique. They were long and spiraling and interwoven, creating a nest of ropes that wasn't actually rope at all, but hair. Its bark was thickly corrugated and its leaves bright and green, though its shape was what made it unique. The leaves formed a kind of halo around not the top of the tree but along its middle, creating a type of robed effect the way it fell gracefully down its back.

The tree itself wasn't that large or even that tall. It was an average tree, maybe fifteen or so feet. Rather slender, in truth.

I wet my lips then stood as still as a rodent watching incoming prey, waiting for that final telltale hint that I was right about just what type of tree it actually was.

I didn't have to wait long. I didn't know if it had sensed me and had stopped moving and my stillness had tricked it into believing it was alone again, but suddenly, the creature was groaning, the sound a distinctive grinding of wood upon wood. There was a great rending sound, then it lifted its roots, which were actually its feet, out of the ground.

The tree inhaled and shivered then gave a long and whistling exhalation. Its rightmost branch reached out for the tree beside it, and it seemed to lean its weight upon it.

The creature had a faery name, one that was impossible for any humanoid mouth not of faery to replicate. Most Grimmers had taken to calling it by its more mundane name, tree spirit.

But that wasn't an entirely accurate representation for it, either. The tree was actually inhabited by the body of a woodland guardian. It was two in one, a symbiotic alliance wherein one could not exist without the other.

Shaping my lips, I sucked in a long breath then whistled as only a siren could.

The shriek pierced the heavens, and the tree spirit suddenly twirled. Its face contorted, with long fangs dripping with venomous resin. It lifted its arms, bark-like claws extended.

And from the front, I could see that its side had been pierced through. Sappy blood trailed in thick rivulets down its side. The creature, then, was the reason for the blood trail.

It was not a mortal wound, but the guardian wouldn't heal quickly from it, either. That Titiana had even placed a guardian here was significant. It meant that whatever she'd hidden inside the stronghold was important enough to be guarded by something very nearly indestructible by anything other than a fae hunter. But first, I had to temper the beast.

"Spirit of the woods, I was sent by the one you would call queen. My name is Arielle, siren of the deep and King Triton's daughter. I seek safe passage through your lands. Might I come in?"

The guardian's eyes were little more than opened slits in its bark face. Like melted wax, its face was a thing of nightmares to a child or the less well informed of the hundred realms.

While they were deadly fighters, the truth was guardians always preferred an amicable resolution. They were watchers more than anything, responsible for relaying to the queen's armies when and if intervention would be needed. So how had this guardian failed in its duties so badly?

There was a quick rush of winds, and upon them, I heard words.

How is it that you come now? Are you them? Are you one of them? Its long, tentacle-like branch wrapped around its wound.

I pressed my lips tight. "Who is 'them'? What has been done here?"

I do not trust that I can speak with you. Again I ask, who are you that you should come now? The queen has told me of no visitor.

Somehow, I wasn't surprised that Titiana had failed to mention my future presence here. I shook my head. "I am as I said, but I am also a detective of Grimm. Titiana spoke with me a few days past, alerting me to some strange activity in this area and that she would like me to check things out for her. That is why I've come."

The winds rustled through the trees, the sound more aggressive, as though the guardian were angry.

Would that you'd come then, Detective, for I fear that my queen will be given the gravest of news this night.

I blinked, going cold all over, gaze returning to the summit and the thick formation of faery bats growing thicker and thicker in number so that they resembled a moving black pillar. Their angry chirps made me feel anxious and sick to my stomach.

"What has happened here, guardian?"

It shook its head. *They are dead. They are all dead.*

"Who?"

The protectors of the mountain. They came in a wave of black feathers, eyes as red as hell flame, slashing and tearing at us all. I was outside when the massacre took place. It is the only reason why I still stand. Once I was alerted, I tried to enter, but it was too late. I was too late, then I was set upon by a murder of them. They struck at me with their venomous claws, immobilizing me instantly. The enchantment has only just worn off, and now I must tell my queen this most terrible news.

"Let me pass, guardian," I tried again. "Give me leave to enter. I must study the scene. I must look for clu—"

It is forbidden!

The guardian's thoughts rolled through the winds like a violent crack of thunder, making me flinch.

The taste of its power on my tongue let me know I was no match for the creature. As powerful as I was, wood could not be enchanted by the sound of my voice. And the strength in its body was ten times that of mine.

"Titiana bade me—"

She said no such to me. You may not pass.

Sighing, I closed my eyes. The fae were incredibly deceitful, but their deceit came more in trickery. Which meant the Slashers had come here.

And if I had come two days earlier, I might have actually learned why. Frustrated with myself, the faery, and even Titiana for being such a heinous bitch, I shook my head. "How long ago did this attack take place?" I asked, opening my eyes and staring the creature.

It was breathing heavily and swaying on its feet. It had taken a far stronger blow than I'd at first suspected. It was a wonder that it was even standing upright.

Barely two hours.

I frowned, instantly realizing that would have been around the same time as Whiskers's attack on the Lost Boys. He'd mentioned to me about coming out of his mountain dwelling and spying the blood and following it.

"Does a dragon make its lair here or close by?"

Aye. An ancient golden one with green bands. It glides the skies.

My heart squeezed, and I wet my lips. That had to be Whiskers. There weren't many dragons in Neverland and none, so far as I knew, as far west as he.

"What did the Slashers want? What did they say? Did you see or hear anything suspicious?"

I saw nothing and heard little, only the screams of my dying brethren. Only that. It shuddered.

I nodded, frustration pinching my eyebrows. "Why were they here? Why would they dare attack a faery stronghold such as this?"

It shook its head. *I must away now. The queen must know of these bleak tidings.*

"Of course, guardian," I said and gestured with my arm that it should press onward toward its destination.

It dipped its head as though it meant to turn, but I held up my hand. "Just one last question, guardian, and then you will never see me again."

It stood perfectly still, looking just like the tree it mostly was, and waited.

"This stronghold, it guards some of the holiest and most powerful of all fae relics, does it not?"

The guardian didn't answer but did dip its head.

I nodded. "How long were the birds within?"

It was quick. Minutes, at most.

"More than enough time to hie off with a relic, is it not?"

Its face remained impassive, but behind its mask of bark, its eyes glowed like flame.

"Did they take something, guardian?"

I did see one fly away with something. But I can't be sure what it was. I was not the archivist, merely a watcher. But it winked like crystal in the sunlight as it flew.

Then it tipped its head one final time before slowly turning. Its ropey fingers began to wind and undulate, and as it did, a fragment of its bark broke off, dropping to the grass below.

Its fingers formed a mesmerizing sequence in the air, and suddenly, a tunnel was opened, one of flashing starlight and glimmering stardust. It slowly moved with the gentle cadence of its kind and stepped inside. Then it and the tunnel were gone.

Wrapping my arms around my body, I looked back at the haunting stronghold. This case would not be mine or anyone else's in Grimm P.D.. But my gut told me that the timing of the heist was no coincidence, none at all.

I would need to speak with Titiana again, but I couldn't speak to her yet. She would need time. A day or two should be enough. Then I would ask her what had been taken. She should know by then.

I turned, ready to head back to Grimm, when I suddenly thought of that fragment the guardian had dropped. Trees only shed when injured. And I wasn't even sure why I should suddenly think of going and grabbing that sliver of wood. It was just bark, nothing special. Yet...

I glanced around me. The guardian had claimed to be the last fae left standing on this land. Which meant if I crossed the demarcation line, there was a good chance I'd not get eaten for it.

And I really didn't understand why I was so hung up on retrieving that bit of bark. But before I overthought things, I was moving, sneaking past the line, heart racing a mile a minute, as I was increasingly aware of what I'd just done.

I was on fae soil. At night. With no guard.

"Feck's sake," I muttered and jogged faster and found the indent where the guardian had been standing just seconds earlier. Miraculously, the sliver of bark rested right on top. There was nothing about it that really stood out.

And I thought myself every type of fool, but even so. Biting my lower lip, I quickly encased the small sliver of wood into a droplet of water. I had nothing else on hand with which to keep it safe. But the water wouldn't erase anything in the bark. It was acting more like amber, encasing and trapping whatever might be in it.

I whipped my key card out of my back pocket and swiped it through the air, and my own transdimensional tunnel opened up for me. The sun was barely a tint of pink upon the horizon, and mushrooms with iridescent blue and green glowing caps began to bloom like a carpet all around me.

Death was in this place, and soon, so would the queen of the winged faeries be. It was time to leave. I had to get back to Grimm, but first, I would make one last stop at Ichabod's.

He opened the door on the second knock, still undressed, his eyes bright and alive, as they tended to be when he was close to cracking an uncrackable riddle. The night was thick, the darkness around us cloying.

"Here." I handed him the droplet of water, and when he took it, the way the candlelight hit the drop, I could almost swear I saw glimmers of blue and gold flash back at me. I frowned, wondering if maybe my stupid hunch might actually have been right. For once. "From the latest crime scene. I don't know if this is anything, but I figured you were the man to hand it over to."

He took the drop, his fingers grazing mine for a split second. Bringing the drop up to his face, he squinted at it. "I'll be damned, Elle," he murmured, "but this does seem just the slightest bit... odd, doesn't it? What is it? Is it... wood?"

I shrugged and shoved my hands into my pockets. "It was found in faery."

His eyebrows lifted, and he gave me a knowing look.

I shrugged unrepentantly. "Maybe it's nothing, but it feels like a wood spirit, and well, I just... I dunno. I grabbed it."

He tipped his head in a nod. "Okay, Detective. Then I'll look into it."

I knew I'd been dismissed. His brilliant mind was already a million miles away. So I didn't even bother to say goodbye. I simply turned, swiped, and left, hoping against hope that somehow, some way, I'd just discovered our miracle.

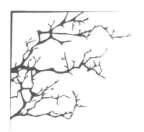

Chapter 11

Detective Elle

I RETURNED TO THE HOSPITAL, wanting to speak with Maddox one last time before I finally got back to Grimm. It was a good thing Bo hadn't bet me that I'd be back in two hours, because as usual, I'd have lost that one.

Shoving my hands into my pockets, I thought about all I'd learned since I'd left him that afternoon. One, the sands at the crime scenes actually appeared to be significant. And two, just as one of the grisliest killing sprees in all the hundred realms for decades was being perpetuated, another crime—and perhaps of far more consequence than I could currently imagine—was simultaneously taking place. A heist—of what, that bit was still murky, but the crime itself was definitely fitting of the Slashers' typical modus operandi.

I pushed open the door, expecting to find Hatter lain up in bed. But he was up and pacing the length of the room. He twirled the moment the creak of the door sounded and looked at me with a mixture of shock, relief, and even a smidge of trepidation.

"Bloody hells, Elle," he growled and marched to me then grabbed me by the elbows and gave me a firm shake before yanking me to his chest. His twin hearts beat in rapid tandem against my breast.

I frowned, not sure what he was upset about. "Maddox?"

"I saw what became of those within the mountain." He blinked, looking haunted and lost in his visions still. His blue eye burned like a flame. "The fae stronghold," he said thickly, voice scratchy and low, "the one you told me the queen wished you to visit. You went, didn't you?"

I should never be surprised by the accuracy of his visions, yet somehow, I always was. Clearing my throat, I gently extricated myself from his grip.

As though realizing what he'd done, he brushed his hands down his hospital-gown-clothed chest and shook his head. "My apologies, Elle. I worried that I would need to call Bo when I saw it. I saw you there, and a guardian. I thought maybe..."

His eyebrows dipped, and again that feeling that he was stuck in a dark vision seemed to grip him.

I placed a gentle hand on his bicep and squeezed. "I'm fine, Maddox. Just fine. But if you had a vision of what happened, please tell me that you knew more than the guardian could tell me."

Scrubbing at his square jaw, he asked, "Such as?"

"The guardian believes the Slashers were successful. It claims to have seen the glint of crystal sparkling in the sun as a crow flew off. Does that mean anything to you?"

He walked back to his bed and took a seat on it, looking weary and tired. His eyes were pinched and his skin slightly gray. He'd not been sleeping well. Hospitals were never easy to relax in, but lack of a soul could also slowly leech the life from you.

Taking a seat beside him, I leaned into his side, as though a lover whispering of sweet nothings.

"When will they discharge you?" I asked softly.

As he glanced at me from the corner of his eye, I could sense his confusion. I wasn't normally so demonstrative, and especially never in public. But I doubted anyone of any significance was looking at us and trying to determine whether they should report us to IA. It wasn't as though we'd crossed any lines.

"Tomorrow morning," he said.

I nodded. "Good. Then come to me first. At my place."

He turned to me full on, his body completely open to mine. I could read the tension in his shoulders and the question in his eyes. He opened his mouth to no doubt ask me why I was inviting him to my home, but I placed a finger upon his lips and shook my head.

"As you wish, Elle." He said the words softly, and I could have sworn there was a note of heady seduction there too. Did he think I'd invited him over to sex him?

And why was my pulse beating so furiously at the thought?

I felt the thrill of his nearness, the heat of his body moving against mine, breaking me out in a wash of longing and goose bumps. We couldn't do it. Yet...

Shivering from the heat of him, I pulled away, placing some much-needed space between us. I really did have to get back to headquarters, and the sooner, the better.

"How did your meeting with the dragon go?"

I shook my head. "As well as could be expected. He claims ignorance of his crime, but there is undeniable proof of it, which definitely complicates things."

Hatter frowned. "Ignorance how? Does he claim an enchantment of some sort?"

I nodded. "Yes. Made mention of golden sands and then nothing more until he awoke hours later, the deed already done."

"Golden sands. Why golden? The sands are usually dun colored that we find at the scene."

I held up my finger, feeling much as Ichabod had as he'd explained the significance to me. "I went to Ich's place after speaking with Whiskers. As you know, he's the one gathering the sands from each scene to analyze."

"Aye."

"And you're right—the sands are typically dun colored. But that's only because the enchantment woven through them has been used up. What makes Whiskers's assertions significant is that we also spotted golden sands at Midas's gala, if you'll recall."

Narrowing his eyes, he looked over my shoulder before slowly nodding. "Aye, I had noticed them. Miniscule granules of it, but yes, it was definitely there. Not that it meant much to me at the time because Midas can turn anything to gold."

I pursed my lips. That part was still bothering me.

Leaning back on my arms, I thought about the strangeness of Midas's request for me specifically to attend the gala. I'd thought our shared history had played a role in it, but what if it was more?

It had been many years since I'd seen Midas last. Was it coincidence that I'd been pulled to play babysitter for a king who was notorious for having the best bodyguards money could buy already on payroll?

"I'd thought the last-minute request an odd thing, but then Midas is an eccentric," I mumbled before looking back at Hatter.

He thinned his lips. "Aye. And the hue of the enchanted sand—is that coincidence, Elle?"

I lifted my eyebrows as impotent rage started brewing through my belly. My claims that the Charmings' were not only responsible for the deaths at their estate but the masterminds of several more, spanning many realms had resulted in me being subjected to hells by my superiors, made me extremely unpopular for months, and put a target on my back with IA to boot. Not an experience I was keen on reliving so soon.

I chuckled darkly. "Are we seriously doing this? Once again considering a royal as the possible mastermind of another high-profile crime? I doubt the commissioner would take kindly to me hurling these sorts of accusations twice in so short a span."

He shrugged. "Stranger things have happened."

"True. Still, I'm not entirely comfortable throwing around such damning indictments. Not without solid evidence to back me up."

Hatter shrugged again but not unsympathetically. He knew what I'd suffered after our first case. Added to the pressure was the fact that I'd had to harbor all those hateful sentiments alone. Not only had I been unpopular, I'd been practically reviled, and had I not been the princess of the deep—disgraced or not was immaterial—I knew I'd have been sacked long ago. Royals didn't take too kindly to their misdeeds being bandied about as idle tittle-tattle for the rabble. It made them cranky. And when royals got cranky, they also got vindictive.

And friendly or not, I had no doubt Midas could be just as petty as the rest of them when pushed to it.

I blew out a heavy breath. "Are we truly seeing a link here, or are we merely trying to shove a square peg through a round hole out of frustration?"

Exhaling heavily, he leaned back, too, his fingers spread wide, his pinky barely grazing the outer edge of my palm. His touch felt potent, like fire and magick, and like a heavy weight bearing down on me, making me aware of the smells and sights and noises all around me: the wild beating of my heart; the drunken waltz of butterflies winging by; and each inhalation and exhalation of his large chest.

I wasn't sure it was a good thing. In fact, I knew it was a very, very bad thing. The last thing I wanted or even needed was a romantic entanglement of any sort, and for some damned reason, I couldn't seem to remember that when he and I were alone. For the past two nights, all I seemed to be able to do was replay in my mind what Maddox and I had done and said at the gala. Maybe if we'd not been so consumed with flirting, we'd have caught on sooner or seen the signs of what was about to take place more quickly. I didn't know. But I had to stop forgetting that. Maddox and I weren't a couple. We weren't anything but partners.

I *must* have been enchanted to remain calm earlier, because that spell was definitely starting to wear off. Trying not to appear too obvious about it, I stood and rolled my shoulders.

Hatter looked up at me, blinking, his intelligent eyes clearly saying I'd not fooled him in the slightest. He sat up and took another deep breath. "I don't know, Detective. Perhaps we are forcing this. But after so many months of nothing but half-baked theories, I'm at my wit's end and ready to consider any eventuality, no matter how outlandish."

I wanted to ask him if he was saying more than the obvious, if maybe he was speaking of us. Was he as bothered by what was happening between us as I was? I studied him.

He was calm, his face composed. Everything about him dripped rational concentration. The madness seemed mine alone to bear.

I dropped my head into my hands and rubbed at my brow. What had Bo learned of her interrogation of other Hook? I felt myself divided by so many different problems all at once. There were times I wasn't sure whether I was coming or going.

"You look worn out, Elle." He said it softly, almost tenderly.

I cracked open an eye. His lips were set, one corner slightly tipped, as he looked at me as though he wasn't sure what to make of me. The worst of it was, half the time, I wasn't sure what to make of myself, either.

I shrugged. "I *am* tired, Hatter. I do not sleep well anymore."

He narrowed his eyes. "You've shared visions with me often. Maybe you should stop."

I frowned. "What? Why would that—"

Clearing his throat, he sat up. "Alice used to suffer strange night terrors, too, soon after we'd begun cohabitating. I don't know that this and that are linked, but..." He let the rest of the thought dangle.

There were a thousand questions I wanted to ask him but none that I could form into any type of coherence and especially not on the sly in that hospital room. Rubbing my hand down the column of my throat, I gave him a nod. *Tomorrow. We'll speak tomorrow.*

"I have to go talk with Bo. Hopefully, she's made some headway with the other Hook."

He licked his front teeth and gave a tight, grim nod. "Indeed. I'll see you in the morning, Elle."

With a flick of my fingers, I turned and swiped open a portal. None of that had been weird at all.

And yes, that was very much sarcasm.

BACK IN GRIMM, I WALKED through the doors and headed slowly back toward Bo's office.

Wanting some coffee, I made a quick detour. The stuff in the office sucked troll arse, but it was drinkable, even if it was cold and more often than not swimming with coffee grinds.

I was only aware of the chatter because of the sudden lack of it. Frowning, I glanced over my shoulder. Everyone was doing busywork, doing and acting the way they should, except I was very aware that I was being watched like a hawk. But the glances were furtive, mostly drive-bys.

Janey, noting my look, dipped her chin. "Detective," she said slowly.

I narrowed my eyes, looking at the others. But none seemed quite as brave as the Valkyrie to meet my gaze.

"Hey, what the hells is going on?" I asked, pretty sure that whatever it was was definitely about me.

Janey, who was still the only one willing to talk with me, got up from her desk and came to stand next to me. Her normally clear eyes were a deep blue today, and her features looked more razor sharp and defined.

I peeked at her back. She wasn't wearing her wings, but she was clearly agitated about something.

Leaning in close to me, she whispered in my ear, "Might want to get to Bo's ASAP."

Frowning, I took a sip of my crappy poop water and frowned. "Is this about the case? Slashers do something else while I was gone?"

She clapped her hand on my shoulder. "Just go, Elle."

Realizing how odd it was for her to call me by my first name, I felt an instant burn of goose bumps ride my flesh. "What is it, Janey?"

She looked confused for half a second, and I knew I'd garbled her name to hells, but she shook her head and rolled her wrists, looking as though she wanted to be anywhere else but here. "It's... it's Hook, Elle."

I shrugged, still not understanding why anyone should think I'd care about a mirage. "Yeah? And? The enchantment been stripped yet? What did we catch?"

She blew out a heavy breath. "I really, really shouldn't be the one telling you this, Detective."

My stomach bottomed out, and ice flowed heavily through my veins. Every once in a while in life, you suddenly knew when you're about to hear news that's going to upend everything you ever thought you knew. This was one of those times. My heart raced. My pulse blasted through my eardrums.

"What's going on, Valkyrie?" My voice was a too-tight growl. My flesh felt charged, electrified, the charge begging me for release.

She blinked, glanced to the side, and stared at a monitor. A black wave swept over me. Because when a Valkyrie of her pedigree looked scared, I knew it was bad.

"What the fec—"

"It's him, Elle. It's really him. It's your Hook. He's back."

I wasn't sure when I dropped into a chair, but I was suddenly sitting in one and breathing in and out like a bellows. "Hook? Hook... but—but... no. It... it can't be."

"It is, Detective." Bo's voice cut like a blade through my mutterings, and I looked up at her, feeling as if I were walking through a haze, confused about what was real and what wasn't because they were telling me Hook was alive, but I knew he couldn't be.

I knew he wasn't.

"He's alive, Elle. And you need to start talking."

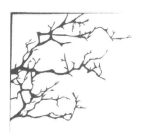

Chapter 12

Detective Elle

BO GAVE ME SEVERAL minutes to compose myself. But even so, when I followed her down the mazelike hall toward her office, I didn't feel as if I was actually walking. Yet somehow, I was moving. Or floating. I didn't know what. My fingers were numb, and my head was starting to ache.

Sighing, Bo stopped and turned to look back at me. But my gaze was fixed on the frosted panel of her office door. Was he back there?

I heard a sound, like that of a wounded animal, and knew somewhere deep inside of me that I'd made it. But even that, I couldn't remember doing.

She took one of my hands into one of hers and gestured over her shoulder with her thumb. "Behind those doors is a man that I swore was dead. A man you vowed to me was dead. So I'm going to touch you with my staff, and you're going to answer my one question. Do you understand me?"

I stared into her warm brown eyes, feeling so damned confused and waiting for the punch line, waiting for someone to scream and laugh that they were just pulling the wool over my eyes. I was almost hoping they would. But apart from a constant buzzing in my ears, it was so bloody quiet.

"Elle, do you understand me?"

"Ye-yes, I... I understand... you."

Worry pinched the corners of her eyes. Then she released my hand, reached inside of her shirt and slipped out the silver staff necklace she was never without.

Bo wasn't a witch. But what she was was a magick all its own. She was like a shepherd and we her flock, obeying her in all things and not because we were commanded to, but because we wanted to. She had a higher-than-average level of charisma. I didn't know where she'd gained it from or whether she was something other than human. So much of her life was veiled in shadows. All I knew was she was trustworthy in a way so few others were.

"Are you ready?" she asked me softly, and I nodded.

Slipping the charm into my palm, she spoke. "Princess Arielle of the Deep, did you see Hook die?"

Immediately, the powers of her staff flared, and the heat of it wrapped around me, my mouth moved of its own accord, and the truth, for that was all I could mutter, poured out of me.

"He died, Captain. In my arms. Turned to sea foam by my own powers. He died."

Taking the pendant out of my hand, she briefly closed her eyes and sighed heavily. "Then I do not understand how this can be, but I've been assured by Matilda that it is so. Behind those doors is the man whose loss very nearly destroyed you."

She held up a finger. "You don't have to go in there, Elle. Understand me. But once Matilda broke through the enchantment over him, the only thing he's asking for is you."

I shuddered. So cold. All over. "But... but this can't be. He died, Captain. He died in my arms. I witnessed his last breath. I felt the soul leave him. He was human."

She shook her head. "I don't know what to tell you, Elle, that can make any of this better or even make much sense, because it makes none to me. Only that we were all wrong."

"How?" My voice cracked, and I glowered down at my feet. "How in the hells did he wind up at Midas's gala? What in the hells is this, Bo? We were yanked off my case because Midas requested me personally to guard him. And not only is there an attack, but suddenly Ho—" I couldn't even say his name. I felt as if I couldn't even breathe anymore, as if my dress, which should have given me air, was the very thing stripping it from me. The floor suddenly shot up beneath me, rising swiftly to meet the roof, and I got abruptly dizzy. I grabbed hold of the wall, digging my fingers in so hard my knuckles blanched.

She pounded on my back. "Breathe, Detective. You must breathe. If you can't do this, then I will tell him so."

I wanted to flee. I wanted to tuck tail and run away like a coward. My feet burned so badly to do it. I needed to shed this skin, this body. Needed to find my waters and swim far and fast away from this. From all of this.

But I had a case. My life wasn't just about me, not anymore. There were people, actual blood-and-flesh people dying every day due to the avarice of a gang grown so violent that none were safe from their wrath.

At all costs, I had to stop the Slashers, or at the very least, do my part to bring them down.

I shook my head, rubbing at my brow as the dizziness finally began to slowly pass. "It's a shock."

"Do you need—"

I took a deep breath, then another, and finally one more before I felt centered enough to open my eyes again. Bo was no longer swimming in and out of focus, and my feet felt rooted once more to the ground beneath me.

"No. No. I didn't expect this outcome, in truth." Because yes, though Maddox's visions had shown that Hook had lived, I'd very nearly had myself convinced that it was only an enchantment of some sort and that the actual person beneath the mask would be just another crow shifter. Because death was final. It was absolute. Even in a world full of magick, there were very few instances in which it was not, and it usually involved spells of the darkest, most vile kind. Magick that had been wholly eradicated ages ago.

So how the hells was this possible?

"He wants to see me?" I asked her softly. "He remembers me?"

"Yes." She nodded. "It appears that way. But, Elle, I feel it prudent to warn you, I did not arrange this meeting so that you two could reconnect. Hook is still responsible for his part in the attack of Midas's gala and many others besides. In truth, he will likely wind up in chains next to Whiskers soon. I am sorry, but I had to call this in. Transport should be arriving soon."

I massaged my forehead. "What else has he done?"

She merely shook her head sadly, asking me with her eyes whether I really wanted to know. And though I did, I also didn't.

Sighing, Bo said, "I've brought you here in the hopes that you might be able to interrogate him further. Learn if there could be more. Why he was even at the gala? Who sent him? And how is any of this even possible? He spoke of his deeds, but when we asked him those questions, he'd merely freeze up and say, 'I want Arielle,' then he'd clam up completely."

"If, as you say, he's been under an enchantment, isn't it possible he might not remember any of that?"

"It is possible, yes. But we're hoping that your shared histories means something." She shrugged. "We're running incredibly low on any good, solid leads, Elle. I don't think I need to tell you that. After what's happened to the Lost Boys, the commissioner is antsier than ever to find the gang and lock them up in the pit. We know he was fighting alongside the Slashers. But why? That's the real question."

Biting my front teeth together, I nodded slowly.

She glanced at the door, a determined look upon her face. "Before we go in there, did you learn anything of value from Whiskers?"

"Has Ichabod told you of the golden grains found at Midas's gala?"

"He's mentioned it. Has he finally figured out what it was?"

"Yes, I believe so. The golden grains appear to be laced with powerful forgetting magick. Once the magick is consumed, they turn back to their familiar sandy color. Whiskers says that right before his memory was completely wiped from him, he recalled coming across piles of golden sands. Then nothing until he awoke hours later, the slaughter already complete."

Worry pinched and lined her forehead. "This is distressing news indeed. I'll send a witch over to Crane's to help him further analyze his finds. If there is a way to reduce the charges on the beast, I vow to you, Detective, that we will do it. Was there anything else?"

I almost said no. In all the fuss, I'd forgotten about my detour to the fae stronghold. But I twitched so hard that I shoved off the wall and rose up on my tiptoes. In a hurried rush, I whispered, "I was asked by the queen of the sprites to check in on her stronghold in Never the other day."

"Why?" Bo shook her head.

I shrugged. "She wasn't ever completely clear about it. She claimed it was because of the dragon skulking about, but I didn't really feel that was completely the truth, either. Her request was that I drop by and check in. I promised I would, but then I got roped into Midas's ball and had forgotten all about that until today, when I realized, in talking to Whiskers, that he lived close to the faery mound. Captain, I have reason to believe that the slaughter that occurred might have actually been a diversion meant to keep us too preoccupied to figure out the Slashers' real motives. And that was whatever was hidden in the stronghold."

Shoving her fists into her jacket pocket, she gave me a stiff shrug. "What are you saying, Detective?"

"The fae stronghold was attacked at the exact same time by a murder of shifter crows, as stated by an eyewitness."

"Who?" She frowned.

"A guardian."

"*Mm*, that's problematic considering the ancient ones aren't given to embellishments."

I nodded. "Aye. It was a slaughter. All dead, save for it. It was gravely wounded, which leads me to believe its tale."

"And that was?"

"That the shifters swooped in, killed them all, and took off. All of it done in minutes."

"But why? Did they steal something? To what end did they attack that faery mound?"

"The guardian wasn't certain, but it remarked on seeing a glint of crystal in the sunlight."

She pulled her upper lip between her teeth and chewed worriedly on it before saying, "We have no jurisdiction on fae lands. But if what you're saying is true, Elle, this is worrisome indeed. The fae have some of the most powerful relics in all of the hundred realms in their archives. Do you think that Titiana might be persuaded to share Intel with you?"

I tossed my hands up. "I don't know. And the fact that I arrived days after she'd requested my intervention could make her less than inclined to ever help me again."

I clenched my back teeth. I was completely not looking forward to that prospect.

"Three high-profile crimes in mere days. Slashers linked to all of them. What does this mean?" she asked. "What the hells am I to put in my report to Draven?"

I shook my head, not envying her job at all. I'd rather gouge my eye out with a rusted spoon than have to deal with that bastard.

"There was one other thing, Captain," I said slowly.

"What is it?" she sighed, sounding exhausted by what she'd learned already.

I frowned and shrugged. "It might not be anything. But the guardian dropped a sliver of its bark on faery soil. I picked it up and took it to Ichabod. He's analyzing it now."

She pursed her lips. "Did you have a guard?"

I grimaced.

Air released in a long steady stream from between her lips, the noise pure aggravation. "Gods, Elle. Why? By the books... did I not say that? And it was just bark. Why risk it?"

Sighing deeply, I shook my head. "I don't know. It was just... a gut feeling. But I wasn't caught, and maybe it'll be nothing, but I figured I'd give you the heads-up. Anyhow, I gathered what I could and took it to Ich."

"Okay." She shrugged. "I guess that's all you could do. I'll follow up with Ichabod later and see if maybe your hunch was correct."

She looked frustrated for a second longer, but then she straightened her shoulders and gave me a firm nod, and as though she'd been spelled, all the emotion she'd so freely shown me just moments earlier vanished, replaced by the hardened and steely resolve of a captain who'd seen and heard it all and still managed to remain cool under pressure.

"You ready now?"

She'd managed to take my mind off of the fact that Hook, my dead lover, sat waiting for me behind her closed door. I was calm once more and centered. Bo swore she had no magick, but I knew she did.

I nodded. "I'm ready."

"All that you say and do will be monitored," she warned me.

Then there was no more talking after that. She quickly opened the door. A blast of cold air hit me square in the face, breaking me out in a wash of electrified goose skin.

I walked in, and the door creaked shut behind me. The echo of its closing sounded like a gun blast in my ears. And there he was, sitting on Bo's ratty old love seat.

I'd not paid nearly as much attention to him at the gala as I would have if I'd honestly believed that the man sitting and looking at me so was the same one who'd whispered his undying devotion to me with his very last breath just a few years earlier.

I planted my hand against my throat, my finger tapping rhythmically against the hollow of it.

He was dressed in orange prison overalls with a black-stenciled number stamped upon his left chest. There were silver chains tied to his ankles and wrists. His hook had been taken off of him. No doubt it had been impounded at his in-processing. His sleeve hung limply over his amputated arm.

His body was big, strong looking, his chest broad and gently moving in and out as he took deep, steady breaths. He was so alive, when the last time I'd seen him, he'd been anything but.

I shivered and flicked my eyes to his face and saw the same black-whiskered cheeks I'd seen back at the ball, but I looked at him through different eyes now. Absorbing every nuance, every scar I'd known intimately, like the tiny one above his lip that he'd earned from a nick of the Pan's blade many years ago, or the little burn mark at his right temple from musket powder that had backfired into his face when he was a child. Things I'd not noticed at the ball because my brain had fritzed from the shock of seeing him again.

His eyes were deep brown and his lashes so long and black that he'd always looked as though he'd shaded his eyes in kohl.

His skin looked smooth, tanned, strong. My mouth opened, but no words came out.

He clenched his jaw, his hand flexing tight by his side as he watched me as surely as I'd studied him. His heated and intense look made me feel breathless and sick to my stomach.

Then I heard my name upon his tongue. Not the one the rest of the world knew me as, but the one only he'd ever dared to call me.

"Ellie?"

Hearing that was like taking a fist to my gut. I bit down on my tongue hard, hard enough to feel my incisors just begin to cut through the nerve-rich meat, hard enough to taste the tang of metal.

Having a full body spasm, I had to count slowly to three in my head before I felt able to actually speak. "How?"

I knew that if he was really Hook, really my Hook, he wouldn't need to ask me to explain what I meant. I prayed that he would ask so that I could place him where he belonged—in the past, tucked away, forever.

He shook his head. His hair had grown a little shaggier than I remembered it being before. He'd never liked it long. Hook had always been fastidious with his appearance.

Sighing, he looked at me for the longest time with those same brown eyes of his that had once been my entire world. "I'm not entirely sure, Arielle."

My lashes fluttered. He rolled my name with his pirate's brogue just as I remembered, caressed the vowels just as he'd once done. I twitched, feeling as though I'd been sucker punched by him.

"That is not my name," I hissed, voice squeezing tight, my airway feeling cut off and pinched.

A muscle in his jaw flexed. "So I heard. You changed it. You've changed a lot of things since we were last together."

A strangled, high-pitched laugh slipped off my tongue. "What are you trying to do? This walk down memory lane, it's not—"I growled. "This isn't happening." I backed up a step.

He shot to his feet, and I felt my body vibrate and my heartbeat quicken, felt my limbs growing loose and soft. I didn't think it was lust or even desire, but it was definitely something. The marking on my forehead began to burn, and my eyes issued lambent radiance.

"Gods," he murmured thickly, "you were always the most beautiful creature I'd ever known."

Again that high-pitched laugh—this time, it sounded on the verge of crazy, and I snorted as I shook my head, trying desperately to regain my composure. We needed answers, answers he might have.

Squeezing my eyes shut, I wrapped my arms around myself and thought not of Hook or our long and very complicated past, but rather of Maddox. Mad though he appeared to be, he was the picture of calm in the storm. Nothing bothered him. Nothing distracted him. I needed to approach the interrogation as he would, as he had with Alice the previous year—impartial and critically thoughtful.

Forcing a few deep breaths in through my nose and out through my mouth, I decided that the only way to get through it was to simply get through it. Rage, pain, possibly even tears—those were for later. I had a job to do.

"How did you wind up at the gala the other night?" I opened my eyes again, piercing him with my no-nonsense look.

Hurt flashed through his eyes. Hook had been one of the deadliest pirates on all of the Never seas. His exploits had become legend. He had been chaos, fury, and extremely lethal when he'd had a mind to be. His passions so easily matched my own.

So it was bizarre for me to see this man, hear his voice, smell his scent, and while everything was screaming at me that he was somehow and miraculously him, there was a side of me that still couldn't accept this, accept that the same marauding pirate could be looking at me as he was looking at me—as though my words wounded him, killed off something in him.

My nostrils flared as I thinned my eyes.

"It's a long story, and parts of it are still missing from my brain."

I shook my head. "I'm not interested in the minutiae. Give me the bullet points. Midas's gala. How? Why?"

Squeezing his eyes shut, he sat. Really more of a graceful slump. His big frame curled over on itself as he stared with a faraway look down at the floor, his good hand gliding along the spot where his silver hook should have been.

"I was spelled," he murmured thickly.

"Matilda said as much," I said with a quick nod.

Brown eyes met mine, steady but also bottomless with a wellspring of pain I wasn't prepared to see or to handle.

I dug my nails into my palms.

"It was like seeing my life through fogged lenses. Being constantly outside of myself yet somehow aware enough to know that something terrible had happened to me. Just not fully knowing why."

"Gala?" I said again.

He snarled. "I'm getting to that, Arielle. Dammit! Do you think that this is fun for me? That any of this is fun for me? Do you think I wanted my soul and body hijacked? Bloody hells, you don't know me at all if you—"

I swallowed hard, trying to push down the lump of heat that crawled up my throat even now. "Hijacked?" I whispered, voice broken and stomach scuttling with feelers.

He squeezed his eyes shut and lifted his good hand to rub at his brow. How many times had I seen him just like that? Hook had suffered terrible head pains, usually after one of his thousands of skirmishes with the Pan. The Pan had never fought fairly. Childlike in his simple thinking, he'd usually resort to some form of treachery to escape Hook's justice.

Hook had been captain of the seas, an authority that held some serious sway in Neverland and especially amongst other pirates. He'd not been a man of Grimm Central law, per se, but he'd brandished his own form of Neverlandian law. He'd ruled fairly, but he'd also had a firm hand and an intractable sense of integrity that had required him to sometimes tap dance outside of Grimm's code of ethics to see that justice was served. Out there, pirate justice ruled the day.

Hook's one rule—no harm could ever come to children or women. Ever. Period. It had been a rule that all the Pans had routinely danced over because though most of them were into their fiftieth year—if not longer—of holding the Pan title, in many ways, they were as mentally acute as an immature fifteen-year-old.

Many nights, I'd had to help Hook get through his pains with my singing, quieting his discomfort with my voice.

My mouth flooded with saliva, and my tongue felt thick and inflated with the siren song swelling within me. But I couldn't open my mouth. I couldn't sing to him. Because it was too intimate and far too personal.

His tan skin looked pale, even a little gray around his mouth as he said, "Aye. I can't explain to you what it is to know all that goes on around you in the worlds but to have no autonomy over your actions. Deep inside of me, I knew what I was doing, but I could never stop it, even if the idea of it was abhorrent."

So the gold dust had not been used on him? It seemed likely, because when Ich had commanded I fetch the tea, I'd had no memory of doing it. Still didn't.

"Who did this?" I asked him.

He opened his mouth, and I waited, expecting to hear him blurt out the name of the person who'd done it to him. But instead, he simply stared at me.

"Can you not say? If so, Matilda hasn't broken through your enchantment at all."

Shaking his head, he scowled down at his feet. "Nay, it's not that. It's just that I feel like you're here to merely interrogate me, and this isn't why I wanted to speak with you, lassie."

I held up my hand, stopping him right there. "That's the thing, though, Hook. I *am* here to interrogate you. Whatever past you thought to exploit, don't." I narrowed my eyes as he flinched, but at least he understood matters. "Now. Why did you go after Maddox?"

"Who?" His eyebrows furrowed, and I heard a note of aggravation in his tone.

"At the ball. My partner. Painted in gold. You slashed at him with an envenomed claw. Why? To what end?"

Dropping his hands, he looked at me through eyes that shone wetly. Deep-purple bags attested to his exhaustion. Red veins crisscrossed the whites of them. I clamped down on my front teeth as he slowly shook his head.

"I wasn't supposed to be there for him."

I frowned. "So it was about Midas's wealth?"

"Arielle..." He sighed deeply. "I was there for you."

My heart fluttered in my chest as if it had suddenly sprouted wings.

"What? Why? Who would want to harm me now? Father's done all he could. He doesn't give a rat's arse what I do now, and I've made no other enemies."

Laying his palm on his knee, he rocked on his seat, his gaze still never wavering from mine. He shook his head. "I'm murky there. All I know is that you're important somehow." He said it slowly, voice scratchy but full of hidden inflection.

I scoffed, but my skin felt electrified, and I rocked back on my heels. "Me? There are far brighter than me here who are on the cusp of solving the mysterious grains of sands, which I assume are the means by which the Slashers take control. So what about me exactly is so terrifying that you'd actually go out of your way to rig such an elaborate trap?"

"Only you can stop her."

I blinked. *Her?* We'd all believed that the head of the shifter syndicate was male, because it had been at the start.

"Her? Hook, what in the hells are you saying? Who do you work for? Who hijacked your body and mind?"

His face was impassive and his voice without heat as he said, "Did you not notice the increase in violence lately? The cutthroat and more bloodthirsty nature of the syndicate now?"

I blinked, knowing there was only so much I was free to discuss with him. But yes, we'd all noticed the increase in violence. "Who runs the gang now?" I asked so quietly I was sure he wouldn't hear me.

His gaze was laser focused on mine as he said, "Anne Bonny, and make no bones of it, lass, jewels are the very least of what she's wanting."

I knew Anne. Anyone in law enforcement knew Anne. The mad rose, she'd been dubbed ages ago. She was a pirate with the uncanniest ability to always slip right through the cracks. Slippery like an eel, she was, flaunting all her crimes in law enforcement faces, getting captured yet even so, somehow always managing to evade the hangman's noose.

"Are you telling me"—I placed my hands on my hips and leaned slightly forward—"that the syndicate that is, for all intents and purposes, a group of shifter crows, is now being run by an interloper?"

He grinned, and the sight of it made my knees go weak, because he looked so much like my old Hook—swarthy, handsome, and just a little bad.

"Interloper?" he said. "Did you not know then, lass? She was Black Angus's only daughter and his first mate to boot. She's no interloper. It was a coup."

I blinked. I'd not known that. In fact, I doubted anyone in law enforcement did. "Black Angus never had a child."

"Aye. He did, lass. Kept her under wraps because of some deep, dark family secret. But she was. And she overthrew him."

"Okay, fine. I'll accept that." I held up my hand. "But none of that explains the magick. Anne's not a wit—"

He cocked his head, thinning his lips, and my blood curdled in my veins because I knew that look.

"No," I whispered.

"Aye. She is, Ellie. She is as dark a witch as they come. And what she's got planned next will rock the hundred realms to its knees. I'm telling you, lass, that I know what's coming down the pipeline, and if you'll let me, I can help you bring the Slashers down."

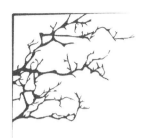

Chapter 13

Detective Elle

THERE WAS A LOUD RAP at the door, and I twirled just as Bo entered with a squad of well-armed cops behind her. My heart skipped a beat. "Already? But I wasn't—"

"Transport's five minutes out, Elle. Good work. Take him to the cell." She pointed at Hook as she spoke to the group of guards behind her.

A large and rather terrifying ogre we'd all affectionately coined Fluffy—on account of the fact that he was absolutely not—grunted as he approached Hook.

"Gently, Fluffy. Not that I should have to add that caveat," Bo snipped, "but..."

The tusked and green-skinned ogre grunted. He'd been on the job less than a month and still had quite a bit to learn about managing his strength.

I said nothing, but I felt sick and stupidly emotional. I watched as Fluffy pulled Hook upright.

So much of it just felt so wrong, but I couldn't stop it, either.

Hook went without argument, only looking at me as he was slowly led out of the captain's office and back toward the underground and warded jail.

I told myself to feel nothing. But my insides were rioting, and my mouth tasted of cotton. I breathed gently through my nose and out through my mouth, telling myself that even if it was him, it wasn't him.

Not really. He and I had been so long ago. That version of the man I'd once loved, it wasn't the same. I'd sensed it, felt it. Once upon a time, Hook and I had been like one soul. That was gone. It was gone.

Closing my eyes, I forced myself to turn back toward Bo's desk and forget about him. She was staring at me with a pinched look, a thousand questions burning in her eyes.

"If you need to ta—"

"I'm good, Captain," I said, voice strong. Though my insides ached. I squeezed my fists tight by my sides.

She grunted. "Well then, good job. I'll send Mulan and Rip to follow up on the Anne Bonny angle."

I thinned my lips, staring hard at the blunted curve of her desk.

"You've done good work, Detective. You should be proud. Much of what he said in here made a certain kind of sense. We'd suspected for a while that there'd been a shift in gang leadership, and the uptick in violence is a deadly reflection of it. Hook being part of the syndicate, his story of a bloodthirsty pirate manning the helm, it ticks all the boxes for us. The clues we've been missing, it all aligns, so why do I sense hesitation in you?"

I clenched my jaw and turned toward her. "I don't like it."

Sitting slowly, she spread her hands over the desk. "Explain, please."

I shrugged, not even sure how to put it into words. "It's... it's a feeling."

She snorted. "You're going to need to give me a little more than 'It's a feeling.' You know the commissioner wants this case closed. And right now, Elle, I won't lie—things are looking pretty good from where I'm sitting."

"Yeah, that's just it. His story is too perfect. I mean, it's so damned flawless, and you and I both know that's not how cases go."

"Sometimes they do. Sometimes you actually can tie a nice neat bow on things. This isn't just about the case, though, is it? Not really. It's because it's him, right? Maybe you should take some leave. Get your head on ri—"

I jerked, snaring her gaze with mine. "No. I don't want it. And unless you force it on me, I'm fine right where I am."

She tipped her head. "Fine. And just to alleviate your fears, we'll question him further, see if we can't make the connection between Midas's gala and Whiskers's rampage and if we can't have someone from the inside link these crimes together."

I snorted. "And the fae stronghold. And why he claims that I was the focus of the attack at Midas's gala. That makes no sense at all. Yes, I'm a powerful siren. But other than wanting to lock their arses in jail, I've got no personal feelings on the gang one way or another. But if what he claims is true, then Midas is likely lying or withholding information from us."

She pursed her lips. "Hm, you might be right. But are you claiming that he, too, is involved with the syndicate? That he created that event to help set up your takedown? You know if I even hint at that with Commissioner Draven, that another royal acted badly without incontrovertible proof, this will go down like—"

"Fetid whale blubber, yeah. I get that."

She snorted. "Not exactly what I was going for, but basically." Her lips thinned to a tight razor line. "I'll call the hospital, reach out to the medical chief, and see if we can't get Maddox released tonight. You need sleep?"

I shook my head.

"Good, because I wasn't planning to give you any. With Hook in custody, Draven is gonna be up our asses more than ever to shut the syndicate down. You have an established kinship with Midas. Use it. Go back there and make him talk. "

Nodding, I made to go, but her words stopped me.

"And Elle?"

Glancing at her over my shoulder, I lifted an eyebrow. "Yeah?"

"Don't do anything I wouldn't do."

I snorted and smirked. "Wouldn't dream of it, Captain."

"Yeah, right." She grinned.

There was a sudden knock at the door, and instantly, we both dropped our grins.

"Captain Bo, is this a good time?" someone with a deeply cultured voice asked.

Turning, I stared straight into the face of an immortal. Draven was a throwback to a different era, another dawn.

His body was tall and lanky, his face smooth but alluring. He was strangely beautiful with his razor-sharp cheekbones, piercing light-brown eyes, skin the color of warm umber, and long, beautiful raven's-wing-black hair that he had tied back with a silky red ribbon. He wore a long black coat that fell to his knees and a bloodred cravat much like Hatter's. I'd never actually seen the commissioner in person, but there was no mistaking who the man was.

He simply oozed vampiric elegance.

"Detective," he said in the hypnotic drawl of his people before gliding past. I shivered at his nearness. I might be a predator that most of the hundred realms feared, but I'd hazard a guess that my death count and Draven's weren't even within the same vicinity. You wouldn't know it, though, to look at his public records. Marcel Draven was probably the only vampire with such a squeaky-clean record. But he was rich, and he had the ear and loyalty of the ultra-elite on his side.

"Elle, shut the door behind you," Bo commanded. "Draven, to what do I owe the pleasure?"

If one didn't know better, one might actually believe the captain happy to see the vampire. But Draven was no fool and chuckled robustly. "All lies, but that is neither here nor there at the moment, Captain. I've been told you have the one known as Hook in your custody. We must talk."

"I rather thought we would," she murmured.

I heard no more after that, as I finally shut the door. I extracted my travel card and swiped it through the air. Thanks to the high-priority capture the Slashers had become, all detectives now had access to the enviable golden key cards. I was so damned spoiled.

I stepped through the transdimensional tunnel back into the witch's hospital and shoved open Hatter's door.

The room that had once been an idyllic nighttime garden was now cold and white and sterile. The bed was made, and there seemed to be no one around.

I frowned. "Maddox?"

"Elle?"

Whirling at the husky sound of my name, I saw him standing in the corner, gathering up what few items had come with him. He was still only in his black trousers and was completely shirtless. I'd forgotten that we'd come here straight from the gala.

He looked confused. "What are you doing here? I was only just discharged."

I wasn't sure when Bo had issued the order, but clearly, she'd meant business.

My gaze roamed up and down his muscular form, and without stopping to think, I walked over to him, took his hand in mine, and pulled him into me, hugging him hard.

He was tense at first. "Elle?" His voice was unsure and surprised. "What is this, eh?" he asked at my sniff.

Overcome by emotions I didn't quite know how to handle right then, I buried my face into his chest and trembled all over.

He stopped asking me for an explanation after that, only hugged me tight and murmured thickly, "It's okay, Detective. Whatever has been done, you're okay now."

Feeling the heat desperate to leak from the corners of my eyes, I squeezed them tightly shut and nodded miserably. I needed to get a handle on my emotions. Right now.

I cleared my throat and grunted several times before I trusted myself to speak. "I'm... I'm fine. But I do need coffee."

Tipping my chin up with his thumb and forefinger, he nodded slowly. "Okay, partner."

Biting down on my back teeth, I forced out a smile I wasn't feeling. But I'd be feeling better soon enough. "After that, we make a quick detour to my waters. Are you okay to—"

"I'm fine, Detective. Don't worry. I've been lain up long enough." His eyes were shaded and pinched. I knew he needed his soul back, and I would give it to him tonight. Then he'd be good to go again.

With a nod of gratitude, I stepped out of his arms, cleared my throat, and held my head up high. We grabbed our coffees, mine with several extra shots of calm, before we headed to my grotto to retrieve his golden soul.

I watched him as he slipped the soul back into his body. His entire frame gave a rolling shudder, and the gray tint that had perpetually hooded his mouth and eyes in the hospital instantly vanished. For a split second, his pores radiated like candlelight from the inside out. Then his soul settled in, and he was simply Hatter once more.

"You ready?" I asked, retrieving my key card from my inside jacket pocket.

And just as I made to swipe, he said softly, "Elle, I know you've noticed—"

I knew what it was. I also knew there was no time for it. I shook my head and gave him a soft smile.

"Think nothing of it, Maddox. The truth is, we all have our skeletons."

He closed his mouth, eyes looking worried and unsure.

I nodded. "I'm your partner. I've got your six, just as I'd hope you'd have mine. Does your soul impact our working relationship in any way?"

He looked thoughtful before shaking his head.

I knew it was the triple shots of calm that were affecting my mood. I'd always heard coffee called a drug. Now I knew it was true. The stuff they served at the Witches' Beans was nowhere near as mouthwatering as what Georgie made, but I was growing an addiction to it all the same. Because Georgie's wasn't pure magick.

"Then that's what matters. Not us, right now. The case the only thing. If you're ever ready to tell me what you are, I'm ready to listen. But until then, we have to stay on task. The noose is tightening. I can feel it."

I swiped the key card and opened a tunnel. We didn't speak again until we'd stepped within.

Hatter glanced at me, and I sensed none of his earlier unease. My words had clearly helped him compartmentalize, and I was glad of it.

"So what do we know so far?" he asked.

That was Maddox's way—he'd think through our cases like a chess match, looking at past moves to help him create a likelihood of what future moves would look like.

Lifting up my hands, I ticked off what I knew already.

"One, the sands, which seems relatively open and shut. The sands are how the Slashers are enchanting their... let's just call them zombies for now. Cognizant to a degree but asleep."

Though I thought of what Hook said and thought maybe sands hadn't been used on him at all.

He tipped his head. "It might behoove Ichabod to try to trace where the particular sands are coming from. Could help us create a sort of grid, where they are bound to meet. They'd have to gather more sand at some point, surely."

I nodded. "He has, actually. He even showed me all the grains he's found."

"And?"

"Nothing. I can normally trace even a granule of sand to a nearly perfect location, but this stuff, it was just nothing, as though there was no point of origin for it, no mineral content in it, very little in the way of personality."

"That's very interesting. Maybe in this case, the lack of identifiers is actually the clue?"

I shrugged. "If I could speak with my sister Anahita, I could probably figure it out. There is no one who knows more about water-based sediment than her."

His eyebrows twitched. "I didn't know you had a sister."

"I have six, actually. And I doubt she'll help, but I could try reaching out to her, though she'd daddy's little pet and loyal to him to a fault."

"Worth a shot."

"I guess." Thinking of my family I could no longer see usually filled me with a sense of profound and aching loneliness. Though Father and I didn't get on at all, it had been quite different for my sisters and me. We'd grown up with a very tight bond between us, and when I'd been exiled, they'd been the only ones truly broken up to see me go.

The coffee was truly a wonder drug. I almost smiled at feeling nothing.

"What else?" he asked, nudging me with his elbow and drawing me out of my head.

"*Erm.*" I shook my head to clear the thoughts and said, "Obviously, the fae."

"Not proof positive that those two cases are one hundred percent connected," he said deeply.

"*Mm,*" I wiggled my wrist. "The fact that Whiskers was at both crime scenes is more than a little coincidental."

"At the very least, it warrants our time to dig a little deeper into it," he murmured. "What else?"

Thinning my lips, I did a mental catalogue of what I knew so far. "Midas probably deceived us."

He pursed his lips. I hadn't yet told him about that latest development.

"I spoke with Hook right before coming to fetch you."

"Ah," he said as though he'd finally understood something that had been nagging him, a long and rolling sort of sound. Not ah so much as *ahhhhhh.*

"And he mentioned that he'd been sent to take me out, basically." I shrugged.

At this, Hatter's dark eyebrows lifted high on his forehead. "Excuse me? You? But why? What have you to do with the Slashers?"

"Beats me." I held my hands up in the universal gesture of "How the hells should I know?" "That's what he claimed, anyway. I'm not sure whether I fully believe him. Though he does appear to have more of his memories intact than Whiskers does. Which brings us to the dragon. Two different bloody scenes he's witness to." I held up two fingers. "One is the bloody remains of something large that had been killed outside his nest. But at the other, he's an active participant of the slaughter. Then that rolls right into the fae stronghold—something was stolen. What?" I shrugged.

He shook his head. "At the very least, it would be worth chatting with the queen about this."

I thinned my lips. "Titiana isn't the most forthcoming of fae. She sent me out there without a guard. I could have been killed. I don't think she would have cared."

He snorted. "You're quite levelheaded about your near extermination."

I grinned. "I know, right? It's that witch's brew. Anyway..." I flicked the nonsensical tangent away. "And last but certainly not least, Draven came."

"And that's of note because?" He let his question dangle.

I snorted. "You clearly have no experience with vampires. Somewhere around their five thousandth year of life, they begin to petrify. Immortal but not." I wiggled my hands. "Which means it takes something truly significant to cause them to leave their self-imposed prison. He came. It's significant."

"Okay," he said as he scrubbed at his jaw. "Okay. I think I'm spun up now."

"Good. Because we're here." I turned, and the tunnel opened at the same moment.

We were not in Hel when we stepped out this time but in a land of glittering rolling gold hills with birds wheeling in the air and winking like molten metal. Trees, homes, the pathway, and even the massive twenty-thousand-acre mansion were made entirely of gold.

It was Midas's safe place where he could come and not be forced to wear his gloves, where he could touch whatever he wanted and not worry about killing any of it.

Demons, of course, were immune to his cursed hands, which was probably why he paid them a king's ransom to guard both him and his home.

Hatter and I slowly walked along the golden-bricked path toward his gilded mansion.

Neither of us spoke. It wasn't safe to discuss an active investigation out in the open if we could help it, especially not in a place we suspected could have a conspirator running free.

"How do we—" Hatter began, and I sniffed.

"Oh, he knows we're here already."

"How can you be sure?"

I pointed to the sky, not even needing to look up to know what I'd find. I'd always been fascinated as a little girl by the angelic and strange beings that floated above. Composed of nothing but pure radiant light, they were mostly just wisps of lambent color, but every so often if you looked hard enough, you'd catch a glimpse of their true shape. They were always guarding the king's skies, alerting him to any potential threats.

I'd never realized how dangerous those beings were until the day I'd seen them become a massive swirling funnel of death and chaos, ripping and clawing at the screaming human trapped within their cyclone until there was nothing left but silence.

There'd not been a trace of him behind when they'd finished with him. He'd simply been gone, as though he'd never been at all. I was still haunted by nightmares from it.

"Are those sylphs?"

I nodded. "Indeed."

Hatter shuddered. "Who in the devil would keep those nasty fae on payroll?"

"Aw, c'mon, they're not so bad. Quite cuddly when they care to be," I teased him.

Then I turned to my right, and there he was, dressed in the clothing not of a king but of a regular man, barefooted, and hanging onto a golden basket nearly filled with golden apples. Midas's hands were completely exposed. In this setting, he seemed younger somehow, freer, as though the burdens of kingship weren't his—at least, not here.

He pointed over his shoulder with his thumb. "My sylphs alerted me. I was in the orchard, picking the first crops of the season. Though I can't claim surprise, either. I expected you'd be showing up sooner rather than later."

He sounded reconciled, and I knew my hunch had been right. Midas had been withholding information from us.

The informal setting, the lack of pomposity typically associated with royals—all of it was calculated on Midas's part to help put Maddox and me at ease, but it was also part of who he truly was as well. Midas hadn't been born privileged. In fact, he'd been a layman in his previous life. The golden touch was what had literally created his kingdom from dust. No one knew what had caused him to become the "golden king," only that he had become one of the most formidable royals in all the hundred realms.

"You're not surprised," I repeated to him. "So if you're not surprised, why didn't you come down to our office sooner? Why wait?"

"C'mon, Elle, you already know how difficult that endeavor is for me. The mobs I have to deal with." He shook his head as he pursed his lips. He wasn't lying—Midas attracted a mob just about anywhere he went unless he oversaw all aspects of his outings. It was part and parcel of the curse he'd been handed. He was a man who could create wealth from nothing, and in a lot of people's eyes, it was wrong of him to hoard such a gift when there were so many in such desperate need.

I knew Midas donated to charity, but as he'd always said, no matter how much he did, it was never enough. Somebody somewhere always thought he could and should do more.

I shrugged. "So you already know why I'm here then?"

"I can imagine." He sighed deeply. "You think me complicit in what occurred at my gala." It wasn't a question, and I didn't treat it as one.

"Wouldn't you? We captured Hook. He's told us everything."

His blond eyebrows furrowed, blue eyes looking soft and sorrowful. "Was the enchantment reversed then? Was it a Slasher mole?"

"You know I can't talk about an active investigation with you."

"Of course." He grinned affably. "It was just a shock seeing him wear the face of someone we both knew and loved."

It had been no secret, Midas's great esteem and affection for my fiancé. Midas considered himself pansexual, fluid in who he developed an attraction to. He didn't see gender so much as the individual. It had been a great pain to him when Hook had taken up with me, and I'd been sorry for it, always knowing that the very man responsible for introducing me to the greatest love of my life had felt similarly and also broken in the end because of it. It was why I'd kept my distance from Midas for so many years. Not because I hadn't cared for him but because I knew that for him, seeing Hook and me together was always agonizing.

Hook's identity wasn't pertinent to the case. I shook my head. "It wasn't an enchantment, Midas. It was him. It is Hook. He lives."

All the blood suddenly leached from his face, and he stared at me with his large golden eyes. I could read the questions scrolling through his head, caught flashes of agony and desire, but then his softly rounded jaw clenched, and he murmured, "I see. So h-he," he stuttered, "he was the one responsible for telling you that your invitation was no coincidence?"

Sensitive to the fact that he'd need to process Hook's reappearance the same as I was—which I wasn't doing a bang up job of, considering I was currently suppressing my emotions with spells—I gently grabbed his shoulder.

Blinking, he stared into my face. "What really happened, Midas?"

He swallowed hard several times and cleared his throat before he spoke. "It happened a week before the gala. I was approached by missive from a dear friend of mine in the province over. He spoke of my hosting a ball to help cheer me up. I've been very blue for a few years now, as I'm sure you know."

I expelled a slow breath. I'd not been the only one to suffer, but my pain had been so great I'd been unable to see beyond myself to the plight of others. For a moment, I could see him caught up in the memories in his head. But as a second ticked by, and then one more, I gently cleared my throat. He blinked, glanced at me, and gave himself a small shake.

"A ball was what he suggested, and naturally, the thought did appeal greatly to me. He spoke of making sure I was safe since Slasher activity was on the rise and I'd be a prime target. He also began to speak of your father."

I frowned. "My father? Who did you say your friend was?"

He shrugged. "I hadn't, but it's not some dark secret. It is Lord Humpty."

"As in Humpty Dumpty?" Maddox rolled in his deep accent.

Midas flicked a glance at him. "Some call him that, yes. But he is my companion and has been for many years. Due to his condition and mine, we share an understanding, you see. He isn't the great love of my life, but I am not his, either. I respect him, though, and I would ask that you both do the same."

My eyebrows lifted high onto my forehead. "So that's who you meant to introduce us to that night?"

"My deepest apologies," Maddox said. "I did not mean offense."

Midas shrugged off Maddox's apology. "Yes, though you know how that went. Anyway, it is of no importance. I'm sure if you asked him, he'd corroborate my story."

"Speaking of that night, ever learn how it was that you were so infiltrated by the Slashers?"

Midas shook his head slowly. "None. Infuriating to be in the dark that way, but I cannot account for how they did that. The only way in, literally, was through an invitation, and I would never have invited them. Not any of them." He blew out a heavy breath.

I nodded, taking an infinitesimal step back. "Just one more question, King, if I may."

"You're always welcome to ask me anything, Arielle." He looked tired, his skin sallow, his gaze shaken.

"Did Lord Humpty actually know my father? And more to the point, what exactly was it that he wrote to you when he mentioned King Triton?"

"I'm not certain of just how well they knew one another. But Humpty owned the largest fleet of cargo ships in all the hundred realms. Because of that, he was familiar with many of the lords and kings of the waterways, and considering Triton is king over all hundred realms waters, it stands to reason that he knew him reasonably well. As to what he said exactly"—he rolled his wrist elegantly—"he simply said that he'd been speaking to the great king as of late and that he sensed a disquietude in him, a restless unease, then he mused that possibly it could be because of you. After all, all have heard of your case in Wonderland. Quite daring, that."

Titiana had also mentioned my father the other day. Was it possible that he was really speaking of me to others? But that didn't seem likely. He was never an open man, especially not with people he wasn't even close to. I shook my head. "The fact that you'd even believe my father could care about me makes me want to laugh. But the fact that Hook mentioned it was no coincidence I'd been invited to your gala definitely gives me pause. By any chance, have you the letter Lord Humpty wrote?"

He sighed. "I do not. It was just a note. I didn't think it all that valuable or worth saving."

"We understand." Maddox dipped his head. Midas thinned his lips.

"I do wish I could have been more help to you, Detective Elle," he said with a soft curve of his lips, sincerity printed all over his handsome face, "and though I'm sure you must hear it often, I was not aware of any sort of conspiracy until after the fact. When I received yet another missive from Humpty, a day later."

I'd been about to ask him how it was that he'd known of the supposed conspiracy. "And?"

He shrugged. "He seemed upset. Told me he'd done wrong. That he wanted to confess to me that he was grateful you were well and that he was so sorry for whatever role he'd been forced to play in this charade."

"That's what he said?" Maddox stepped forward, into my line of sight. "Forced? That was the word exactly?"

"Indeed. And *that* letter, I do have, Detectives. If you'd care to see it."

"Of course."

He set down his basket of apples then turned and led us to the back of his massive golden castle and through a hidden doorway in a maze of hedgerows. Our footsteps sounded nearly deafening in the spiraling golden staircase.

As one might imagine, every square inch of Midas's home was gold, from the ceilings to the floors, to the walls, and even the framed artwork and the suits of armor that had been placed out on display.

I trailed my finger along the cool, shining surface as we walked up what felt like an eternity of steps, oddly drawn to the slick metal, even as I found it just the slightest bit gauche too.

"This is my private entryway. Few know of it, only my most trusted advisors." Midas spoke over his shoulder to us. "I've never had chance to use it for its actual constructed design, an escape route should I ever find myself under attack." He chuckled lightly. "Though anyone would be a fool to try, considering I have a small army of high-caste demon warriors at my disposal. My private office is just around this corner now."

True to his word, we finally stopped our eternal climb, and I knew we had to be easily several stories high. The heavy door to his office moved on silent hinges when he pushed it open.

Unlike the rest of the castle, Midas's room was a study in understated elegance. And there wasn't a bit of gold in here.

There were bookshelves loaded with leather-bound tomes, a desk that had a pewter-colored cage resting on it, and two gorgeously plumed finches singing merrily within, green and orange with bright-yellow tail feathers. They hopped around wildly when Midas approached.

He murmured tenderly under his breath as he slipped on his leather gloves that he clearly always kept on him and pulled open a desk drawer to extract a small tin.

"The note is on my desk. As you can see, I've only just received it. In fact, I hadn't even had a chance to respond to Humpty's request to meet up tonight. I'm rather torn on what to do, to be honest." He popped open the tin and pulled out two hopping bright-green crickets and proceeded to feed them to his birds.

Candlelight played lovingly around the room. It felt very much like Midas's true living space. There were books opened everywhere, reams of thick paper, ink, and quills. Even a couple of robes were strewn over the back of his plush and elegant couch.

Maddox and I read the note together. Midas had related its contents nearly word for word to us.

I picked up the note with the very edge of my dress, careful not to transfer my fingerprints onto it, and turned it over to study the wax seal. It was the crest of the Ainsley clan, that of a knight's helmet sitting atop a shield bearing a Maltese cross. It was definitely Lord Humpty's.

"We'll be needing to keep this as evidence, have it brushed for prints, whatnot," I said to him.

"Of course." Midas, who'd pulled one of his finches from its cage, was gently rubbing its head with two of his fingers. "You should also know—though I vow to you that I'm merely telling you this because I want you to trust in my transparency with your department—I was asked by Lord Humpty many months ago to help him with a delicate matter."

I frowned. Hatter tipped his chin.

"And that was?" I prompted him.

Midas groaned. "You must know that I loathe the very notion of speaking of money. I find the endeavor to be so gauche. That said, Lord Humpty was having some difficulty making back a loan he'd taken out against his fleet. He did not tell me why he'd taken the loan, only that he had. I assumed the loan was to your father, but that is only an assumption. Either way, I did enchant several rum barrels' worth of sands for him. I've heard tell of golden sands being found recently, much at my own gala, and I do not honestly know what to make of this or whether it is even my sands. But…" He inhaled deeply. "I thought it worth mentioning at the very least."

So neat. That was my first thought. That explanation ticked all the boxes and was so very neatly done. Midas had just introduced enough reasonable doubt that even if he were involved further, without the proof, he'd never be indicted. He was an old friend of mine, but I'd always known he was a clever man.

Whether that was proof of innocence or not, even if we somehow traced him to the golden sands, he'd just given himself the perfect out. Even I couldn't argue with his rationale.

"Interesting," I murmured softly.

He shrugged. "I just thought you should know. Now, is there anything more I can do for you? Tea? Cookies? I was just about to take my repast."

I knew a dismissal when I heard one.

"No, we really need to be going. Thank you, and if we have any further questions—"

"Then you know where to find me," he said, smile stiff. "And… and should you see Hook, tell him that I'm glad he is well. And that he was missed."

I reached over and clasped Midas by the shoulder. I'd gone over there so certain that Midas had played more of a key role in what had taken place with the gala, but as was usual when I got around him, it was impossible to think anything but kind thoughts about him. I still wasn't sure that he wasn't guilty of more, but I couldn't prove it either way.

He took my hand in his gloved ones, brought my knuckles to his lips, and dropped a gentle kiss upon them. "It is truly a shame that such terrible tidings were what brought us together. Don't let this be in vain. Visit me more, girl. I rather enjoyed our quiet nights spent together."

I wasn't prone to hugging. Not in the slightest. But Midas had always been more of a father figure to me than my own father. Leaning on tiptoe, I gave him a hard but swift squeeze.

He went stiff for half a moment, not used to touching others or being touched in return. With his gloves, on he was perfectly safe, but that didn't stop others from fearing him regardless. He patted me twice then cleared his throat.

"If you do see Humpty, tell him that I'll accept his invitation for dinner, would you?"

"Of course." Hatter held out his hand to him.

Midas, looking suddenly shy but also pleased, took Maddox's hand, and they swiftly shook on it.

Swiping my key card through the air, I opened a transdimensional tunnel, and Maddox and I didn't speak again until we were safely ensconced within.

"Do you believe him?" we both asked at once.

Hatter scrubbed at his bristled jaw with his long, elegant fingers. "I think I do, or he's a very clever liar."

I snorted. "He is clever. Do not doubt it. His cursed hands aren't the only reason why he's reigned as long as he has. What he did was a stroke of genius, really, owning up to his part in all of this but only just enough to keep him innocent in the eyes of the law. Especially a law that is inclined to always let royalty walk. Still, I don't think he was as deeply entrenched as I suspect Lord Humpty was. Did you see Midas's shock upon learning of Hook's return? As good as he is, that was definitely real emotion we saw there."

I felt Maddox's studious look upon my face, and I shrugged. "I'm fine. Really. The spells are doing a wonderful job of keeping me quite levelheaded about all of this."

"And when it wears off?"

I laughed. "Then I'll just take more."

"You can't remain drugged forever, Elle. At some point, you'll have to confront this."

I clenched my jaw, feeling the tiniest bit annoyed, which let me know the spell was already starting to wear off.

He sighed and quickly switched the subject. "Lord Humpty's then?"

I knew I had to keep focused and think not with my heart but with my head. Lifting an eyebrow, I said, "Yes. The seal was definitely his. I just want to verify he actually did write this letter, and then if we learn that, why? Unlike Midas, I'm not very familiar with Humpty at all."

"Is he really an egg? That's what I've always heard of the male. That he was an egg. A rather rotund one at that. And I'd like to know this so that I might not offend when I am finally confronted with the legend."

I chuckled. "No, I don't believe he is. Though he suffers from a condition that makes his skin as fragile as an egg's shell. Thus his moniker. He lives his life mostly in a bubble to protect himself. But I can understand why Midas and he might be drawn to one another. Though for all intents and purposes, I hear that Humpty isn't the most attractive sort of fellow."

"*Hm.*"

The tunnel opened, and immediately, we found ourselves in the middle of a busy and elegant Victorian-themed town. Brownstone homes with inviting front porches and encased in thick, elegant black gates sat at even intervals—save for one. A creamy egg-white-colored brick face stood out boldly. The home was understated but refined, affluent without being overly gaudy.

"That must be his place, no?" Maddox jerked his thumb at the white-bricked home.

I shrugged. "That's my going theory, anyway."

Women wearing elegant rider bustles and satin corsets in every color of the rainbow sashayed slowly by on the slick cobblestone street, their white-lace parasols held aloft to help ward off the slight drizzle that fell from the gray skies above.

A few of them gave Maddox long appraising looks before passing by.

He grinned as one pretty blond, bolder than the others, winked and pursed her coral-pink lips at him.

I licked my front teeth, feeling quite like kicking that trollop's arse right now. "Should I question Lord Humpty alone, Maddox? In need of a tart to warm your bed this evening?"

He frowned and turned on me. "Whyever would you say that?"

He sounded genuinely scandalized, which mollified me a very little.

Walking in the direction of the white home, I shrugged. "Oh, I don't know. Maybe the way you undressed her with your eyes. You lit up like a pine tree at Yule."

He frowned. "Don't be ridiculous."

I snorted.

And he grinned. "Is this jealousy, Elle?"

Scoffing, I walked through the open gates and marched up the five steps with purposeful stomps of my booted feet. "You wish, Detective. I can't feel anything right now, anyway. I'm high on spells."

But his grin, rather than grow smaller, only grew wider. "You *are* jealous."

"Gods' sake," I snarled and rapped sharply on the door with my knuckles, though there was a perfectly good wrought-iron door knocker in the shape of a demonic gargoyle resting on its front.

"Deny it," he said in a low voice.

"Don't push me, Detective," I hissed.

He chuckled softly.

I knocked again, this time picking up the heavy knocker and giving it three hard booms. But after almost a minute and still no one bothered to answer, I stepped back and frowned, shoving my fists into my jacket pocket.

"Is no one home, you think?" Maddox murmured. "But surely a butler should be, especially at an address like this one, no?"

"Indeed." Getting a rather strange feeling, I studied the house again. It was a gothic Victorian, with large windows with well-constructed shutters upon them and flower boxes that bloomed with large, gorgeous red flowers. I looked at the lawn—Well maintained and manicured.

I pursed my lips and looked back at the gate. It had been open, which hadn't much bothered me at the time.

"Who lives in a community this affluent and leaves their gates just hanging open that way?"

"They don't," Maddox said instantly. "Lord Humpty," he called out, placing his hands around his mouth, "we are Grimm PD. Please open up. We have a few questions to ask you."

When there wasn't even a rustle of sound from within, he raised his fist and banged on the door with the side of it. "Lord Humpty, we've been sent by Midas to check up on you. Open."

It wasn't true, but Humpty might be more willing to speak with us if he felt that we had come on Midas's request.

But still... nothing at all.

That bad feeling in the pit of my gut only grew stronger. I shook my head. "I'm walking to the back, Maddox. You keep banging, okay?"

He nodded but continued his banging and calling out to Humpty.

I jogged rather quickly around the side of the house, noting how everything seemed to be orderly and in place. But that gate was open. In communities with such wealthy patrons, there was an almost obsessive code of conduct that manifested from one realm to another. The wealthy didn't like to mingle, not even amongst themselves, though they often did in order to lord their wealth and accomplishments over one another.

When I got to the back of the house, I saw there were no lights on in the windows, and the nut trees in the grove behind me were creaking in the rising stiff wind. A terrible feeling of foreboding crawled over my flesh.

"Lord Humpty," I called out as calmly as I could, lifting my voice just a little but keeping my tone moderate. "We've come only to ask a few questions. Please open up."

As I said this, I quickly peered into the windows and noted the tasteful décor of each room: the sitting room, the drawing room, the study, etcetera. Then I moved to the last room, and I saw legs poking out from behind a massive mahogany desk.

Unmoving legs.

"Maddox! Come here. Come quickly."

"Elle!" he cried, then I heard the rustling of grass and the heavy breaths of his run, and he was suddenly there, wide-eyed and harried and looking at me. "What is it? What's the matter?"

I pointed at the window, noting the paint chips on the sill and the small crack in the base of the wooden frame. As though someone had forcibly opened the window.

Frowning, I stared back at the trees behind us. Then I spotted a pair of beady black eyes. "Maddox, there's a crow." I pointed.

At my words, the bird cried out loudly and shot from the tree, winging off powerfully.

Maddox growled. "Do you think—"

"Yes. Yes, I do. That was a watcher. They were here and not long ago at that."

Protocol said we couldn't enter a domicile uninvited unless we were certain someone within was incapacitated and in need.

"It's going back to its leader. Shouldn't we stop it?" he asked.

But I shook my head. "You and I cannot fly. That shifter is long gone."

Banging on the window with my fist, I called out, "You there! Are you okay?"

I waited a good two seconds. No response.

"That's it. I'm crawling in."

"Let me go first."

I snorted. "Don't play hero, Maddox. I'm smaller than you. This will be far easier for me than for you." Then I set my hand upon the frame and tried to move it. It did move but only a little. It got caught on something inside.

There was just enough room for a bird to comfortably slip through or a petite child to wiggle through and pray they'd not get trapped.

Thankfully, I was a very petite female.

I shrugged out of my jacket then turned and handed it to Maddox. He crushed it in his large hand, staring silently at me.

I nodded once. "You see anything, Maddox, and I swear to the twin hells, you'd better warn me."

"Elle, I don't bloody like this."

"And we don't have time to discuss this further." I grabbed hold of the sill and hopped up, arms already trembling because the damned window was a bit higher than I'd expected it to be.

Hatter shoved on my bottom, helping to push me through. I groaned as my head popped through.

"Bloody hells, that pulled out hair," I snarled as my scalp tingled from the shock.

He chuckled, but his words were calming. "Just relax, Elle. Think thin thoughts."

"*Pft,*" an indelicate sound spilled off my tongue. I could barely catch a proper breath as my chest passed ridiculously slowly beneath the torture device. At one point, I couldn't breathe at all and almost had a panic attack.

Perceptive, as he usually was, Hatter shoved me through hard.

I felt a nail dig into my side and rip. I grunted as I felt the thick gathering of crimson begin to spill.

"Elle, bloody hells, you're bleeding!" he hissed, grabbing at my heels.

I was in down to my thighs and wiggling like a fish on a hook to get through. "I swear to all the gods that if you pull me back out, I'll gut you like a sea carp," I snapped, sweating, bloody, feeling as though I'd done ten rounds in a pugilist's ring. Why the hells hadn't I just broken the glass?

Oh yeah, because I was on thin ice, and the last thing I needed was an irritable Lord filing a complaint with commissioner Draven—or worse, BS.

His hands were suddenly off my ankles, and just like a child being pushed through the birthing canal, I finally popped free. I landed face first, hurting all over and realizing that had probably been the stupidest thing I'd ever done in my career.

"Elle, are you alright?" Hatter demanded.

But I couldn't move. I could barely even draw breath. Everything bloody hurt.

"Elle!"

I growled and shoved myself up on my shaky arms. "I'm fine, you big devil. Give me a second, damn it all."

Squeezing my eyes shut and very aware that I'd made enough noise to actually wake the dead, I groaned as I gingerly made my way up to my feet. I turned and looked at the window and saw why it hadn't wanted to budge. There was a big nail hammered into the frame.

With a little snarl, I pulled the damned thing out and dropped it at my feet with a soft *plink* on the hardwood floor.

Hatter shoved the window up with force, his blue and green eyes bright with worry.

I grabbed onto my side and grimaced as I felt the tackiness of blood. "C'mon then," I whispered hoarsely, and when I turned back around, I again saw the legs, and the entire reason for my breaking and entering was suddenly front and center.

Moving on aching legs, I called out, "Sir, are you well? Do you need a medic? Do—"

But I stopped talking the moment I rounded the desk and caught sight of broken pottery shards and dust. Lying stomach down on the thick and golden Turkenish rug was none other than Lord Humpty himself.

His head was completely gone, his hands like broken pottery that was crisscrossed through with veins of black. Broken but not quite shattered. Beside him lay a long black crow's feather.

It was obvious it was a retaliation killing. But for what? And why exactly? For attempting to tell Midas the truth or to cover something up? Sadly, I wasn't sure I'd ever know the answer to that question.

I sighed and shook my head. Poor Midas. Ever unlucky in love.

Frowning, I thinned my lips. "Maddox, call this in, please. I'll look through the rest of the house and see if there are any other bodies or clues."

He nodded. "Be careful, Elle."

I pulled my gun from its holster and held it out before me and said, "Always."

IT WAS HOURS BEFORE we finally left the crime scene, but much of what Midas had claimed had been easily corroborated.

Letters between the two of them all but proved most of Midas's innocence in the matters. And we'd also learned how the Slashers had gotten into the gala.

Hidden in Lord Humpty's safe was one of Midas's golden stamps. When we put two and two together, it was easy enough to figure out that he must have been the one to write the invitations to the Slashers, and with the stamp on their invite, they'd have easily slipped through alerting none of the guards to their presence there. We were going to dust the stamp for prints but I had no doubt they'd be a perfect match for Humpty.

And though I'd found a few letters in my father's hand to Lord Humpty, I'd not seen anything that would indicate it had been Triton who'd brought me to Humpty's mind. Those letters had been of nothing other than business matters. Humpty owed a great deal of money to my father, which would account for Midas's story of turning sand into gold.

My father didn't give a rats arse about me, but even if he did, he'd never have spoken of such private matters to someone he clearly didn't think of as more than a mere business acquaintance.

No, Humpty had been told about me by someone else. Maybe Anne Bonny, maybe someone else. But if I could just figure out who that someone was, I had a feeling I could probably even solve the case.

We were close. I could feel it in my bones.

We just weren't close enough.

Not yet.

But we would be. We would be.

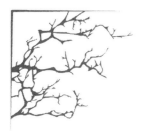

Chapter 14

Detective Elle

I BRUSHED DOWN MY VERY shredded dress, feeling stupidly anxious and nervous for some reason.

Maddox grabbed my wrist. "Relax, Elle. She'll be here soon. Don't give her any power over you."

Sighing deeply, I shook my head and nodded. The rolling of waves crashing along my perpetually deserted shores calmed and soothed my frazzled nerves. I really wanted to take a swim, but I didn't have time. Not that I needed the water, but the water always comforted me.

"It's just something about all of this feels—"

"Wrong," he said, not as a question. "I know. It does. Why kill Lord Humpty? To what end? What did he know that we don't? And how the devil was he mixed up with the Slashers at all? He was a respectable businessman."

Wetting my lips, I looked over at him and shrugged. "Was he? Clearly, he had dealings with the Slashers in some capacity. They must have had dirt on him that they were able to exploit."

"*Hmm*," Maddox mumbled and scrubbed at his jaw, in his thinker's pose, as I liked to call it. His eyes burned but not with vision. He hadn't had another one since leaving the hospital. "What burns me more than anything is how you're mixed up in this. What are you to them? Why the schemes? The games?"

"I wish I knew. But then only one person has said it was me they were after, and how much can we afford to trust him?"

Maddox looked down at me and gave me *the look*, the one that said he didn't believe a word I said, and my stomach trembled with nerves. I bit my bottom lip, pulling it between my teeth.

"Why won't you say his name?"

The spells were wearing off rapidly. My pulse was thundering in my ears.

"It's Hook, Elle," he said softly. "Why would he lie?"

I scoffed. "Are you seriously asking me this? What do I know of him?"

"Everything, I'd imagine."

"Once upon another time, maybe." I snorted. "But that man in there, that's not my Hook. I don't know who that man is. Why is no one else bothered by the fact that he's been brought back to life when all would say that's an impossibility?"

"Dark magick could—"

"That's been stamped out, ages ago. When all the realms unified for the first and only time and fought as one to bring down their great evil. You know this. You know Grimm's history. This is impossible. So no, I don't give much credence to what that man says. I don't believe him. And neither should you."

Maddox pursed his lips. "I'm not saying we blindly agree with everything he says, but it does make a certain kind of twisted sense, Elle. And I think that's what bothers you most. Look, if you want, you can work another case, a different angle. I'd be happy to take point on this one."

I sighed. "No. No, that's not what I want. I just... I really don't want to talk about him, okay? I just don't."

He held up his hands. "Understood."

We stood in silence for several heartbeats, and with each second that ticked by, I worried not only that Queen Titiana wouldn't show but also that the constant bickering between Hatter and me had to stop. I didn't know why we couldn't seem to just stay neutral with one another. It was as though we were both incapable of keeping ourselves solely focused on business.

I tapped my foot in the sand.

"You're like a restless tiger trapped in a cage, Elle," he said in a low voice, turning to stare at me with those eyes that saw too damned much.

I tossed up my hands. I told myself to say nothing, that it was none of my business, but damn it all, he was constantly picking at my scabs, and I was just petty enough right now to return the favor.

"Why have you a golden soul? Who are you really? Does Bo know all this? I know I said I didn't care, but I do, dammit."

As I asked, his eyebrows rose high, and he looked at me in a way I'd never seen him look at me before, like he was disappointed in me, in what we were devolving into.

Groaning, I pinched the bridge of my nose and shook my head. "Forget I asked. I don't care."

"Oh, but I think you do, Elle. I really think you do."

I couldn't tell whether he were simply stating a fact or being uppity. Dammit, I couldn't tell anything. Why? Because Maddox was right—I was worried about Hook, worried about who and what he had become. I had felt a different man in that office, but I'd be a liar if I said it was simply about Hook.

Squeezing my eyes shut, I whispered, "My life feels like it's spiraling. Ever since that day you told me he still lived. I've not felt right. I hurt. All over. My sleep is nothing but nightmarish visions of his death. And I relive it over and over and over," I confessed, voice tight and gritty. "I... I need some sense of... I don't know what I need." I laughed mockingly, hating myself, wishing I'd never said anything.

Then I felt his warm hand grab mine. I opened my eyes and looked up into his burning blue and green ones.

"Control," he said succinctly. "You need control. I get it, Elle. I do. I know what it feels like to be a kite spinning in the wind with no anchor to hold you down. But..." He clenched his jaw. "I—"

Whatever he'd been about to say was forgotten as his green eye blazed with fire. Gasping, I slid my hand up his arm and pushed back his loose sleeve so that I might grasp his tattoo, and when I did, I felt as if my entire body had been yanked backward by a mighty hand.

I was back in that darkness swirling with light and chaos. There was music,

haunting music everywhere, like the screams of the dying coalescing into song, a strange litany of macabre beauty that pricked at my ears and my heart.

I'd heard it once before. I was so sure of it yet not sure at all. It was as though I sensed what would come next in the aria, though I wasn't sure how.

I felt something inside of my head slink and move, slither through me like a serpent—a memory of great and distressing darkness that was so far down deep I'd even forgotten it was there because until just now, it had been locked away in a vault I'd never even known existed inside of me.

The skies were gray above me and clapping with thunder. I stood not upon land but water, water that rushed in a torrential current, roaring as though it crashed over a steep cliff to the land below.

Why was I seeing this vision through my eyes? It was different from Hatter's normal visions. I was only ever a spectator looking in, but this time, I was the active participant.

Looking down, I saw that my feet were in water. I should have been forced to shift because of the contact. Yet I was human, and I sensed that it wasn't fear that kept me trapped in that form but that I actually could not shift. The heart in my chest was beating rapidly, far too rapidly.

"Hatter?" I called and heard the echo of my voice. It sounded odd, disjointed, as if I wasn't really there in physical form but rather a spectral of that form. As if I were a... ghost.

Wrapping my arms around myself, I blinked and looked up, down, and around. I was all alone in the darkness. The roaring and singing grew louder.

Where was I?

The skies lit up with lightning and quaked with thunder. Dark, evil-looking black clouds rolled in. I needed to get away from there. I needed to find shelter, safety.

But there were only miles of pitching and angry waves and that ever-present roaring and song buzzing in my ears like angry hornets.

I walked left first, and the roaring began to grow faint. Something inside of me told me my only hope for safety was to walk not away but closer to the noise. So I stopped and turned and walked in the opposite direction, and each step I took made my heart bang in my chest, my skin prickle, my head ache. Then my heart began to stutter, and I clutched my chest. I was dying.

Wait, I was dying?

I looked down at myself with a frown and saw that I was coated in a netting of silver—a spell.

It was dark magick.

Shaking my head, I pressed on. My vision grew dark and full of spots. I was just barely clinging to consciousness. I could feel my body swaying like a drunkard with each step I took. But the roaring, it was so close.

So very, very close.

One more step.

Then...

I saw it. A doorway, in the water itself. It was open, and eternity beckoned to me.

I couldn't go through that door. It might kill me. I would die if I did. I just knew it.

The singing was changing its tune. I could hear words... thready and just barely there, but if I held really still, I could hear it.

You must do it, Elle! You must trust us!

I blinked, thinking that maybe I'd recognized the voice but not exactly sure how. I shook my head, backing up a few steps, able to take easier breaths when I did.

Arielle, this is the escape. This is your way out, love. Jump! You must trust me, damn you. Jump!

A different voice, also familiar. Also not.

"No," I muttered. "No. I'll die. He'll kill me. He'll—"

Trust. Us.

Then I felt myself being watched again. But this time, even the air seemed a malevolent presence. There was death waiting for me.

With a gasp, I looked up and saw a ghostly white specter, no face, no body, just a ball of glowing light, and I began to hyperventilate. My knees went weak. I dropped to the ground and kicked back on my heels as I desperately tried to scrabble away.

But the ball of light laughed, a terrible, wicked, and low laugh.

"*You poor, unfortunate soul*," it said in a voice that was deeply feminine, then it screamed.

With a gasp, I pulled away from Hatter's arm. A soft glow still emanated from beneath his sleeve, but it was fading fast.

I was gasping, choking on air, looking at him and shaking my head, having a hard time severing myself from the vision we'd just shared, and still feeling trapped by that evil, knowing that soon I would die.

His hands gripped my shoulders, and I screamed, flailing at him to get off me, desperate to jump into my waters, to run away, feeling as though I'd been tainted somehow.

"What? What?" was the only word I could manage to say.

He was moving me, hefting me in his arms as I felt my skin begin to roll. The panic was shredding at my insides, raking at my innards with claws that eviscerated and bled me dry. I could almost smell that blood, thick and viscous and full of iron. There was a tang of it on my tongue.

I still felt her touch. That evil, it was spreading through me. It would never stop.

"Water, Elle. You need your water. Stop fighting me!" Hatter snapped in my ears, waking me up just a little.

Blinking, I finally took note of his face. He was clawed up, and there was blood dripping down my nails. I licked my mouth. There was blood on my tongue.

I shivered violently, suppressing the desperate urge to continue fighting him as he quickly undressed me.

"Go to your waters, Elle. Right now. Jump into your waters," he said softly but firmly.

My back teeth chattered violently as I nodded and turned, moving on autopilot as I somehow swayed my way toward my waters. The first touch of its coolness against my flesh made me explode out of my skin.

My legs shifted instantly, the change so painful because of its brutal swiftness that I cried out, but I didn't stop. I let my waters drag me in deep, then I flicked my tail and gained a powerful burst of speed. The instant I cut through the cool depths, I felt myself slowly begin to regain myself, felt that demonic entity release its grip on me.

What the hells had that vision been? Had that really been a vision of me? In trouble? His green eye had flared, which meant that was a future not yet seen.

I swallowed hard, trembling all over as I thought about my isolation, my fear, and the terror when I'd seen that... that thing that somehow I recognized even though I knew I'd never seen it before.

I swam for several more minutes, breathing in deeply through my gills, purifying my mind and purging myself of the remnants of those emotions. When I finally emerged topside, I flicked my tail and swam for shore. I'd gone several klicks out.

What had that been? What in the devil had I seen?

By the time I was halfway to shore, I felt lethargy start to creep up over me. That vision had wrung me dry. I'd burned through all of the adrenaline and was simply depleted and exhausted. The calming spell long worn off.

Then I spied light, bobbing, dancing, beautiful light, and I gasped.

"Godsdammit, the queen!" I hissed. How the twin hells had I forgotten why we'd come here in the first place?

Forcing my weariness to the back of my mind, I put on a great burst of speed. I could feel Titiana's gaze burning a hole right through me as I jumped clear of the water, vibrating my tail so hard that I dried myself off instantly and reformed myself so that when I landed, I stood on my own two feet.

But changing so swiftly, so quickly, and with all that adrenaline I'd consumed too, I was dizzy. I swayed on my feet. Maddox was instantly by my side, grasping hold of my elbow to steady me.

Titiana had come with only a small contingent of her guardsmen. Only two, but I recognized them both. Cute and childlike, they looked, one with skin as dark as night and the other as golden as the day, both with eerie red eyes and holding onto no weapons—because they *were* the weapons.

The dark one was called Niht and the golden one Dae.

"Queen Titiana," I said quickly, upset by the gravel in my voice.

She narrowed her eyes. The queen was robed in a gown of flowers and thorns. She sat in her bee-led chariot, staring haughtily at me.

"You requested my presence, and then you make me wait." she hissed, "I should kill you where you stand." Her teeny voice trembled with that promised violence.

"I meant no disrespect, Titiana," I whispered, my throat feeling swollen, as if I'd swallowed a stone.

Maddox shook his head. "There are matters of most greatest urgency, fair queen of the winged folk."

The fire that had been licking at the center of her pupils dimmed as she turned her gaze upon Hatter. A small smile curved her lips like a sickle, showcasing the tips of her elegantly pointed fangs.

"Ah yes, ye must be the fabled mad one I've heard so verra much about," she purred heatedly.

I glanced at Hatter from the corner of my eye. He wore a smirk, too, just barely there but enough to turn him from already sexy to something slightly darker and far more appealing.

"In the flesh, beautiful one."

He released his grip on my elbow, and I swayed only a little, feeling far more in control of myself. He crossed one arm over his stomach and gave an elegant bow.

I had to hand it to him. Hatter knew how to play the game—well.

She tittered. "Oh, I do like ye. I've always wondered what it would be like to bed a human." She cocked her head, her dark eyes raking over him boldly before she sighed longingly and said, "Though not quite so human, after all. I sense a god in ye, mad one."

I bit my bottom lip, telling myself not to turn and look at Maddox's reaction. We weren't here so that we could unearth each other's deepest, darkest secrets. We were here for the case and only the case.

Even so, I did look. He still wore his arrogant smirk, but his spine and his shoulders were stiff. He hadn't liked her saying that.

"You can try to figure me out, queen. Many have, though none have succeeded."

I frowned. Was this truth or bluff? What the devil was he talking about?

"Oh, I do love a challenge."

I stepped forward and held up a hand, eager to end whatever nonsense this was. "My most sincere apologies, Queen Titania, for the *unfortunate—*"

Hatter twitched, just barely, his hands clenched by his sides, and I knew that he was thinking the same as I was about my use of that word. I could still hear the ghostly echo of that evil ringing in my ears.

"Delay. I took rather ill of a sudden and needed to heal myself in my waters."

Her eyes cut to mine. She looked me up and down then pursed her lips. "I sense no untruth in your statement. You may continue. But do not ever do it again I am not a dog that can be summoned. Next time, I might not come at all."

I nodded, hearing the threat quite clearly. I needed her enchantments. She did not really need me.

"My *ornë*..." She said the guardian's name in the native tongue of her people. "Told me of your being."

I dipped my head, glad the guardian had mentioned me but bristling all over again when I thought about how she'd planned to send me through fae land with no guide. I hated the fae bastards.

She smirked, and I couldn't help but think she knew exactly what I was thinking.

"What was stolen from you, Titiana? What was taken?"

She stared at me, never blinking, her tiny, beautiful face looking vexed and furious.

"You waited days after I told ye to visit. To go. To see about me people. Why should I give ye anything else?"

I'd known that would come up. I'd been prepared to defend my actions, knowing full well she might still deign to not answer me. I'd kept to my bargain but too late. She could not kill me for breaking an oath, but I'd curried no favor with the queen.

I opened my mouth, but Hatter gently touched the back of my wrist and stepped forward.

"Even in faery, you must know of Grimm's troubles. The syndicate has grown bold. Dangerous."

"The dragon," she whispered, fires licking at the center of her pupils again. "Aye. I ken what's been done to that poor beast."

My ears perked up, detecting a note of sadness in her tone. "Do you know anything about what was done to Whiskers? He will hang without sufficient proof of his innocence."

She laughed, the sound like demonic tinkling bells. "The beast kills children, yet it is not for them that you fight now. I'll grant ye, them Lost Boys were naught more than wildlings. Yet they say it is faeries that be heartless."

I clamped down on my tongue. She was goading me, but I would not take the bait.

"Can you help him, Queen Titiana?" Maddox asked in his deep accent.

She rolled her eyes. "I suppose I could. I saw what was done to the beast. I can prove his words, now that I ken he were acting against his will. But again, why should I help ye?"

"Just for once, for one damn moment could you fecking—" I growled, but again Hatter clamped down on my elbow and this time he squeezed hard, telling me to shut the hells up before I blew it for us both.

Snarling, I turned on my heel and marched back and forth in the sand, temper right at the surface of me. Bloody faes were sometimes impossible to deal with. Everything was a tit-for-tat sort of nonsense with them, and tonight, I was just too damned impatient to play the game.

Her laughter grated on my nerves.

"Titiana. Or could I call you Tati?" Hatter murmured as a lover would, and the queen purred.

I glowered at them both. Bloody hells, we didn't have time to pacify the bitch. We had a syndicate to stop. Something big was coming.

I felt it. I knew it in my bones. I'd been a detective long enough to sense when there'd been a shift in the winds. An uneasy feeling was curling through my body, my bones. Something grave and terrible was headed our way. And very, very soon if we could not—

My eyes almost popped out of my head when I turned and spied Titiana—flower-wreathed head—bent over Hatter's thumb and sucking lustfully on it.

"Godsdammit, Maddox," I muttered under my breath. Giving blood to a fae was a terrible idea. The wee bitch could kill him if she had a mind to.

As if realizing I was spying on them, he glanced over his shoulder at me, a bored expression on his face now that Titiana was occupied, and slowly shook his head.

And I shook mine back. *You know what? Whatever.* If he had a death wish, then who I was to stop him?

I crossed my arms and glowered.

He merely rolled his eyes and turned back around.

Seconds later, she unlatched from his finger. Her mouth was coated in red. She looked like a demonic child with her glowing red eyes.

"Gods above, what power," she whispered. "You have kept to your end. Now I shall keep to mine." She continued to speak with that blood still painting the lower half of her face.

I grimaced.

"A slipper. Cinderella's glass slipper, to be more precise. That's what was stolen from my stronghold."

Niht and Dae sidled in closer toward their queen's side. Then without a bit of warning, they both leaned in and began to lick her clean.

Gods, the fae were nasty lil' bastards.

My stomach rolled.

Titiana laid a hand on the backs of each of them. Judging by the looks of it, I knew they were quite comfortable sharing their queen. Not that I cared, but... I really wished they'd done it someplace else. Not everyone enjoyed blood with their sex.

"A slipper? And this is significant why?" Maddox asked, in full-on detective mode once more.

She snorted. "Gods, are you even of Grimm that I should have to spell this out for you?"

He said nothing, and I cocked my head. Well, that was interesting.

What else was there in the universe but Grimm? There were a hundred realms. Surely, Maddox was of one of them.

"Happily ever after," she snapped. "Whoever possesses the slipper will gain their happily ever after. It's one of our strongest enchantments."

My entire body suddenly tingled with unease, and I stopped thinking about the mysterious origins of my partner.

"Why the hells was something that dangerous not destroyed?" I snapped.

Titiana rolled her eyes like a petulant child. "Because it's mine. And I would kill anyone that dares to steal from me."

"Yet someone did just that," I replied tersely. "Successfully."

She hissed.

Maddox stepped between my line of sight and hers, holding his hands up. "This helps no one!" he thundered, looking between the two of us. "Get yourself together, Detective. Whatever this is, stop it now."

Furious that he would take her side over mine, I very nearly picked up handfuls of sand and tossed it at him. But then that would be proving him right, that I, and not Titiana, was being the petulant crybaby.

Maybe I was. Hells if I knew. But he was my partner, and he should have taken my side.

I knew it sounded silly the second I thought it. I sighed and clenched my hands into fists. It was me. Godsdammit. It was me.

"Sorry," I muttered.

He took a deep breath, looking at me for a moment longer than normal. I shook my head.

"Rest assured, Detectives, that when I find the arsehole responsible for this crime, I will personally be the one to remove its head from its body. No one steals from me. Least of all a thing not even fae at all."

She sounded more upset by that fact than by anything else.

"Word of warning, Mad One." She looked at him. "If they stole the slipper, whatever they have planned... it's big. It's big, and it's nasty. And if they succeed, we're all fecked."

With those words, she, her chariot, and her guards vanished.

Maddox turned and looked at me. "I'm sorry. I... I don't think I handled that we—"

I held up my hand. "I'm a wreck right now, Maddox. The spell is wearing off. Your vision has got me sick, and now I think we might not be in time to stop whatever it is that's coming for us. We've missed something. A clue. Something big. There is no time for this. For bickering. For making up. There is no time for anything right now. We have to stop this. We have to speak with Bo."

He nodded. "Aye. We do."

But he didn't sound glad of it, and honestly, neither was I. I wasn't sure what was coming for us, but in my bones, I knew that if Bo or Ichabod hadn't figured out something new for us, just as Titiana had said, we were all fecked.

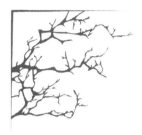

Chapter 15

Detective Elle

THE INSTANT WE ARRIVED back at Grimm headquarters, Bo was waiting for us. Commissioner Draven stood tall and regal behind her, his hands crossed behind his back, aloof and haughty.

"Detectives," Bo said, and I knew, only because I knew her so well, that something was most definitely up, something I wouldn't like—at all.

Her shoulders were tight, her eyes pinched and her lips pursed. She was in a foul mood. And I had no doubt it had everything to do with the male standing behind her.

"Come with us." She crooked her finger.

Hatter and I glanced at one another, wearing identical worried frowns. But we followed like the good sheep we were.

We all walked back to her office, none of us talking or even looking at one another, the tension so thick it was palpable.

"You know, the escort was a little overkill," I said with a high-pitched chuckle, mostly because I wasn't sure what else to say. My nerves were a hot mess inside of me, my ears were ringing, and all the emotions I'd blocked out for hours were starting to come at me with a vengeance.

No one said anything, which only further compounded my anxieties.

By the time we actually made it to her office, I was both relieved and ready to puke.

Bo took a deep breath and pushed the door open.

"Really, all this cloak-and-dagger is unnecess—" I began and instantly stopped the moment my eyes landed on a sight I'd never in a thousand years thought I'd see.

Agent Crowley, dressed in his familiar shades of black, glanced our way for less than a second before turning quickly back to the task at hand, namely, fitting Hook—my Hook—with a wire. The miniature black listening box was taped to the side of Hook's chest. As flat as a paperclip and not much larger, it would be nearly undetectable if someone brushed against him. Because most boxes were now wireless, there weren't any actual wires to speak of, but he would have to wear an auditory chip so that he could hear the directions being given.

I cocked my head, noticing instantly that Crowley and Hook were basically wearing the same clothes—tight-fitting black pants that left very little to the imagination and a long-sleeved black cable-knit shirt that while not skin tight wasn't loose, either. As if aware I was watching him, Crowley smirked.

I shook my head, jaw going just the slightest bit slack as that bad feeling I'd had since getting here began to really erupt into pools of unease. Why was Hook out of the orange jumpsuit? Why was Hook out of his holding cell at all?

Hook's "hand" gleamed silver in the sterile fluorescent lighting of Bo's office. They'd given him back his hook, which told me a lot. Whatever he was dressed for, he was going out. I twirled on Bo, eyebrows lifted, silently urging her to tell me what was happening, immediately.

"Captain?" I asked.

She nodded and looked as if she meant to speak, but Commissioner Draven lifted his hand.

"Detective Arielle Trident, I feel as though I know you personally. I've heard so much about you." He chuckled softly.

He didn't say it in such a way that I took it as a compliment. I lifted my eyebrows, waiting for more, but there was no more.

I crossed my arms, and I felt Maddox looking at us both. I shook my head. The commissioner was an odd man.

There was yet another knock on the door, then Ichabod suddenly popped his head inside. "Boss?" he asked crisply before looking around. Once he saw me, his eyebrows twitched. "Elle? What? Why are you—"

"Come in, Detective Crane," Bo said wearily with a hand gesture. "This concerns all of us. Shut the door behind you."

He did as asked, a worried look on his handsome face as he gave me a quick but more shuttered look. I'd worked with Crane long enough to know when he was hiding something, and he was definitely hiding something.

I thinned my mouth.

"Did you bring it?" Bo directed the question to Ichabod.

"*Mm*," he said with a nod as he walked toward her and made to hand her a vial of sand—not nearly as much as what he had in the ones he'd shown me earlier, though. And this sand was just the slightest bit different from the others. I caught glints of blue whenever the vial would turn and catch the light.

My eyes instantly hooked on his. I frowned. "What is this?"

"It's what I scraped off the sliver of bark you brought me earlier, Detective."

I cocked my head. "Sand? Blue sand at tha—" I gasped, and my gaze shot to his very worried one.

Because I recognized what it was. Sands were as distinctive as fingerprints, I'd always said. And Anahita had always drilled that into me. "*This is from the sky isles. And this is from Hell. But this, dear sister...*" Her voice was a ghostly echo in my ears. "*This blue sand, it's from Nowhere, and gods help us all if it is ever found again...*"

There was no way in the twin hells that was what I thought it was.

Ichabod gave me the merest fraction of a nod, and my heart felt as if it had literally skipped a beat. I clutched at my breast. I felt Maddox's questioning look, but I was frozen, staring at that blue glinting sand.

"I called you in here, Detective Elle," Bo said, voice carrying easily, "because of your powerful affinity to water. I had to verify what Crane had told me he'd seen. And I see that his guess was sadly..." She sighed. "Accurate."

My hands balled into tight fists. Blue sand. Oh gods.

"Will someone please tell me what in the twin hells is going on here?" Hatter all but growled, and I could feel anxious energy coming off him in waves.

"There is only one place in all of the hundred realms where one can find sands of that shade. But... it's impossible to reach." Legend said the bridge to Nowhere had long since been destroyed.

Agent Crowley had sidled over to Bo's side and was reaching out for the vial, as though he meant to snatch it from her hand. But she whipped her hand down by her side and glared at him. He pursed his lips but didn't argue the matter.

"I may not have any say on what's happening here, but this evidence stays with me, Agent," she snapped, showing the fire inside of her that made her such a damn fine captain—the best, in my humble opinion, we'd ever had.

The irritating special agent smirked. "As you wish, Captain Shepherdess."

Draven moved... more like glided... to the center of the room and addressed us all. "The finding of these sands means that no longer is this simply a Grimm PD matter. It is obviously no secret now why Special Agent Crowley is here. With the discovery of these blue sands, we have been required to form an interagency task force."

"What does this mean exactly?" Maddox rumbled softly, standing close to me and as still as a board. He didn't like it. Welcome to the club, because neither did I.

But at least I knew more than Hatter did. I glanced at Hook. He was looking back at me, eyes soft and his long, dark lashes shading his thoughts from me. I shivered and quickly glanced away.

"Agent Crowley, would you care to do the honors?" Draven asked in his silky voice before giving a small but elegant bow.

Crowley wasn't smirking as he customarily did whenever the bastard was around me. Instead, he was completely serious, which gave me a chill down my spine.

It was as bad as things got if Crowley couldn't even find the humor in gaining the upper hand over me.

"It means, Detective," Crowley began in his rough burr, "that I am now in charge of this investigation. For some months now, my department has been sussing out the coordinates of the gang based on where they struck and when.

At first, the pattern was random, seemingly nonsensical. They would go to a museum and leave a fifty-trillion-valued diamond alone but take a grain of eternal rice. Their heists completely baffled us, making it impossible for us to really guess where they'd hit next. Which always placed us one step behind and one second too late. But lately, in the last several months since they began upping the body count, a pattern finally began to emerge. The devil's in the details, as they say. And with the theft of the slipper—"

I jerked, I'd not told anyone yet what the queen had told me. In fact, that was why I'd come back.

Spotting my reaction, Crowley finally smirked, as he was oh so fond of doing.

"Ah, I see you already knew about this, Detectives Elle and Maddox?"

Bo frowned. "You knew this, Elle?"

I nodded. "We only just learned this, not even an hour ago. Might I ask, how in the hells did you know this already? It was like pulling teeth to get the queen to tell us this."

"Impressive." Crowley's stretched grin looked genuine, which I didn't trust at all.

I narrowed my eyes to slits.

"The queen is notorious for keeping tight-lipped. Though she does have a fondness for male flesh," he said then flicked his dark eyes toward Hatter, as if he knew exactly what Maddox had had to do to get the Intel. And it made me wonder if Crowley had done the same. If so, that meant the wee queen had played Hatter and me for fools.

Maddox's jaw was set, and his nostrils were wide. He was not happy, no doubt having come to the same conclusion as I had.

"But no matter. The bureau has our ways too. We learned of the theft early yesterday morning. Then the phone call about the sands, and suddenly, it was all crystal clear. We are dealing with..."

At this, Crowley trailed off, and for once, the smirking bastard wasn't smirking. In fact, he looked sick and not at all happy about what he was about to say.

But he didn't need to say it, because I already knew, just by his look alone. And the blue sands that should never have been.

I rubbed my temples and squeezed my eyes shut. Fear didn't make me weak or pitiful. Fear made me angry. And I felt that sick demon crawling all the way through me. My throat was tight, my skin prickling. I wanted to become that killing monster of the deep, because if I was a killer, then nothing could harm me. Nothing could hurt me, least of all that bitch. A bitch long dead, but even the legacy of what she'd done was enough to make even the most hardened of criminals want to piss themselves.

I shook. "Bonny's trying to resurrect the deepest darkness, isn't she, Agent Crowley?" I asked, my voice surprisingly calm considering I was anything but. "What dumb bastard would do such a thing? What fecking bitch would try to raise something so wholly evil?"

I went still all over, thinking about everything I'd seen, all that I'd learned, and my nails dug like claws into my palms. It all fit. That was the missing piece, why I hadn't been ready to call the case closed as Bo had earlier: the sands; the zombie-like devotion of the Slasher sycophants; spelled grains of golden sand that tied directly to Midas; Lord Humpty's role in all of it; his fleet of ships that somehow mattered, though I couldn't quite yet make the connection; and the ability, the almost witch-like mystique of each and every heist gone off without a hitch, especially the way they'd broken into the fae stronghold. Just as Hook had said, Anne Bonny was a witch, but she wasn't just that. She had to have gotten her hands on some form of arcane knowledge, knowledge that she planned to use to try to resurrect a monster.

"Godsdamnitall!" I hissed. "How did I fecking miss this?" It all seemed so obvious now.

"Elle, talk to me," Maddox whispered heatedly. "What is going on here?"

I whirled on him. I didn't give a damn if I was cutting into Crowley's speech. Maddox was my partner, and he deserved to know the truth—from me.

"She is a legend amongst my people. Something so purely evil that even the children grew up knowing her name."

"Don't say it," Crowley warned.

I snapped at him. "Do you think me a fool? To say her true name is to feed even the spirit of her greater power. We stopped worshipping the sea witch millennia ago, but even so, father destroyed her body and exiled what was left of her to the forgotten realm, one so dead that not even water can exist, only the sands of it. The endless grains of blue. There mere fact that Bonny's gotten her hands on those blue grains means she's been there once before already. And the resurrection clearly didn't work then. But if she's going back with the slipper, then it means she thinks the resurrection could work now. We have to stop this. Right now!"

Maddox's nostrils flared, and his blue and green eyes were fixed on my face. Unspoken between us was a thought—the vision I'd shared with him on his arm, the lashing, whipping, and torrential rains and the endless expanse of gray waters and black clouds churning angrily with thunder and lightning. A water realm full of fury and rage. And I'd been trapped in it. But Nowhere wasn't that. Nowhere was nothing but blue sands and not much else.

So it couldn't be Nowhere. Not to mention that last I'd heard, the bridge to Nowhere was shattered, meaning travel to that forgotten realm was impossible, even for my father.

Right?

I grabbed my stomach and rubbed at it with nerve stretched fingers, suddenly feeling queasy. I shuddered. I'd never been to the forgotten realm. No one had, save my father. But every naiad, huldra, mermaid, siren, selkie, and every other genus of water elemental knew of its dark legend. There'd been no sand in Hatter's vision, only the water—the endless stretch of water for as far as the eye could see. So was I really thinking of the same thing? Or was that as yet a different clue to something we'd not yet learned?

Agent Crowley licked his front teeth, now far sharper than they'd been before. "This will not be easy, and in order to slip in, we must keep our numbers small," he said.

"It's impossible!" I declared. "Nowhere is impossible to reach."

"Yet you see the sand!" he snapped, gesturing at the captain with a free hand, glowering with red glowing eyes at me.

"No!" Then softer, I said, "No."

Crowley's jaw worked from side to side. His look was hard but now no longer so heated. "We have to ascertain whether Nowhere is now a threat, siren. You know we do. Those sands only come from there."

I squeezed my eyes shut, no longer able to hold his concentrated stare. How was it even remotely possible? It wasn't. Yet... Hook was alive. And that was an impossibility too.

I opened my eyes and stared at my silent ex-lover. "Is this possible? Do you know anything?" I whispered. "Anything at all?"

For a second, it was as if nothing else existed but us. His dark eyes searched my face, and in them I read only honesty as he said, "I heard whisperings. Mutterings. It was what I'd tried to warn you of earlier, lass. Bonny wants power, and the only way to gain it is to bring the monster back. She claims that by raising it, she can control it and, by so doing, will control all of the hundred realms."

I trembled and wrapped my arms around myself. How did he know all this? How could we afford to trust him? Yet how could we afford not to?

Crowley grunted. "There's no time to waste. We leave as soon as the bureau gives the all clear."

"We?" I asked, my voice cracking a little. But deep down, I already knew.

"We. Me," he said and pointed at his chest, "Hook, because he's involved in all of this still, and now... you." He pointed at me. "Detective Arielle. Daughter of a king and princess of the deep."

The fact that he'd so formally said my title let me know just how deep in shite we really were.

I swallowed hard.

Maddox grunted. "No way. No way in hells."

I shook my head. "Stop, Maddox. You know I don't—"

His voice sounded more like a beast when he said, "This isn't happening. I'm coming too. I don't know what the hells you're planning, Crowley, but you're not getting your hands on—"

"Detective Maddox!" Captain Bo snapped, and we all jumped at the sudden authority in her voice.

Maddox was breathing like a bellows, looking furious, and I knew why. Crowley was no fan of mine. In fact, everyone here knew of his deep-seated hatred and prejudice toward me. But I couldn't shirk my duties.

"Do not forget your place," the captain snapped. "You're not lovers. Family. Or otherwise. You are a detective of Grimm PD, and you will do *exactly* as told!"

Maddox's jaw clamped shut, and his throat moved with his hard swallows. He was pissed. In fact, Maddox was starting to burn. I could feel the heat of him singeing the fine hairs on my arms. His flames were invisible, but they were there.

My pulse skittered in my veins.

I had to help calm him somehow. I didn't know how much Bo or even Draven knew of Hatter's true identity. I wasn't even sure what he was, and though I would really, really like to know it someday, this wasn't how it needed to be found out.

"May I speak with my partner?" I chimed in quickly, seeing Hatter start to tremble with the need to explode with his power. "Alone."

Bo lifted an eyebrow, but Draven flicked his fingers. "Go. Five minutes. Prepare as you must. You will all leave soon. Crowley will fill you in on the rest once you do."

"Come with me," I snapped, latching onto Hatter's hand and yanking him behind me. Steam curled between our palms as his invisible heat lapped at the water-rich flesh of my body.

I felt Hook and Crowley's eyes follow me out the door, and to a lesser extent, even Ichabod's.

I marched us into the blessedly empty filing office across the hall and closed and locked the door behind me. Then I snapped my fingers and shot a jet of water at the hidden cameras around the room.

And only once I was sure no one would hear or see us, I whispered, "Go."

Maddox said nothing, but he jerked violently and then flamed on. He burned like the golden god that I suspected he truly was.

"Godsdammit it, Elle!" he snapped, still shaking powerfully, not able to stomp and roar and destroy, as I was sure he would wish to.

I shook my head, leaning against the door, knowing my slight weight wouldn't hold anyone out for long but also knowing that he needed to release it before he could go back out there.

He burned like a majestic phoenix, flames so hot that I felt my hair go limp. But I watched him, heart in my throat, wishing I could touch him, hold him.

Now that I was leaving, I was coming to the very startling realization that I didn't want to go, not without getting some things off my chest first.

I let him burn for just a little longer before I finally whispered, "Look at me, Maddox."

His eyes blazed like jewels when he did, but his fire wasn't a nova of pure energy anymore. It was simply warm, comforting.

"I didn't want to speak of Hook for so many reasons. But the biggest and the most important one was because of you. Because of how I felt for you."

His fires died out completely, and he looked broken. The whites of his eyes were red and his skin slightly more golden, as though he'd been out in the sun all day.

"What?" he asked softly. "What are you doing, Elle?"

I shrugged. "Hells if I know. I just need to say it. I need to—"

"Don't," he said softly but with conviction. "Don't say it."

"But—"

He shook his head. "Tell me when you come back. Don't say this now. Don't say this, because it means you don't expect to make it back, and gods-damnit, Elle, if you don't come back to me, I'll"—

I didn't let him finish speaking. I rushed at him. He looked startled when I placed my hands on his chest and leaned up on tiptoe. I kissed him, as if it were the first and the last time. Because I didn't know that it wasn't. And because if it was, I didn't want him living with the same regrets I'd had with Hook.

Hook—the man of my heart, my dreams, my desire, everything. The man I kept pretending wasn't there anymore. The man I kept shoving away. Because the loss of him had very nearly killed me the first time. I squeezed my eyes shut. It wasn't time to think of him. Not even now.

Definitely not now.

I dug my fingers through Maddox's hair and hung on for dear life. He wrapped his arms around my waist, squeezing me so tight that I was sure if will alone could have kept me with him, I'd never have left him. He moaned, and so did I. Everything we'd kept bottled up, it was pouring out of us. But there was no more time.

I felt the ticking of the clock and knew we had seconds before they came looking for us again. I trembled all over, clinging to him with my fingers.

I opened my mouth, but he placed a finger over it and shook his head. His face looked haunted.

I palmed the corner of his cheek, letting my finger trace along the outer edge of his full mouth, heart still hammering wildly in my chest.

"Forewarned is forearmed. I saw it, too, Hatter. And if I saw it, then maybe I can somehow not suffer the fate your vision has shown us."

He trembled, and I patted his chest.

He groaned loudly and murmured, "If something happens, I won't stop looking for you. You have my word." He placed his hand over mine and put them upon his heavily beating dual-hearted chest.

I nodded, and he gently placed a finger beneath my chin and tipped it up.

With one last hungry moan, he stole my mouth for his. I wanted to live in this moment with him, just us together, and never have to leave it.

There was a knock at the door, and we broke apart guiltily. I shivered violently, still tasting him on my tongue.

"Detectives, your five minutes are up. It's time to go. Now," Crowley growled, and I nodded.

"It's time to go," I said softly, almost like a whisper.

He nodded back at me. "Yes, Detective. It is. Just make sure you come back."

I grinned, but I knew the smile didn't reach my eyes. "Of course."

I turned on my heel, still trembling all over. But the tremors were small, unnoticeable to all, and only felt by me. When I opened the door, there were Crowley and Hook. Both of them looked at us, Crowley with suspicion and Hook with pain.

He knew. And somehow, that made him so much more real to me.

With a careless toss of my hair over my shoulder, I lightly laughed. "Let's go catch a villain, boys."

It was so much easier for me to slip into a role, to pretend to be someone I wasn't. But the truth was, I was barely keeping myself together. One strong wind, and I'd snap.

Hook's arm brushed mine, and I knew it had been intentional. I also knew that he knew I wasn't well. At all. But he said nothing about it, and I said nothing, either.

Sometimes it was just easier to ignore the truth. I felt Hatter's stare like a brand on my back as I followed Crowley out the door, but I didn't look back. Because I couldn't.

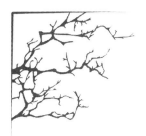

Chapter 16

Detective Elle

I HAD NO IDEA HOW IT had happened, but somehow I was standing on the stern of a large wooden ship, facing the endless expanse of the waters as the sun set slowly before us, headed toward only the gods knew where and the gods knew what.

If the bridge wasn't fixed, we might very well sail off the very edge of the universe and be forever trapped in a time loop. I didn't know if that was even possible, but I didn't know that it wasn't. And if the bridge was fixed, if somehow it was possible to reach Nowhere, that might actually be even worse.

Tapping my fingers on the wooden railing, I gazed deep into the waters. We'd acquired use of an enchanted ship from the bureau. The way it cleanly cut through the waters, moving at speeds not even I could keep up with, it was a technological marvel. But even so, the thrill of wanting to shed my skin and race it was a budding obsession.

Once upon a time, I'd simply been a girl, a princess of the deep, free to roam and frolic and do whatever the hells I wanted because I desired to do it. When had I become this person? Uptight? Serious? Weighted down by the cares of the world?

I'd once laughed, swum, drunk, and sexed whatever the hells I wanted when I wanted. Now all there was for me was an endless tidal wave of case after case, bad guy after bad guy. And somewhere on the damn ship was Hook, my Hook, and it was impossible to ignore it or forget it.

"Fecking hells," I snapped, tapping my toe on the deck as I wished for the millionth time that I could just jump in and never come back.

"Don't even think about jumping in, fish. All I need is one reason to slap my cuffs on you, and you'd better fucking believe I'll do it too."

I turned at the sound of Crowley's gruff words. Crowley was a wolf shifter, meaning he was stealthy and silent when he wished to be. But considering we were the only three on board, I wasn't exactly surprised to find my solitude had been breached.

Glancing at him, I noted the surprisingly not unpleasant musk of his cologne—woodsy and piney—and the way his thick, dark hair ruffled in the strong breeze. I lifted an eyebrow as he slid off his ever-present mirrored sunglasses.

His irises were a strange hue, sometimes bright green, like Hatter's "future" eye, yet when he turned, I'd also catch a glint of deep and bloody red, not unlike a feline's or a canine's when the light would catch their eyes just right.

I wondered if that was why he always wore his glasses, because of how unnervingly unhuman he looked when they were off. But Grimm was full of unhumans like us, so I doubted that was it, either.

The truth was, though, I knew next to nothing about who Crowley was, other than a constant thorn in my flesh. Who he was, what he did for fun... not a clue. Eat children, I'd imagine. He was such a fecking bastard most of the time that in all honesty, I didn't give a rat's arse one way or the other. But we were trapped together for the foreseeable future, and it was either talk to him or keep thinking about Hook.

I sighed, staring back at the waters. We were getting set to enter the golden triangle, an invisible spot on the geographical map of Grimm's coastal waters where the transdimensional portal for water travel was at its strongest peak. The circumference of it wasn't actually all that large, but the convergence of earth, water, and wind magick was greatest at the very center of it. It was how boats with special access to other dimensions could travel from one realm to the other.

I didn't have to see the coordinates Crowley had inputted to know—my affinity to water made it obvious to me.

The sun had very nearly set. Nothing but a blaze of orange and purple hues lit up the skies. The waters were a deep blue, almost black color. Already, I could see the pinpricks of starlight.

At no point in my life did I ever imagine I'd find myself on a ship to Nowhere, literally, with only Hook and Crowley for company. Sighing, I shook my head slowly. I felt so fecking off, and I couldn't understand why. Maybe it was all that damn coffee with its potent magick shots, which had worn off and was forcing me to feel ten times what I had previous to ingesting the damned spells. I tapped my fingers on the banister, feeling like a junkie desperate for her next hit.

I just wasn't in the mood to verbally spar with the bastard. I didn't want to take Crowley's baiting. I didn't want to fight. All I felt was a giant ball of unease. And it was destroying me like a cancer from the inside out.

Crowley frowned, and from the corner of my eye, I caught him move just slightly closer to the railing, filling my lungs with the not wholly unpleasant scent of his body.

"What's the fucking matter with you, Arielle?" he asked gruffly, sounding a little put out, as though he wasn't even sure why he was asking me that, like the very thought of it was shocking to him.

I looked at him side-eyed. "Are you really doing this?"

He snorted and shrugged, looking put out and as confused as hells. "Fuck if I know."

He sighed deeply, and I heard the exhaustion in his voice, the strain of long days and nights finally starting to catch up to him, weighing him down. I felt his look burn into my profile.

He stood silently for a while until he softly said, "But usually when I taunt you, you don't roll over like a little bitch and let me keep doing it."

He didn't ask me again what was the matter, but I heard the question threaded beneath the words.

I snorted, feeling the slightest bit of annoyance but not enough to bother working up to any kind of true anger. So I shrugged instead. "How sure are we really that a mere slipper can actually help her raise this evil? Feels to me like there should be more, like we're maybe missing something, right?"

He looked startled by my questions, as if he'd not expected them. And I was surprised that he no longer taunted me but rather gave me an intelligent and thoughtful response.

"The Slashers, we now know, hid their whereabouts by not doing as we expected. Their home base was never above the clouds, as you'd imagine a group of flying shifters would have it."

He was still looking at me as if I surprised him, but I was surprised that he was actually not giving me shite for once. Crowley was actually treating me like an equal.

Somewhere, pigs were flying.

"Instead," he said in a thick, gravelly drawl, "they made the waters their home. It's why they eluded us for so long. Everything that we expected they should do, everything history has told us should happen, none of it did." He slapped his palm on the railing, obviously agitated. "The damn birds didn't fly, save for when on the job. The rest of the time, they'd learned to adapt to a new way of being. Fucking smart, that's what they were."

"I rather think," I said as I glanced straight ahead at a world more purple than orange, "that had they never gotten too big for their britches, we might never have stopped them. Black Angus was a clever bastard."

Crowley snorted then chuckled softly. "That, he was. A fucking thief. But honorable in his own warped way."

I grinned. "Hindsight being what it is, I'd have to agree. He was a fecking thief but not dangerous. No one died under his watch. But this shite—"

"It's fucking dangerous is what it is," he snapped. His eyes gleamed, switching between green and red before settling back to their soft-green shade.

Suddenly, I had a thought. A long shot, but it could fit. "You know, I keep thinking about Lord Humpty. Why he was aiding the syndicate. They had something on him, right? But what? He owned a fleet of vessels. Nothing inherently illegal about that. What is his role in all of this? What was Midas's, at that? Just to get me to the ball?"

Crowley frowned, looking a touch lost, and for once, I wanted to smirk.

"Oh, I see Bo didn't tell you that part, did she?"

His eyes narrowed to slits. "Got something to share, fish?"

I snorted and turned, leaning casually against the banister with my elbows. "I wasn't with my informant the night of Midas's gala. I was there. At the damned ball. At his behest. Why? Because he got a note from Lord Humpty, all but telling him to invite me there."

"Why?"

I wasn't sure whether he was wondering why I'd been invited or why Bo hadn't told him, but I shrugged. "Hook came for me, Crowley. That's what he said. They were there not there for the jewels, but for me."

"And you believe him?"

I rolled my wrist. "I don't know. Makes as much sense as anything else, I suppose."

He licked his front teeth. "That is interesting. And does suddenly make me wonder whether you should have stayed back in Grimm."

"Hook's not going to be an—"

"I'm not speaking of Hook. He's been wiped of the trace on him. He's whatever the hells he was before." He gestured dismissively. "But this is Intel I damn well should have been told first."

He glared at me, as though it were me that had kept it hidden from him. Which just pissed me the hells off.

"Excuse me, but if I were trying to hide that from you, what possible reason would I have had for revealing it now?"

He opened his mouth and held a finger just beneath my nose, his big body practically vibrating with fury. But then he quickly deflated, and he shoved his fingers through his hair. "I'm not happy that you're here. In fact, I'm not even sure why we're talking, you and me. You piss me off more than anyone I've ever known before, *princess*," he snapped.

I was pretty sure that in his own warped and roundabout way, that had actually been an apology. I lifted an eyebrow. "Okay then. Got that out of your system?"

He grunted then heaved a long-suffering breath. "I think Lord Humpty's role in this was purely wrong place, wrong time. He was a weak, pathetic male. Easily blackmailed."

"You knew him?"

"I know the type," he said with a roll of his lips as though he were disgusted. "They got dirt on him, clearly."

"What?"

He blinked. "Does it matter? He was a filthy elitist who would die if anyone knew the really dirty, dark truths of him. He liked to fuck pigs when no one was looking. Hells, I don't know."

I couldn't help it. I chuckled a little. Which set off Crowley, who made a weird noise I would swear was actually amusement. But then he was back to looking stern and mean and grumpy all over again. The man was entirely confusing to me.

"Good guess, I suppose. So you think he got found out and decided better to work for them than to not?"

"That's generally how these things go," he said, sounding bored. And he was right. Occam's razor said the simplest theory was usually the correct one.

"Okay, so he gets in a pinch, and his lover, Midas, has to bail him out by turning sand to gold?"

Crowley sniffed. "Guess it's my turn to enlighten you, fish face, but gold is one of the best conductors for magick. Especially when you don't have a witch fully in control of her spells to create a refined and elegant incantation."

I hated to admit that I didn't know that, especially to him, but... "Hells."

He chuckled.

"Arrogant bastard," I said but not spitefully.

At first he looked unsure about how he should take that, but his shoulders relaxed, and he moved in closer toward the railing.

"That accounts for the gold grains, I guess. And Bonny, obviously dabbling in some form of elementary witchcraft."

"Strong enough to create a gang of loyal zombies. I'd say the girl is far from mere elementary."

"Touché." I sighed. "So they, what? Take one of Humpty's vessels, make it their own? Sail the high seas. Going unnoticed for decades. The equation was obviously working. And well. Why escalate things? Why now? What's changed?"

"Greed," Crowley guessed. "That ever-present obsession with humans for more."

My eyebrows gathered. "Not just humans, Crowley."

"Fine. The less enlightened."

I snorted. "So wolves aren't greedy? Is that what you're claiming?"

"Can't speak for all of them, but I know when I've had enough."

"Fine. Say, for argument's sake, it is just greed. Human weakness. Why the witch? Why try to resurrect that thing?"

He pinned me with a sharp and very intelligent gaze, leaving me feeling odd. I almost felt as if I were seeing Crowley for the first time in some ways.

"Have you considered, for one second, that maybe she's not trying to resurrect the witch?"

I chuckled. "Well, there is obviously no reason to go to Nowhere otherwise."

He shook his head, looking at me blankly for a long enough time that I started to wonder if I was trapped in some sort of nightmare and I wasn't even there at all, but asleep, passed out somewhere after all.

"I would think you were trying to make a fool of me, but I can't scent any deceit in you right now, and it's messing with my fucking head, fish. How can you be of Undine and not know this?"

"What?" I snapped, shoving off the railing. "What the hells are you getting at, Crow—"

"Time, Arielle!" He rolled his wrists, giving me a "Now do you get it?" look.

But I totally didn't. Stiffening my neck, I widened my eyes and said, "Yeah? So?"

"Fucking hells," he growled. "Your daddy didn't just dump the shade of the wicked in there for no reason."

"She was trying to take over his realm. Yes, that, I know. Why didn't you just say so?"

"Arielle," he snapped, sounding impatient, "no, it was so much more than that. The witch swallowed a sliver of eternity. Trapped inside of her incorporeal form is literally time. It's why when the great culling of dark mages occurred, she wasn't killed. Because to do so would literally unravel time itself. Any place—and not just place, but to be more precise, any moment in history—will be Bonny's to command if she's somehow figured out a way to snatch time from the witch. Now do you get it?"

I looked at him, just looked at him, feeling nothing but a strange, twisting darkness rolling through me. That same slinking energy I'd felt earlier but stronger, brighter. And for just a second, I caught a glimpse of colors. Bright flashes of it. None of it made sense. But I was hearing laughter, bone-chilling and demonic laughter, echoing all around me.

"Hey," he said and grabbed my elbow. "You still there?"

And I jerked, flinching so violently I nearly fell flat on my arse. "What?" I blinked, the image scattering as quickly as it had come on. My head felt suddenly thick and full with fuzz. I rubbed at my now pounding temple. "What?" I said again, softer.

He had his head cocked and was looking at me as if he wasn't sure he could trust what he was seeing. "Arielle, are you—what the fuck was that?" he finished, sounding hard and gruff again, but beneath it, I was sure there was a thread of worry there too.

I shook my head, not even sure myself. "I. *Mm.*" I patted my dress, which had definitely seen better days. "I think I'm tired, Agent Crowley. This case and... other things..." I shivered. "Have been keeping me up at night. I'm..." I frowned. "I'm sorry."

He looked confused and tired himself. And he was staring at me as he had been earlier, as if he was no longer so sure about me. "I know the feeling. This case has been fucking hells."

"Aye," I agreed with a nod as we settled into a not so uncomfortable silence. I watched the wake of the ship, becoming mesmerized by it, trying not to think about what had just happened.

I'd been doing a lot of that lately, trying not to think—about anything. Made me wonder if maybe my problem was that I needed to stop not thinking and start thinking. I sighed.

"The... the girl," he said softly into the lulling quiet between us.

I looked at him, trying to figure out what he was saying. He shuddered, and I heard the demons he normally kept leashed trying to come out of him. All cops had our demons. It was just that most times, we were damned good at keeping them our dirty little secrets.

"So broken." His voice broke.

That was when I realized he wasn't talking about Anne Bonny, not with the pain he wasn't even bothering to hide. I turned more fully toward him, taken aback by the sudden softness he was openly exhibiting. Since when did Crowley act like that? With me? He was a hard-ass, grade A prick.

The girl.

Suddenly, it all clicked in my head. "You were there, at that scene, weren't you? You saw Holly Th—"

He snarled, chest vibrating with a harsh lupine growl.

I held up my hands, trusting that an agent of the law wouldn't commit cold-blooded homicide, but then again, we were all alone in the middle of vast waters with no witnesses around—none that would be considered trustworthy in a court of law, anyway. And it was a well-known fact that I was

Crowley's least favorite person in all the realms. Who'd know? It would be the perfect crime, really.

I narrowed my eyes, and he shoved off the railing, clenching and unclenching his fists.

Silence stretched uncomfortably between us as he took deep and even breaths. Finally, with a hard crack of his neck, he seemed to get himself together.

"Are you... o-okay?" I asked, not even sure what to say to him. I'd never dreamed I'd see any kind of actual whatever that was from someone like him in my life.

"We're not friends," he snarled.

I shrugged. "I never claimed to be," I said.

His nostrils flared, and I was struck all over again by the surreal nature of our situation. I hated him. He hated me. So how the hells had we wound up there?

Once more, he grabbed hold of the railing. "Sometimes I can't sleep, thinking about what happened to that poor girl. I don't give two shits what you think about me, fish, but you should know I have a line. I don't keep with murdering children. And there's been too damn much of that lately."

"Lost Boys aren't really children. They only look like it. But I'm not trying to minimize what happened to them," I said quickly, realizing how cold I'd just sounded.

Crowley snarled.

"Fuck me." He rolled his eyes. "Stop, okay? Just stop. I don't need you to try to make me feel better. Hells, I don't even know why I'm telling you this. Any of this. Godsdamnit it."

"Bloody hells," I snapped, "riding the crimson wave tonight or what? Don't forget you walked over to me. You want to stop talking, fine. Good. Go. I didn't ask you to—"

At first, he looked seriously pissed. But as I kept talking, his face began to slowly change, from severe and feral to humored, and finally, he chuckled.

"Shit, I'm riding the crimson wave? Okay. Yeah, good one, fish." He snorted but couldn't seem to stop chuckling, and watching him lose his usual sharply controlled demeanor like that was startling to say the least.

"Have you lost your damned mind tonight?" I asked, thoroughly confused by him.

"Shit," he said on a sigh as he finally stopped laughing. "Trapped on a ship to Nowhere with my least favorite people in the world. I'm in a fucking nightmare."

"Pretty much my idea of the worst first date ever," I said, chuckling softly.

At first, he grunted, then he began to chuckle again. "Don't you wish, little siren. Don't you just fucking wish."

"Not really," I said but couldn't help but grin. Because what the hells—we must have sailed through to some alternate dimension where Crowley wasn't an uptight arsehole but a somewhat decent unhuman being.

Rolling his eyes, he stared out at the horizon, and I followed suit just a few seconds later, and somehow the silence between us no longer felt so weird.

"Why the hells are we riding toward what is likely to be our certain doom again?"

He snorted. "You've got a point, dammit. Which is annoying as all fuck." He glanced at me, a strange look upon his handsome face, as though he couldn't quite figure out why we were still even talking. He gave his head a slight shake. "But you're not entirely right, either. Anne's the reason why we can finally put a stop to the syndicate."

"You really think so? After ten years of dealing with this gang, you really think this could be the end of it?"

"Don't you?" he asked, sounding confused. "For once, we might just actually be a step ahead."

I licked my front teeth. "Seems too easy. I dunno. All of this." I shook my head. "I just... I don't... know." I frowned, not even able to coherently put my thoughts and feelings into any semblance of order. I blew out a harsh breath and gave a self-effacing laugh. "I just fecking need sleep. Why do you always have such a hate on for me?" I asked, and I froze, because I'd not expected to ask him that, but we'd actually been civil to each other for longer than a minute, and I was sleep deprived and so damned confused and it just sort of came spewing out of me. "Wait, I don't—"

The strange and surprisingly easy banter between us suddenly felt icy and tense again, just as it usually was with us. His nostrils flared, and his green eyes suddenly seemed to glow that shade of bright, eerie red that made my blood run cold.

"I hate you because I know who you are. I chased you. Me"—he pointed at his chest—"for three years. Hunting you down like the fucking spoiled fish you were. Finding one nasty mess after another left in your wake. Fucking monster," he spat.

I winced. Because he was right. I had done that. My past was dark. I could not deny it. So I wouldn't even bother trying.

"Then I catch you. I fucking bag the biggest bad in the hundred realms. I did it. Me. Then Daddy Dearest," he growled, "with all his pomp and swagger and pull, somehow gets you off the hook, and now, not only are you free, but you're a fucking lawman to boot. It's insulting. Makes me sick. Makes me want to break you. Because you know what, Arielle?" He leaned in, a deep growl reverberating from his chest and making mine tremble. "Fish don't change their scales. Deep inside of you, that she-bitch still lives. You're not changed from that same monster I tracked all over the fucking realms. That's you. And that will always be you. And I'm gonna be right there, ready to take you down, the day she comes back out. That's why I ride shotgun on you, why I'm always there, always foiling whatever the hells you've got up your sleeve. Because soulless monsters like you, they don't change. Ever."

With those words, he pulled back, but his eyes gleamed like a wolf's in midnight, and his skin looked darker. I could see his fur just below the surface ready to break free.

I swallowed hard, feeling surprisingly raw by his words. He'd picked at a very deep and secret fear of mine, that inside of me where there was nothing but shadows and darkness, my evil still lived, still breathed, just waiting on me to call it back out again. "My father had nothing to do with that. And if you think he did, then you're an even greater fool than I thought."

Standing upright, he laughed loudly and heartily, as though greatly amused. Crowley had been my greatest adversary since I'd joined the ranks of Grimm PD. Always there, always giving me the sense that he wasn't just waiting but actively attempting to prove to the world that a leopard was incapable of changing its spots, making my life absolute hells as he always moved against me to impede my cases and my progress. And deep down, I'd always known that was why. But hearing him say it somehow felt like a relief, as if I wasn't a conspiracy-theory nut job. He was wrong, though. What he thought he knew, he was dead wrong. And I could correct him—hells, I could even prove it to him—but what was the godsdammed point? Even with the proof staring him right in the face, I doubted that man would ever become my ally. His obsession with bringing me down was as strong—possibly even more so—as it had ever been in the beginning.

"If you think," he hissed, now all serious, his starkly handsome features looking twisted with barely checked anger, "that your father wasn't behind it, then it's you that's the fool, not me. Wake up, princess."

He tapped me on the forehead with his finger, and I snapped, swatting at his hand angrily, but he'd already pulled it back to his side.

"I will always have my eye on you, Princess Arielle. And someday, you will be in cuffs. I vow it."

With those last words he turned on his heel and walked angrily off, fading into the deep shadows of the night.

There was a roaring of water off in the distance. The golden triangle. We were close. Soon, we would be sailing through the deep, defying the conventions of science and order as we headed toward a destiny that was increasingly making me queasy.

I should turn in. It would take us several hours at least to get there. Nowhere was exactly where the name implied, literally nowhere. An island unto itself. So far removed from the realms of Grimm, it was almost an afterthought. I could finally get the sleep my body so desperately craved and needed.

But now that I had the time to do it, I couldn't turn my fecking brain off. All I could think about was the damned case and how strange and weird it all was: Lord Humpty's broken body; the stolen slipper; the senseless deaths; the possibility that the sea witch might actually come back in some way, shape, or form; and Hook.

Where was he? What was he doing? Why was he even a part of all of it? I'd watched him fade to sea foam. Why bring him back? Why him? Of all the dead that could have been resurrected, why him?

I smelled darkness, and my body grew tense. I gripped the railing so hard that I felt the groan of its wood beneath my fingers.

"What are y—"

"Don't turn around, I... I just need you to listen to me, Arielle."

I shivered, hearing the delicious burr of Hook's rum-soaked voice in the darkness. I closed my eyes, trembling all over as I felt the blanket of his heat press up against my flesh.

"What are you doing here, Hook? You should be below deck. You should—"

"Crowley released me," he said slowly.

I sucked in a sharp breath. "What? But he... he can't do that."

Hook's rumble of laughter was so familiar and titillating that I felt my nipples grow hard and my thighs weak. I shuddered.

"We're out here in the middle of nowhere, Ellie. Who could stop him?"

I groaned. Hearing the sound of his pet name for me on his tongue was bringing it all back, the highs and the lows of our relationship. What Hook and I had, it had been so damned forbidden, and I'd known it.

Sirens never mated with humans. Not ever. It was my father's one sacred law, never to be broken, not even by his own flesh and blood. To do so would incur his everlasting wrath and swift and brutal punishment. My sisters had been smart enough to never fall for a human, but I'd never had enough sense in my head to keep away from danger. Somehow, I always seemed to run headlong into it.

"What are... what are you doing here?" I whispered.

"You don't trust me anymore?" he asked silkily, softly.

I clutched at my lower stomach. For days, I'd been doing everything I could to ignore the giant elephant in the room, keeping busy, running from one realm to another, drinking coffees so heavily spelled to make me numb, all so that I could pretend this man was not real, not here, not a ghost sent to haunt me again and again and again.

Heat burned my eyes, and my throat was clogged and thick with a giant lump that no amount of swallowing seemed to get rid of. "No, I don't trust you. I don't know you."

"But you do, Arielle. You do know me."

I growled, unable to keep from looking at him another second.

The tiny scar above his cupid's bow that I used to kiss with wild abandon whenever I could. The ever-present dusting of a black beard that shaded the sharply cut lines of his bold square jaw that I used to always touch whenever

I wanted to. The intensity in his dark-brown eyes, which only looked at me the way they looked at me now.

A sound tore from my lips, came crashing out of me, mortifying but also brutally honest.

He shivered, dark eyes growing deep with shadow.

"Am I so off putting to you now, lass? Is that what this is?"

Looking at him hurt so damn badly. Peering into his eyes felt a lot like slipping deep into his soul all over again and giving him access to mine. Once, it had felt honest and real between us, but now... it fecking hurt like hells. So I cast my eyes down at his booted feet and shook my head.

"Ellie, gods," he murmured. "We canna pretend we don't know one another. Not after everything we've been through together."

My head snapped up at that, and I didn't know what happened, but suddenly, I was the one unleashing the demons inside of me. Tears, thick and blinding, came pouring out of me.

"I left you! Don't you fecking get it? To look at you physically hurts me. To see you, it makes me remember. Remember everything. How it felt to be with you, how it felt to be touched by you. Gods above, I can't do this. I can't—"

I turned on my heel, desperate to get away, desperate to find my room. He gave chase, and if I'd really wanted to, I could have made him leave me alone. I could have blasted him with water, shoved him into the oceans below us. I could have gotten away, but I didn't stop him.

Instead, I ran and listened with all my heart and soul as he ran just behind me. When I opened my door and slipped through, I didn't close it behind me.

It softly shut with a *snick* just a second later, and there he was, breathing heavily, sharing my oxygen, in my dark, cramped quarters, with only low dancing fairy light hovering above us, creating deep hollows and shadows in his face, making him look like the devil come to snatch my soul, and my body thrummed with power and energy.

His dark eyes roved up and down my trembling body. "I missed you, Ellie, every second of every day, every minute I was forced to breathe and you weren't there with me. Deep in my soul, I could never forget you."

I shoved my hand into my mouth, biting down on the tip of my pinky finger until it burned with a red-hot flash of pain as my fang pierced through and a drop of my liquid essence sizzled upon my tongue.

"I still love you, lass," he murmured tenderly with that wonderful dark burr of his that never failed to make me weak in the knees.

He started walking toward me, but I held up my hand.

"Stop."

My command was weak, but he did stop.

I shook my head. "Why are you doing this? You need to go."

He flinched as though I'd physically slapped him, but my words came out pinched and tight. I didn't mean it. I also knew that whatever this was, it was a bad idea. A very bad idea.

"If that's what you really want, then I'll go, Ellie. But if you think you don't know me, then you're only lying to yourself."

Latching onto my anger was as easy as breathing, and since that was all I had right now, that was what I did. "You died! I saw his lightning tear through your side."

He flinched. "Aye, it tore right through me, split me right down the middle, lifted my soul from my body, and I gasped in your arms, silently roaring at you that I loved you, that I would find my way back to you, that I'd promised you fecking forever and godsdamnit it, I would do it, some way, somehow. That's why I think Anne could bring me back—because I was willing. I wanted this, Ellie. I wanted you, one last time."

Words that should have made me glad didn't. They made me sick, angry, violent. My skin prickled. Deadly music was trapped in my throat.

"That's not possible!" I didn't know how I was suddenly beside him, with my hands on his chest and shoving him back hard. He fell onto the edge of the bed, not fighting me at all, just staring at me with those eyes, those bloody eyes that made me feel as if I'd just been split open.

Tears slid silently down his cheeks. But his bright gaze was unwavering as he said, "I think I loved you from the moment I spied you feasting on the soul of a dead man laid out before you. But I knew I did the night of your awakening. That first night when you first saw me and said, 'Hello—'"

"'Pirate,'" I whispered along with him. I shuddered. I'd never told anyone how Hook had first seen me. Only he could have known that.

Sickness spread through my stomach, and I pressed a fist against it, moaning from deep inside my chest. "I said goodbye. We said goodbye. You can't come back. You can't. Anne should never have done this thing to you. You've been brought back by dark means, Hook. You... you must return."

Pain glittered brightly in his eyes, but he didn't fight me. My words were true. Bringing back the dead was a power that few possessed. If not done right, if every part of the spell wasn't spoken correctly, there were always consequences to be had. Because where souls came from, it was darkness. Void. Empty. And if not pulled back by a true and mighty power, the dead always brought that darkness back with them.

But he looked at me like my Hook. He spoke to me like my Hook. I shook as I fought the tears fighting inside of me for release. "The worst days of my life are the ones I've been forced to live without you," I confessed, hating myself the moment I did it.

But like a dam on the verge of bursting, I could no longer contain my pain. Hook's jaw clenched.

"I hated you for leaving me."

He grimaced but sat there and said nothing. And I knew I shouldn't say those things, but they came out of me, anyway.

"I hated you for being so frail, so very human. I hate you." As I said it, tears finally spilled down my cheeks. I stood before him, as rigid as a statue. Nowhere in my mind or heart had I imagined that I'd say those words to him.

A reunion should have brought me joy. Peace. I felt none of those things, only despair and abandonment.

And that pain was a bottomless wellspring that had no end and no beginning. It simply was.

"Oh, my beautiful lass. I see you, Ellie. Even on the other side of that veil, I never stopped thinking of you. Of us. Hoping. Praying. Dreaming for one more chance to say I—"

I shot my hand up and held up a finger, my posture rigid. "Don't say it. Don't you bloody say it, you damned bloody pirate!"

If I heard those words, if he ever said them to me again with that delicious inflection in his voice and the bright sincerity in his eyes, I would break. And I didn't want to break. Because we were about to fight for our lives and that was the last distraction I needed.

"This doesn't make sense!" The dam fissured just a little bit more. "What are you to this? Why are you here? Why did they just abandon you? Don't you understand, Hook, that this isn't right? That none of this makes sense? You say Anne wanted me. Is that why she brought you back then? Is this her play? You? Am I supposed to weaken again and fling myself at you then you'll turn around and—"

Shoving up from his seat, he rushed me, and this time, I couldn't stop him. My thoughts were poisoning my mind. Anne hadn't sent him to me as a gift. He was not that. He was my own personal devil, sent to haunt me, to kill me.

His arms were around me and he was holding me close, and I wanted to fight it. I wanted to fight him. I didn't want his arms, yet I did. I struggled with my wants and desires, telling myself I was ten times a fool to let him touch me this way, yet all I could do was lean into his strong, towering body. He'd been so broken, so very broken the last time.

But he smelled of Hook, and he murmured to me just like my Hook. And his touch... the way his hand slid up my spine, the grip firm and caressing... it was. All. Him.

"Ellie, I told you that I was not controlled by the sands as the others were. I couldn't be. Not if Anne wanted me to be believed. She did send me here to find you. That day, at the gala with your... partner," he mumbled, and this time he was the one who trembled, and I could no longer keep my hands from touching him. "I was sent for you, Arielle. That venom on my hook, it was meant for you. Stonefish venom wouldn't have killed you, only incapacitated you long enough for me to take you with me. But I fought her compulsion with everything I had in me. That was why I nearly killed your partner, because if I didn't do it to him, I'd have done it to you. And I would rather die a thousand deaths than ever hand you over to that monster."

"Anne?" I breathed.

"Aye." He looked deep into my eyes, brushing his knuckles down my cheek. "Aye. Anne. She's mad, Ellie. Mad with a dark power that I've never seen before. She controls the waters like only a siren of the deep could. I saw her, every night, in her cabin, candles flickering around her, muttering softly, and I swear that I heard a voice muttering back. Wicked. Unnatural. You're right, lass—none of this makes sense."

I shivered, digging my fingers into his spine, our chests pressed so tight to one another, close enough that I felt the beating of his heart move against my flesh.

"What voice? What did it sound like?"

He shook his head, his eyes faraway and haunted by visions I couldn't see. "I am dead, Ellie. Have been for a while now, and I recognize the dead when I hear them. Whoever she speaks with, whoever she's gained her twisted powers from, they're not part of the living, lass."

I swallowed. "What's her end game?" I asked into the expectant hush that filled the room.

His jaw flexed. "She didn't trust me, Arielle. I think she always sensed that I wasn't fully controlled. I fought her manipulations. It was hells, but I was able to keep a part of me me. And I knew that no matter what, I would find you and I would fight like the damned devil hisself to get back to you. I don't expect you to trust me, Ellie. I wouldn't trust me if the boot were on the other foot."

I sniffed, because how many damned times had I heard him use that ridiculous turn of phrase? Exhaustion clung to my bones, my body. I'd tried so damned hard to prevent it from happening, knowing full well that if I opened myself up to the possibility that my Hook had actually returned, it would not end well for me, that I would find myself falling prey to him once more.

"Why do you say you're dead?" I asked and brushed my hand up his warm flesh. His skin prickled beneath my touch, and I felt things, things I'd fought so hard to ignore. But he was here. I was here. He was the man I'd once loved with my whole heart and my whole soul. Dead once but alive again.

"You're not dead, Hook. I feel you, your smell, your touch, your voice. I want to keep lying to myself, but I can't. You're here. And I still can't fathom how this could be."

His cheek replaced the touch of his hand upon my face. Somehow, we were sharing air, nuzzling and touching more. And that fire, it was spreading like a slowly moving inferno through me, blazing and burning and setting me ablaze with the old feelings, the old desires, rekindling a passion I thought I'd never know again.

"You wondered why Crowley would release me, why no one seems all that bothered by my returning? Have you wondered why I've been sent on this mission with you both? Ask yourself, Ellie, why an agency known for handing down severe and swift punishments would dare let me walk so freely."

I frowned, hearing the bitterness creep into his voice. Leaning back in the circle of his arms, I shook my head. "What?"

I knew that if I could think rationally, I would already know the answer to these questions, but my head was full of too much—worry about the case, worry for Hook, even worry for Maddox still, knowing that he, too, must be worrying for me back in Grimm, sick about his visions, wondering what might become of our partnership.

His eyes squeezed shut for half a moment before reopening and looking at me with something a lot like agony. "Ellie, I'm not meant to walk away from this. I broke away from Anne's manipulations, but Matilda didn't break Anne's hold on me completely."

I froze. "What are you saying?"

He pulled his bottom lip into his mouth and worried it with his blunt teeth. I'd seen him do that a thousand times before. Whenever he was stressed, whenever he felt too much, he would hurt himself, give himself bruises even. I touched the corner of his jaw. Since I'd given myself permission to touch him, it seemed so normal again, so right, so damned easy.

"You will make yourself bleed, my..." I couldn't finish the words, because they still didn't quite seem mine to say.

His anguished dark eyes held me spellbound. "They kept the tether in place, Ellie."

I shook my head. "Why? That would mean she can still take you back, make you hers once more. Why would they do that?"

He shook his head slowly. His hook was warm from touching my back for so long. Using just the tip of it, he gently rubbed at my spine, breaking me out in a heated wash of desire.

He'd always known just how to touch me, how to hold me that would make me sing for him.

"Because with that tether there, I can still find her. I feel her, Ellie." He patted his chest. His long fingers brushed against my breasts and though my soul was sick with grief and worry, my body yearned for more of him.

"In here," he said softly as he tapped at his chest. "And she feels me too. She knows I'm coming. In the end, I think it's what she wanted and why she won't fight our going. I vowed to never bring you harm, Arielle, and I'm taking you to the one place where—"He shuddered.

I shook my head, finally starting to make sense of the missing pieces. It was amazing how much you could still feel pain, how it could literally seem to cleave you in two like a knife through hot butter, even when you thought you could never feel such agony like that again. I chuckled darkly. "You are all using me as bait, aren't you? You suspected this all along. It's what the gods-damned tête-à-tête was about, wasn't it? You told them exactly this, didn't you?" I hissed softly, but when he didn't answer, I banged my fists on his chest and snapped, *"Didn't you?"*

His eyes squeezed shut, and his jaw worked furiously as he repeatedly swallowed, as though he were tamping down the words that were desperate to break free.

My laughter grew wilder, and I froze in his arms, needing to get away from him.

You fecking pirate bastard," I hissed. "You all played me for a gods-damned fool, and I—" I was like a deranged madwoman, tears spilled down my cheeks unchecked as my laughter grew deeper and harder.

He yanked on my flailing wrist, holding me tight, squeezing so hard that the flash of pain snapped through my insanity.

"Let me go," I snarled quietly, "or by the gods, I swear I'll rip your other hand off too."

"No!" he barked. "No! I will not have you believing that I don't care. I promised you no harm would ever come to you, Ellie, and godsdamnit it, I mean it. I will lay my life down for yours. You must know this. You already know this!"

I gasped, remembering why he'd gotten one of my father's bolts through his side. That bolt hadn't been meant for him at all, but for me.

His touch gentled as I stilled, but only a very little. I could break free, but I was bolted in place, unable to turn or to leave.

I was breathing hard, and so was he. The whites of his eyes were large and wild, frantic.

"I have loved you and only you all my life and now into death. Yes, I suspect this is why she left me there at that gala, why she never fought to claim me fully. Because of my dark and constant craving for you. Ultimately, I think we played right into the bitch's wee hands. But I won't let her kill you, Ellie. Because I'll—"

"Stop saying that!" I snapped. I was still pissed at him, but I didn't want to hear him speak of death, especially not his.

His nostrils flared, and his handsome face turned severe as he said, "I can't. Because I'm not meant to walk away from this, lass. This is why Crowley released me to you. I'm meant to return to the veil in Nowhere. The second he kills her, I cease to be. This ship will only return with two."

"No," I whispered passionately.

His face crumbled. "Ellie, stop this. Accept reality, lass. Understand that if there were another way, I'd never leave ye. Ever. I was brought because my tether to Anne means we can find her in the vast void that is Nowhere. And once I do, have no doubts that I won't take breath for much longer."

"No! No! I won't let him. I won't let Crowley destroy you. I'll kill him. I'll—"

"Arielle, listen to me!" He shook me fiercely, rattling my teeth, his panic for me to understand and accept feeding mine that I would do anything, even break the very laws I'd vowed to uphold to keep his heart beating. "Even if Crowley doesn't pull the trigger, once they hang Anne for her crimes, anything she's reanimated, it's all gone. We're all gone." He slapped at his chest. "Returned to the dust from whence we came. I was never going to survive this, Ellie. We only have this. We only have now."

The terrible visions of his last moments came surging out of me like hot vomit, and I didn't realize I'd fallen to my knees on the floor until I heard my broken wails.

But he was right there, and he was grabbing me, holding me so tight, patting my hair, my cheek, my body, making me tremble and yearn and burn and need as I remembered all over again how he felt when we moved as one—how he breathed and smelled.

"Arielle. Ellie. Please, luv. Don't do this. Don't do this. I... I can't bear this."

"Then... then we don't let her die. Because this can't... this can't happen again, Hook. This can't happen again. And I'll be damned if Crowley kills you. I vow it to the sun, moon, and stars that I will end anyone who dares take you from me again."

His eyes shone brightly in the moonlight.

"Oh, my lass. My beautiful siren." He framed my face in his one warm and one cold hands. His eyes pierced straight through my soul. "You know very well we cannot stop the hand of justice. Not this time. Anne will swing by the neck for what she's done, if not by Grimm justice, then by vigilante. What she did to Black Angus—you can't stop this, Ellie. And that's not why I'm here. I'm here so that we can have our goodbye, the way it should have been, how it was meant to be. A good one this time, my sweet girl."

I hiccupped, then I stopped fighting it. Because there would never, ever come a moment in my long life when I would not want, need, or love this man.

With hunger that had been suppressed for far too long, we attacked each other. Our lovemaking wasn't sweet or sensual. It was raw and wild and even cruel. So much pain for us both, it came pouring out of us. But we could handle it. Because we always had.

His kisses were drugging, like wine laced with crystals, making us high and crazed, wild and frenzied. I ripped at his clothes, and he shoved at my skirt. Fumbling with his pants, I was less than patient as I helped claw them out of the way.

And when his hard, steely thickness slid deep into my warm wetness I shuddered, and so did he.

"I love you, my girl. I love you. Always will I love you," he murmured over and over and over.

All I could say was, "Don't die again, Hook. Don't die."

I came, and so did he, like a blaze. Tears blinded my eyes, and he held me so tenderly, cradling me in his strong arms.

I would never be the same again. I wasn't even sure I could ever love again. Being with Hook reminded why we'd worked for so long, why I'd loved him as fiercely, wildly, and passionately as I had.

And when we were done and all I wanted was to marvel in the fact that I had the love of my life back in my arms, all we could do was sleep. His big, strong arms wrapped snugly around me. My legs slipped between his. We must have looked like mating octopi. And though it was as uncomfortable as all hells, neither one of us wanted to move.

I sighed. He kissed the crown of my head. I traced the S curve of his hook, and before we knew it, we were both gone to the world.

The next thing I knew was that the ship gave a great shudder, and I heard Crowley's raspy voice call out, "We're here."

Chapter 17

Detective Elle

WHEN HOOK AND I STEPPED out of my cabin, Crowley looked us both up and down, saying nothing and with no emotion on his face.

Hook clearly hadn't lied when he said that Crowley had released him. A part of me wondered if it had been some kind of olive branch for how he'd lashed out at me the night before, but I wouldn't ask because I knew he'd never admit it. Also, I hated him. More than ever.

And I let that hate simmer in my eyes, let him know it, see it. I would be damned if BS thought for one second that they could take Hook from me. I curled my hands into fists, glaring death up at him.

I expected that same fire to be back in his eyes, but it wasn't. He simply looked at me for several moments. Then he turned on his heel and walked swiftly up the ladder steps to the deck.

Hook reached for the ladder, but again that same feeling of disquietude I'd been wrestling with for days came over me. I grabbed his elbow, stopping him.

"Ellie, what—"

With a hungry growl, I leaned up and stole his lips, kissing him passionately, giving him all of me in that one kiss.

When I pulled back, we were both breathing heavily.

"Don't die," I whispered.

He reached over and very gently brushed my cheek with his knuckles. A multitude of words were spoken between us in silence, said in a nanosecond of infinite time. Then he turned back once more and was gone. Finding my center wasn't easy, but there was still a job to do.

I had personal stakes in this case too. Not only would I stop whatever Anne was doing, but I would also save my lover. No matter the cost.

When I finally got up on deck, I'd expected to hear Crowley giving me guff about taking so damned long, but he wasn't. He was staring straight ahead with a furious look on his face.

My heart sank when I realized why.

An endless sea of blue grains stared back at me. The bridge hadn't been destroyed after all. We were here.

"Do you feel her?" Crowley asked, voice full of grit and gravel, as though he'd spent the entire night drinking.

I clenched my jaw. I hoped like hells that bastard never slept at night.

Beside me, I felt Hook nod. "Aye, mate, I feel her."

He sounded tired to my ears but also not so heavily burdened, as though he'd freed himself of it already. Hook was ready to end it. But I wasn't.

I never would be.

I reached for his hand and laced my fingers through his. He squeezed once, and when he tried to let go, I refused. I wasn't letting this man die again. Not again.

Crowley reached into his jacket pocket and extracted not a golden key card but one even rarer.

I'd never actually seen a black diamond card before. In fact, I'd always thought them nothing more than tall tales. Diamonds, but especially black diamonds, were gems of great power and significance, favored by the highest practitioners of light magick because of the way diamonds refracted energy. With a black diamond card, it was said, transdimensional travel wasn't only unnecessary, it was also an antiquated mode of travel.

Crowley looked at us. His face was hard, his eyes inscrutable. "When you are ready, Hook, you simply have to touch the card and think of her. Arielle, you must also be touching the card. Otherwise, you'll be blasted someplace else entirely."

I snarled when he said my name, wishing I could pound my fist through his face.

Which he must have known, because he suddenly lowered the card and looked at me. "Fucking say it then, fish," he snapped. "Get it out of your system."

Hook, without warning, shoved Crowley back on his heels. Crowley, who wasn't wearing his glasses, glared at him with eyes gone fully red.

"You don't talk to her like that... mate," Hook snapped, and I knew that it wasn't just because of me that he'd reacted as he had.

I had to get my emotions under control, for his sake. And though it galled me to admit it, so much of Hook surviving meant we had to have Crowley on our side. It wasn't easy, but I had to figure out a way to tamp down my fury at not just Crowley, but also Draven, and even to a greater extent, Bo, for using us both as they had. At the end of the day, we weren't friends, even if sometimes it might actually have felt that way.

Plastering on a tight smile, I shook my head. "I'm just fine, Special Agent Crowley."

His eyes narrowed to slits. His jaw worked from side to side. I could see a thousand thoughts spin behind his mask, but I couldn't decipher any of them.

"I'm sure by now that you know what's about to happen. And I'm not going to apologize for this, Detective. But you should know, I'm not a fucking monster. No matter what you might think. And just for the damned record, you should also know I wanted no part of this godsdammed idea. But at the end of the day, you and I wear a badge, and that means we have to do whatever the fuck we have to do to make sure assholes like Bonny get stopped. So if you're done acting like a petulant child, we've got a fucking job to do." He scrubbed at his jaw with his fist.

I hadn't felt like an arsehole before, but damned if I didn't now. As much as I hated to admit it, we had no autonomy in our jobs. We were told by our superiors what was what, and whether we agreed or not, we had to do what we had to do.

"Fine." I nodded hard once. "Agreed. We have a job. But... all I'm going to ask is this: don't kill him. And don't kill her."

The muscle in his jaw twitched, and his large frame vibrated as though the wolf wanted out. "I can't make you a promise like that, Detective. You know this."

I shook my head. "Not good enough. You used us like bait. You didn't even fecking warn me about it. You owe me, you bastard, and you know it."

His pupils dilated, and the wolf peeked out for just a moment—wild, reckless hypnotic. I shivered.

His voice was a deep growling drawl as he said, "Call it even for all the years of shit you put me through. Now, if you're quite done, we have a demented psychopath to take down. Can I trust you, Detective?"

The meaning was quite clear. I was going out on a limb, trusting that a man who'd given me no cause to ever trust him before would be my ally. But I wasn't the only one. Hook and I were partners. I had faith in him implicitly, as he had in me.

Crowley was an island unto himself, and he knew it. By giving me that time with Hook, he'd given us our bond back. But he wasn't part of that bond. We could just as easily turn on him.

I unholstered my weapon but kept the safety on and held it loosely by my side, my anger completely spent. "Let's get her," I simply said.

He looked at me for a heartbeat more then lifted the card and tipped it toward us. "Everyone hang on. Hook, keep your thoughts on Anne and only Anne. Got it?"

He nodded. "Aye. I've got it."

Hook and I touched the card at the same time, and it was as if the vacuum of space suddenly picked us up and spit us out.

From one blink to the next, literally, we were standing deep in blue sands, and there standing before us was the infamous Anne Bonny herself.

I'd recognize the mane of fiery-red hair anywhere. Though I'd never personally seen her myself, she was said to be a legendary beauty and as fierce as she was gorgeous. Dressed in skintight leggings, boots, and a loose and billowing top, she looked like a pirate through and through. Her green eyes were shaded, and her face was set. No emotions could be seen on her face.

She shook her head and I frowned, because that hadn't been at all what I'd expected to find when we got here.

"Anne Bonny, you're under arrest for the..." Crowley began to give the spiel, but I was worried and confused.

I looked up at the gray sky above, which had not one cloud hanging in it. Black birds, at least a hundred of them, wheeled acrobatically above us. If they were shifters, and I couldn't see why they wouldn't be, we were not only outnumbered, but also outgunned.

So why weren't they attacking? Why were they moving in that same kind of repetitive formation?

"What say you?" Crowley finished.

Finally, I looked back at Anne, and still she just stood there, looking at us, but there was emotion on her face, a look in her eyes that scared me to my very core.

My breathing began to come in short, sharp bursts. And carefully, so as not to draw attention to myself, I sidled in toward Hook's side. Something was wrong. Something was very, very wrong. It had been too easy. Too damned easy.

"You should never have come back," Anne said, voice so soft, sounding almost like a gentle breeze moving over waves. But she wasn't talking to Crowley or me. Her gaze was on Hook's alone.

I whipped my head around, looking at Hook with round, fearful eyes. His face was set, but I could see the curl of his hand from the corner of my vision.

Crowley growled, sounding more feral and like his wolf than like the man. "What have you done?" he asked. "What have you done, you flame-haired bitch!"

Tears were starting to form in her now large and glassy eyes.

I clutched at my throat, looking around us again. A chill wind had crept in from the north, and the sands were starting to roll as waves would.

"You woke her up," I whispered, voice tight and broken.

"*On the contrary, my dear, I was always the one pulling the strings.*"

A voice, ancient, old, and full of pure evil, echoed all around us.

Crowley immediately backed up. Hook and I did the same, pressing ourselves against one another. Crowley had a weapon in his hand, and my safety was off.

The birds continued their careless glide.

"Who... who are you?" I asked.

Anne began to sob. "I didn't ken. He told me not to, but I didn't believe him." She was muttering the words, sobbing between her crazed laughter, and that sound was chilling, something I'd hear in my nightmares until the day I died.

"You know who I am, Arielle." The female voice was lilting, full of terrible laughter, air, and pure venom.

I shivered. "I... I don't know you."

"Oh, but my darling, you do."

Then she was there, a thing of macabre beauty, standing beside a visibly trembling Anne, dressed in a gown of diaphanous white, moth riddled and turned a dull yellow in spots. Her hair was nothing but streamers of hissing and snapping electric-blue sea snakes, her skin as pale as moonstone, her face so perfectly formed and beautiful.

She smirked with lips as red as the reddest rose.

"Hello, daughter. Miss me?"

My heart froze. My soul trembled inside of me, and I heard Crowley growl. I shook my head.

"How very unsurprising of Triton." She smirked. "Let me guess—I'm a monster. Nightmare wrapped in dark beauty. Am I close? A soul-sucking creature who only wishes to destroy and maim? Tell me when to stop, darling."

I shook my head. "Who are you? What do you want with us? Why are you here? And how are you even here? You were naught but a shade—"

"Wrong!" she screeched, and the sands lifted up beneath us, making us all cry out as we tossed out our arms to steady ourselves. Her face had contorted into a vision of death, going from taut and beautiful to something sharp and deadly and full of hollows. Her skin no longer gleamed like moonstone but was a desiccated husk stretched over gaunt bones. "That bastard has only ever lied about me! I was so much more than just a shade. He couldn't control me because he wasn't strong enough to do it. Bet he didn't tell you that, now, did he? He had to trick me here. And so here I've sat, for an eternity, every day growing just a little bit stronger. A little bit more"—she glanced down at herself—"corporeal. Until the day I saw a girl who didn't have enough. Enough money. Enough power. Never enough."

She placed her hand on Anne's shoulder.

Anne began to openly sob, and I shook my head, disturbed to my soul by what I was seeing. We'd all been so wrong. Anne had never been in charge at all. She'd merely been a puppet in all of it.

I stepped in closer toward Hook.

The witch's eyes glanced between us. A knowing light filled her gaze as her thin lips curved upward just slightly. "So I made her deal, did I not, fair Anne?"

The pirate, who'd always been known as one of the most vicious and brutal to ever sail the hundred realms, dropped to her knees. Her wails were pathetic and pitiful, and I saw that her skin was also beginning to look more like a husk, just like the witch's.

Hook grunted, grabbing hold of his chest. My heart jumped. I stared between him and the witch. Her grin only stretched wider.

"Don't do this," I pleaded, knowing it was entirely in vain. I'd thought Crowley my adversary, but I'd been so fecking wrong, about everything.

Crowley moved in slightly closer to my side, his weapon trained on the witch and unwavering. But I knew, as I was sure he did, that if it was truly the great darkness, our weapons were all but useless against her.

"I was given no choice, you see. He fooled me. And I thought myself so in love that I did not realize it in time. And now I hate him."

My ears pricked at the confession, and it took me a second to realize she wasn't talking about Hook, or even anyone else I'd had on my radar, but someone else entirely.

"Wh-who?" I stuttered, needing to be sure my hunch was correct.

Her laugh was full of hate. "You know who. Your seed bearer. He told me he loved me."

I flinched and shook my head. She sounded like a mad child. "You're lying."

She tossed her head back, and the snakes upon her head hissed in agitation. "Oh, am I? Why do you think he hated you so, Arielle? Why do you think that he banished you as he did? So good to his other daughters, wasn't he? So kind. So loving. But every time he saw you, he cursed your name. Wanted to kill you, didn't he? But he couldn't. Just like with me, he wasn't quite strong enough. Though he made you think he was, didn't he?"

She glanced at Hook meaningfully. My blood ran cold through my veins. Darkness was spreading through my vision, and a strange roaring sounded in my ears.

"Don't listen to this crackpot, Detective," Crowley hissed. "She lies. She—"

Her eyes hooked to his, and they were pools of inky darkness. Suddenly, I heard a croaking sound, and he was being lifted off his feet, held in the air, gasping and clawing at his neck, weapon lost as his skin turned a dark shade of red.

"Stop!" I screamed and flung out my arms, one against Crowley's thigh, one at her. "Stop! What are you doing? What is this? *What is this?*"

She smirked and knelt beside Anne, who looked alone and lost and empty already. Then without a word of warning, she punched her hand through Anne's chest and ripped out her bloody, still-beating heart.

Hook roared then instantly dropped to the ground, silent, so deathly silent.

"No!" I shook my head, blinded by fear and panic that clawed away at my insides like a poison. I didn't think, only reacted.

Song spilled out of my throat—the siren song. He wasn't dead yet. I could still reach him. I could still reach him.

But I didn't sing to Hook. I sang to Anne—Anne, who held my lover's soul inside of her unmoving, bloody, and broken form.

Hundreds of souls came ghosting out of her, wailing and crying as they vanished back into the oblivion of the veil.

The witch laughed. "Go ahead, little siren witch. Find your male. Find him, child. I will not fight you on this."

Her words made no sense, and I didn't care. I simply sang to Hook's soul, and though he fought like the devil to return to the land of the dead, my powers were too great for him to ignore. He was compelled to obey me, to come to me. His glowing blue orb floated like a beautiful dancing light into my hands, and I held him, rocking him and sobbing, kissing his light. He was safe. He was with me. He was safe.

"Safe," I breathed and shuddered as I shoved his warmth into me, being filled with his humanity and feeling life as I so rarely knew it running through me like fire. I knew this was bad. I shouldn't trap his soul in mine. There were consequences for this, but it was the only way to save him.

Crowley was kicking with his legs back and forth, growling deep in his chest, and when I looked up, I saw why he'd begun to grow more agitated. While I'd been occupied with saving Hook, the witch had glided toward his side, and her hands were on him.

"Get your fecking hands off him!" I screamed, shoving to my feet.

She shook her head, still laughing. "You still don't get it, do you, child? You." She pointed at me with a long-tipped claw. "None of you can stop me. I am too powerful now. I stole a sliver of eternity. I can fix this. I can reclaim what was once mine."

Her inky eyes would be forever burned in my memory banks. I'd seen evil before, or at least, I thought I had. But I'd never stared into the beautiful face of it as I was now.

"I only lack one thing. You, Arielle. My very own flesh and blood."

I hissed, "I am no daughter of yours. Mara was my mother."

Again, she laughed. "Is that why you look so different from your sisters? Come on, Arielle. Deep down, you must have always known. Your craving for darkness, your hunger for souls—do you really think that was just your siren's blood? Your sisters are sirens. Did they ever do as you did? Did they ever craft a throne of bones? No, my child. You are mine. The dirty little secret Triton was so very desperate to hide."

"I am not a witch," I said, feeling outside of myself as I said it.

She grinned. "Oh, but you are. Untrained, but my blood runs wild through your dark veins. You know..." She cocked her head, looking almost fondly at me. "I meant to kill you. I was banished from Undine, you see, a bloody curse I've been unable to break because I am no siren. I cannot enter. I need royal blood, and well, daughter, I'm sorry, but you were it. But you look so much like me before I met that faithless, feckless bastard," she hissed, and her snakes writhed like an angry ball upon her head. Her black eyes found mine again.

I shook my head.

"Denying it doesn't change the facts, Arielle. You are my daughter. And I will avenge what Triton's done to me. But I won't kill you. Now that I see you, now that I know who you are, I will do what your father could not. I would love you, cherish you. I will train you to become all that you should have been. Only give me your soul."

I clutched at my chest. "No."

Fires began to lick and burn around her form. She moved away from Crowley, and he was kicking, clawing at his face and neck, as though trying to break the invisible hold, grunting and groaning.

She stood in front of me, smelling of death and glaring at me with eyes that burned through my soul like hell's flame.

"You don't need it, Arielle. You are a witch. Embrace that side of you. Be your darkness. You can survive without it."

I shuddered, squeezing my eyes shut. All that I'd learned, all I'd heard—I didn't believe it. I couldn't. Yet deep down, very deep down, I was starting to think it had to be true.

For the past few days, all I'd done was deny the obvious, and that strategy had been less than effective for me.

She reached for me. "Give me your soul, and we can finally gain our revenge."

I felt the warmth of Hook's soul, beautiful and big and lovely. I shook my head. He loved me because of my humanity, not because of my lack of it. "If you go back and undo this, then you undo me. Why would I ever allow that?"

She snorted. "I like you, Arielle. You are the only child I have ever borne. I think we are more alike than you could possibly imagine. All this time, fighting who you really are. The pain that must cause you. The agony you must feel. I could heal you, daughter."

She grabbed my hand, and I flinched, expecting more pain and more fire. But I didn't feel that. What I did feel was peace, comfort. It flowed through me like gentle rolling waves, and I shuddered as I leaned in toward her.

"He treated you like vermin," she said softly, almost tenderly. "Give me your soul, and I vow to you that I will come back here for you. I am your mother, Arielle. I would never abandon you like he did. You must trust me."

Trust. That one word was enough to make me have a violent reaction. I hissed and snatched my hand back.

The peace of moments ago vanished as I fully heard what she'd just said. I looked at the broken body of Bonny, the pirate I'd been chasing after for months, lying there, just a pathetic shell. But I'd known of Bonny's legacy. She'd not become so feared for nothing. Her legend had been steeped in truths. She'd been bloodthirsty, absolutely ruthless, and cunning like a fox. Yet there she lay, nothing now, her legend unable to keep her from falling prey to the hands of something so lethal and dangerous that not even a siren like me or a shifter like Crowley could come against her.

I shook my head. "You think me a fool? All the lies you've spouted." I chuckled darkly. "Even if you were my mother, I would never trust you."

She hissed, and her snakes snapped at me, so close to my neck that I felt the wash of their breath tingle upon my flesh.

Then she grinned, and before I could even catch my bearings, Crowley was no longer dangling in the air, but she held him in front of her. She, a tiny insignificant-looking woman and he, a massive pedigree of man, but it was obvious who the more powerful of the two was.

Crowley was gritting his teeth, veins in his neck swollen and distended as he hacked and coughed, growling like a frenzied wolf as he tried to shake her off him. Her snakes were all pointed at him, staring him down. One word from their mistress, and they would attack.

"Give me your soul, Arielle, or he dies too."

She couldn't take it. For reasons that I couldn't quite understand, I suddenly realized she couldn't just steal my soul. Maybe it was part of her curse. I wasn't sure. But she'd had no problem teaching Bonny how to steal souls. No, somehow it was just mine that she was unable to snatch without consent. I felt as if there were blanks here, as if I didn't fully understand how she was doing what she was doing or even why. Already, I knew my father had lied to me. He'd told me the witch was nothing now, a mere shade, useless, pathetic. But he'd never told me that she'd swallowed time. He'd never said that.

So many lies. So many things I did not know. What was true and what wasn't? I hadn't a clue.

I placed my fist over my heart, feeling that darkness inside of me begin to stir once more.

Crowley laughed. His lips were swollen from the pressure she exerted on his windpipe, and I could see pink mixed in the spittle at the corners of his mouth. He was a shifter and harder to kill, but the witch wasn't even breathing heavily.

"You're a fool, witch, if you think Arielle would ever hand over her soul for me. You know nothing at all."

"Ah, no, shifter," the witch crooned as she dragged a black-tipped claw down the side of his cheek, her nail so sharp that a ribbon of blood was left in its wake. "It is you that is the fool. You believe my daughter heartless. A fish, you call her. Soulless. But she has a soul. She has a heart. Though I will eventually destroy it. She will give me her soul, or you will die."

His laughter was full of incredulity. "Tell her, Arielle. Show her just how much you care. I dare you!" he taunted, eyes wide, veins throbbing.

He really did think I would hand him over to her. And sadly, he wasn't totally wrong, because I wanted to. I really wanted to. I didn't want to give her my soul and not just because it would hurt, but also because I understood the ramifications of what might be if I did.

My father's kingdom would be in peril. My sisters... I shivered. That darkness in me, it was growing stronger, gaining ground. I felt its terrible hunger. But I felt something else in me too.

There was another soul in me, one that would stave off that darkness, at least for a little while. Because that soul had loved me enough to believe me good.

I looked at Crowley, and there must have been something in my eyes because he was no longer laughing. He was shaking his head.

"What are you—don't be a godsdamned fool, Arielle! Don't you fucking dare do this, fish! Don't you dare."

I clenched my jaw, tuning out his hateful, ugly words. The witch smirked.

"Such a weak thing you are, my daughter. Yet I have hope for our future."

I flinched, hugging my arms to my waist. "If... if I do this—"

"Don't!" Crowley said again. "Don't do this, Arielle! You know what will happen if you—"

His words instantly ceased when the witch breathed upon his cheek. He gasped, as his skin began to turn a shade of gray and the veins to black.

"You killed him!" I cried.

She shook her head. "I did not. I will not. Though he does not deserve to live. If you honor your word, I will honor mine and prove to you that I am not faithless like the man you call your father."

I clenched my jaw, watching as Crowley slowly turned to stone before me. His eyes were glued to mine, and from them welled tracks of blood. My nostrils flared, and I squeezed my eyes shut.

"If I give you my soul, I die?"

"No. You simply become... human but more." She laughed. "You don't even know who you are, do you, Arielle? But I'm sure you've sensed it, that power in you, untapped, unclaimed. So much power." She wet her lips, eyes alight with avarice and lust for said power.

I shivered. "What will you do?"

"I will merge our forms. I will make it painless, daughter. For you. Because I love you."

Hearing something so evil speak of love was the stuff of nightmares. "Do I have your word that you will not steal Hook's soul from me?"

She shrugged. "I don't want it. And he wouldn't want to be bonded to me, anyway. He only came to Anne because of his great desire for you. But once he found you, he betrayed her. He'd do the same to me. Keep him if you must. Though I'd suggest consuming his light and being done with it. Just me, though."

"Give me your word. Bind it in magick. You cannot steal him from me."

She laughed, looking perplexed but intrigued. "Fine, you silly child, I bind it in the very darkest of magicks. May I shatter into oblivion if I take him from you."

The air quickened with her vow, and I breathed a sigh of relief. "So mote it be," we both said at once. To break her vow would mean the end of her.

I bit down on my front teeth, saying nothing, thinking nothing.

With one last breath, I whispered, "Then do it."

A wail like the souls of the dead rising from below screamed through the heavens. The witch flew at me, and I had no time to brace for impact. One second, I was me, and the next, I was not.

I felt her in me, breathing, moving, taking, siphoning. I screamed. It wasn't painless. It wasn't easy. But I'd known she'd lied. I'd been expecting it.

I felt her glee, her greedy ephemeral hands stealing more and more of me, the last bits of my light. For a siren to be soulless was to become a monster true.

But I had Hook in me. And his little light, it shone like a beacon, keeping me sane, clearing my mind of the pain, the lies, the questions. I only thought one thing.

She had eternity in her form. And if she could steal from me, then I could steal from her.

I let her drink until she was bloated. I let her become satiated, drunk on my power. And just before she began to separate, I found that spark of time.

It was a golden glittering rod settled snugly in her dark soul, a mere sliver of eternity, and just as she tore herself free of me, I snatched it free of her.

She screamed, eyes widening, grabbing at her breast and whirling just as I sank the sliver into Hook's soul. His warmth encased eternity.

"*What have you done?*" she cried, clawing at her face, bleeding herself so profusely that thick rivers of it ran from her flesh to the blue sands beneath. Sands that were growing softer, turning from solid into liquid. They began to rise and wave and roll.

"You can't take him from me, and now, witch, you can't control time, either."

"I'll kill you," she snarled.

I grinned. "You kill me. You kill him. And thus, you kill yourself. So go ahead. Do it if you must. And this all ends here."

She smiled, but madness burned in her bright eyes. "You think you've bested me, little girl, but you have no idea what I can do. Anne was a good little girl, she got me all that I needed. And now, time or no, none of you can stop me. No one!"

I shook my head, thinking of all the items she'd stolen. The slipper, but also the ones that Crowley had mentioned on the ship, and I finally saw the bigger picture. The witch had thought of everything, and I was so stupid it had never once occurred to me that someone as dark and wicked as her could play the long game. But play it she had.

"You won't win," I whispered, because that's what I did. I denied the obvious. But this time, I meant it. This time I would stop at nothing to make sure she never got her happily ever after.

"*Ahhh!*" She screamed so violently that whatever last bits of tensile strength had remained in what had once been sand became no more.

I sank into the waters, and my legs did not turn. She'd stolen the siren from me. I had no tail. I was human. But I had two men I had to save. Struggling to keep my head above the tempestuous waves, I very quickly shucked off my jacket, no longer even thinking about the witch. I rolled my sleeves, trapping them with air, creating a floatation device that I quickly tied off at the bottom so no air could escape. Then I swam.

I might no longer be a siren, but my body knew how to cut through the water. I struggled with my inability to breathe under the waves, but I was strong still, and I moved like a missile.

I found Hook first, sinking with his arms floating above him. I rushed us to the surface and wrapped the makeshift float around his waist.

Then I went for Crowley.

He was a massive weight of dense muscle and stone. He'd landed on the bottom. Thank the gods, the bottom was only ten feet down. I wrapped my arms around his waist, kicked off the sand with all my might, and rocketed to the surface. When my head parted the waters, I gasped for air, my chest heaving. I looked around, praying, hoping, and wishing for an island—anything that I could swim us toward.

Crowley was heavy, even in the water. His body was nearly all stone. The witch was gone, which surprised me. I'd expected her to kill us. But clearly, she wasn't done with me yet. That, or she simply no longer cared one way or another whether we lived or died, and it was looking very likely that any of us would make it out of Nowhere alive.

So I switched course, and I swam for Hook, backstroking with Crowley's massive weight resting on my chest. The waters had finally stopped rocking so violently and were nearly smooth by the time I reached Hook's lifeless bobbing body.

I was gasping when I finally got to him, my muscles so tired that it was a struggle just to remain afloat.

I tried to access the sliver of time in Hook's soul, but his soul would not release it to me as the witch's had so easily done. I'd hoped to turn back time, that maybe by some miracle I could have taken us to the point before we'd ever even left Grimm.

"Bloody hells!" I snapped. "Can nothing be easy?"

Then I thought of Crowley's time card and frantically reached my hand into his coat pocket. If that was still there, then we might still be saved. But just as I'd feared, the card was gone, no doubt sucked into the raging waters when he'd been dragged into it.

"*Argh*!" I screamed, releasing all the pent-up fear, anger, and worry that felt as though it was choking me. Once I'd exhausted myself even further, I knew I could not afford to do that. I was the only one who could save us, which meant I had to find focus, had to not give in to the panic and fecking think.

Above me, the sky grew thick and angry with storm clouds. Lightning streaked the darkness and rain dumped down in buckets from the heavens. The birds were all gone. Hatter's vision had come to life.

I shook my head. I was a siren stripped of her powers. I'd consumed the soul of one male and was now struggling to keep the stony frame of another from sinking into the sands below.

I shook my head again, this was probably the lowest I'd ever been in my life.

"Crowley, if you can hear me, please, please say something. Please just say something."

The sky was furious, rumbling and flashing, as though an angry god were tearing it in two.

There was a soft coughing grunt. I gasped and glanced down at him, my heart hammering in my chest. How could he still be alive? His eyes shifted, and he looked at me.

A gentle smile touched my mouth. "I will save us. Okay. I will. I won't let you die."

He coughed weakly, and I knew I'd just lied to him. Because I was almost one hundred percent certain that none of us were getting out of here.

But I hugged my arms to his body and continued to lie to him, whispering to him softly until he no longer looked at me, until he'd even stopped breathing. I didn't know if he'd died or if he'd merely turned to stone. But he was not flesh and blood anymore. And I don't know how long we'd been floating, but my skin was wrinkled and itching.

It would be so easy to close my eyes. I was so tired, and the sky still screamed at me.

I thought of everything that had happened to get us here: chasing nothing but red herrings and imagining the big bad was Anne Bonny, when in truth, the big bad had been playing an infinite game of chess. I still didn't even really know why or when or how. But floating on that endless sea with no land in sight and no hope of salvation on the horizon, I also knew it didn't matter.

I wouldn't be there to save Whiskers. Hatter would never find me. No one would. I'd sentenced him to the same kind of fate that...

I went still all over. Thinking of Hatter made me suddenly think of something else.

All of Hatter's visions were true. All of them.

I'd seen myself standing over a doorway in the water.

A burst of energy I'd never known suddenly rushed through me as I jerked, looking left and right, listening for the roar of the falls, knowing it had to be here somewhere. It had to be. His visions were always right. Salvation was just around the corner.

But where was the music and the voices? This vision only felt half realized right now.

Then I thought of something so outlandish, so ridiculous that I would never have even bothered believing in it except that I literally had nothing else to believe in.

She'd called me her daughter, told me of the darkness within me, the flame of the witch that breathed in me, just as it did in her.

She'd left this place—with magick.

I hissed. Could I do that too?

I closed my eyes. I had no idea what I was doing. I wasn't a witch. I'd never been trained to be one. But I'd been around enough of them, and always, they'd say, "It's all in the fire. You find the fire, you find the source."

I floated, and I thought of that fire, pictured it in my mind's eye, falling into a hypnotic trance, thinking of its burn, its mystic draw, remembering Hatter's burn, picturing it so completely in my mind.

But seconds ticked by, then minutes, and finally hours—and nothing. No fire. No burn.

With a cry, I slapped at the water. I was so tired. So damned tired. I looked at Crowley and at Hook. They were gone to me. I was alone. It might all be for nothing.

Then I felt the slinking of dark fingers spread through me, and I trembled.

The witch was an ancient evil. She wasn't merely a black witch. She was a dark mage. Did that mean that maybe that darkness within me... that maybe, just maybe that was my source?

But if I tapped into that, what would it do to me? Who would I become? I looked at both men and squeezed my eyes shut. "Gods forgive me."

And one last time, I cleared my thoughts, and this time I didn't go looking for a fire that did not exist. Instead, I turned toward that yawning black and bottomless pool and said simply, "Come."

The darkness crawled over me, latching onto my leg, my waist, my arms, my neck, before finally covering my head, and I knew I'd awakened something terrible, something monstrous.

I knew I should have been scared. But all I felt was... power. I laughed as it sparked through me, making me feel more alive than I had, maybe ever. So much power. The water began to sizzle around me.

I snapped my fingers. Then there it was—a doorway, lifting up from the waves beneath—and I grinned. All three of us were shoved up and out of the water and stood on a platform of solid ice.

I felt myself glowing, but my light wasn't lambent blue, not anymore. It was black, as black as the glittering night.

"*Anahita, come*," I cried out, calling out to my sister with a voice that trembled like a demon's.

I felt the shuddering of movement beneath the waves. I'd saved us.

But at what cost? The gods only knew...

THE END IS ONLY THE BEGINNING...

There will definitely be more Elle and Hatter. In fact, should all go well I'll be releasing book 3, A Witch and a Fish, in early to mid 2019. So keep your eyes peeled to my Jovee Winters FB page for further updates about the Grimm Files. And if you loved this book, leave a review. I've decided that 2019 is all about feeding the beast. Meaning, if you (my readers) want more I'll write more. But the only way I can know that is through reviews. I'll be drafting up my 2019 writing schedule based off of interest generated by my readers themselves, so again, if you want more Grimm leave your reviews!

In the meantime, I have plenty other UF titles to whet your whistle while you wait. If you're looking for something edgy and dark consider starting with my Completed Night Series. All 4 books have been released and deals with the physical manifestations of the 7 Deadly Sins. Or if Berserkers are more your speed check out my Completed Tempted Series. If you like Shifters and Vampires, then you might just love my Southern Vampire Chronicles. All 3 of those series are completed and published.

Remember keep an eye on my FB[1] page for further updates! Want to know when the next Grimm Files book releases? Make sure to sign up for my newsletter[2]!

1.   https://www.facebook.com/joveewintersauthor/

2.   http://eepurl.com/xo-bj

More Books!
The Night Series written as Selene Charles

The Complete Night Series Collection, a boxed set of all 4 books!

With over 2000 four star reviews on Goodreads alone!
The Night Series originally written as Marie Hall, I'm now writing as Selene Charles. Fully Completed Series! Written by the USA Today Bestseller of Crimson Night.

<u>NO CLIFFHANGERS</u>

Welcome to the carnival of the damned. I'm one of the seven deadly sins, they call me Lust, but you can just call me Pandora. This is a story of darkness. Redemption. Hope. And betrayal I never saw coming.

A reaper's found me—deadly to my kind—and though I know I shouldn't be I'm as drawn to him as a moth is to flame. But I don't have time to indulge in my fantasies of stripping him down naked and having my dirty, dirty way with him. Because there's a prophecy going round. Real end of the world type stuff. And somehow this little demon is at the heart of it all. I'm thousands of years old, but I'm starting to feel like my numbers finally come due...

COMPLETED SERIES!!
Tempted Series by Selene Charles YA Urban Fantasy (Spin-off set in the Night Series world)

Welcome to Whispering Bluff, Tennessee. Where the guys are hot. The girls are sweet. And nothing is what it seems...

Forbidden, Book 1
Reckless, Book 2
Possessed, Book 3

COMPLETED SERIES!!
The Southern Vampire Detective Series written as Selene Charles (Loose Spin-off set in the Night Universe)

Meet Scarlett Smith, Southern Vampire Detective...
Well at least that's what she is today. Not too long ago she was just a regular
Southern Belle in love with her soldier, dreaming of a life full of babies and
white picket fences.
Then she died...

Whiskey, Vamps, and Thieves, Book 1
Fae Bridge Over Troubled Waters, (short story) 1.5
Me and You and a Ghost Named Boo, Book 2
The Vampire Went Down to Georgia, Book 3
COMPLETED SERIES !!

Made in the USA
Middletown, DE
04 November 2019